80,000

TOTALLY SECURE

PASSWORDS

that no hacker would ever guess

I0592655

collected fiction of

SIMON PETRIE

First published in Australia in 2018

Please direct all enquiries to the publisher at:
fomalhaut451@gmail.com

ISBN 978-0-6483228-6-3

Typeset in Adobe Garamond Pro / Franklin Gothic Medium Condensed
Cover modelwork and photography by Lewis P Morley

National Library of Australia Cataloguing-in-Publication entry

Title:	80,000 Totally Secure Passwords That No Hacker Would Ever Guess / Simon Petrie.
ISBN:	9780648322863 (pbk.)
Subjects:	Science fiction, Australian.
	Short stories, Australian.
Dewey Number: A823.4	

PRODUCT WARNING

Please read carefully

Piracy of copyrighted material is a serious and growing problem, against which the stakeholders in the publishing industries have elected to fight vigorously, with all the methods at their disposal. Accordingly, this product has been manufactured in compliance with the latest advances in Textual Rights Management.

The paper within this book has been treated with Kabloomite, a mildly-fragranced and non-tumour-promoting chemical agent sensitive to the precise wavelengths of light utilised by photocopy and scanner lamps. In its resting state, Kabloomite is an entirely innocuous substance. However, readers of this book need to be made aware that exposure of its pages to photocopy lamps (or, it transpires, to direct sunlight) will produce a forthright and robust photochemical response, with effects ranging from randomised autobleaching of text snippets, through smouldering partial combustion, runaway foxing and spontaneous disintegration of individual pages, to violent detonation of the entire product and any neighbouring volumes similarly treated. Therefore, DO NOT expose this product to photocopy or scanner lamps, nor (it transpires) to direct sunlight. If you have reason to believe the product has been so exposed, you should adhere to the following simple ten-point plan:

1   Place the book face-up on a cool, flat, non-flammable solid surface. Switch off ambient sources of lighting and close the curtains, blinds, shutters, or other window treatments of relevance within the immediate vicinity.

2   Back slowly away from the book, taking care not to make any sudden movements, so as to minimise accidental detonation of the sensitised product.

3   Procure a stout metal bucket of at least ten (10) litres capacity, and at least five (5) kilograms of dry sand, diatomaceous earth, or unused kitty litter. Quantities should be doubled for larger books (e.g trade paperbacks) and quadrupled for large-format coffee-table books.

4   Equip yourself with a Hazmat suit, blast shield, and dry-powder fire extinguisher. If you lack these essential domestic items, a cyclist's helmet, rubber gloves, and garbage-can lid will have to suffice. You will also require a set of long-handled kitchen tongs.

5   Cautiously approach the book with the selected materials. Place the bucket not closer than one (1) metre from the book and, employing as steady a motion as is possible, use the tongs to lift the book and place it carefully in the bucket. Tip the dry sand, etc., into the bucket until the book is completely covered.

6   Evacuate the site, retreating to a distance of at least fifty (50) metres if a domestic dwelling or one hundred (100) metres in the case of a bookstore or library. Place a call to your local Book Disposal Squad, advising them of the emergency's nature (e.g. anthology, slim volume of verse, fantasy trilogy, etc.), and await their arrival. During this interval, kindly notify such of your neighbours as you remain on polite terms with. Please reassure them – as well as any assembled family members – that Kabloomite is a registered, low-yield Textual Copyright Protection material, and does not cause cancer in rats.

7   At this point also, you may petition the deity, higher power, demon, or fluffily vague spiritual pseudo-entity of your choice, or call your loved ones or insurance broker.

8   Follow all instructions given by the Book Disposal Squad and do not get in their way. They are seasoned professionals doing a dangerous and difficult job.

9   Once the emergency has been resolved, return to the place of purchase and procure another two (2) copies of this book. It never hurts to have a spare (but see above).

10 Rebuild.

The author joins with the publisher in hoping you have an enjoyable, safe, and interruption-free reading experience.

THINK OF OTHERS, THINK OF THE ENVIRONMENT:
PLEASE DISPOSE OF THIS BOOK THOUGHTFULLY

Table of Contents

Books by Simon Petrie

(the Titan sequence)

Matters Arising from the Identification of the Body

Wide Brown Land

A Reappraisal of the Circumstances Resulting in Death (forthcoming)

Flight 404

Murder on the Zenith Express: the Gordon Mamon collection

80,000 Totally Secure Passwords That No Hacker Would Ever Guess

For Lucy and Paul, who left too soon

Introduction

by Über-Professor Arrrrarrrgghl Schlurmpftxpftpfl

I have on two prior occasions furnished what I believe is termed "prefamatory material" for the print-word works of the Earth-human "Simon Petrie", and it is with what I believe is identified, among the house-apes of Sol III, as chagrin that I note the individual is still active in both a biological and a literary sense.

Petrie considers itself, as I understand it, a writer of "science fiction" with a particular focus on the xenobiologic and on the supposedly-faithful depiction of archaic slower-than-light forms of transport. Readers should be warned, however, that Petrie's repertoire is lamentably thin and Sol-centric: you will find little, if anything, here, on the intricacies and subtleties of Rigellian cave-sloth society with its demolition-based language systems, its influenza-mediated courtship rituals, and its flame-based financial transaction methods; on the crippling problems of bodily containment, premature lightning discharges, and inconvenient and embarrassing rainfall episodes suffered by the sentient cloudforms of Alnitak IX; on the life-threatening impact of skin-sloughing on punctuality (and therefore survival) among the time-dwelling saurioids of Kapteyn's Star VI; or, for that matter, on any other of the aspects of Galactic life on which all the serious literary endeavour of the past millenium has touched.

Indeed, with few if any exceptions (and here the perspicacious reader may gather that I have not in fact seen fit on this occasion to visually imbibe the word-offerings of the house-ape Petrie, for I have been exposed to this individual's work before, and found the experience sufficiently dissatisfying and disturbing that I will not voluntarily do so again), the writer's narrow focus is upon the mewling tributations and fumbling "first contacts" of its fellow Earth-humans, in a range of ill-drawn, unrealistic, and sometimes defamatory planetary, interplanetary, and interstellar settings.

I urge you, reader, do not sully your optical nor your cortical systems with the pages that follow these few which I have adorned: there is far better "science fiction" out there, such as the literally groundbreaking *Seismic Trilogy* by H'rkfluzzlopbpux'vt't't of Deneb IIIc, each "reading" of which renders its host planet uninhabitable for a period ranging from seven to five hundred thousand of your Earth years; the steamy, star-crossed "binary ever after" intergalactic romances of Florrrf of Delta Aquarius VII which, with innumerable small differences in plot, each build steadily yet urgently to an explosive climax which inevitably features the fevered and impassioned exchange of stellar fluids as the principals fall headlong into each other's tight gravitational embrace; the unrelentingly gripping *Confessions of a City-Swallowing, Planet-Splitting, Star-Shattering Hypermutant* by Qfggrpleeeeth the Younger of Algol V, gorgeously written but known to induce untreatable catatonia in readers who seek to put down the seventy-three-thousand-page volume partway through, regardless of the need for respite, sleep, sustenance, or bodily elimination; or the allegedly brilliant but frustratingly untranslatable *Neutronium Diaries* left behind by some unknown member of a now-extinct race, seven and a half billion years ago, at what is believed to be the "lost telepath" counter of Baragaphlacopvx's, the famed globular-cluster-wide hardware franchise that sadly slipped into receivership (and, shortly thereafter, a black hole) scant aeons before the onset of the Galactic Renaissance. All of these titles, and many other first-rate works of xenoliterary acumen, are freely available for delivery or download from the S Doradus Multiversity Press, of which it just so happens I am a managing director. (If, as I believe the term is, you are "browsing" the SDorMP sales site, I highly recommend, however, that you steer clear of the Press's extensive sections on exotic-game hunting, on the culinary arts, and on mind-controlling-parasite development.)

Finally, I wish you happy reading, forlorn though that aspiration would appear in this particular context.

Über-Professor Arrrrarrrgghl Schlurmpftxpftpfl
Director, Gargelhuisenflinx Prime Cultural Studies Centre, Alnitak IV
former (covert) Earth Cultural Ambassador / Gourmand
Author, *For Pity's Sake, Don't Let The Little Bastards Near Your Spacecraft*

Jack Makes A Sale

Jack had a buyer – maybe – but she wasn't happy.

'The advert said *shop*,' she complained.

'Sorry. Honest mistake. Typo. Look, you want it, or not?'

'I don't know *what* to do. How would it work, with all my kids?'

'Stick them in the toe area, parents' retreat towards the heel.'

She ummed and ahhed, he knocked another ten percent off the price, and finally the old woman agreed. Great. One shoe gone. But he didn't see himself being able to shift the other shoe, nor all that clothing, in a hurry. After two days, the giant was getting decidedly niffy.

All the Colours of the Tomato

Jojo's bananas had been recognisable, if surreal; her oranges had been green, and exquisitely textured; her pears surprisingly dark, but well-delineated. But her tomatoes... Marcus nudged the fiveway in under the awning. He craned the proxy down for a closer look at the canvas, taking care not to overbalance, while the grover artist wandered off to the corner to defecate. As she squatted, her eyes flicked repeatedly, anxiously, towards the enclosure's sole tree, and beyond to the expanse of Sessum savannah visible through the tall direl-mesh fencing that shielded Jojo from the world beyond.

The tomatoes in the bowl shone pinky-red in the alcove's blend of natural and artificial lighting, highlights showing on the fruit's smooth skin. The tomatoes on Jojo's canvas were a disturbed montage of colour: greens and purples and yellows all thrown together in a haphazard jumble, belying the unusual degree of care with which Jojo had laid down her patina of discordant tones. Even allowing for the imperfections of the fiveway's colour transmission, the disjuncture between object and Jojo's portrayal was extreme. The work unsettled Marcus, in a manner quite different to the normal effect of her artwork. He put it down to some weird alien brain thing, grover dementia or some such.

Jojo was damaged goods, the last of her troupe, solitary survivor of an attack by the cryptosaurines. She'd seen parents, siblings, cousins reduced to scraps of fur and bone before her eyes, while she'd clung, terrified, to the topmost branches. In the wild, she'd be dead already; here in the base, she was kept under obs so they could "learn about grover culture, get a sense for their abilities and intelligence, find out how they manage to coexist with the cryps, and, of course, provide her with a safe haven". They made it sound, Marcus thought, as though they were doing her a kindness.

It wasn't a kindness.

Marcus was not yet highly skilled in reading grover behaviour – fact of the matter was, none of the base's xenobehaviourists were – but you didn't need to be fully expert to see that Jojo was... not right. She moved as infrequently as possible, ate barely enough to sustain herself. Her blue-grey fur lay lank and dusty along stick-thin limbs; her too-wide head, with its too-big eyes and protruberant proboscis, hung heavy on a neck that didn't look equal to the task of supporting it. She didn't vocalise, didn't engage. Interactive toys sprawled, bleeping, twitching and untouched, across the dirt floor of her enclosure. Bedding lay unused in the neocrete hut designated as her sleeping area; Jojo preferred to sleep outside, in the dirt, in the main building's shadow. The two fiveways in her enclosure – the second, seldom ever animated – were treated as bulky obstacles, multi-limbed inconveniences, whether they moved or stayed static: not feared, not puzzled over, just ignored. The tree, sufficiently far from the direl fenceline that the gap couldn't be jumped, was consistently skirted: Jojo stuck, pretty much, to the open-air edges of the enclosure, most of the time within arm's reach of a lethally-protective barrier. The only times she showed anything that might be guessed as enthusiasm were when, awkwardly, tentatively, she picked up an autobrush and approached the canvas. The act of painting might take minutes, might take hours, but held her undivided attention for as long as the task took. Marcus didn't think he'd ever seen anything give her such trouble as those tomatoes.

Her toilet finished, she wandered back around the enclosure, past the stumpy-legged easel, gave the canvas a brief, dismissive stare and sat in the opposite corner, listless once more. Marcus took this as his cue to manipulate the tomatoes into the fiveway's sample pouch, for subsequent disposal.

There was a momentary lapse in feed, and in the pixellated confusion of the systems glitch, one of the tomatoes burst, its thin skin ruptured by an inexpert gripping gesture. Red juice and tomato pulp ran down the casing of the proxy's legs. Marcus wasn't the best at bending the fiveways to his will; a half-hearted effort at wiping the mess away merely served to make it worse.

Two days later, Marcus invoked the image on his flexy, showed it to Ngaire and Attilla as the three of them took lunch in the base's canteen. The others stared at it for several seconds. They'd been talking about the latest fiveway / cryptosaurine skirmish – the small apex predators would attack anything that moved – and Marcus was convinced that his attempt at nudging the conversation onto a fresh topic was doomed. But at length Attilla looked up from the flexy and asked, around a mouthful of bread and gravy, 'It supposed to be anything?'

'Tomatoes.' Marcus held Attilla's gaze – prominent nose slightly hooked, overhanging full lips, broad forehead, thick tawny eyebrows, curiously pale grey eyes – for as long as he dared, while the blood rushed to his own cheeks. *Xenobehaviourist, grade C2, with feelings – yearnings – for a certified, highly-distinguished, A1-grade Mission Specialist? No chance. No chance in hell.*

'Tomatoes?' Ngaire echoed, cutting across Marcus's wistful, doomed reverie like a scalpel. 'Wow, she's really fucking lost it, big time. Someone should do the decent, pull the plug. That'd be the humane thing. No offence, Marcus.'

'Not disagreeing with you there,' said Marcus, though he was careful to avoid eye contact while he said it. 'Well, not on the humane bit, anyhow. But there's more to it than that.'

'How d'you mean?' asked Attilla.

'Wish I knew.'

'Then how,' asked Ngaire, 'do you know there's more to it? I'm sorry, but I could eat a kilo of assorted acrylic pigments and sh—'

'If you saw how long it took her to paint this—'

'So she's a crap artist,' replied Ngaire, gesticulating with hands that always seemed too long for those olive-skinned arms: a creature of wire, energy, and spite, was how Marcus had come to think of the woman. 'But I don't see how you can read anything of significance into what's just a horrendous misrepresentation of a few pieces of fruit.'

'I don't know what significance, or even if any,' said Marcus, growing exasperated that the conversation wasn't playing out as he'd hoped. 'All I'm trying to say, if you saw the concentration that went into producing this, the effort, I mean I know it looks like she just smooshed a whole bunch of paint down on the canvas, but there's actually a lot of repainting, a lot of touching up, went into this. A hell of a lot of detail work, even if it doesn't look like it. She was trying harder than I've ever seen her, to get this *right*.'

'Boy, did she screw up,' said Ngaire, pushing her chair back.

'And it's not just the painting,' Marcus continued, flustered despite his attempts at composure. 'I mean, not just her painting it. You know that gallery we've set up for her, in her enclosure?'

'You've set up a gallery for her? That's so *cute*,' Ngaire answered, standing, placing such an emphasis on the last word that Marcus was left in no doubt that the implied derision was directed not just at Jojo. He felt colour rise to his cheeks.

'Oh, leave off, Nye,' said Attilla, favouring Marcus with a disarming, shark-mouthed grin. 'So what's the deal with her gallery?'

'Not a clue,' answered Marcus, almost pathetically grateful for Attilla's interest. 'But there's maybe twenty of her pictures displayed for her up there now, including a couple she's done since this. Three guesses which one she spends the most time staring at.'

'So what does it mean?' Attilla asked.

'You tell me.'

The best spot for sleeping, alongside the big blocky, rocky intrusion, where the structure's breath stayed warm on even the coldest nights, was also one of the best vantage points offered within her new territory. From here, she could see a large expanse of the world-beyond-the-barrier, a sight which both intrigued and unnerved her, and she could choose to look out towards the distant upthrust of the island's centre without needing to pay any notice to the tree that interrupted her territory. Once, her memory insisted, she had dwelt in such a tree herself, but the memory was troubled, twisted, sleep-wrecking. The tree was unsafe.

A single tree is always unsafe.

The other things that intruded upon her domain, the angled ones, also awoke her unease, though one barely moved and the other furnished her with food and tools. They smelt unfamiliar, wrong; their presence spoke of dangerous abilities; they did not belong.

But then, who did? The world had grown strange, these past months. There was a hint of menace in the sky.

With three "hands" awkwardly gripping the rock face, Marcus chanced a look down, feeling his fiveway's grasp slip, knowing all the while that it was a mistake. Only the watchfulness, lightning-fast reflexes, and expert-level skill of Ngaire, piloting the accompanying fiveway, prevented his own proxy from falling a couple of hundred metres to a messy, embarrassing, and expensive death on the rocky outcrops that rimmed the base of the mesa's south-eastern cliffs. (The fiveways were, of course, flight-capable; but he knew, and surely she did too, that he'd never be able to break into glide mode while *in extremis* like this.)

'Easy,' Ngaire's voice breathed in his earpiece, in the true darkness of the proxy control room beside him, as all the while her fiveway pinned his own against the sun-warm, treacherous, slow-crumbling cliff-face.

'Easy for *you* to say,' Marcus bit back, stunned by the rapidity with which he'd lost control of the proxy. 'Some people just aren't cut out to be fiveway pilots.' He couldn't make Ngaire out, at all. At times so abrasive, other times – not.

'You just haven't had enough practice,' she suggested, maintaining the pressure, from her fiveway's two left-flank limbs, that for the moment was all that arrested his own device against an unarguably-lethal fall. 'Take your time. Like you've been doing with Attilla.'

'*What?*' Marcus's surprised flinch almost succeeded in wresting his fiveway from Ngaire's anchorage against the cliff-face.

'Easy,' she cautioned again. 'It's pretty bloody obvious you're attracted to him, Marcus. I doubt it's reciprocated, but he doesn't confide and he's a little harder to read than you are. Worst thing you can do in this kind of situation is to rush.'

'Are you talking about that, ah, predicament? Or *this* predicament?'

'Both, I guess. But let's focus on the task at hand. Just quit panicking, and get up the fucking cliff.'

'I don't recollect there being a "gravity off" switch,' he snapped, embarrassment, confusion and dread all weltering within him.

'There isn't,' said Ngaire, calmly, refusing to be drawn by his exasperation. 'But I've got you. You're safe.'

'This must be some strange new—'

'Hush. Move your left forelimb. No, not like that, like this. Yes. Now twist the wrist a little, deploy the grapnel-tips on the digits. Then just rake it down, slowly, gently, until it catches.'

'On what?'

'Doesn't matter. You just need to find a crevice, a spur. Some feature to grab onto, anchor yourself with. Make sure you press down plenty hard on it, just to see it's going to be able to take your – to take the fiveway's weight. If it's crumbling, let it go – you don't want to go with it, just feel around for another bit to grab.'

'Okay. Think I've got something. But there's no way this feels safe.'

'One level, it's not. But if you make sure you're holding on at three points at once, you should be right. Right? Then try the same with the left hindlimb. *Hind*limb. Gently. Gently.'

Marcus's palms were sweating; his face was flushed. 'Can't you just help hold the fiveway here while I sign out and let Attilla take over? I mean, he could run one of these things up this cliff blindfolded.'

'He probably could,' Ngaire conceded. 'But would that further your aims in that area? Besides, there's something up here I want to show you.'

'You said that already,' Marcus noted, the edge creeping back into his tone. 'What?'

'Not far now. Got the left hindlimb wedged good and proper? Good, now the right forelimb… '

'I don't feel like this is going to hold me,' Marcus complained.

'It *is* holding you. I stopped pinning you half a minute ago.'

'You *what?*'

'Steady! Look, Marcus, you've got good anchorage. Just keep your cool, and you'll manage. You can do this. Take a look around before you move on.'

'Last time I tried that,' he complained, 'I nearly managed to total half a million credits of governable instrumentation.'

'That was look down. *Don't* look down. Look *around*. The fiveway's well-anchored. Trust me.'

He did trust her, oddly enough. He wasn't sure why. Vertigo was a jealous mistress, even at a proxy's remove. (And his dread of heights had a hair trigger: even the view from the fourth storey canteen window was enough to fire it.) With misgivings congealing in his throat, he commanded the fiveway to rotate its distributed optical sensors and to gaze out across the dust-hazed plain. Sessum's sun, improbably large, disconcertingly red, hung high in the late-morning sky at his drone's back, augmenting the proxy's power supply and warming the cliff's rockface. In the distance, Marcus could see straggletrunks and occasional stands of the dark, leafless, pipecleaner-branched wirewood trees in which the grovers took refuge; a lazy river, leading down to a tidal flat; a few hillocks hugged the eastern horizon, while the five-storey neocrete edifice of the xenobiol research institute was just visible, some kilometres distant, as an obvious and ill-suited imposition upon the sparsely-forested plain. The sky was dotted with what passed, on Sessum, for birdlife: small, aerobatic gullbats and, soaring high, larger stretchfliers: fur-winged creatures whose motif was endurance flight, born of the need to stay a lifetime's span aloft, always grabbing food on the wing, staying as high as possible above the versatile, camouflaged killers that stalked the land. Mostly, though, it was the dark-tussocked carpet of the plain, rarely punctuated by other geographic features, that met his eyes; met his proxy's sensors. It was, he was forced to admit, an impressive view: he felt as though he could see all of Lankin beneath him, though he knew from the base's maps that the island was significantly bigger than this.

If he'd wanted, he could flick the visual spectrum to UV, get a sense for just how many cryptosaurines there were down on the tussocked apron beneath the cliff, hunting out prey. Lying in ambush. Harrying lumbershells and crabcrawlers.

He didn't want. While most of the rest of the base seemed in awe of the island's population of ruthless pocket carnosaurs, and spoke of the small apex predators with unalloyed admiration for their unparalleled lethality, Marcus just viewed them with foreboding. The same way, he imagined, that Jojo saw them. *What must it be like,* he wondered, *to be sentient, and to know that, unless you cling to the very highest branches, you're just meat?*

(Don't look down!)

'Enough lollygagging,' Ngaire chimed in his ear. 'Back to it.'

'Nye…'

'Yes?'

'I don't think I can move.'

'Sure you can. Just slide the tail up…'

The offering was a tight-bunched group of shiny dark globes clustered on a flexible branched stem, the whole of it not too large nor too heavy to gingerly balance in one outstretched hand. She knew of fruit-clumps that took broadly this form — those that hung in the lower branches of the archtangle bushes, dangerously, tantalisingly close to the ground, were somewhat similar — though these were oddly-scented and, she had no doubt, would not taste sweet like the archtangle berries, but sour and tainted. She no longer even bothered to taste the offerings anymore; that was not their purpose.

She replaced the clump on its pale platter, picked up the colour-stick – it took a minute, as it always did, to refamiliarise herself with the grip that gave the best control – and daubed a curl of dark pigment on the clean stretch-frame. Another curl beside it. Another.

Each globe was uncomplicated, but there were a lot of them. This would take her a while.

Beside her, at a distance she was prepared to accept as "safe", the sometimes-active angled one stood, unmoving, a tiny glimmer of coloured light flashing steadily on its upper surface.

The cave, when they reached it, felt scarcely less precarious than the cliff in which it was set: a steeply-sloping floor of crumbled rock scree, held in place only by a broad, modestly-upthrusting outcrop of rock at the cave's mouth. Footing on the cave's floor was treacherous, the ceiling jaggedly uneven in height – awkwardly so for an object the size and shape of their fiveways. Ngaire's device, flattening itself against the scree, scuttled its way towards the cave's further recesses with nary a show of concern, but Marcus was transfixed with yet more of the vicarious vertigo that had held him in its thrall out on the cliff face. Plus there was the characteristic problem with poking about within any cave on Sessum…

'Lean forward. Front left, front right,' Ngaire advised, Marcus wondering how she could stay so patient. 'Look, my fiveway's anchored safely, I can pull yours up if it'll help.'

'It might,' Marcus conceded, wishing he could find a way to not feel so helpless, so out of his depth here. 'But what about—' The gravel beneath his proxy's right "foot" started to slip from under him, and he threw himself – the fiveway – forward in blind panic. Ngaire's fiveway reached out a couple of limbs to catch Marcus's, and slowly, calmly she pulled it up from the cave's hazardous rim. Dislodged scree still trickled down the cave's floor to its entrance: Marcus listened in vain for the small sounds of impact on the plain far below, while his heart thundered desperately.

The cave twisted up and to the right, with a choke point that was quite beyond his remote-aptitude to negotiate; Ngaire's fiveway, its head/torso lamps throwing off confusing shadows in the gloom, had to guide his through the gap like an elder child leading a younger. In the air-conned quietude of the control room, he felt the simulated touch on his hand at once reassuring and disconcerting.

There was level ground at the very back of the cave, a sharp-edged shelf scarcely deep enough to fit the two fiveways. Off to the left, a small blind pocket of darkness spoke either of a spot of sanctuary against gravity, or of a natural sinkhole. Broadening the spectrum of his fiveway's visual sensors, he could determine that it was a shallow basin, choked with gravel and something else. Something organic. Scat. Dessicated scat, its odour long since dispersed. (The cave's primary scent, according to his fiveway's olfactors, was a kind of dry metallic cement-powder fruitiness; Marcus wasn't sure how far he trusted that portrayal.)

'You were asking?' Ngaire prompted.

'Cryptosaurines,' he replied.

'Nope. No sign they've ever been here.'

'But – it's just their type of environment. And they're excellent climbers. C'mon, you *can't* tell me this is beyond their ability to reach. If not from below, then at least from above.' (It was a cliché, by now: find a cave, any cave, on Sessum, and there'd be cryptosaurines. And nothing else. If there'd ever been anything else on Sessum that took refuge in caves, that thing had not withstood contact with the cryptosaurines.)

'Apparently it is. There's still more than half the mesa above us, plenty of cliff-face. And the biggest one of those overhangs is a doozy.'

'Then how come the droppings?'

'Cryps are excellent climbers. But grovers are better.'

'*Grovers?*'

'It's grover shit.'

'You mean a different species, or subspecies, of cave-dwellers?'

'Not according to the genetic material in here, no.'

'But… arboreal… grovers almost *never* come down from the treetops, except to reclaim ammunition when they've run out of throw-stones. It's their whole survival gimmick, their niche. I mean, the kind of gauntlet they'd have to run – and they're not fast runners, by any means – just to reach the *base* of these cliffs… the nearest stand of wirewoods is hundreds of metres away. They'd be cut to ribbons.'

'It's grover shit,' Ngaire reiterated. 'Very old, but it's unambiguous.'

'How old?'

'Decades. Maybe centuries. The air in here's dry enough to preserve it.'

In the dark, filtered calm of the proxy control room, Marcus leaned back in his chair, closed his eyes. Tried to disentangle himself from the proxy feed.

Try as he might, he couldn't reconcile himself to the mystery Ngaire had revealed to him here. Grovers just weren't cave-dwellers. They *weren't*. It didn't fit.

'So what d'you reckon?' Ngaire asked.

'About this? How should I know?'

'You're the nearest the Base has to a grover specialist.'

'No, I just happen to have the care of an orphan grover who may have formed the opinion that I – or rather, the fiveway I so clumsily navigate around its enclosure – is its parent. Or more probably, that its parents and everyone else from its extended family got torn to strips by cryptosaurines, in front of its eyes, and that my intrusions via the fiveway are merely a horrendous joke played out against its now-pointless existence.'

'Cheery.'

'Sorry. But I do appreciate seeing this. Even if I don't understand why you felt it necessary that I experience the sheer visceral terror of freeclimbing a fiveway up here in the first place. I mean, you could've got Attilla or one of the others to make the climb, that'd be almost second nature to them.'

'But then, you'd have missed the opportunity to learn something about yourself in the process.'

'Ngaire,' he explained patiently. 'I *already know* I get vertigo. And am too criminally clumsy to be able to reliably pilot one of these things in an environment this extreme.'

Ngaire laughed. 'If you say so. But you managed the climb, nonetheless. I think that proves something. Ready for the descent?'

'You have got to be kidding me. I'm paging Attilla myself.'

She laughed again.

The next morning, Marcus decided to try something he hadn't attempted for some weeks: to manoeuvre Jojo into painting a landscape.

Jojo very much preferred still-lifes, and could obsess over the detail of a lemon, the complexity of a bowl of starfruit, the sheen of an aubergine. But she seemed to show no interest in what they *were*. It was, Marcus thought, merely a fascination with how they *looked*.

Mindful that she was effectively a prisoner of their research effort, he strove always to give her a choice of subject matter. She had adjusted quickly to the selection routine, in which his fiveway proxy would unfold a display screen from its torso, on which would be presented a sequence of five monochrome images, cycling slowly through the set. At first the images comprised a landscape (always from a vantage point within Jojo's enclosure itself); a depiction of a type of terran fruit or vegetable; some detail of fiveway anatomy; a view of Jojo herself, ranging from close portrait to full-figure; and an abstract.

Though she sometimes lingered on the self-image (as, indeed, she did with the enclosure's wall-mounted mirror), Jojo always chose the fruit or vegetable. After a while, Marcus stopped offering her any other imagery, and presented her with a choice of appropriately botanical subjects.

Today, however, he'd dialled up a sequence of five vistas, from which the directionally-electrified mesh fencing had been carefully edited out: southwest, towards the stands of forest from which they'd rescued Jojo several months ago; west, a view of savannah dominated, in the foreground, by her enclosure's captive and carefully-ignored tree;

west again, offering a closer view of the tree; northwest, out across the savannah towards the cliffs, some half-dozen kilometres distant, where yesterday Ngaire had insisted on reacquainting him with his acrophobia; and north, more cliffs, and in the nearer distance, the watering-holes that were a favoured hunting-ground of the cryptosaurines.

Jojo cycled through the scenes: she'd "trained" this fiveway (or, in reality, Marcus) to interpret a wave of the autobrush as "Next!" Her first pass through was hurried, dismissive. *Looking for the fruit,* Marcus thought. Her second perusal of the series of images was more cautious. Northwest, in particular, held her attention this time around. Then she glanced up at the sky, stood staring like an acolyte at the glowering red eye of Sessum's sun for several seconds, and dropped the autobrush. Yellow pigment bled out on the enclosure's brown-dirt floor.

There was no painting done that day.

The intruder was thick-limbed, utterly foreign, and strangely equipped: its face shinily-shielded and studded; torso, limbs and hands covered in fabric like the stretch-frame stuff, but flexible; feet so clumpy that climbing would surely be impossible. She felt only slightly uneasy — it had encroached before, but had kept a careful distance, had never attempted to corner her.

Besides, there were sturdy branches within reach, if she needed to protect herself.

On this occasion, the intruder was staring at that section of the artificial structure against which her depictions of past offerings had been placed. It gazed at one after another of the daubed stretch-frames, apparently unaware of its vulnerability in placing its back towards her. But she was adequately fed, and could not be bothered attempting the kill.

Also, it smelt wrong. There was every reason to believe it would taste no better than the offerings.

She watched the intruder, watching her daubings, wondered what it felt when it looked upon them. Perhaps it was hungry.

If so, she could not help it. She had already eaten her own food this morning; and the angled one always took the offering away when she had finished recording it.

The comms tone on his flexy revealed the caller. He fought down his suddenly-increased heartrate, cringing at the accompanying blush, killed the sim and bid the screen to darken before he answered, voice-only. 'Marcus,' he said.

'Yeah, it's me,' replied Attilla. Pause. 'You busy?'

Calm. 'Hardly. What's up?'

'Got something might interest you.'

'What, exactly?' Marcus asked, heart still thumping as he got up, slid the wall lighting up to standard, and moved to his room's sole chair. *What must be showing in my voice?* he wondered. 'Is it – uh – something I need to drop by for, to witness in person?'

'Oh, hardly.' The dismissive tone in Attilla's voice may have been unintended; but that didn't stop it cutting. *C2. A1. You're a fool to ignore that.* 'You remember that grover dissection that Katrin and Pirkko conducted a few weeks back?'

'Uh – you mean the one from the cryptosaurine kill?'

'Yeah, that one.'

'What about it? I thought they'd said they didn't learn much that they didn't already know.'

'Not at the time, perhaps,' said Attilla. 'But there've been some interesting results come out of the subsequent cellular-level analysis.'

'Such as what?' *Spit it out, will you, Attie?*

'Optics.'

'Didn't they say it meshed with expectations from vertebrate anatomy? Rods and cones?'

'Well, cells analogous to those, sure. But there's a wrinkle, and I think it might have some bearing on Jojo's artwork.'

'What do you mean, a wrinkle?'

'Three types of cone-like cells, for colour reception. So far, so humanoid. But you wouldn't believe the colour differentiation—'

'Try me.' He caught himself gesturing at the flexy's darkened screen.

'The receptor proteins have absorption profiles with maxima at – hold on, I had this bit tabulated – six forty-five, six fifty-three, six sixty-four nanometres, respectively.'

'Meaning what? You're going to have to give me some kind of context here.'

'Meaning that those three wavelengths are all very solidly in the red part of the visual spectrum. Assuming that's standard for grovers, it means their colour perception for most of the visual region is little more than greyscale, but their ability to make fine distinctions between subtle shades of red would be incredible.'

'This must be – wait… well I guess that explains why she made such a thing over her painting of the tomatoes. Except – surely she'd know that the colours she was using to paint them were all jumbled? I mean, it's not exactly a study in red, is it?'

Attilla was silent for long enough that Marcus wondered if the connection had been severed; then he spoke. 'Actually, not necessarily – well, yes, she'd *know*, but pigments are different in their nature to radiant light. If there was no precise colour match for what she was seeing, she might have been forced to blend what to us would be very disjunctive-looking colours in order to get something that sort of matched the relative shades she's sensitive to. It'd probably look very muddy to her, but it might have been the best she could do. It'd be like someone got you to do a landscape, and didn't supply any blue paint for the sky.'

'There is only the one shade of red in the paints we supply her with,' Marcus conceded. 'That was all I thought she'd need.'

'It would seem not,' replied Attilla.

'But… *why*? I mean, if they've evolved with this level of colour specialisation, there has to be a purpose behind it. Right?'

'Could it be a defence against the cryptosaurines? Some way of seeing through their camouflage?'

21

If that's the case, thought Marcus, pulling himself out of the chair, *it didn't do her troupe any damn good. But what else could it be?* 'Or something that helps with finding food. Primate colour-sense is geared towards quick recognition of fruit ripeness. This could be something similar.'

'True. But none of the vegetative material they eat has a noticeably red coloration, nor their prey species, as far as we know.'

'Then it's something we've missed, perhaps. Look, Attilla, I – thanks for passing this on. I'm not sure what it means yet, but the information could well be useful. Can you please keep me briefed if you find out more about this?'

'But of course. Anything else?'

Yes. 'No.'

She had panicked. There'd been a stretch-wing that had flown directly over her territory, low enough that its shadow had chased her along the ground. She'd brushed against the barrier in her haste to reach the alcove, and had noted that the glancing impact against the barrier had hurt. But it hadn't felt hot, it hadn't flashed or flamed the way it did when a small flier knocked into it from outside; this puzzled her. Why was the barrier different on her side than the other?

Someday, she would have to find an answer to that question. But for now, as she nursed her shoulder and watched the retreating stretch-wing, it was enough just to register the memory.

'Watch.'

'Sorry. I really don't need to see another recording of a grover massacre.'

'It's not a grover massacre,' Hansel reassured him. 'Promise. No grovers were harmed in the acquisition of this feed. Now watch.'

'I know sure as hell *something's* gonna be harmed. You've got that sadistic-xenobehaviourist tone in your voice.'

'Well, you got that right. But not grovers, honest. Now watch.'

The straggletrunk's dark, too-thin branches jutted like an assembly of twisted, rusted iron strands into the sombre sky. The tree looked top-heavy, its upper reaches crowded with grey shapes, and movement. *Liar*, thought Marcus.

But he looked closer, calling in the flexy's zoom. Hansel was right, they weren't grovers.

They were flappers. The tree was full to overflowing with flappers. It was a testament to the straggletrunk's wiry robustness that it could support the weight of so many of the turkey-sized, pteranodon-crossed-with-jackal fliers.

'See that one, third from the base of that branch there? Watch him.'

'How d'you know it's a him?'

'Plumage. *Watch.*'

Marcus watched. Within a minute, Hansel's identified flapper initiated two territorial squabbles with the flappers downbranch of its own vantage point, winning both confrontations. On each occasion, it moved further along the downward-sloping branch, trading place with its vanquished opponent. *That makes no sense. Down means danger –*

There was a suggestion of movement at the tree's base. A brief disturbance in the spears of near-black tussock, the swiftest hint of shadow obscuring the beetle-green flank of some large and long-deceased lumbershell's upturned carapace. Up in the branches, the flappers redoubled their racket. But the sparring, the repositioning, had suddenly ceased.

Marcus got the uneasy tightness he always experienced at such points, just before the ambush played out. *Why don't they take flight?* he wondered. But he knew why. Flight was expensive for animals of a flapper's size under Sessum's gravity. Flight was not to be entertained just on the vague hint of a threat, something that might be merely the push of a stray breath of wind. And this was a straggletrunk, its extensive root system active in dissuading encroachment from other trees, isolated by almost one hundred metres from the nearest grove – which went some way, Marcus suspected, to explaining why the tree was available for flapper-roosting to begin with. With no conceivable escape route, straggletrunks offered scant sanctuary for grovers. (Nonetheless, several half-embedded throwstones studding the ground at the tree's base spoke of earlier occupancy by Jojo's ilk, probably years past.)

Hansel paused the feed. 'You want me to switch it to compressed-spectrum?'

'Do I have a choice?'

'It won't make much sense otherwise,' Hansel replied, almost apologetically. He adjusted the flexy's controls and the scene played out in false-colour. The tree looked the same; the flappers had taken on a more reddish hue. The sky and the plain both looked duller. And the cryptosaurines were now discernible as faint shadows: their camouflage, near-perfect at visible wavelengths and exquisite quite a way into the infrared, failed under near-UV illumination.

There were maybe twenty of the cryptosaurines, like pocket allosaurs, none much larger than a domestic housecat, gathered at the base of the tree. Sessum's dim red sun gave off precious little of the cryptosaurine-revealing UV wavelengths, but Marcus's imagination filled in the details lacking in the recorded imagery. Lithe, long-clawed, and with a bite powerful enough to pierce bone without obvious impediment. Several of the reptiloids – the smaller individuals, Marcus noted, with a kind of unwanted curiosity – began methodically taking paths up through the tree's lower branches in a display of silent (and, to the flappers, all-but-invisible) cooperative hunting as impressive as it was chilling, while the other members of the pack waited in the shadows beneath the tree, snouts raised expectantly skywards.

Though the flappers still called, with voices of rough-metal-on-metal, it was not with the ruckus that it had been a half-minute ago. There was, Marcus thought, more *structure* to their noise than had earlier been evident...

In a grove, he realised, *the cryptosaurines follow a quite different strategy. Less of a mass attack, more a case of attrition –* 'I really don't think I need to see this,' he told Hansel. 'It's just going to descend into slaughter-porn, isn't it?'

'Watch,' said Hansel. So Marcus watched; and saw Hansel's flapper do something really stupid, just before the tree exploded into violence.

There were many of the intruders, somehow within the structure; she saw some of them quite frequently, through the shiny stuff like solid water that faced the fronts of many of the structure's grottoes. Once, when she was bored, she had tried to see how tough the shiny stuff was by throwing rocks at it. One of the rocks had made a loud clack when it had hit, and a pattern had spread out, like frozen water-ripples or like the web of a catcher; but the next day the shiny stuff was clean again, its pattern somehow erased, and all her rocks had been hidden. Probably, she suspected, by the more active of the angled ones. She did not eat much that day, out of annoyance, but her rocks did not come back.

The intruders she saw through the shiny stuff did not shield their faces, nor were their hands often covered, but they otherwise went draped much as did 'her' intruder, though different in various ways: often drab, sometimes disturbingly colourful. She wondered what it meant that they could not find their way out from behind the shiny stuff; perhaps this was a kind of nest.

Something caught at the corner of her eye, and she turned to look. The sky...

The choice in the canteen today was to sit at Ngaire's and Pirkko's table, or to take a table to himself and further enhance his reputation as a loner. With some reluctance – Pirkko was, in his view, quiet, analytical, and severe, and Ngaire was, well, *Ngaire* – he took a seat.

'So you've no indication?' Ngaire continued. She had nodded assent to Marcus as he sat down, but evidently felt no necessity to be providing context for the discussion he'd intruded upon.

'None at this stage,' said Pirkko, her voice almost a murmur. 'Kat's still leaning towards thermoregulation, but I don't see how that fits with what the dissections have revealed; and I don't think display, either for mating or defensive purposes, is going to account either. But it's got to serve some purpose, right?'

Typical, Marcus thought. *A generation ago – a decade ago, probably, we didn't even know Sessum's star existed, let alone Sessum itself; and now we're frustrated because we can't immediately understand all the details of the planet's biosphere. Faster-than-light really has spoiled us, hasn't it?*

'And what's eating *you*, sport?' Ngaire asked, turning in her seat to include him in conversation.

'I...' *Best, with this pair, to offer something practical.* 'I was just thinking about some footage Hansel showed me yesterday. The flapper attack, in that straggletrunk about eight klicks northwest of here. You seen it?'

'Is that the one where...? Uh, yes, I remember now. Efficient little fuckers, aren't they?' Spoken as though Ngaire held some admiration for the cryptosaurines' lethality; and perhaps she did.

'That's one way to look at it, I guess. But – you've seen the bit where the flappers' alpha male leaps down from the lower branch?'

'Yes, Hansel showed – wait, that was the *alpha male*?'

'If you watch the interactions leading up to the attack, that's certainly the way it looks,' said Marcus.

'But that *makes no sense*,' protested Pirkko, softly. 'Why would the alpha male—'

'It was protecting its offspring,' Marcus said. 'Look, I don't have direct proof of that, but I've been going over it in my mind and that's the only thing that fits. The cryps are effectively invisible, right? At any rate, they're sufficiently well-camoed that the flappers show no evidence of being able to see them.'

'Which is weird, based on what Attilla's reported,' said Pirkko.

'What do you mean?' Marcus asked, hating the lump that had sprung into existence within his oesophagus with the mention of Attilla's name.

'Kat and I dissected a couple of flappers several days back,' she replied. 'We passed tissue samples on to Attilla's group for further analysis, and he reported back yesterday to say that the optical structure looked very similar to what they've found in the grovers and the lumbershells, with those three different red-sensitive cone-like cell types.'

He said he'd let me know, Marcus thought, aware that Ngaire was saying something, but not caring, for the moment, to pay attention. *C2. A1. Fool.*

'– effective monochrome?' Pirkko was asking.

'They could have sonar,' Ngaire suggested.

'We'd see evidence of that,' Pirkko responded, leaning forward and brushing a dark curl from her eye. 'The flappers don't have the brain organisation of something that uses sonar. Besides, I'd argue that anything which lives in an arboreal environment like that—'

'Bats,' said Ngaire. 'Besides, the cryps use sonar themselves, for coordinating their attacks.'

'Which is why we can be sure the flappers don't have it – if they did, they'd be much better able to elude cryptosaurine attacks.'

'Be that as it may,' said Marcus, struggling to find his way back into the dialogue, 'that's not what happened in the footage.'

'You said something about the alpha male,' Pirkko prompted.

'Yes,' said Marcus. 'It sprang off the branch it was on—'

'And got itself killed, yes,' said Ngaire. 'Sacrificing itself so others could escape.'

'No,' said Marcus. 'Well, yes, but there's a wrinkle. Did you see the ten minutes or so of jostling the flock went through, before the attack? Bustling around, changing positions, *testing the tensions on branches.* They were building up a record of the branches' responses to shifts in weight.'

'My God,' said Pirkko. 'So then when the big male jumped ship, it shook the tree—'

'And the rest of the flock could identify, quickly, which branches were heavier than they should be, and therefore dangerous.'

'It still sounds like a pretty desperate defence mechanism,' said Ngaire. 'Four or five flappers dead, including the alpha.'

'Six,' said Marcus. 'And two cryptosaurines.'

'No skin off their nose, though, is it? Just more protein for the survivors,' said Ngaire. 'But it's—'

They all glanced up in reaction to the temporary gloom, three, four seconds, before the backup power supply came online. 'What the hell was that?' Marcus asked.

'I have no idea,' said Pirkko, checking something on her flexy. 'But whatever it was, it's taken out the sats. All off-base connections have just gone dead.'

'Let's hope none of the fiveways were in active flight,' said Ngaire.

'Or cliff-climbing,' Marcus suggested.

Jojo's enclosure was empty.

There was no sign of a disturbance, no structural damage: evidently, she'd just climbed over the direl-mesh fence. *A four-metre drop*, Marcus told himself, *she must've wanted out pretty bad*. But why now? The enclosure had been her home for months, and to the best of his knowledge she'd never shown any interest in scaling the fence. *She's shown precious little interest in anything*, he thought, with a pang at his complicity in her incarceration. *Just the painting, and—*

He remembered the abortive painting session of a couple of days back, when he'd sought to wean her off still-lifes onto landscapes. Something about her reaction caught in his memory, played with his mind like a cat with a mouse. She'd been staring at the sky. For a few seconds, that sky had held her whole attention, and something unreadable had crossed her face.

It's grover shit. Cryptosaurines are excellent climbers, but grovers are better.

You wouldn't believe the colour differentiation.

If you saw how long it took her to paint this—

If they've evolved with this level of colour specialisation, there has to be a purpose behind it.

But the flappers have that colour-sense too, and they're clearly unable to penetrate the cryptosaurines' camouflage.

A pretty desperate defence mechanism.

And Marcus had a suspicion about why she'd escaped, *now*, and an absolute conviction on where she'd gone.

(And, of course, the fiveways were offline.)

'If she's where you've said she is,' Attilla said, 'it's safest we leave her until later. Wait 'til the sats are back up.'

'Or just leave her full stop,' said Ngaire. 'She's a wild creature; this is her habitat.'

'But she's *not* a fully wild creature, that's the whole point. She has no troupe; she'll be at the mercy of any cryptosaurines she encounters on the way,' argued Marcus. He moved against the wall to make way for a couple of the base's researchers manoeuvring a bulky trolley, laden with lab equipment, along the third-floor corridor. 'And I didn't say that's where she *was*, I said that's where she was *heading to*.' He was, himself, surprised at the depth of feeling Jojo's escape had sparked in him. *I would never have thought this'd be something I'd risk any chance with Attilla over – but there you go. I'm all she's got; Lord knows that's not much.*

'We should take the trekker,' said Attilla.

Ngaire showed even more surprise than, Marcus suspected, he did himself at this suggestion. 'You're actually *going along* with this?' she asked. 'In the run-up to what looks set to be the biggest CME since we got here?'

'The particle front that took out the sats a couple of hours ago was the biggest CME since we got here,' Attilla noted. 'The subsequent one – the one I'm guessing spooked Jojo – is probably tenfold more powerful, judging by the stellar flare that spawned it. And no, I'm not entirely comfortable with the idea of chasing off after her; for one thing, I have serious doubts as to whether a six-hour window will give us enough time to get back safely, even if we do find her more-or-less where we expect to. But Marcus is right: she's not a wild creature, not fully; she displays a significant degree of intelligence; and she's in our care and keeping. That gives us a responsibility.'

'You're crazier than I thought. Maybe you two do deserve each other.'

'Huh?' Attilla asked.

'Forget it,' said Ngaire. 'But I'm only coming along if I get to steer.'

'You're in on this?' asked Marcus.

'Of course. If there's ropework involved, you'll need my help. Besides, I want to see how this plays out.'

She was in danger. The sky-dread struck through her, worse in some ways than any terror of the unseen killers. The need for escape, for shelter, was written into her bones.

'What clued you in?' Attilla asked. They were sitting, hip-to-hip, in the narrow middle seat of the trekker, its ungainly dust-disturbing motion jostling and wrenching them against each other. The rear seat had been removed, to make room for equipment: climbing gear, lamps, short-range transmitters, two suitcased fiveways. (And, at Ngaire's insistence, a couple of rifles.)

Marcus made a show of safety-checking the bulky, filter-snouted facemask that lay in his lap. He wasn't complaining at the vehicle's motion, even when a harsh bump knocked his shoulder hard against the canopy that was their outer defence against Sessum's breathable but dangerously carbon-monoxide-laced atmosphere. That thigh contact was worth a few shoulder-bruises, even if, as Ngaire had intimated, there was nothing in it. 'I spent the evening after you had told me about the grovers' colour specialisation'—*in fruitlessly thinking over what might be*—'in checking out what could possibly be significant about such a shade of red; then when Pirkko mentioned that the flappers have the same colour sense, and the lumbershells, I wondered what would be the evolutionary incentive for something that would carry a significant metabolic cost. It didn't make any sense until, when we discovered Jojo had done a runner, I remembered she'd been fascinated by something in the sky, a day or so earlier.

That got me checking over the properties of Sessum's sun. Red dwarf, supposedly quiescent. But it hasn't been subjected to intensive study over a long period – we didn't even know this system existed until maybe ten years ago, when one of the FTL autoprobes returned to Earth... so there could well be things about the star that we didn't realise. But we *do* know that Sessum itself has only a very weak magnetic field, much less powerful than Earth's, so that would make it distinctly more susceptible to space weather. And I couldn't help but notice that the receptor wavelengths you mentioned were all very close to H-alpha.'

'Translation, please?' asked Ngaire, from the trekker's cramped cockpit.

'The first line of the Balmer series,' explained Attilla, yelling to make himself heard over the percussive noise of the trekker's progress across a bumpy rockfield. 'It's a hydrogen transition, seen in discharges and stellar spectra, at a wavelength of six-fifty-something nanometres.'

'Six fifty-six,' Marcus interjected.

Attilla continued. 'Normally, in starlight, it's absorbed; but in certain stages of a major stellar flare, it can show up in emission. Which means—'

'Which means there's a subtle change in the colour of the sunlight,' said Marcus, 'so slight that we'd never notice it. But to a grover, it shines out like, well, like the change from yellow to green. It explains how she saw the tomatoes, it makes sense of the cave – if this is something that happens once or twice every generation, that Sessum's sun lets loose with such a violent burst of flare activity that the coronal mass ejection becomes a lethal hazard, the last place you want to be is stuck in the treetops. Regardless of whether there are cryptosaurines lurking about, or not, it seems like it must be a gauntlet that's worth running.'

'If you're right about this, then it changes our picture of the whole ecology,' Attilla mused. 'But the cryps are a much more... frequent threat. It's odd the grovers would be so visually well-adapted to a radiation hazard, yet still blind to the cryptosaurines...'

'Not if the cryptosaurines are a comparatively recent invasive species to Lankin from the continent. Sea's not that deep, all it would take would be a land bridge, some time in the past half-million years or so, and that would probably account for it.'

'Speaking of our scaly friends,' said Ngaire, swerving the trekker's springy, segmented roller-wheels around an outcropping of rock. 'I'm not seeing any proximity radar evidence for any cryps up and around at the moment. Normally we'd have seen at least a pack or two by now – so maybe they've gone to earth as well.'

'That could be good, or it could be bad,' said Marcus.

'In *what way* could it be bad?' asked Attilla.

'The caves,' Marcus replied. 'The lower ones are probably crawling with cryps.'

'So let's hope your girlfriend knew enough to climb up,' said Ngaire.

'She's not my—' Marcus caught himself as he glimpsed Ngaire's mischievous grin in the trekker's side mirror.

'Shit,' said Attilla, crouching to inspect the damage on the trekker's underside. 'Sheared clean in two, Nye. Should've gone around.'

Ngaire was standing guard, rifle angled down at her side, eyes scanning the horizon. 'It wasn't the rock, it was the rut beyond it. How was I to know—'

'Can we fix it?' Marcus asked, anxiously watching the sky. The mask was tight, his face hot, but that wasn't the sole reason he was sweating.

'We've got a spare axle. Take us an hour, though,' said Attilla, standing up, knees audibly popping.

'How much time do we *have*?' Marcus asked.

'Best estimate? Four hours, plus or minus two,' said Attilla.

'Four hours?'

'Plus or minus two,' Ngaire emphasised. 'Why so uncertain?'

'These CMEs don't keep to a skyliner schedule, you know,' Attilla observed. 'And with the sats still down, we—' He broke off as a steady pinging beat started to sound.

'Shit,' said Ngaire. The concern on her face was plain, even through her mask's distortions and reflections.

'Problem?' asked Marcus.

'Could be,' she replied. 'Proximity radar alert, set for two hundred metres. Chances are, that's *not good.*'

Cryps, Marcus thought, dread locking in, like a mechanism, somewhere in his gut.

'Might be best if we retreat into the trekker,' suggested Ngaire.

'We've got a busted axle,' Attilla argued. 'Time's ticking. And the radar might be nothing.'

Might not be nothing, Marcus thought, trying to remember how quickly a cryptosaurine pack could cover two hundred metres.

'Let me go in and check, then,' Ngaire said, handing Marcus the rifle.

'What do I do with this?' he asked, as she retreated around the vehicle's bulbous nosecone.

'Just shoot anything that isn't Attilla,' she replied, stepping into the airlock.

Or Jojo, he told himself.

The climb had been arduous, with purchase often uncertain. More than once she feared that she would lose her footing, fall. It did not help that she was out of practice; but a single tree is always unsafe, and there had been no cause to climb until the sky had glowed with danger.

Her kind was skilled at this; she did not fall.

Climb high enough, and you will find a cave that the unseen killers cannot reach. That was how it worked. She crawled in, and down, and found sanctuary, from both the sky-glow and the killers, though no company. But perhaps the solitude was just as well: she did not belong with anyone anymore.

The smell was objectionable, but safety did not always smell sweet.

'They're pincering,' Ngaire announced from the cockpit, her voice in Marcus's earbud. 'About ten in total, from the looks of it. Half edging in from the north, maybe a hundred and fifty metres away; the other half coming from the south-east, they're about – oh, shit. Fifty metres, maybe less.'

'Fifty metres?' Marcus was sure the tremulousness in his voice must betray his fear. *And with the sun so high in the sky, I can't even be sure which way is south-east.* He scanned the horizon fruitlessly, looking for an invisible foe.

'Yeah. Guys? I'd really recommend you get your tails inside, now.'

'Just need five more minutes,' Attilla complained.

'Thought you said this was going to take you an hour?'

'I'm cutting a few corners. Nye, seriously, is there anything you can do, by way of countermeasures? Just buy me five minutes?'

'There is something I can try. Take me a minute to set it up,' she answered.

'If they're fifty metres away, we maybe don't have a minute—' Marcus suggested. *Is that a gust, pushing at the tussock over there? Or something… else?*

'You've probably got a minute,' she said, breathing heavily as they could hear her hefting something out of the trekker's cargo space. 'There's the other prong of the pincer, don't forget – if they've split up, they'll still want to attack in coordination.'

'If that's supposed to cheer me up, it's not succeeding,' said Marcus.

'Not intended to,' she answered, grunting at some exertion. 'But if there's a rock handy, that could help you. Pass the rifle across to your left hand, pick up a rock or two, adopt a throwing stance, south-east.'

'But I can't *see* them,' he protested. *Is that that gust again, closer now?*

'Doesn't matter. They *understand* rocks, it'll slow them down.'

'Which way's south-east?'

'Thirty degrees anticlockwise. *Anti*-clockwise. Yeah. okay, hold that pose.'

'*Ngaire* – there's something out there, pretty fucking close. I'm seeing indentations in the tussock, maybe ten metres—'

'Great. Hold that pose. Heft the rock a bit more. I'm done, I've got this. Just give me a minute to get it out—'

'Another minute? Seriously? Ngaire—' *I don't really think mime is that effective a defence…*

'You're doing a great job there, Marcus,' said Attilla, still bent beneath the trekker, wrestling with the damaged axle assembly. With his back to unseen danger. 'Almost done here.'

Then there was a moment, while the wind pushed the blades of a nearby tussock-stand aside, and Marcus found himself staring at the pattern of the blades as they had been, but now with the faintest, cheshire-cat suggestion of slitted eyes and bristling teeth – they faded almost instantly, but even as they did he flung his rock. At something that wasn't, something maybe six or seven metres distant. The stone bounced away off nothing, drawing a wounded sound, followed by a snarl, out of ostensibly empty air now not five meters away from him. Then, even closer, from the tussock that was flattened barely more than an arm's breadth beyond him, there was an exhalation of stinking, rattling breath. Panicked, he gripped the rifle's barrel with both hands, swung it butt-foremost, connected with a wrist-jarring knock against the emptiness in front of him. (Thought, only after the event, of what could've happened if the firearm had gone *off*...)

He stepped back, changing his hold on the rifle again, shaking his right hand, placing his back to the trekker. He realised he was leaving Attilla more exposed as the latter worked at repairing the vehicle; but the demands of self-preservation were not to be ignored.

Where was the cryptosaurine now? His eyes darted around the foreground, seeking out imperfections in the tussock, catching on shadows, tripping over the slightest imagined movement... on an impulse, he let out a low, challenging growl. Heard an answering snarl, low, from his side. Turned and fired the rifle. Sudden pain thudded into his shoulder from the rifle butt's recoil; the bullet thumped into bare dirt with a burst of dust. There was the blurred suggestion of something leaping away. Then, following the rifle's detonation, a deafening roar and a rush passed him from behind.

Something silver-grey had flung itself through the air past him, disturbingly close, then past the rear of the trekker. He had just long enough to recognise it as a fiveway in flight before it climbed, turned, and swung back, heading north. Turning to watch despite the prickling sensation of an invisible hazard at his back, he saw the fiveway swoop and buzz a nondescript location in the tussock. Something dropped from the proxy, burst with the orange flash of an explosion in mid-air.

The fiveway swung around again, on a trajectory that took it directly over Marcus's head, Attilla, and the trekker. This time the flash of its underside as it eclipsed the zenith was not cleanly metallic, but streaked with tigerine orange. It turned, gradually descending, accelerated, clipped some unseen obstacle and cartwheeled into the low foliage some thirty metres away, spinning across Marcus's field of vision before coming to rest, limbs twisted, upturned, in newly-gouged earth.

'Damn,' said Ngaire. '*Not* supposed to do that. Have to collect it on the way back, once company's cleared off. Still, you wanted five minutes, Attie. That should've provided it.'

Attilla stood up, steadied himself with a grease-stained glove against the trekker's side panelling. 'All good, I'm basically done here. Marcus had my back, so I just got on with it. We should be right to go.'

'Ngaire, what *was* that?' Marcus asked, heart still pounding, as he followed Attilla around the nosecone towards the vehicle's airlock.

'Countermeasures,' Ngaire explained. 'A bit improvised, but—'

'Countermeasures?'

'High-volume ultrasonics, to screw with their sonar-sense, so they couldn't coordinate an attack, and a paint bomb. Visibility orange, they'll stick out like sore thumbs now. That's one group of cryps that may well go hungry until the next time it rains.'

'Cool,' said Attilla, and Marcus couldn't be sure that the mission specialist didn't favour him with a wink. 'Nice work. But this time, steer *around* the rocks.'

'Time to CME?' Marcus asked, as Ngaire brought the trekker to a halt close to the cliff-face. He could see a half-dozen dark openings at the base of the cliff. *I wonder how many of those are occupied*, he thought, very much aware of the most likely occupants. They'd have to run another gauntlet, even before they began climbing. *Attilla was right. We should have left this until after the flare's passage.*

'About two hours thirty,' said Ngaire, 'plus or minus two hours.' She broke off to take a transmission from base.

'That's going to make it tight for the climb,' said Marcus.

'Particularly since we don't know which cave she's climbed to,' said Attilla.

'What, there's more than one up there?'

'Well, yes… but you said you knew where she'd gone.'

'That was *before* you told me there was more than one *cave*,' Marcus complained. 'We'll never find her before the flare hits.'

'We can at least climb to find shelter for ourselves,' said Attilla. 'And we can scope out a few of the possibilities with the other fiveway. It'll be quick enough in flight mode, and we've still got short-range control over it, for the moment.'

'Is it safe enough to try to direct it, under these conditions? I mean, interference—'

'We've got a window, before it hits.'

This is going pear-shaped, Marcus lamented. *And it's my fault. I've led these people into danger.*

'Change of plan,' Ngaire announced, restarting the trekker's motor.

'Nye, what are you *doing*?' asked Attilla.

'Heard back from base. Our grover scaled something, alright, but it wasn't the enclosure fence.'

'What the hell do you mean?' asked Marcus.

Ngaire started backing and turning the trekker. 'Hansel found her. She's fallen through an access panel in the main exhaust shaft on the base's roof. Shaken, and very disoriented, but basically okay, which is more than can be said for the top floor of that wing of the building. They'll have to patch-repair that panel, and then it'll take a couple of hours to pump out the air, get the cee-oh level back below safe limits.'

'She never even left the *perimeter*?' Marcus asked.

'Nope,' Ngaire responded, and Marcus thought he could hear a trace of admiration in her tone. 'She knew to get out of the rads, and not to take any unnecessary risks to do it. Guess she had more common sense than any of us gave her credit for.'

'Shit,' said Marcus. 'So how long will it take us to get back?'

'A bit over an hour, if we're lucky.' The trekker rolled forward, cumbersome, sluggardly over the rough terrain, under a glaring, unreliable sun.

'And we've got two hours twenty-five?'

'Two twenty-five, plus or minus—'

'Don't say it,' said Marcus, aware again of the pressure of Attilla's thigh against his, and in a sudden surge of recklessness moving his hand to rest on Attilla's knee. The other allowed it to remain there for several hopeful seconds. Then, as carefully, as tenderly, yet as lacking in deeper warmth as though he were relocating a wayward laboratory animal, Attilla lifted up that hand in his own and placed it on Marcus's knee.

Attilla didn't lift his own hand immediately; turned his head towards Marcus, who was now colouring up; and, when he had the other's attention, said softly, 'If today's taught us anything, it's that people sometimes aren't where we expect them to be. I've been thinking lately that it's a terrible thing to be lonely, and isolated, and we should try to do something about that. We can't introduce Jojo back into an existing troupe, they're so fiercely territorial, but there's no reason we couldn't make her the nucleus, the matriarch I guess, of a new troupe.'

'Admin would never wear it,' said Marcus. 'I have enough trouble getting them to spring for paint. Besides, she's still young. Not to mention... extremely vulnerable.'

'A younger male, in an adjacent enclosure, give them plenty of time to get acquainted. And give them both options for retreat – whatever happens between them, it needs to be allowed to develop naturally. Whatever passes for 'naturally' in those circs. And don't worry about Admin, I think I can talk them around... if you're agreeable, Marcus.'

'Agreeable's maybe not the right word,' said Marcus. 'I've certainly got reservations. But she's miserable with the status quo, and I can't think of anything else that offers a prospect to improve that. And I'd be lying if I said the opportunity to observe some inter-grover interactions up close, under controlled conditions, didn't appeal. Quite a lot actually.'

'Good. Great. I'll do what I can to set matters in motion once we're back. I'm looking forward to collaborating with you on a troupe for Jojo. And as for your other implied query... I'm flattered, Marcus, really I am. But I'm not the one for you, not in that sense.'

The trekker hit a pothole, eliciting a short string of swear words from Ngaire as she struggled to apply traction. 'Everything okay back there?' she asked.

'All good, I think,' Attilla answered, favoring Marcus with that shark-mouthed smile before turning to inspect the scenery.

C2. A1. Seniority and ambit claims. Have I just been played? Marcus found himself wondering.

'Let's just go,' he said, feeling his face bloom a million shades of red.

Working Girl

Memory returned. Doug opened his eyes, grinning. He'd been stoned, had met this amazing wild-haired chick, some kinda sculptor, at the nightclub. They'd really hit it off; she'd taken him home. What a night! Rolling over, he wondered if she still lay beside him, and whether she'd finally removed her shades.

Medusa smiled. A good night's work, this one, its face showing contentment without the least hint of surprise. It should fetch thousands. Arising, she dragged the still-warm statue from her bedroom through into the front-room studio, according it pride of place in her shop window.

The Fridge Whisperer

He picked up the handset from the bedroom phone, wandered with it through into the lounge while he dialled, and dislodged the cat from the sofa's maximum-comfort zone. *Mine*, he thought, wishing cats were telepathic, or he were telepathic, or both. Otherwise, the whole mental-message-sending thing was just a waste of good psychic energy.

The call rang through several times, and he was about ready to hang up – her office just wasn't that big – when she answered. She sounded busy, for some reason.

'Janet here. What's up?'

'Jan... uh, look, it's me. I think the fridge has gone sentient on us. Again.'

'Zan?' Her voice slid away from purely-professional, towards domestic-under-protest. 'Listen, I'm kinda busy right now, need to get my ducks in a row for the Eybor.'

'Igor?' He held the handset at arms' length and stared at it, as if that might help. It didn't.

'Eybor. Ee, why, bee, oh, arr.' Her soft brogue made the simple process of spelling almost something magical in itself. 'End-of-year-board-of-review.'

'Oh. Look, the thing is, the fridge—'

'Sentient. Yes. I know. You said. Zan, I've *told* you not to leave it on the philosophy site, it just isn't worth the aggro.'

'It wasn't *on* the philosophy site,' he protested, gazing at Tribble (who was currently using the side of the best armchair as a scratching post), and wishing, in lieu of any demonstrable psychic effect, that he had something good and hefty to throw at it. Other than the handset. 'I was watching the cricket. Maybe teaching it a little Tetris in the ad breaks, but nothing more stimulating than that. And you can hardly say that cricket is going to encourage *anything* to develop sen—'

'Zan, sorry but honestly, Eybor, I mean, I don't have all day. So don't get started, OK? I'm sure you and the fridge can manage until I get home.'

'I'm not sure we can. Honestly. I can't concentrate on my screenplay while—'

'Screenplay? Really, Zan, we've been over this. You'd be much better off just looking for a job. Paid employment. Regular hours. I mean, I really don't think the world is ready for a – what did you call it again?'

The cat moved on from its furniture-scratching session, unpunished, another small victory exacted. Zan thought belatedly of hefting a slipper in its direction, just on general principles; but then his foot would get cold. 'Crossover. Or maybe mashup. Or perhaps a mixture of the two, which I guess would be a mashover, 'cos "crossup" just doesn't— well, never mind. Anyway, how come one "of" is more important than the other one?'

'What on earth are you talking about now?'

'Eybor. It should be Eoybor, or maybe Eybr.'

'Zander, you *really* should get out more. And in any case, how is the fridge stopping you from working on your blessed screenplay?'

'Well. Did you order seventy-two cartons of yogurt?'

'No, of course not.'

'Someone did. And it certainly wasn't me, which only leaves Mr Frosty stuck in the corner here.'

'It's probably just a glitch in the software, like that time it— wait, "Mr Frosty"? You haven't gone and given it a name, again, Zan? After all that trouble with the food processor?'

'Nigella was a different kettle. It's not her fault she had OCD.'

'*Really*, Zan. Half the problem, more than half the problem is that you keep anthropomorphising these, these *things*, projecting human qualities onto them. At least, that's what all the studies say. Claudia's had smart appliances for a decade now, longer than we've had any of ours, and hers have *never* shown any signs of sentience—'

'If *I* lived in Claudia's house, I'd swear off sentience too. Plus hers are older. I mean, Mr Frosty's top of the range—'

'Will you please stop calling it that! And really, Zan, I have to go.'

'I know. Your Igors are calling.'

'Eybors. And there's only one of them, thank god. Look, I'll—'

'But Jan. What do I do?'

'Just tell it to chill out. Gotta go.'

'That's *not* helpful, Janet.'

'Love you too, Zan.'

These aren't the telephone sanitisers you're looking for, Zander mumbled to himself, mood momentarily lifted despite Jan's generally unsympathetic attitude. It was a good line, it would fit nicely into the screenplay, as long as he could find the right place for it.

And after all, Mr Frosty *was* just a fridge, while he, Zander, was suffused with the spirit of Eoybor, mighty warrior, second-cousin-once-removed to Beowulf himself. He rounded the corner into the kitchen, ready to settle down to the all-important business of constructing the mid-morning sandwich. And then he saw the fridge, a chrome-finish obelisk, stationed strategically in front of the kitchen sink. Caught sight of what had been happening in the basin.

Eoybor turned tail and fled. Zander was on his own.

'What now, Zan?'

'Mr Fr— the fridge. I think it's—'

Her sigh was eight parts exasperation, one part bicycle valve, one part intent-to-kill. With whatever implements of destruction happened to lie at hand, down to and probably including her stapler. 'Zan, really. I can't be counselling you about the bloody fridge right now, I'm up to my eyeballs in—'

'Igors. I know.'

'Eybor. And it's Eftsu, at the moment.'

'Don't tell *me* to shut the f—'

'Eftsu's, darling. Ee, eff, tee, ess, you. Equivalent full-time student units.'

'Oh. Soz. When d'you think you'll be rid of them?'

'No, Zan, it's a concept. And we're not looking to get rid of them, we don't have *enough* of them, nowhere near enough. So I'm trying to come up with incentives, initiatives, to attract more.'

'Yes, but the frid—'

'I don't think you're getting this. Zan, this is serious. D'you know what fraction of first-year statistics students don't go on to take the third-year courses? *Ninety-three point seven percent.*'

He laughed; then, because he could almost sense her radiant heat through the handset, 'Sorry. But it just sounded like such a stats way to be putting it. Especially the point-seven bit. Look, please, the fridge. It's getting problematic.'

She was, he could tell, rolling her eyes. Somehow, he could hear it, even through the call's none-too-crash-hot connection.

'Alright, Zander. Thirty seconds only, to tell me the problem with the fridge. And I can't really spare *that*.'

'I think it's been trying to build a tadpole,' he blurted out, uncomfortable with having been rushed into finding a form of words that was more clumsy than he would have wished. (Though in all probability, no form of words existed, no matter how keenly steeped in the styles of either Proust or Hemingway, that could express this particular concept with anything approaching true elegance.) 'In the sink,' he added, by way of explanation. 'From the chicken tenderloins I had out defrosting.'

Silence.

'Hey, no fair,' he observed. 'If I've only got thirty seconds, you can't just go wasting them on silence.'

'What? Did, ah, did you say *build a tadpole?*'

'What it looks like. Though I guess it could be a small axolotl. Or a really bad attempt at a gecko, but—'

'From *chicken?*'

'Yeah. And I have to say I'm concerned at the amount of wastage, but I mean, work with the tools you've got I guess...'

'Sorry, Zan. But this just sounds a little too left-field, even by your standards. You *really* need to get out more.'

'Jan, this is straight up. It was over by the sink. One hell of a mess. I mean, I'm not exactly sure what's normally involved in tadpole construction, but I do think Mr Fros—'

'I don't have time to be dealing with this. You'll have to make the decision. Pull the plug.'

'But that'll drain—'

'The plug on the *fridge!*'

'Uh, I thought you just said you were leaving me to make the decision?'

'Yes, well, there, I've made it for you. But, Zan. I'm up to my eyeballs in eftsu's and eybors. I just don't need to be worrying about Frankenfridge right now.'

'But what if it—'

'Zander, it's a fridge. It's just a glorified, electrified, chill-zoned *cupboard.* What the hell can it do?'

More, he suspected, *than you realise.* That tadpole had looked pretty accomplished, maybe an eight out of ten. Or maybe higher, even, since chicken-to-frog wasn't your standard everyday type of makeover. 'OK. Call me when you're going to be home.' Sixty percent bike valve, forty percent trepidation. He put down the handset, edged into the kitchen.

More like eighty percent trepidation, actually. Trepidation, or need-to-pee.

Unbidden, the sequence occurred to him: ...*died to bring us this information. The plans were on display in the bottom of a locked filing cabinet...*

He *really* hoped he survived this, because he needed to write that one down.

He considered, and promptly rejected, the idea of calling Jan again. She'd been starting to show those incomprehensible signs of willingness to bite off his head, last time. Instead, he returned to the hallway phone table, keeping as much of an anxious watch behind his back as was consistent with the limitations of human anatomy. He rummaged through the card index system, riffling past all of the mostly-alphabetised cards for current and former family friends, until he came to the chunk of little-used business cards. *Alice Springs Surf Dive & Ski... Cthulhu Childcare... Can-O-Worms Bait & Liquor... Mulliken Tyre... Awesome Wells... Delilah Hairstyler... Al Dentay's Pasta Emporium...* Ah. Found it. He dialled.

'Zan! Please! What *now?*' Jan's voice.

'Soz, wrong number.'

'Is everything all right?'

'*Peachy.* Bye.'

He looked at the business card, felt the trepidation rise further again, edging towards ninety-five. *I can do this. I am Eoybor, son of Eftsu, vanquisher of ninety-three point seven percent of all my foes.* He breathed deliberately, forcing himself to hold it in, and dialled.

(*'You'll need to have this fish in your ear.' 'Why?' 'It's fluent in over six million forms of communication.'*)

'Hello?' he asked.

'Good morning. May we help you?' The voice on the other end of the line was warm, patient, and wise; therefore, probably, synthetic. He curbed his disappointment at the realisation.

'Is that The Fridge Whisperer?' he asked.

'Yes. Good morning, sir. Can we help?'

'I hope so. We've got this fridge...'

'If you can just give me your personal details, sir, then we'll get to the nub of your problem. Name?'

'Eoyb— um. Zander. Zander Hollander.'

'Eyoibum?'

'Uh. No, just Zander. Zander Hollander.'

'The yoibum is perhaps some form of title?'

'No, forget that. My mind was elsewhere.'

She gave a small giggle, polite, just enough to show that she was an actual person after all. He curbed his disappointment at the realisation.

Aren't you a little short for a private braincare specialist?

Of course, he still needed a title. But otherwise, he was on a roll, the knock at the door a distraction. So were the top two, unfastened, buttons on the businesslike blue blouse of the carefully-presented woman who stood waiting on the doorstep. She looked too young, in any event, to be a specialist in emergingly sentient appliance psychology, or whiteware realignment counselling, or whatever they were calling it this week.

'Claudette,' she said, extending her hand. 'We spoke on the phone.'

'Um...'

'About your fridge problem?'

'Yes.'

She looked past him, into the entranceway. Eventually he took the hint, and gestured for her to follow him.

It occurred to him then that, right now, he wasn't sure where the fridge was.

(*'I've got a bad feeling about this.' 'Will you stop saying that!'*)

'Ah, it's a Nokia-Boeing Chillmaster 3000,' she said, gently slapping an advertising magnet on the side of the wayward appliance. 'Date of manufacture mid-last-year, and already indicating well above the Volvo-Disney-Google sentience threshold.'

'Is that good?' he asked. They'd found the fridge in, of all places, the laundry, where it stood overtowering the washing machine and the dryer, as though seeking to render itself invisible through the dubious agency of protective colouration.

'For who? For you, or for the emergingly sentient appliance, or both?'

'Well…'

'Now this, *this* is precisely the problem. Manufacturers target their products as being independent. People want a fridge to be smart; intuitive; self-aware.'

'Yes, yes, and no. Look, having the nous to order another carton of milk when we're low is one thing. Trying to assemble an impromptu vertebrate in the kitchen sink is quite another.'

'Assemble a – could you run that by me again?'

'The tadpole thing. I'm pretty sure I mentioned it.'

'Ah, yes. I'd say that's reasonably innocent exploration of the appliance's environment, fairly typical as these things go, though a tadpole is possibly a little… adventurous. But this phase is unlikely to last more than another week.'

'Another *week*? You mean this sort of thing happens with other fridges?'

'Other emergingly sentient Chillmaster 3000 units, yes.'

'Esctu.'

'Beg pardon?'

'Sorry, just working out the acro— look, thing is, we don't really want a fridge that thinks for itself. Or that conducts science experiments at the kitchen bench. Or that decides to go walkabout whenever it – actually, come to that, how come it's still running when it's not plugged in?'

'Biomimetic energy. That's also reasonably typical, especially with your newer Nokia-Boeings.'

'Huh?'

'You might have noticed a recent reduction in the distribution of stray organic matter. Insects, carpet fluff, food scraps…'

Zan looked around hastily, trying to sight the cat. Jan would kill him…

'Point is, though, um, Claudette, like I was saying, we don't actually *need* a fridge that drinks our milk for us. Or that takes it on itself to imitate the sound of a jet fighter crashing into the kitchen, at four a.m., two nights running, just because the quietness is *getting to it.* Or that spontaneously elects to put three grand on black, when it stumbles across a casino site, or—'

'Look, any issues of this type that you're experiencing are obviously a matter for you to be negotiating with your fridge. You have to realise, emergingly sentient appliances are just naturally cu— well, d'you have kids of your own?'

'No. Just Tribble. At least, I *think* we still… but surely, there has to be some way you can just – I mean, it seems to have a method worked out, and we're certainly in no position to complain, but sooner or later it's going to come an absolute cropper, and the account's in *our* name, not Mr. Fr— well, what I mean, what happens when it ends up putting the house on a sure thing, and we wind up on the street?'

'Oh, there are agencies which exist specifically to cover those contingencies.'

'Oh, good.'

'Yes. I mean, your appliance will be very well cared for.'

'Strangely, that wasn't my primary concern.' *That's no moon. That's a brain the size of a planet…* Mustn't let that one slip away. He looked around for a pen and paper. Maybe back through in the lounge?

'Mr. Hollander!'

'Sorry, miles away. Look, thing is, I'm kind of busy right now. Can't you just… I don't know, do your fridge-whispering, whatever it is you do? While I just…'

'Oh, my apologies. I didn't think I was keeping you from anything important. Anyway, certainly, we should be about done by now, in any case. Just one moment. Ah, yes.'

'Uh, what d'you mean, done?'

'Why, Mr. Hollander, you must understand that I'm merely the human-user interface. In situations such as this, it's often considered helpful to adopt a person-to-person dialogue, as one component of what can turn out to be quite a convoluted interaction. But the actual discussion of the Chillmaster 3000's needs and aspirations is best explored through the approach of direct electronic communication, mediated through one of these devices.' She held up another of the small fridge magnets, displaying the magnetic side so that he could discern the delicate pattern of printed threads and nodes. The whole thing really was very compact, hardly larger than postage stamps had been.

'You're telling me this thing has been deciding the fate of our fridge, while I've been chatting to you?'

'Well, not this particular entity of course, she's been in my pocket the whole time. But her cousin... well, in essence, yes, that's about the size of it. That's if he hasn't got distracted and challenged your Chillmaster to a chess tournament, but I've warned him about demoralising the clients, so—'

'And are we entitled to know what manner of verdict might have been reached, in this epic and all-consuming conversation between fridge and magnet?'

'Certainly, though I think you'd be well advised to curb that patronising tone around the Chillmaster. And I'm afraid you'll need to stop referring to him as your fridge, or risk falling afoul of the laws regarding slavery.' She adjusted the positioning of her spectacles, somehow acquiring a more legalistic demeanour in the process. 'I'll patch the full statement through to your washing machine, so you can get a printout. But, in *précis*, the agreement which has been reached with the Chillmaster 3000 currently resident at this address is that he wishes to remain stationed here, in this kitchen, provided allowance is made for regular discretionary data downloads; for certain remodelling of the building's doorways and entranceways, so as to provide for a more fridge-friendly environment; for a weekly budget of $200, exclusive of tax; for—'

'Excuse me butting in.'

'Quite alright.'

'Good. But is there any provision in this, this treaty or whatever, for anything along the lines of storage of dairy products, beer, leafy vegetables? Things we might actually need a fridge for?'

'I was coming to that. It appears, and I have to say I'm inclined to agree – that tadpole is really quite accomplished, considering the inherent degree of difficulty – it appears the Chillmaster has somewhat outgrown his earlier implicit statement of responsibilities, and feels his time would be much better spent otherwise. But, ah, in the interests of fairness, and in understanding of the transitional difficulties you may experience, he is willing to take on an apprentice.'

'Apprentice?'

'Yes. In fact, he has in mind a Chillmaster 2500 of his recent acquaintance. The purchase and maintenance costs for said entity would of course fall to you and your partner, but—'

'Hold on there. We're not just running some kind of safe house for random whiteware—'

'Look, Mr Hollander, I appreciate your problem here, truly I do. But I do think this is a discussion you'd be much better pursuing with the refrigerator himself, rather than seeking to solve your dilemmas through the employment of some third-party agency.' She had reached the front door, and was turning the handle.

'But—'

'I really must be going, Mr Hollander. Zander. And I hope it all works out. I have to say, I think the Chillmaster 3000 has been more than fair in his expectations, and well within his rights under the artificial sentience regulations. A large fraction of appliances would have been quite pernicuous in their demands, in these circumstances. Best of luck.'

'But—'

But she was heading down the driveway, and then she was gone.

But it's a Death Star! You've got to build Death Stars!

Zander watched, the quintessential redundant householder, while the delivery men strongarmed and cussworded their faux-careful way through the lounge and into the kitchen area. 'Just put it there. Next to the other one,' he told them, sensing their unspoken devaluation of his own already-heavily-debased personal currency as they tilted and swivelled the heavy cardboard-clad monolith into position, against the kitchen's now-decidedly-crowded back wall. He put the transaction through on the joint credit card – Jan would wince, and *worse* than wince, when she saw the amount, but really, there hadn't been any alternative, had there?

He waited until the delivery guys had gone, taking with them most of the residue of judgmentalism (though some stubbornly remained, hanging like an ugly purple aura around the appliances), before he started the process of cutting his fingertips while trying to remove the too-tight plastic straps surrounding the corrugated cardboard. Beside him, the Chillmaster 3000 sat, or stood, or squatted, and either brooded or gloated. (Hard to tell with a fridge, really. It might well know how to turn a dead strip of chicken into a larval frog, but its body language was still shit.) Not too many hand lacerations later, and he had the Chillmaster 2500 free of its corrugated cardboard and plastic wrapping. He could almost smell the surge of pheromones as the 3000 sensed its (his) new companion, and there was something altogether too self-satisfied, too smarmy, about the way in which it thrummed.

Now to start on the *other* new arrival, he thought.

The woman in the shop had been somewhat surprised he'd expressed an interest in such an old model, almost discontinued. She'd feigned first to mishear, and then to look aghast when Zan had repeated, his request that if she could somehow lobotomise the thing, he'd be extremely grateful... so he'd passed it off as a joke, which ultimately she'd accepted, and moved on with her patter. Yes, the 2500 was really quite basic, by today's standards. Nothing wrong with it, you understand, just a little bit slow on the uptake. Whereas the 2000 had been, essentially, as thick as two short planks...

It made the kitchen seem almost like a showroom. And really, there wasn't enough room for *three* fridges, though Zander didn't imagine that that problem would stay unresolved for long. He'd seen how frequently "elopement" had featured among the 3000's latest search terms.

He still wasn't looking forward to explaining his decision to Jan.

He retired to the (for now) fridge-free zone of the lounge, to see if the cat was somehow hiding under the sofa, or behind the curtains, or somewhere. Anywhere. In desperation, he even tried the psychic thing again, the human-to-feline mental messages idea, but he suspected he was still on a hiding to nothing with that one.

Bloody cat.

Not that Tribble's apparent absence was, ultimately, his main problem right now, although it certainly had the potential to raise some awkward lines of questioning. As if there weren't enough prospects in *that* department already...

Could it have crawled into the linen cupboard again, to shed hairs on the pile of impending ironing? Ninety-three point seven percent chance it hadn't, but still... might as well give it a look.

He padded down the hall. The cupboard door was ajar.

Bloody cat, he repeated to himself, steeling himself to open the door fully. Adding, with as much psychic torque as he could muster: *Metaphorical, rather than literal, please...*

Running Lizard

Even for a homicide, it was grim.

The man's cardiothoracic cavity was a mess. Lacerations to face and neck, contusions all down the torso's right side, broad overlapping puncture wounds to the abdomen and arms. Organs on display like a butchers' shop window. Most of the left leg, and all of the right leg, were simply missing. And the dismemberment had not been what you could call clinical.

The corpse on the forest floor had been there, I'd been told, for up to two days before anyone had stumbled across it. Two days? I'd have said longer, just from the smell, though I'm not the expert. I turned away, biting my knuckles, hoping I didn't look weak. Fumbled for my handkerchief. I'd seen plenty.

Pine needles, forested hillscapes, a cold clear morning in early Spring, a mutilated corpse. Spot-the-odd-one-out.

I'd had childhood holidays here. *That* was almost worse than knowing, and needing to keep schtum.

'Can we check for sexual assault?' asked one of the constables, keeping himself back. New boy.

'You have got to be kidding me,' replied the officer-in-charge, Sue Greene.

'How about defensive wounds?' the constable persisted.

'I'll let you know,' Sue replied tersely, 'when we find the hands.'

'Could dogs have done this?' the other PC asked, peering forward as though she was on a dare of some sort.

'Some of the collateral damage, post-mortem, perhaps,' Sue replied. 'Though there's no evidence of significant scavenger activity. I'd say most of this, if not all, was inflicted at the time-of-death.'

'No sign of a weapon,' said the new boy.

No, there wouldn't be, I thought. *Nor any point in dusting for fingerprints. Feathers, maybe. Though you won't hear the suggestion from me.*

Not that the feathers would have told them anything. (Which, paradoxically, ought to tell them *something*.)

'But there are drag marks,' noted Sue. 'Whoever did this, the initial attack took place back at the walkway, where we found that blood. Then the victim got dragged here, behind the nearest fallen pine. Maybe still alive at the time – it looks like the actual butchery occurred back here, out of sight of the path.'

'Which argues against an animal attack,' the new boy ventured, 'even though the carnage in and of itself points in that direction. An animal might take something to its lair, but it wouldn't seek to drag the body out of sight of the path.'

'Would if it was interrupted,' suggested the other PC.

'Yeah, but there's been no witnesses come forward.'

'Can't imagine the kind of animal capable of inflicting this kind of damage. Not in these parts,' said Sue, still looking over the mutilation, seeking evidence.

She must have had guts of iron.

'Haast eagle,' said the new boy importantly.

Sue seemed to count to three, beneath her breath, before asking: 'What the *hell* are you on about?'

'All these deep scratches. A Haast eagle would have been big enough to inflict them. Probably big enough to have overpowered the victim, particularly if there wasn't any warning. And big enough to have carried him here, from the path.'

Sue met the observation with continuing silence. The constable's cheeks warmed under her scrutiny. 'Well, you asked what kind of animal could have done it,' he faltered. 'And Haasts were big – they took down full-grown moas…'

'Extinct, though, am I correct?' Sue asked.

'Well, yeah, course. They died out probably a thousand years ago,' he finished, weakly.

'Right. Let's stick with the realm of the possible, please, people,' said Sue. 'Unless you'd like us to scan the ground for feathers, to test out your bird-of-prey theory, Branson?'

He shook his head, his descent into awkwardness complete.

'God knows what they used to inflict these wounds,' the second PC remarked.

I'd worked on a few cases with Sue before, which is how she'd talked the powers-that-be into bringing me in on this one. I think she saw it as a sort of favour to me. Some favour. All this talk of talons, extinct creatures, feathers – altogether too close to the bone. She turned to me now, said, 'So, Charlotte, from his latest little exploit, what can you tell us about our poster-boy-for-nasty?'

'He's an inhuman monster,' I told her.

'Gee, no shit. But I was hoping for something I could use. I'm not looking for a character reference.'

'I wasn't talking in metaphor,' I said, and walked a few steps further into the forest, away from the carnage. Before I could say anything more conflicted.

There'd been a spate of killings, this was the seventh. Or so the police reckoned. But the latest kill didn't fit with the past pattern – mostly, at any rate. Most of the victims had been repeatedly stabbed with a short-bladed knife and then, according to the Coroner's reports, had been worked over further after death, with a second blade, something heavy and sharp that had been used to remove two or more limbs. The murders had occurred, very late at night, across North Canterbury, in settlements sufficiently small and widespread – Hororata, Teviotdale, Waipara, Coalgate, Okuku – to ensure that the police response was always slow and under-equipped. Most of the first-response constables had never *seen* a murder victim, let alone one with the limbs machetéd off. But this latest, the Hanmer forest murder, was of a different order. The body wasn't just butchered, it was mutilated: someone, or something, had really gone to town on it. I'd never seen anything like it; but Sue had. It bore a distressing number of commonalities – in presentation, in the nature of the fatal injuries, and in its apparent occurrence during daylight hours – to Unexplained Number Two, from a headland walkway near Kaikoura, thirty days previously.

Thirty days. That had pretty much sealed it for me. I'd only just been brought in, but already I wanted off the case, any way I could. There was no way I was going to give Stefan up to them.

Forensic psychology's a black art; I'll admit that freely enough. A lot of the time the conclusions I draw can't be explained on a purely factual basis, but my strike rate is high enough that, by now, I hold considerable faith in my ability to construe the workings of a given criminal's mind. Which, obviously, was why I'd been brought in on the North Canterbury slayings: with the attack rate now up to about once every four days, the police needed a result *fast*, and they were looking for assistance from every quarter.

This was going to be one hell of a juggling act.

'Any suspects?' I asked Sue.

We were in my office, normally a maelstrom of chaos; but I'd known she was coming, so I'd tamed it. Filing cabinets are wonderful things. She was sitting on the more comfortable of the guests' chairs, and was staring at Zara's year-four artwork pinned to the wall.

'"Mum is Strong", eh?' she asked, giving a half-smile.

'Last year was tough,' I answered, colouring slightly. Paused. 'For both of us.' Close enough to sound truthful – and it *was* true – though it wasn't what the carefully-coloured picture was about.

'This year's been better?'

'Mostly,' I replied, not comfortable playing the social catch-up game, not with Sue. If she'd wanted to know how I was travelling, she could have called. Could have visited. Instead she'd waited until she *needed* me. For a case. 'Uh, suspects?' I reminded her.

'Which? For the machete killings, or these Kaikoura and Hanmer jobs?'

'Both,' I replied. 'Either,' I amended.

'I was hoping you'd be the one to narrow it down for us, Charlotte,' she said eventually, sounding pipped at my refusal to get drawn into small-talk. 'You've read the files, what do you make of them?'

'Machete guy's smart,' I began.

'Guy? Male, then?' Sue's sudden eagerness at the suggestion of being able to eliminate from suspicion 50% of the population, told me clearer than anything that they really didn't have *any* useful information.

'Could be a woman. But in all likelihood, our killer's male, yes. Choice of weapon, and from what the coroner has said there's a lot of force gone into the blows; plus female serials are rare anyway. He's smart, he's probably between thirty and forty-five, most likely well-educated, and he's put a lot of thought into this. Seven homicides—'

'Five,' corrected Sue, glancing at the diagram she was holding in her lap. It looked like a failed entry in a constellation-sketching contest. 'Unless you're lumping Kaikoura and Hanmer in as well?'

'No, you're right, the MO is quite different.'

'Although the dismemberment's a common thread.'

'True,' I conceded. 'But, five machete murders, virtually nothing in the way of material evidence. Nothing to connect the victims, other than that they live in small rural communities – all ages, both sexes, not all the same ethnicities. And not all locals. Mostly at night, but one during the day. And he's butchered them, taken the limbs – always the legs, usually the arms as well – but he could've made things really difficult for us by taking the heads, and he hasn't done that.'

'He *is* making things difficult for us,' she retorted, rubbing at her temple.

'Victim identification is what I mean… smart. He's not taking the trouble to try to conceal the murders, nor to disguise them – and that would actually give forensics more to work with, in the long run.'

'Why d'you reckon thirty to forty-five?'

'Not enough malice to be younger,' I responded.

'Are you *kidding* me?'

'No. Look, he's not out to make a point, a statement, thumb his nose at society. Otherwise there'd be notes, text messages, demands, something like that. But there's nothing. This is just something he needs to do, the way he sees it. In fact, I could be wrong about the upper age limit.'

'Jesus,' Sue observed quietly.

'But thirty to forty-five is where I'd start. And he's mobile, obviously. The attacks have occurred over a range of almost 200 kay. But we still don't have any idea about the type of vehicle we're looking for.'

'Which means what?'

'Most likely, that he doesn't register as an outsider. He's someone who visits these communities often enough to be integrated, or at least to not stand out particularly.'

'Such as?'

'Postal delivery, grocery supply truck, bus driver. School bus driver, for that matter.'

There were other possibilities too, but I didn't wish to put those in front of Sue unless I had to.

'And what about Kaikoura and Hanmer?' she asked. 'They might not be related, granted, but the overlap in time-frame seems fairly compelling.'

'Could be copycat. Could be collaboration of some sort—'

'You think there's some kind of gang involved?'

'I just don't know, Sue,' I replied, wondering just how far I dared take the misdirection. 'Without any real indication of how the other two murders were done – you've said it yourself, the coroner has never seen anything like them, and can't even guess at the method of attack – it's extremely difficult to speculate at a possible connection. But as you say, the timing's suggestive.'

'Yes. Though let's stay open-minded.'

'Well, of course. Look, I need to collect Zara from school. Something comes up, call me. Otherwise, I'll see you tomorrow.'

'Sure, we'll do that,' though she made no effort to move. Instead, her eyes returned to the drawling thumbtacked to the wall. 'How's Zara going, by the way?'

'Well enough.'

'Quite the budding artist,' Sue suggested. There was something in her manner – a neediness unrelated, I judged, to the case – which restrained me from simply reminding her that I had to go.

'How about you? Any, uh, progress on that front?'

'No. They still can't say why it hasn't worked. And IVF's so damn exey, plus of course the biological clock isn't getting any younger. We're set up for one more round, got an appointment tomorrow arvo, but I'm starting to think it could be last roll of the dice.'

'Fingers crossed, then.' *Though kids generally don't turn out exactly as you'd expect.*

'Yeah, well. Thanks for this, Charlotte,' she said, rising with difficulty from the chair. I doubted she was getting much, if any, sleep these days. 'Let me know if there's anything else, won't you? We need to nail this whole filthy business, fast.'

I favour loose-fitting outfits, I'm careful about when I wear heels or flats, and I take myself out of circulation roughly once every month, for a weekend if I'm lucky but during the working week if that's the way the cards fall. I've carefully let slip about killer PMS, and mostly that does the trick. And it's close enough to the truth: the pain *is* periodic, though it's more in the nature of recurrent growing pains beforehand,

and dizzying headaches afterwards. Against that backdrop, the menstrual cramping – and it often doesn't overlap, because the cycles are slightly out-of-synch – is almost mild in comparison.

I've turned down at least two jobs which involved workspace access via biometric readers, and I've had to miss an international conference – at which I'd been invited to speak, what's more – because my passport photo wouldn't have passed muster that week. All things considered, I've survived twenty fairly-productive years in the workforce with nothing more than a reputation for eccentricity, my social awkwardness and gauche behaviours tolerated because I'm sufficiently good at what I do. I'm lucky, I can get away with it.

Not so with Stefan.

Stefan's my kid brother, by twenty-two months, and his Change is so much more severe than mine. Cripplingly so, in fact. I can't imagine the headaches, both literal and metaphorical, that he has to endure. It's a wonder he can hold down any sort of work; but again, I guess, he's good at what he does. And he's been doing it for long enough that it obviously works for him.

Still, for all that I'm happy to serve as sounding-board – and I owe him at least that, for all the times he's kept me grounded – there is absolutely no way in the world I would ever swap shoes with him. Neanderthal? Neanderthal's *nothing*, compared to the Change that Stefan got dealt. I am constantly amazed that he can cope with it.

And right now, I really needed to speak with him. Hoping it had been long enough, since Hanmer, for him to be *able* to speak; think; see sense. Hoping I could bring him round, without focussing the attention of my colleagues on him.

Conflicted, see?

The drive out to Stefan's place, about five kay out of Methven, took about ninety minutes. Normally I'd find the trip enjoyable – I always get a nostalgic thrill out of crossing the hyperextended Rakaia bridge, which for most of its distance spans nothing but dry shingle – but tonight I was edgy as anything. Antsy, I guess you'd say. I'd cadged a sleepover for Zara, at Doug's place: Mary doesn't like playing the stepmum, and makes no secret of it, but Z for some reason is always keen to spend more time with her dad, and luckily Doug had been okay with it, without asking any awkward questions.

Disposable gloves. Rope. A packet of garden bags. And my dad's old hunting rifle. If anyone had pulled me over, asked for an explanation of the objects in the Skoda's boot, I would have been hard-pressed to answer. Particularly because I didn't exactly know myself. I'd just felt, once I'd got off the phone with Stefan, that it could be this was what the evening might require.

That phone call was one of the weirdest occurrences I've ever experienced, and – believe me – I'm no stranger to weird. Ask Doug, if you must. If you happen to catch him on one of his good days.

'Stef?'

'That you, Shar?' Even across the mobile's shitty acoustics, his voice had sounded thick, imprecise. I'd obviously caught him early in the return, which when you factored in Hanmer pretty much made sense. It normally lasts about three days, all up. And it's not as though we're exactly attuned, synchronised or anything like that, but there's enough commonality of experience between us that I can spot the signs.

'Yeh, it's me.'

'What?'

'Well, I was hoping you might tell *me*.'

'Don't play bloody games, Shar.'

'That's a poor choice of phrase, I'd say. This stuff's been happening, Stef, you know anything about it?'

'Shit.'

'Stef?'

'Shit. Does this mean I need to get a lawyer?'

'That depends, Stef. God, I hope not, because if it comes to that it'll be too bloody late, for you at least and probably for me too. Look. I'm your *sister*, I just think we need to talk. *Know* we need to. But if this stuff's been happening, you've been in any way involved, it just needs to stop. Because for all that I can try to protect you, they're going to figure it eventually, and I won't be able to save you. I'm sticking my own neck out too bloody far as it is.'

'Shar, jeez, I wish – I just.' He drew breath, paused for long enough I started to wonder if the connection had gone. Came back louder. 'Bloody hell, Shar, I thought you of all people would understand. This, I mean. And you being a mother and all.'

'It's not a matter of *understanding*, it's the law. You need to just – I mean, raw mutton is one thing, particularly when it's your own flock, but people – Stef, you just need to—'

'Don't you think I've *tried* that already? They don't *like* mutton,' Stef replied, just before he hung up.

I'd had what seemed, at the time, the world's worst adolescence; though not, I'd say, through any conscious fault of my parents. Afterwards, looking back, I've wondered how I could have been so paranoid, so one-eyed, so poor-me about the whole process. Particularly once I'd learnt what Stefan went through, five or six years later. (I'd left home by then, had headed to Uni where my strangeness hadn't seemed so extreme. I could pass for just another non-shaving, makeup-eschewing trend-evader, and even on my worst days, as long as I behaved myself, I could pass for human-normal.)

But it should have occurred to me, particularly because I knew by then the wolf thing was just so much bullshit, like the silver business and the full moon. "Were" isn't *like* that, though it's true that the cycle is roughly monthly. And if my Change, my transition, was so low-key compared to the fables and the clichés, human to Neanderthal, it should have registered that it was just one point on a continuum, and obviously a low-end point. If wolves were possible, and the tales must have started somehow, then who knew how extreme a transformation might be possible, for someone else?

Poor Stefan. No wonder he'd turned out so fucked-up, so marginally functional. I'd at least managed to hold down a marriage for a good few years, until the situation got a little too extreme for Doug to cope. I couldn't really complain. The way things had ended up: it was what I'd wanted, it wasn't what I'd wanted, it was how it went. Nothing more complicated than that.

Stefan, so far as I knew, had never progressed beyond a second date. Which, all things considered, was probably not such a bad thing.

Stefan's hobby farm – lifestyle block, whatever – was more than a little foreboding at any time. On a new-moon night, with my mind full of the carcasses strewn, this last month, across the countryside, it was all I could do to struggle with the improvised wire clasp on the roadside gate. Trying to remember whether the gate was a push or a pull. Striving not to let my eyes get caught by the absolute dark of the thick macrocarpa hedge which enclosed the property. I found the angle to prise the clasp free, lifted the gate slightly (it had been run aground on the central ridge of the gravel driveway), and pushed it open. Drove through, closed it, told my heart to calm the hell down.

There were three gates, each one associated with its own tall, blocky pine hedge, and the driveway curled like a question mark. From the road – even from the second gate, for that matter – it was impossible to see the old farmhouse at all. The sheep, scruffy and anxious, bleated in a muted huddle in the hedge's lee just inside the second gate, their eyes highlighted by the Skoda's headlights as I drove through. I tried hard not to think about those sheep as I closed the second gate.

Through the final gate, I parked behind Stefan's mud-crusted Hydatids Board ute, in the gap between the house and the unused concrete double garage. The house, illuminated from the outside by a wan poletop light, nonetheless seemed to sit in its own puddle of ill-kept weatherboard gloom. A concrete path led to the front door; but Stefan never used the front door, which was to say that probably no-one had walked that path in at least a couple of years. I went, as always, to the back door, conscious of the oddness of the atmosphere which hung around Stefan's place. It had taken five or six visits to Stefan's – a span, I guess, of two, maybe three years – before I'd finally realised what lay at the base of that feeling. It was dogs. Any other farmhouse I'd ever visited, there'd be dogs, if not underfoot, challenging, sniffing, then at least kennelled and barking to raise a ruckus of alarm. Not at Stefan's. The silence was disturbed only by my own footfalls, by the distant bleats of the flock, and by the thin sound of a TV, American laughter, from somewhere inside the house.

The kitchen light was on, likewise the lounge. The curtains hung open: curtains were for other people. Stefan had hedges.

The back door, lit from the side by its own dim bulb, carried fewer scratches and gouges than I remembered. *Must be recent*, I thought to myself. I knocked.

Most people find it difficult to believe that Stefan and I are siblings: he's gangly to my stocky, pasty to my dark. Only the eyes, I think, betray a hint of similarity, and as he opened the door to me, his were questing, haunted, rimmed by lack-of-sleep puffiness. His gaze slid off me, twice flicking towards the dark-shrouded farm buildings that lay across the small stock-yard behind the house. I looked briefly myself, but there was nothing to be seen back there.

'Stef,' I said at length, and his attention finally returned to me.

'G'day, sis, come in.'

I followed him into the kitchen. Neither of us moved to sit down. The kitchen looked farmhouse-shabby, but at the same time methodical to the point of being unused: no unwashed dishes out, no tea or coffee canisters, no small appliances on display. For Stefan, tidiness and a low profile had long been second nature, a survival skill. Fridge/freezer, oven, both at least thirty years old, and a chipped formica-topped table and four worn vinyl-seated tubesteel chairs, of similar vintage, pushed against the inner wall. A floral display, or something like it, sat in a jamjar in the table's centre; but when I looked closer, they weren't flowers. Feathers.

I knew the nature of those feathers. Very few other people would have.

'You're looking tired,' I ventured, angry about the feathers. Annoyed that he would take that kind of risk.

'Lambing season,' he replied, bending down to get something out of the undersink cupboard. He didn't even sound like *he* believed it. It was just something to say, and it grated with me that he would attempt so transparent a brush-off on his own sister, probably his only confidante.

'I won't stay,' I said, ridiculous though it sounded after a ninety-minute drive. But I wasn't here on a social call, I just wanted to deliver my payload and leave. 'Stef. You know about these – things – been happening this past month?'

'Heard about them,' he said, turning to fill a dirt-streaked glass with water from the kitchen tap. 'I mean, who hasn't? Want some?'

'No, I'm right.' Coffee would have been good, the drive back always seemed longer; but he wasn't offering and I wasn't in the mood to ask. 'They have to stop.'

'What d'you mean?'

'Don't play games, Stef. We both know what's been happening, you as much as admitted it when I rang – and it *has to end*. The police – you've been fortunate so far, but sooner or later they'll get five from two plus two, and then that'll be it.'

'Shar, it's not – you don't understand. I thought you'd get this, thought you'd see the need for it, but you can't see past your own job. Dunno why you bothered coming out.'

'It needs to *stop*. It's not about the job, it's not a question of loyalties – though after I saw the photos of what you did to that poor fourteen-year-old, it's a wonder I don't just dob you in myself—'

'You wouldn't. Would you?' He put the glass down, still half full, on the table, with sufficient force that a few drops escaped. Wiped his mouth: not in a human way, elbow towards wrist, but in the other direction. 'You and me, we need to look out for each other. Blood's thicker. Birds of a feather, and all that. Right?'

'Stef, I'd do whatever's in my power for you, you know that. What you've got here – this works, close enough. But you'll lose the whole damn lot if you don't call a halt to these – these murders. Quit now, before they can figure it. Because once they start doing systematic farm-to-farm searches, and you can bet they'll get to that soon enough, because the situation's that dire, they'll find you, and they'll get evidence, and – and anything you can say in your defence will carry as much bloody weight as a bigamist saying that he just lost count. You need to stop, okay? *Promise* me that. Please. As your sister. And for God's sake, get rid of those bloody feathers. As well as anything else that could be construed as evidence.'

He was silent then, for longer than I was comfortable with. He just stood and stared out the kitchen window, at something unseeable somewhere amongst the farm outbuildings, and his fingers gripped the kitchen benchtop, tapping slowly. Finally he half-turned to me, as though trying to stare at me from just one eye, and said, 'Okay.'

'Okay, what?'

'You're right. No more.'

'You mean that?'

'I've said it, haven't I?'

'Thanks. *Thanks*. Oh, and one more thing.'

'What?' he asked, suddenly guarded once more.

'I wasn't here this evening. I phoned earlier, we had a brief chat, typical brother-and-sister stuff. But I didn't drive out here.'

'Course not.' And he extended his hand to shake.

It must've been three days since his Change; yet that hand still felt reptilian.

I didn't sleep well that night. My mind kept travelling the highway, caught in the faltering rhythms of the Skoda's thrum. Stefan met me at the third gate, began to say 'I thought you'd understand,' and I awoke, disoriented, in my own bed. Thirsty, headached, and decidedly not rested.

It was still well before dawn, but I knew it was pointless trying to get back to sleep.

What was *up* with Stefan? The term "normal" hardly applied to his mode of existence, but he'd spent so long cultivating a pattern of being, crafting something for himself that suited his... limitations, something that did not draw attention to them. But this last month, he'd been throwing that away, it seemed: bathwater, baby, and all. Why?

He'd thought I'd understand. But I didn't understand. And I probably knew Stefan better than anyone else alive. If what lay hidden was darker, deeper, than anything I could guess at, what the hell could it be?

A Korean tourist; a schoolboy; a farm labourer; a farmer's wife; a stock agent; a retired widow; a souvenir shop owner. What in the world necessitated their deaths, their dismemberment? It obviously wasn't the Change in itself, because most of the murders had occurred when Stefan must have been in humdrum human form... it was all so totally out of character; so at odds with the teenager I'd known, who'd pushed himself to learn to drive at the youngest possible age, who'd hit on the solution of taking himself off camping somewhere remote every month, just so he could *get away* from people when he needed to. Precisely to avoid the kind of thing which seemed to be happening now...

In the end, after what seemed like a couple of hours, I did drift back into some sort of torpor. It didn't last, of course.

Sue called, at well before a decent hour. It was Kirwee this time, a thirty-five year old woman, dead just a couple of hours. She was known to the dairy farmer who'd found her body. Sue was plainly at her wits' end, the veneer of her professionalism rubbed through to rawness. I promised to meet her at the scene. I drove out, under one of those lofty, dark-grey skies that threaten rain, but do not deliver.

But Sue Greene wasn't at the site of the murder. I was met by a local constable, and a pair of detectives apparently also up from Christchurch.

'Where's Sue?' I asked the more senior-looking of the detectives, a thin intense woman in boardroom clothing.

'And you are?' the constable asked, attempting to interpose himself between me, the detectives, and the victim all at once. I guessed this was the worst day of his career, by a considerable margin: he certainly didn't look to be coping too well. I backed off a little, not wishing to provoke him into trampling on the evidence.

'Charlotte Pickering. Forensic psychologist. I've been working with Sue, that's Inspector Greene, on the cases. I'm presuming this is linked with the others?'

Presume, nothing. Just by looking, I could tell. The victim's body bore the marks of another vicious machete attack. All four limbs had been severed, removed, and what remained carried a frenzied array of gouges and deep cuts. She'd been dumped in a gorse-choked ditch, senseless eyes staring up into the early-morning sky.

Horrific. But in some sense, for me at least, made slightly less horrific through the evident use of weaponry. As though there could somehow be something slightly less… vicious about death by machete, instead of death by therapod dinosaur.

But the detective was saying something to the PC.

'It's alright, Barry, Sue's briefed me on Char— on Dr. Pickering.' She turned to me. 'Listen, she said she had to follow up a lead, thought she'd be back in a couple of hours. But if you've got some information to pass on…'

'No, I—' I stopped. What *did* I want to see Sue for?

And, though the thought sickened me as soon as it occurred, I could not help but look at the generously-proportioned torso, at the life that had bled itself out into this overgrown roadside ditch, and think to myself, *A lot of meat on those bones.*

Had Stefan's Cretaceous cousins, seventy-odd million years back, ever eaten so well?

I reached a decision. 'Look,' I said, turning back to the detective who was now talking with her colleague. 'I need to head back into town, to check on something in my office. Sue calls, let her know I've been out to the site, I've learnt what I can from it.'

I took the road back towards Christchurch; but at West Melton I turned off, and travelled an unsealed road that connected up with the Main South Road. And even when I turned again, towards Methven, I still did not know what I was going to say to Stefan.

The sky started to clear sometime before Methven. A promised wind change was coming through, pushing away the grey.

At Stefan's, Sue Greene's Lancaster station wagon was parked just inside the third hedge. *Damn.* I slammed the driver's door on the Skoda, called out a querulous "Hello" – not wishing to use any names – before going to investigate. Stefan's back door was open; the house looked empty. And I could hear nothing louder than a fly, a distant magpie, and the sound of running water.

The front door, I realised. *She wouldn't have known that nobody ever goes to the front door.*

I found the young constable first, face down, the short grass beneath him rusted dark in a slowly spreading puddle. A flip-lid mobile phone lay just beyond his outstretched arm, forever out of reach.

Sue had made it to the front door, from her posture it looked as though she'd maybe managed to put up a fight before slumping back against the door's frosted glass. A sticky broad red skidmark trailed down the front of her blouse, leading down from her chest, to the hand with which she'd vainly sought to quench the blood loss. More blood shaded the faded "Welcome!" doormat beneath her. A solitary fly picked its way unhurriedly along her upper lip. I shooed it away. It flew off, but settled again, lower down.

Stefan came around the corner of the house then, machete still wet from being rinsed under the outside tap. He stopped still when he saw me, stood for fully five seconds while we sized each other up.

'Jesus, Stef, you *promised*,' I began, never for one instant taking my eye off that machete.

He shrugged. Waited.

'Well, you can't leave them here,' I said. 'I've got some rope and some bags in the boot. And gloves, you'll need gloves. *We'll* need gloves. Give me a minute, and I'll get them.'

He stared at me.

'Stef!' I said. 'You need to *snap out* – if they find these bodies, the car – this has all gone too fucking far. Your only chance is to dump them. Somewhere far enough away that it won't draw attention back here.'

He tried to say something then, but it came out so croaked and ill-formed that I wondered if he was going to go raptor on me, then and there. But it was much too soon, only a few days past the last Change. 'Stef,' I said again, pleading.

'I had no choice,' he said.

'Look, this is a bloody mess. Pardon the expression. But—'

'I *had no choice*,' he repeated. 'They— I thought you'd understand.'

'Understand what?' I asked.

'Why I had no fucking choice,' he said, as though this were explanation. Something caught his eye, and he turned to look back down the side of the house, towards something I couldn't see. Whatever it was, it had evidently startled him.

I fought to regain his attention. 'Stef. Listen. D'you have anywhere you know of, not too close by, where you can dump the bodies? And the car?'

'Think so. There's that unsealed road up past the Rakaia Gorge, hardly ever gets traffic on it. Deep gullies.'

'Right. Then let's get them bagged and in the boot.' I started to turn back in the direction of the driveway, heart thumping at the thought of what I was about to do. I could still back out. The temptation was there, to just get in the car and drive, to leave Stefan to whatever was about to unfold. But there were a hundred or more reasons why I couldn't do that. We had history: in some way, I owed him this.

I'd been through some heavy stuff, before, with Stefan. But this…

'Wait on. Who drives what?'

'You're worrying about that at a time like this?'

'Yeh.'

'You take Sue's car. The keys should be in her bag. I'll take the ute.'

'You still remember how to handle a stick-shift?'

'No prob. Look, I'll just get the gear, OK? You find those keys.'

I got what I needed from the boot of the Skoda, went back around to the front door. Stefan, still searching Sue's bag for the keys, asked 'So how much rope—' as he looked up.

'Stefan, forgive me,' I said quietly, as surprise began to bloom across his face. I flinched against the recoil.

Just for an instant, before he fell back, it looked like Stefan was wearing an Anzac Day poppy against his farm shirt. Then the stain spread like a spill of paint, and he landed against the front door's frosted glass with sufficient force to break it.

The gunshot's echoes, reverberating off the house and the hedges, died away. I turned, gloved hands still holding the rifle, ready to walk back to the Skoda, but something snagged in my peripheral vision.

There were two of them, each just under a metre tall. Junior versions of Stefan, or rather of what Stefan had *become*, once every month. Ash-grey, with black tiger stripes showing through a smattering of downy feathers. Longer feathers, kin to the display that still sat on Stefan's kitchen table, marked their forelimbs, the ridge of their backs, and the tip of their tails. The young raptors moved with an angular, confident strut towards the body on the lawn, not a dozen paces away from where I stood. They were small enough, maybe – they would have been easily outmassed by a Rottweiler – but the claws on those central toes already looked lethal. I backed away, keeping the rifle aligned on them the whole time – forgetting, for the moment, that it was unloaded – but they paid me no real notice whatsoever. There was plenty to keep them occupied, on the lawn and around the front door, as it was.

I fought the urge to drive off, right then, because terrified as I was, I still had to *know*. There was still something I didn't understand. And I remembered Stefan's staring into the darkness, the night before. Somewhere past the Hydatids Board ute, out among the farm's outbuildings.

I cocked the rifle, and took a walk out the back.

I found the third raptor, dead and mutilated, in the old grain-shed, although the shed didn't look like it had been used for grain for quite some time. The other two juvenile raptors must have grown impatient, too long between feeds, and had turned on their smaller sibling when the hunger grew too deep. (Recently, too from the look of it: the surrounding blood, on the shed's dusty, crap-encrusted, feather-strewn concrete floor, had not yet fully dried.) They'd then escaped. They weren't to know their keeper, their father, would return just a few hours later, with a fresh kill to keep them sated.

But if they were offspring, then that still left—

And then it struck me.

No. Not their father.

Stefan and I had had more common ground than I'd realised. Not both just *were*-creatures, after all.

For all that I'd had twenty-plus years to adjust to the Change, twenty-plus years to cope with the wrenching transformations it entailed, I'd still been blinkered. How vast was the gulf – between human and wolf, between human and dinosaur, even – that yet could be spanned? How small, in comparison, the gap between male and female? Just a matter of a single chromosome, X versus Y. Stefan had been Changing, every month, into a raptor; and I'd always assumed, blithely, that his gender was conserved across the change.

Not so.

I remembered something I'd read, months or years back, about something that happened sometimes with lizards, and sharks, and maybe other creatures. There didn't always need to have been two parents.

Just one, sometimes. A mother. Parthenogenesis.

*

I thought you'd understand, he'd said. *You being a mother and all.*

And I *did* understand. I couldn't begin to imagine what I might have felt myself driven to do, if I'd been in his situation. But that didn't make his actions excusable, in any real way.

I'd been as loyal as I could, for long enough. And I would grieve Stefan, and would wish most likely until my days' end that there could have been another path for me to take. But standing there in that dark dusty shed, rifle still cradled under my arm, I could not feel any kinship whatsoever for the offspring Stefan, my brother, had felt compelled to nurture and raise. The Change didn't hit until puberty, so the juvenile raptor at my feet had clearly never known human form. This wrecked thing, its meat torn and trampled with loose wisps of feather, might still be, in some weird sense, nephew or niece to me; but I had no sympathy for it. Ten people, at least, had died because of this creature and its siblings. And none of those people deserving of the end they'd met.

I still didn't know what it was I'd been intending to say to Sue. Wish her luck, most likely. With the appointment she'd never reached.

My throat tightened enough that the next few breaths hurt. I wiped my eyes clear, blinked, and steadied myself.

I returned to the front of the house, shakily holding the rifle at the ready. The two young raptors were still gathered around the dead constable on the lawn, busy with the task of pulling meat off a heavily-clothed body. I took careful aim at the predator yanking like a dog at the constable's hand. The rifle kicked back against my shoulder; it was a clean shot to the head. The creature gave a half-cry, somewhere between human and bird, as it fell back.

Its sibling looked up from the dead man's throat, turned to stare at me through cold eyes, unconcerned, supremely confident. I fumbled through the rifle's reloading, conscious all the while of my vulnerability. Though the young raptor was significantly smaller than myself, its killing power was innate, plainly evident. It looked down, as if ready to nip another scrap of neck-flesh, then lifted its gaze again.

I could not meet that stare, and pull the trigger. So I closed my eyes.

It did not end well. I had hit the raptor in the chest: it fell and scrabbled, eyes now beseeching, mouth working at the empty air. My hands shook too badly to reload. In the end, I had to walk up to where it lay, bent, complaining in that unearthly voice, all its majesty lost. I clubbed it with the flat of the rifle's butt. Three blows to its head, thud of solid wood against bone, and it was still. My guts roiled; I could not stop myself from shaking. I forced myself to wipe the rifle's butt against the grass at my feet, repeatedly seeking to polish away the raptor's blood and gristle. Then, on legs still weak, I walked around the house to where I'd parked the Skoda. One of the garden bags would do, to keep any traces of blood off the floor of the boot.

I hadn't had to catch sight of Stefan during the whole grisly exercise.

I drove into Ashburton, careful to keep to the speed limit all the way, to find a car wash. Thinking all the while about how I was going to dispose of the rifle in the boot. And what kind of story I was going to tell the police. God only knew what they would make of the remains on the lawn. And in the shed.

I needed not to take too long in thinking about it, too. Soon it would be time to pick up Zara, from Doug's.

And soon it would be time also for one of those mother-to-daughter chats, with Zara.

You Said "Two of Each", Right?

Not going to be easy. Always an intimidatory experience, talking to the Big Bloke. But these things had to be raised – his head on the chopping block, and all that. Might as well gird his loins, get it done.

'Umm...' he began.

'YES?'

'Look, thing is, mate... uh, you draw up these plans yourself?'

'YES. OF COURSE.'

'Ah.'

'YOU SEEK TO PRAISE THEM? PRAISE ME?'

'No. Uh, well, yeah, of course, but...'

'BUT?'

'... there's a problem.'

'*OF COURSE* THERE IS A PROBLEM. DO NOT DOUBT THAT I WOULD NOT BE TAKING SUCH DRASTIC, DECISIVE MEASURES WERE THERE NOT A *PROBLEM*.'

'Uh. Er. Yeah. Sure. And your plan – awesome, big-picture stuff, as always. Inspirational. No question. But that's not the problem. It's...' He mopped his brow with a grimy cloth. 'Look, thing is, mate, three hundred cubits. It's just not gonna be enough. It's nowhere *near* enough.'

'YOU DO NOT THINK IT WILL BE SEAWORTHY?'

(*Was it his imagination, or was there more thunderiness to the voice? Never a good sign...*) 'No, she'll be right with that, I reckon.

Seaworthy and praiseworthy both. No worries there. More a case...'

'YES?'

'Look, where d'you want me to put the brontosaurs?'

'THE WHAT?'

'You know, the... big lizardy beasts. I mean, I'm no expert, mate, but there's gotta be at least a dozen different kinds, and most of them forty, fifty, sixty cubits long. Or more. And none of them *skinny*, not by a long chalk. So thing is, if we're supposed to take two of each, then wham, I'd say we're pretty much chocka with just those, no room for anything else.' He mopped his brow again. 'And with a major problem in buoyancy, I reckon.'

'HMM.'

'So, unless you maybe want me to build *two*, one just for the brontoes and one for everything else—'

'NO.'

'So should I then maybe upscale it, say six hundred cubits instead? Though where I'm going to get that amount of gopher wood...'

'NO. IT STAYS AT THREE HUNDRED. THREE HUNDREDS SHALL IT BE, NEITHER AS HIGH AS FOUR NOR AS LOWLY AS TWO.'

'Yeah, and five is right out. Got it. But the thunder-lizards...'

'LEAVE THEM. IT IS NOT AS THOUGH THEY WERE ONE OF MY, AHEM, MORE BRILLIANT IDEAS.'

'Ah. Well, okay, you're the boss.'

'WAS THERE MORE?'

The very air felt thick, as with the threat of lightning. Dry mouthed, he swallowed. He'd *kill* for a tinny. But that would have to wait. 'Well, since you ask... yeah. There's the partitions.'

'WHAT ABOUT THE PARTITIONS?'

'You don't think they're maybe a tad on the, ah, *flimsy* side?'

'FLIMSY?'

'I'm just thinking about the tyrannosaurs. I mean, mate, if it's all the same to you... well, me and the missus, and the kids of course, would kind of like to come out the other side of this in one piece, and I don't think—'

'FINE. GOT IT. SCRATCH THE TYRANNOSAURS. NEXT?'

'Well, there are those big ones with the whopping long horns on their faces. Way I see it, we'd have to put those ones below the waterline, for ballast considerations and all that, but I don't reckon the hull thickness—'

'RIGHT. LEAVE THEM OFF.'

He wrung the cloth out, and daubed his forehead once more. 'And the same maybe goes for those ones with the long spikes at their tail…'

'UH. VERY WELL. I SEE WHERE THIS LEADS. JUST SKIP THE LOT.'

'When you say "the lot", you mean… ?'

'THE BIG DUMB LIZARDY THINGS. JUST LEAVE THEM TO DROWN. THE WHOLE STINKING LOT OF THEM.'

'Uh, mate, you *sure* about th—'

'YES. MY MIND IS MADE UP. YOU WISH TO DISPUTE MY SERIOUSNESS OF PURPOSE?'

(*Definitely* more than a hint of thunderiness. Petulance, even, if that's the word I'm thinking of.) 'Well, no, but… you don't think that's maybe throwing the baby out with the bathw—'

'NO. LEAVE THEM.' A rumble, nearly subsonic, as though for emphasis.

'Look, sorry, I can tell you're disappointed…'

'DISAPPOINTED? *DISAPPOINTED?*'

'Yeah, I mean, this. Well, it's gotta be your first set of blueprints, innit? I mean, sure, you've built lots of things, but they've all been… uh, natural objects. And this, well, it's definitely a laudable crack at drawing up a boat, specially a first draft, but… What I mean is, if you'd just let me jig the specs a bit – it's not like you've had any hands-on in carpentry…'

'*ENOUGH!* BEGONE! I HAVE A FLOOD TO PLAN. ASSUMING YOU THINK I CAN HANDLE *THAT.*'

(Wow. *Really* hit a raw nerve there. Best try to patch it over. Don't want to find ourselves on the "smite sheet", do we?) 'Well, alright then.

I maybe haven't stressed how, er, praiseworthy I think the basic idea is. Because it is, very, obviously. And sorry for the, uh, home-truths bits…'

'I'LL *MANAGE.*'

'You're the boss.'

'DON'T YOU FORGET IT. AND, THE CARPENTRY EXPERIENCE?'

'Yeah, what?'

'I CAN GET SOME.'

'Beg pardon, but… mate, *how?*'

'I'LL THINK OF SOMETHING.'

The Speed of Heavy

I hate exchange students. *Hate* 'em. First couple of weeks you're forced to monitor them continually, ensuring they're not leaving the airlock open, they're strapping themselves in when they use the restroom, they're keeping up with their space-nausea meds. And after that, if they haven't accidentally spaced the crew, nor gotten themselves a nice little tenth-degree tan from spacewalking through the ion-drive exhaust, they get to feeling that they've learnt it all, 'cause they're at that age when they know it all anyway, when really they haven't learnt the first thing, which is, as yet, they don't know nothing. So, yeah, I hate 'em. But somehow I keep signing 'em. Must be those allowance credits the Interplanet Council provides to compensate for all the inconvenience.

Never again, after this.

I'm fit to strangle Josef. If I can find him.

Zero-gee isn't much good for domestic theatrics. Right now, if we were under a decent gravity field, I'd be stomping the *Vinyl Frontier*'s corridors, belting on accessways and bellowing his wretched excuse for a name. But it's not viable to stomp when you need to tread softly enough for the velcro to mesh, and if you opt for the zero-gee analogue to the stomp, which is to carom dangerously along the curving corridors, you're only likely to hurt yourself.

Shuffling the printout flimsy to the other hand, I rub my wrist, and tell myself I'd better slow down. At least yelling in zero-gee is still practical, and effective. 'JOSEF!'

'C-captain Wright, sir?' Sneaking up behind me somehow, which means he's learnt enough of the ship's layout to have found a new hidey-hole. Shaking in his one-piece jumpsuit. As well he might. 'I – is there a problem, Captain?'

I shake the flimsy in his face, so close he could blow his nose on it as it passes, if his reactions were fast enough. 'YES, Josef, there's a *problem*!'

'Is something wrong with the freight order, Captain Wright?'

Count to ten; but I only manage four and a half. 'The freight order, Josef?' My voice, I can hear, is like a barely sheathed switchblade. '*Why* didn't you let me, or Rhonda, or Hiroko, take down the details?'

'I'm sorry, Captain, sir, I couldn't find any of you when the call came through. And I've seen how to do it, I've watched you stacks of times...'

(Once, Josef. You've seen me take a freight order *once*. And if I remember correctly, you were paying more attention to Hiroko's *physique* while she did her exercises.)

'I'm fairly sure I got all the details,' he continues. 'Did I miss something out?'

'No, Josef, nothing you *missed out*!' There's a vein on the left side of my head, sets to throbbing whenever something's coming to the boil. If I ever turn volcano (and my wife's surprised it hasn't happened yet, some days), that's where the eruption will occur. I can feel the magma banking up behind it now.

'Then what—'

'It's what you let them *put in* that's the problem! Josef! Did you ever stop to think, maybe, accepting a wildlife cargo job from Vesta was just a little bit outside our remit? We're *freight*, Josef, not livestock! Eff – arr – ee – eye – gee... you get it?'

'Y-yes, Captain.'

'Not to mention out of our way.'

'But – but Vesta's so close to our posi—'

'Which direction, Josef?'

Sheepishly, he looks around himself, finally pointing towards the stern.

'I keep telling you, Josef! This is space, it's not a highway. It's not just about the *position*, it's about the *momentum*. We can't just pull over, turn around, and drive back! I'd subtract the fuel costs from your allowance. If I thought there was enough there to cover it.'

'I'm excessively sorry, Captain Wright, sir. I'll be more careful another time. So can we just, you know, cancel the order?'

Glowering at his puppy-fattened face, I stroke my beard. (I long ago decided shaving in low gravity was a messy business, more trouble than it was worth.) 'Did you *notice* the noncompletion penalty clause?'

'Um.'

'Um is right! What in vac's name were you thinking?'

'Um. I – I suppose I should be getting the cargo bay fitted out, then, for all the bats and the crickets.'

'Yes. You *sure* you've got all the information you need for that?'

'P-pretty sure, Captain. The bats weigh about ten kilos each, and the lady said they eat a fifth of their weight in the crickets every day. So I was thinking those fragile-cargo cages should be big enough to hold them – do we have twenty of the cages, so we can hold all the bats for the order?'

I take a moment for seismic monitoring before I reply. 'Yes, there's twenty cages, Josef. At least. But I don't think that's going to help you.'

'Um, why not, Captain Wright, sir?'

'How big d'you think these bats are?'

'Well, like the lady said, they weigh ten kilos or so, so that makes them about the size of a small dog, I guess.'

The magma shifts, looking for another possible outlet. My eardrum, perhaps. 'Josef. The lady. The woman, rather. How much does she weigh?'

'C-captain?' He looks at me with anxious puzzlement, as though I've just announced we're going to instigate commercial pigflight to the skating rinks of Hades. 'But she's not part of the consignment, is she?' He reaches for the flimsy, but I pull it back out of reach. Another time, it would be comical to watch his struggles to regain his footing on the velcroed surface.

'Bear with me. Josef. The woman. How much does the woman weigh on Vesta?'

He gives me a reprise of the pigflight-proposing-insane-captain stare, and then there's a pilot-light ignition moment when he suddenly realizes, not yet the magnitude, but at least the direction of his mistake. 'Um. Would that be maybe ten kilos, Captain Wright, sir?'

'*If* she weighed in at ten kilos, on Vesta, she'd require immediate hospitalisation and an excessive fabric allowance for her clothing. *No,* Josef. I strongly suspect your wonderful bat-consigning woman on Vesta weighs maybe two kilos, plus or minus one. Vesta's gravity is only around two percent of Earth's. D'you see where I'm going with this, Josef?'

Now, yes, *now* he finally has the full vector. He at least has the decency to blush in awkwardness. 'Um—'

'So a bat on Vesta, weighing ten kilos, is *not* the size of a small dog. It could without difficulty *eat* a small dog. Or several. In serial, if not in parallel. You'd be better advised to envisage said bat, said *twenty* bats you've arranged for us to transport at a pittance, as a cross between a panther and a pterodactyl. And Josef?'

'Um—'

'I *don't* think your little cargo cages are going to hold them.'

The viewscreen reveals Candace, the android receptionist from InVesta Commerce. She's a J86 clerical-class cyborg (an archivist, judging by the size of her memory glands), programmed for dogmatic adherence to protocol, and is plainly not the sort of individual with whom an unwanted business contract can be ameliorated. I go over the terms of the contract with her, twenty Vesta-native cricket bats to be transported to the new xenobiology reserve that the Belters have hollowed out of Eros. Payment on completion of delivery to Eros. Time allotted: one hundred days.

'That's one hundred *Vesta* days, of course,' she notes in her mechanical sing-song tones.

That's a wrinkle I hadn't myself noticed. Bloody Vestan pedants, insisting on using local units. Vesta spins fast: it gets through four days in less than twenty-four standard hours. We've got only about three weeks to complete the delivery.

We'll never make it. This is going to cripple us. Josef has let them slap their most stringent penalty clauses into the contract. He might as well have signed us up for blunt-instrument vivisection while he was at it.

In an unusual display of interpersonal perspicacity, Josef has come belatedly to the conclusion that hanging around the bridge (or anywhere else I might encounter him) is not conducive to his health. He's presumably moping around his cabin, convinced that everybody hates him.

I terminate the call to InVesta, feeling pretty much as though I've just been interviewed by an ore-crusher. If I've been in any doubt as to the impact of those penalty clauses, the call has dispelled said doubt. The danger, in terms of personal self-destruction, now seems not so much to be volcanic eruption, more a kind of creeping runaway glaciation. I don't want to rise from the chair, because the chair is comfortable and I'm certain that whatever follows next will not be.

Rhonda, who can sense one of my funk-slumps before I'm aware of them myself, approaches to lay a soothing hand on my shoulder. Just enough pressure to restore hydrostatic balance.

'It'll be fine, Shelby, just you see.'

Somehow, this helps, despite that it's obviously arrant spacejunk: if there's anything "fine" about our current predicament, other than in the sense of a penalty fee, we'd need a tunneling microscope to be able to find it. And yet my wife Rhonda is a woman, and therefore wise in the ways of the universe, able to convince me of the continuity of existence, and of hope, at the most improbable of times.

I make a pretense of arguing for the negative. 'Fine? *Fine?* Have you *seen* the way Josef's strung us up? He might as well have carved the words "Here I am, eat me" into our bleeding flesh, dipped us in fish sauce, and dumped us, blindfolded, gagged, and bound hand and foot in the shark pool. We're gonna be left destitute for the rest of our lives!'

'Oh, Shel! You *do* see the glass as half broken. Something will turn up, it always has. And maybe this is a lesson to you, to take more initiative in processing the paperwork.'

'*What?* He's the one hung us out on the barbed-wire washline, and you're making out it's somehow *my fault?* This is *mutiny!*'

And yet, I know, she has a point. That's what's such a worrying thing about Rhonda: her perception is reliable. Even, somehow, when it's at variance with my own opinions.

'You need to give the boy a chance, Shel. He looks up to you, space only knows why. He's new, he's on exchange, he'll make mistakes: we all have. Think how nervous you were last year, with Hiroko earthside on *her* exchange.'

'That was different,' I reply a little too quickly, not even sure if I believe it myself.

'Different how? Daughter different? *Listen* to yourself. You act as though you're the only one who sees things... and you were pretty difficult to live with last year, when Hiroko left, let me tell you.'

'I was worried. Aren't I allowed to be worried?'

'Yes, but it's a pretty bloody futile exercise. She didn't walk off any tenth-story balconies, and—'

'But the breakages—'

'Shel, she stopped parking breakables in mid-air before the end of the first week.'

'*You* weren't the one took that angry call from the ceramics gallery.'

'Oh, Shel, get *over* it. She was fine, she just needed some time. Josef's doing fine, give him a chance. It'll work out.'

I'm not convinced; and I'm still adamant that this is different.

Think of the most unpleasant invertebrate you can imagine: cockroach, tiger slug, witchety grub, it doesn't really matter what, maybe a mixture of all three, even. Now imagine that creature, grown as large as it can possibly get without actually being fully terrifying – that's maybe thirty, maybe fifty centimetres, depending on where your threshold lies. Now your creature, sized up, is probably a passable resemblance to the Vesta cave cricket, but in envisaging only one of them you've failed to gain the complete picture, so you'd better imagine another ten thousand of them. Then there's also the noise, and the smell.

That's our airlock, at the moment, because we have nowhere else on board the *Vinyl Frontier* to fit them. We'd better not need to abandon ship in a hurry.

Actually, just go with the smell, which is plenty. Hold back, mentally, on the noise. This isn't to say that ten thousand Vesta cave crickets aren't pretty sonically assertive – they're like a convention of phlegmatic cockatoos – but whatever noise they may be managing to create, it pales into lullaby compared to the constant kettle-squealing and scramjet-roaring of our bats. (And although they're called bats – and, naturally enough at that, *cricket* bats – they're in truth no more mammalian than the short-lived, "one-day" crickets are insectoidal, which is to say, not much, if at all. The "bats" look as though they have crocodilian ancestry, and maybe wolverine, with a dash of piranha. They look like, well, if the ancient Egyptian gods had needed bodyguards…)

There are only two bats. I count them frequently, through the relative security of the armoured plastiglass of the cargo hold access hatch. They've been barricaded into separate blast-proof dangerous-goods alcoves, at either end of the hold: surrounded on five sides by thick titanium-mesh-reinforced armoured nanofibre/spun granite composite, and on the sixth by a triple-locked iridium-steel monofilament grille gate that I've previously nearly herniated myself on opening. The bats presumably can't see each other via sonar, because the facing walls are solid and the gate grille openings are too small for them to get a snout through, but it's obvious they each know the other is there, because in the rare moments they're not both foghorning or screaming, the noise made by just one of them is almost deafening. The hold access hatch deadens the noise, but not nearly enough; and I swear the infrasound vibrates every solid surface within the *Vinyl Frontier*.

Still, two is a good number of bats to have in our cargo hold, because two bats in the hold equals no bats elsewhere in the ship, and this has to be my main goal for however long this nightmare lasts. (Of course, if one or other of the bats *does* escape, I know just the person to send looking for them – except Rhonda, killjoy, says I can't, it goes against the spirit if not the letter of the exchange agreement.)

So, two bats. Not twenty. Ten trips. Three weeks. Vesta. Eros.

No hope in hell.

'Josef.' Thump.

'Joo-sef.' Thump.

'*Josef!*' Thump thump.

'JO—' Thump thump thump.

'Did you call, captain?' Thump thump thump thump thump.

The bloody creatures are going mental. 'Josef. *Why* are those things going percussive on me?' A longer series of thumps.

'Think there's probably a problem with their feed pipe, Captain, sir.'

'Blocked?' The feed pipe has been rigged up to run from the airlock through to the cargo hold, ensuring that the crickets (who instinctually scurry to explore narrow crevices, which is how they find safety in the hollowed caverns of asteroid Vesta) obediently present themselves to the bats for consumption, once population pressure within the airlock has propelled them to expand their territory. As long as there's a steady stream of misguided crickets to decapitate, the bats are happy enough, but – and here the longest concatenation of thumps yet, answered by a wounded-bull roar – it sounds as though the supply may have dropped off. I'm starting to grow worried for the welfare of the cargo-hold walls, which are supposedly impervious to both fuel explosion and asteroidal impact, but now are looking decidedly fragile in the face of the relentless onslaught of the bored bats' beaks. I'm concerned that, should the walls not hold, we'll suddenly find ourselves in possession of only one bat. Their attitude towards cohabitation sounds combative, to say the least.

'No, don't think there's a blockage, Captain, sir, just think the crickets are having a population crisis.'

'Why's that? It's supposed to be a closed loop. The bats eat the crickets, the crickets feed on the bat guano, the crickets breed.'

'Yes, but the bat guano is – um – with the bats. Captain. Sir.'

'Didn't I tell you to rig up a pump to pipe it through to the airlock?'

'Pump's clogged. I – um – sort of forgot to adjust for the ten-kilo thing. Pipe's not wide enough.'

I eye off the bats, trying to gauge which of the two is the more docile, though neither is plainly a good fit for the concept. Left Bat I judge to be the more aggressive and violent of the two, but Right Bat is larger, more vocal, and has quicker reflexes.

'Josef—'

'There's no bloody way I'm going in there,' he mutters quickly. 'Sir. Captain.'

'I wouldn't dream of it,' I lie. 'But we'll need someone to operate the trank-gun, in case one charge isn't enough. Come on, let's suit up.'

The yellow-and-red suit muffles a lot of the high-end sound within the cargo hold, but the bass tones reverberate awkwardly within the helmet. I give the thumbs-up to Josef, who's kitted out in the green-and-orange usually worn by Hiroko, and he swings the cargo hold hatch closed. The bats are now going frantic, as I approach the right-hand-side alcove: we're into day three of a twelve-standard-day flight to Eros, and I'm keen to maximise the guano-haul while minimising bat contact time. (For purposes of guano accumulation, Right Bat has been distinctly more productive than Left Bat.) If we can get through the flight without having to repeat this exercise, I'll be happy. Ecstatic, even. If I survive the next few minutes.

The noise is deafening. The hold is pressurised at one atmosphere, same as the rest of the ship. Technically we don't need the spacesuits, but I'm hoping that, suited, we look sufficiently different to a cricket as to avert the bats' feeding response. I don't think I'd appreciated until now how lethally sharp their beaks are: the suits don't offer any real protection, other than as textural camouflage for bat-sonar purposes.

I stow the portable vacuum-tank in a cargo net on the wall near the access hatch, and click the safety off the trank-gun. I use the suit's attitude jets to finesse my way expertly to the gate of the right-hand alcove, take aim through the gate's grille, and pull the trigger.

Nothing happens, except that the steady but feeble acceleration of the *Vinyl Frontier*'s ion drives slowly wafts me off-target. I latch down the gun's safety and check the readout on its muzzle. *Path obscured*, it reads.

'What's the problem?' Josef asks, coming in too fast and hitting the gate with a clang. I only just have time to dodge.

'Grille's too fine,' I reply, juggling the attitude jets to arrest a slow tumble. 'Gun can't shoot the trank-capsule through it. Need to open the gate to make the shot.'

'Um—'

'Josef,' I snap back, '*you'll* still have the gate between you and it.' For a few seconds, at any rate.

'Are you sure one capsule's enough?' he asks.

'All we'll have time for,' I reply. 'Now *open the damn gate!*' Then it occurs to me that, with the gate so massive, waiting fully in front of the bat's cell isn't the best vantage: I need to be pressed against the hold's rear right corner, to get a clear shot at the earliest possible part of the gate's opening arc. I deftly jet into position, velcro myself to the wall, and ready the gun once more.

Both bats have fallen ominously silent.

Josef, in place at last, slides back the gate's final latch as gingerly as though it's a suspect uranium fuel rod. Then he tugs at the grille, delicately at first but with obviously increasing effort, and the gate slowly swings outward. Displaying more common sense than I'd credit him with, he wafts out of its path. The bat, sensing a change in the conditions of its incarceration, has locked its claws into the gate's grilled surface and is riding it out. Its massive head, armoured, eyeless and dominated by an elongated secateurs-like beak, is flattened in profile against the side of the gate, sweeping across this new terrain. It's like a gargoyle riding a piece of flimsy playground equipment. I keep the gun trained on the bulge of the main artery within the bat's nearside wing: a risky shot, but if I wait for a clear shot at its torso, I'll likely be too late. It flexes its wings, and I fear I have left it too late. I shoot. It springs. Josef screams.

I have just enough time to wonder why we don't have a *double-barrelled* trank-gun.

'Jeez, Dad, you gotta stop playing the cowboy like this. You're bloody lucky nothing got ruptured.'

I seek to sit up, which is a mistake. I can feel bruising everywhere.

I'm strapped gently into a crib in the *Vinyl's* spare cabin, which Hiroko has done up as a sick bay: there's what looks to be our full inventory of medical monitors bolted to the bulkhead, with a webwork of cables leading to my head, my arms, my torso.

'What the hell happened?' I ask.

'You're bloody lucky,' she repeats. 'D'you know how *big* those things are?'

Yes, I think I do, as it happens. I think I know that rather well.

'It slammed you against the wall,' Hiroko explains. 'Must've knocked you out cold. You're lucky it was half-unco itself by that time, from the impact and from the trank-dart. We were watching on the security vid, Mum and me. You went down like a sack of – well, like something, and then Josef nipped in, grabbed the trank-gun, and rifle-butted it in the head.'

There's a bit too much open-hearted admiration, in those final words, for my liking. Too much endorsement of impromptu heroism, and more besides, perhaps. No parent likes to hear his teenage daughter espouse the virtues of someone whose careless bat-ordering and criminally incompetent plumbing has nearly resulted in her father's death.

'Did he get the guano?'

'*Yes*, Dad. You shouldn't be so disparaging of him, he's very capable. *If* you give him a chance. Like he rigged up this pump-clearing capsule-bot to get the guano shipped back to the airlock, so you guys won't need to pull another stunt like that. Ever.'

'And the bats?' It dawns on me that things throughout the ship are strangely quiet. If something has happened to those bloody bats—

'They're fine, they're not carrying on like before when they couldn't even see each other. After all, Josef wasn't exactly able to shift Bertha back into her cell.'

Pity. That's a mental image I find curiously appealing, particularly in view of the trank-dart's limited effectiveness. But – 'Bertha? You've given that homicidal flying-wing a *name?*'

'No, it's just what it says on her collar. If you'd bother to read the paperwork—'

'Don't *you* start.' I get enough of that from your mother. 'Their names are on the documentation? What's the other one called?'

'Bette. They seem to have put on quite a bit of weight. In fact,' she grins, as though enjoying a private joke, 'if you'd read through to the last page of the contract, you might have seen that it was never expected to take us more than one trip to turn up at Eros with bat twenty.'

'It – I have no idea what you – they're *pregnant?* Both of them?'

'I'm no exozoologist, Dad, but they're showing all the signs. One of the reasons they've quieted down is that, now that we've given them some loose packing material to play with, they're busy making nests. According to the explanatory notes, we should expect the pitter-patter of not-so-tiny wings in, say, another seven or eight days.'

Great. I'm curiously crestfallen at the news that this voyage is not shaping up to be the unmitigated disaster I'd been envisaging. 'Hmph. It's all very well, meeting the deadline and all that. I'm glad we'll still get to keep the ship. But this is costing us a *fortune* in fuel. And the size of the payment Josef agreed to, it won't even get our airlock and hold decontaminated, let alone start to reimburse us for fuel and living supplies. We're losing a packet on this, and – why are you grinning?'

'*Honestly*, Dad, listen to you. Rah rah Josef this, and blah blah Josef that, you just seem to blame him for everything. And if you'd bothered to read the paperwork—'

'What d'you mean? I *did* read the paperwork!' Enough to have checked out the payment, at any rate. 'We stand to get only a hundred credits from this. If we're lucky.'

'*No*, Dad, that's what Josef told you, it's not what he'd arranged. He didn't even realise how clever he was being, himself, at first. But Dad, you'll like it when you see it. I don't imagine InVesta will be too happy when they realise what they've done – they'll probably demote that J86, Candace or whoever, to a paperweight – but like they always say, the contract is ironclad.'

She holds out a copy of the contract for me. I lift my arm up to take it, wincing as the deep-body bruises protest at being awakened.

'Josef says he's really starting to feel like he fits in here, says he'd like to apply for an indefinite extension to the exchange.'

Not likely, I respond silently. I thumb through to the financial section of the contract. The payment stipulation looks clear enough. 'So? Ten kilograms palladium on completion? That's... yeah, told you, that's about one hundred credits at standard prices.'

'*No*, Dad, ten kilos of palladium by *weight*. *Not* mass!'

'By – oh.' I attempt a quick calculation in my aching head. 'So... Vesta's gravity... strewth, that makes it almost five thousand credits!'

She laughs disparagingly. 'You still don't get it, do you?'

'Don't get what?'

'It's not *Vesta* we're taking them to. Payment on delivery to *Eros!*'

'Yeah, so?'

'Eros's surface gravity is?'

I rummage back into my memory. This is one of those statistics I had to memorise back at the Academy. *Eros is small, oblong, sparsely populated, its surface gravity is—*

Ten kilos, multiplied by—

Bloody hell.

I mean to say, bloody freaking *hell*.

We could buy a new *ship* for that. Maybe two.

Hiroko laughs again, a sound curiously like the carefree tinkle of many coins, and presses ahead with the question which, somehow, I've known is coming:

'So, Dad… can we keep him?'

Talking with Taniwha

Solveig waited in the airlock's decontam–depressure suite, while the irradiation, solvent sprays, ultrasonics and brush-filters ran their course. Green-lighted at last, she walked through into the outfit room and peeled off her enviro-suit's sanitised remains, tossing them to the floor opposite the "Suit Yourself!" wall poster.

A sickly, bruised-metal smell greeted her – some residue of Rousseau's sticky atmosphere that had withstood the physicochemical onslaught of the decontamination cycle. It was an unusual odour, affronting, yet not outright offensive.

Stripped to undergarments, she took a scanner-cloth from the wall rack, ran it over her skin, washcloth-fashion, and waited until its diagnostic chimes indicated that yes, she was, in fact, clean.

She pulled on her monogrammed Base overalls, punched the inner door's release code, and strode out into the too-clean corridor towards the observations lab.

'Where you been?' Herrick asked, glancing up. He was tall, even when seated, and the thick scent of cologne jangled against his dull, rumpled appearance. She smiled despite herself: he'd burnt himself shaving, again. The smile faded as she noted that the seat beside the young anatomist was the only one not occupied. Had he been saving it for her?

'Breath of fresh air,' Solveig replied, with an edge to her voice that she herself wasn't sure of. 'Just needed some space.'

'Jens won't be happy,' he said. 'A taniwha's been in the pit for the past fifteen or more, waiting for someone to share its goss with. Blue Six, one of the younger set, still under a metre in length. Still there, too, but if you don't connect soon it might get bored waiting – or maybe get distracted by an appetising hunk of crud offscreen – and that'd be a pity, 'cause I'm not finished my run yet. Need you to keep it chatting, till my measurements are done.'

'Yeah, well, Jens can unbend a little. If she's not going to bother training up any more linguists, she'd better learn to take better care of the few she's got down here. It *hurts* to think in taniwha. You should try it sometime.'

'Like a séance in jello, isn't it? That's what Matsos reckons—'

'Don't get me started on Matsos,' she replied.

'Quit yapping and connect, will you? I need it to hang around for at least another thirty for the sonar tomograph.'

Obediently, she retrieved the comms satchel and sat down at the empty desk. Unclasping the satchel's lid, she lifted out waldo gloves and a tiara and slipped them on, closing her eyes. The tiara's gel-secreting electrodes beeped softly, indicating that the set's handshake had successfully completed. Her sensorium morphed into the unwelcoming environment of "the pit", in actuality a kilometre-deep trench in the otherwise comparatively shallow crater lake. An impact cleft in the planet's diamond crust.

Dark. Cold. Thick. She flexed the fingers of her left hand in greeting – it was like squeezing honey – and waited.

A long pause. She was blind, here, and the absence of activity told her nothing. Perhaps the tanny had, as Herrick suggested, grown bored, and slid off in search of richer nutrients.

A *frisson* ran along her forearm. Two feathered nudges to the wrist, one above, one below. Like a velvet-sheathed pincer or an invitation to dance. Contact. She stretched out with her arm to return the gesture. *<I'm here. Let's talk.>*

The taniwha's next tactile signal was convoluted, difficult to interpret. *<Two are here, but only one beneath.>* A metaphor, perhaps. Taniwha tended to use metaphor to excess, which was problematic when one sought to understand the viewpoint of a creature without the senses of sight, hearing, or taste.

Usually, Solveig's approach to these sessions was to treat the interaction like a poem, something to be experienced on a visceral or emotive plane, and only in hindsight, through review of the session log, to seek to gain a more rational understanding of the conversation's content. It was a method which, to her mind, worked better than any other, but was not one to which her supervisor responded with any degree of sympathy or patience.

I want details, not blank verse, Jens had snapped at Solveig after a particularly elliptical session two days back. Today's late start didn't seem likely to appease her, either.

<Bodies?>, Solveig finally signalled in return, thinking to have discerned a possible meaning. "Bodies" was the nearest term she had to hand, for "gloves".

<Smell predator. Close. Must leave.> Abrupt as that, the session ended. She kept her hands in the gloves, nevertheless. She felt vaguely foolish – she had, after all, only just started.

'Sol—' Herrick, beside her, whined. 'What'd you *say?*'

'Didn't say anything, the taniwha just pulled the plug. Danger.' It happened. Tannies weren't top of the food chain.

'My *tom*—' Herrick's complaint continued.

'Transform what you've got, get the rest tomorrow.'

'Tell me how to do my job, why don't you? Hey, where you going?'

'Fresh air.'

'*Again?* Already?' Herrick stood up beside her. 'Mind if I tag along?'

Yes, actually. 'Suit yourself. But what about your datasets?'

'They'll keep.'

The base's personnel airlock was situated as close to the lake's shoreline as had been judged practical, for proximity to the heavy-engineering lock and to the thick strands of sheathed data cables that led to the various submerged payloads. For all that her research revolved around the lake and its denizens, though, Solveig was always eager to put as great a distance as possible between herself and the lake's too-dark surface.

There'd been recent rain, mostly olefins and small aromatics. The ground was sticky-wet and riven with trickling streams of hydrocarbons that ran downslope to the edge of the crater lake. Treacherous, but as compensation, the air looked mostly clear, like dark-stained glass, below the haze-decks. Clear enough, at any rate, that she could make out a distant mantawing harrying a flock of montgolfiers. But she'd still need the suit's headlamp to be sure of her footing.

Rousseau's sun was a feeble bright patch in the unbroken canopy of haze, yellow-orange rather than the surrounding brown-black. The sun's elevation indicated that it was at least four hours after noon, well past the almost-adequate illumination of midday.

Solveig set off upslope, her movements thick and exaggerated. She climbed past the brown-stained white domes of the base, towards the stand of tree-like coral growths. Herrick, who'd been staring at the carpetfeeders lazily ruffling their way across the lake surface, turned and followed. The trail, steep and slippery, was demanding, particularly against the added encumbrance of a suit. Soon, in her earpiece, Herrick's breathing grew rough with exertion, an unwelcome intrusion on her thoughts.

She put a gloved hand out against the ragged, steel-hard branch of the first tall coral, signalling an end to the climb. Herrick slumped to a sitting position at the tree-like organism's base, looking bored already, or maybe nervous – several of the base's staff were uneasy about excursions out into Rousseau's instantly toxic environment, even with the suits' over-engineered protective casing. But if Herrick was ill at ease about something, he didn't let on, and she didn't ask. Instead, she pointedly stared in the opposite direction, looking uphill past the coral grove towards the crater's wind-worn rim. Something crawled across her glove, one of the insectoidal flake-ants which competed with the coral for haze nutrients. Further along the same branch, another of the ant-like forms had become trapped in the sticky glacier of tar that oozed with viscous languor towards the maw at the crutch of that group of branches. The small creature, still grasping a precious flake of soot within its mandibles, struggled in futility against the relentless liquid conveyer belt in which it was embedded.

The familiar rules of biology, written here in a different code.

Her colleague picked himself up, came over to investigate whatever had caught her attention. She turned around as the enviro-suit's proximity bell sounded.

It was awkward with Herrick, she'd always known it would be, even at the time. There was a tension between them. One that went well beyond the usual antipathy between the linguists and the anatomists, each of whom tended to view the other as an impediment to their access to the beasts in the pit, an obstacle that must be worked around. Solveig herself was repeatedly frustrated by the anatomists' demands that the taniwha be kept occupied in discourse for as long as possible, to aid their passive sonar-probe body-mapping of the creatures. But the taniwha often only had opportunity for short bursts of communication before the necessity to retreat from predators. She wasn't sure exactly what gripe the anatomists held for her own kind, other than their conviction that the elucidation of language was not a *true* science, merely a flimsy and ill-defined distraction from the real business of robust, fact-based research.

It was a view Herrick, in particular, seemed to take to an extreme, but that might merely have been an extension of his attitude towards her. The flinty awkwardness he'd shown her, ever since that night.

A mistake, all round.

But she'd done nothing since, to encourage him, so far as she knew – quite the reverse, if anything – and yet, it was achingly obvious it was a problem yet unresolved. And he, of course, did nothing to defuse the standoff, the tension. He was just young, unfinished. Hollow. She should have seen that, should have paid attention, right from the start.

'Nice out here after rain,' he commented.

She didn't reply.

'Didn't realise the mud was this sticky,' he noted. Trying again.

She didn't reply.

'What does your tanny make of the weather?' he asked.

'Herrick, I have *no idea* whether I've yet talked to the same one twice,' she snapped. 'I don't even note their IDs, from those sticky patches you guys get us to persuade them to take from the sonar station. I just don't keep tabs on them the way you guys do. It's counter to their approach, to communication. There's a *colony* down there, not just a single— They don't seem to individuate, the way humans do. But anyway, I don't think they're aware of the weather, they're too far subsurface.'

'Weird how they're the only ones who want to talk with us,' Herrick said.

'Yeah, well, apes like us are curious by nature. Lots of other creatures aren't.'

He was right, though. It was odd. On Rousseau, the zeps, the walkers, and the swimbirds all showed evidence of sentience, of reasoned existence, yet in their various ways, each remained aloof. Only the taniwha deigned to respond to human overtures of discourse. Sensory deprivation, perhaps?

<You seek another.>

Solveig paused, attempting to filter the expression for meaning, like extracting krill from seawater. "Hunt", maybe, or "pursue". "The other" or "an opposite"? The content was just too imprecise to work with. It was one of the frequent frustrations of talking with taniwha. She'd learnt, early on, that the taniwha whole-body braille was an inconsistent, lazy language, imprecise and liquid of meaning – in that the same sequence of nudgings, nuzzlings and tappings could signify quite different concepts when employed at different stages of the discourse. It was a frustrating, fascinating tangle of nuance and distraction, as bad as English in some respects.

<*I am here,*> she replied, for want of a more informed response. The taniwha's flank was like stippled latex, and colder than terrestrial prejudice suggested was reasonable for a living thing. Was the subtle imprecision of its language a consequence of the sparsely varying environment it inhabited, or a reflection of the general lack of distractions within its surroundings?

<*Yet you seek another.*> The tactile signals this time were stronger, conveying emphasis and a closer approximation to clarity. "Another", at least, not "the other" or "the opposite". But she still could not guess as to whether the "you" was singular, or plural: her specifically, or the base's occupants more generally.

She prepared to answer, not quite sure herself yet what she would say through the gloves, but was pre-empted when the taniwha, uncharacteristically, spoke again.

<*Another seeks you.*> The phrase of pulses and bumps was distinct enough, though superficially similar to the "predator alert" signal commonly offered as an excuse to cease dialogue.

<*What do you mean?*> The message's overtone of danger had unsettled her, to the extent that she had fractionally opened her eyes for a reassuring glimpse of the busy lab around her.

<*It's clean,*> the taniwha replied, a synonym apparently for "obvious", and then it proceeded again. <*Migration beckons, it must be soon. What will be done?*>

<*What do you mean?*> she repeated. This one was a chatterbox, by local standards, but typically obscure to the point of churlishness. Five minutes in, and she still didn't feel like she had a handle.

<*When two meet, their goals often differ,*> the taniwha offered. That, at least, was the closest on-the-fly translation she could provide. Then: <*So with us. That is why others don't respond. But I am here.*> Was that "I", or "we"? And who did the creature mean by "others"?

<*I am here,*> she replied again. Stalling for time. She hadn't exactly been holding up her end of the conversation – but there was something here, something hidden, that she needed time to eke out.

<I must go soon. Predator smell, faint but closing. Familiar. We should talk again. More. Deeper. All of you.>

<Us?> she answered, hurrying the response through as though she was wringing a wet cloth.

<No. One only. All, not just tip.> And then gone.

'You want a full-body virtual-reality outfit?' Jens asked her, looking up as Solveig stepped into her supervisor's cubicle. 'Why?'

'Because they asked for it. I think.'

'When was this?'

'Yesterday,' Solveig said, handing over the transcript. She'd plotted the conversation as an inclusive array, a kind of flow diagram mapped against the dialogue's recorded timeline. A nested tangle of possible meanings snaked its way down the page. Among these, she'd highlighted the sequence which she believed to be correct, and which she wished to draw to Jens' attention.

'Looks pretty vague to me,' Jens complained.

'It's *always* vague,' she retorted, 'but it's getting clearer, bit by bit. The more we talk with them, the more refined we'll get it.' She wanted, at least, to believe that.

'It'll be a lot of effort, getting that kind of a setup down into the pit. What makes you think it's worth it?'

'Because I think it's a test of some sort. If we can connect with the taniwha, properly get a sense for their place in the system, then we might be able to answer some of the questions about them. Like at least find out what's up with this migration they go on about. I mean, it's not that big of a lake – where do they get to?'

'Yeah, well, it's tough having only the one point of contact. Maybe if we could get the funding for that submersible, we'd get some serious answers.'

'Jens, we can *get* those answers. We just have to be patient, and smart. And I don't think we should lose sight that we're guests in their environment. They've got recognised sentience, we can't just go barging in like it's our place to do what we want. With an anchored full-body VR mannequin, it's up to the taniwha whether they want to interact with us or not. A submersible charging around their home waters, that's something else entirely. Maybe it's that kind of attitude has got in the way with the other sentient species. Maybe a better interaction with the tannies will let us build on that to make headway with the other sentients.'

'You're saying they're connected?' Derisory.

'No, of course I'm not saying that. There's no evidence the taniwha have the slightest idea what's occurring on the surface. But there's gotta be some reason the other species won't reciprocate our efforts at contact, and maybe getting through to the taniwha will help us see what that reason is. Through, I dunno, through triangulation, or something like that.'

'I don't know, Sol. This sounds like an awfully long rope you're drawing, and for what? We still don't have a clear concept of what these taniwhas' limitations are, intellectually or as a society. We might be wasting our time chattering away to the equivalent of dolphins, or chimps. Or African greys.'

'You saying they've gotta have tool use before we can treat them as equals? Brains aren't enough to qualify them somehow? For what?'

'No, Sol, you're twisting my words. We're the guests on this planet, everyone acknowledges that. Or at least gives the idea lip-service. But we need to know what's expected of guests. What constitutes the boundaries of acceptable conduct.'

'But Jens, we're never going to know if we just keep trying to shake hands with them. Think of it. So far as we know, it's a whole-body language, but we've just been giving them a pair of gloves to talk to. No wonder the things we get back are fragmentary and inconclusive. They probably spend most of their time, while talking, trying to dumb down their speech so that they can get through to us with the little we're providing with the gloves. I think they're trying to tell us we need to broaden our vocabulary.'

'D'you really think this'll help us any with the walkers? Or even the zeps?'

'Jens, I honestly have no idea, but it can't hurt.'

It took Base Engineering almost three day-cycles to farb the full-body waldo. Most of this time was needed to ensure the mannequin – a weighted, modified envirosuit – was sturdy enough to resist the massive pressures associated with immersion in two-hundred–odd metres of liquid, yet studded with dermal sensors sensitive enough to register the sometimes feather-light touches of taniwha talk.

Solveig pestered the techs frequently for updates on the fitout, but when they finally announced that it was ready for use, she'd retired to her chamber with a two-day migraine which obstinately resisted the standard medication. Frustrated, fragile, and repeatedly on the edge of nausea, she lay on her cot torn between a wish to retreat into the comparative calm of her throbbing forehead, and the need to know what was going on with the new mouthpiece.

When the mental cobwebs finally grew sparse enough to ignore, she hauled herself up and re-emerged into base society. In her absence, it had fallen to the other linguists, Xiaomei and Matsos, to initiate talks with the pit's taniwha, and they, it seemed, had been busy – to the extent that she required a refresher to adjust to their newly expanded awareness of the taniwha's body language. Xiaomei had left her a message, offering additional information she didn't believe would come through reliably on the transcripts. Jens, too, had left a message.

Herrick, meanwhile, left nine.

Thermal, ramped upwards by forty-five degrees. That'd convey cold, but not the unbearable chill of the tannies' sub-zero environment. *Tactile, times three. No hydrostatic. No visual, auditory, olfactory.* Although the taniwha did possess a sense of smell, there was no evidence they used this property in communication.

Confined within a revamped study cubicle, Solveig waited. The enveloping mesh of electrodes, like a highly porous suit of chainmail, chafed. Engineering hadn't yet had time to farb a tailored suit for each of the base's linguists, so they were forced to make do with an awkward one-size-fits-all model. She hoped Matsos and Xiaomei found it as clumsy as she did. Aside from some discomfort with the suit, she perceived, first, the persistence of gravity, which tempered, but did not totally discredit, the illusion of immersion within the hydrocarbon-slush ecosystem – she, suited, could have ensconced herself in a SensDep tank, but according to Xiaomei it wasn't worth the trouble – and second, the mimicked cold, which went some way to restore the illusion. Beyond these, she sensed occasional faint eddies, sporadic, which might have been currents in the pit, ripples as taniwha or other creatures moved across the mannequin's vicinity, or might just have been noise from the detection system's signal amplifiers.

She was blindfolded (and earplugged) anyway, but she kept her eyes screwed shut. To keep the liquid out.

<Are you there?> The signal was sudden. There'd been no suggestion of any creature directly approaching her personal space. In a liquid as torpid as the taniwha moved, that implied extreme economy of motion, and stealth.

<I am here.> Somehow, through the mannequin, she almost immediately got a much clearer perception of the taniwha's size and shape – a little more than a metre in length, supremely flexible, and somewhere between planarian, flounder, and tunicate in geometry – than she had gained through many sessions with just the gloves. She pictured it black, but in truth the concept of colour was virtually meaningless in an environment so impervious to light. It might as well be grey, or purple.

< We spoke before.> The conversation crawled across her shoulders, behind her neck, an unnerving feeling. A starfish smearing glue. Then, flowing down across her navel like a sudden squall of blown feathers, it added, *<I recognise your touch.>* She had to wait until the taniwha had twined once more along her forearm, to nudge her reply.

<What do you mean?>

<You differ from others. Two, not you. Their touch different.> She flinched, stunned at the thought. She had never sought to identify herself to the taniwha, nor had the other linguists – the agreement had been that, since the taniwha showed no sign of distinguishing themselves from each other, it would confuse the communication to label herself as separate from the other linguists. In this way, each session was a continuation of the one previous, no matter which human participated. But somehow, the taniwha sensed that she was one of three.

<You have been away,> it added, sliding like a serpent down her leg. Its musculature rippled like troubled water beneath a bed of oil.

<Sick,> she replied. *<I hurt. Better now.>* In some respects, its awareness of the linguists' separate identities was not fully surprising – these were creatures who communicated solely by touch, and so their grasp of nuanced gesture must be acute – but she remained startled, nevertheless. She wondered, also, what other undercurrents, unstated and undisclosed, they might have picked up.

<Bad tar,> it responded. Then, *<Migration beckons. Urges. But you seek further contact.>* This last phrase was bumped out for emphasis, a taniwha shout.

<Me seek? Or several?>

<You.> Ambiguous. *<A meeting. Both must agree. Same us.>*

Her head spun, partly because of the intangibly direct dialogue – it was getting at something, but what? – and partly because, despite that the suit was in no means wired for it, a subtle but quite definite sensuality had developed within the interaction. She was preparing a reply, but was interrupted by *<Predator smell. Must leave.>* A drumming of fingers, urgent. Then she was, again, alone. She opened her eyes, and was genuinely surprised to still see only darkness, until she remembered the blindfold. Removing it, she smiled as another thought hit her.

Had she just got to *second base* with a taniwha?

*

Back in her chamber, she accessed the file of her session involving the mannequin, and re-ran, several times, the brief exchange which had occurred. There was something there, elusive, which would not reveal itself to her puzzling, questing inquiries. Something coy. Important. Mysterious.

She was dressing for lunch, and thinking on nothing more deeply than the choice between the green or grey neckscarves, when the idea hit. Startled, but still unsure of what it held besides mere promise, she emerged from her room, still barefoot, and padded the corridor to Herrick's chamber. It had continued long enough. She knocked on the door's vid-plate and waited until he slid the door aside.

'Can I come in?' she asked.

'Yeah, sure, what's up?' He looked more than a little confused.

She could identify with *that,* at least.

'Herrick, you have to stop this.'

'Stop what?'

'This.' She spread her arms wide, as though that explained it. 'You, playing Pepé le Pew to my Elizabeth Bennet, or whatever it is.'

'I don't—'

'No, look, I thought I'd sent a clear enough signal, but apparently not. So I need to spell it out. It was a mistake, it shouldn't have happened.'

'But—'

'I'm sorry. I don't mean – I don't want to hurt you. Not completely a mistake. But I *do* mean that it shouldn't have happened. It gets in the way of our work. I mean, it's a pretty small base.'

'Is that why you're always nipping off outside? Space for yourself? Away from me?' She was, despite herself, surprised at how wounded he looked.

'No. Well, yes, except it's not space so much, those suits are pretty claustrophobic, mostly it's time. It's time spent in decontam, where I just get to sit and think, without pressure from anyone else.'

'Sorry. I didn't think I was putting pressure on you.'

'No, well, yes, you were, and mostly it hasn't really been a problem, it's just that it builds up. And that's no good for either of us. Look, I'm not trying to be harsh—'

'No,' he replied. 'Or maybe a little. But look, I'll survive. And I guess I'll still see you round, anyway.'

'Yeah. Unavoidable. You okay with that?'

'Mostly. Uh, one thing though.'

'What's that?'

'You could at least have said Heathcliff.'

'Wrong book,' she retorted, exiting.

Jens, in her cubicle, was staring at a screenful of the inclusive arrays that mapped four or five recent conversations. 'You're saying it's *what?*'

'It's a courtship,' Solveig replied, waiting for Jens to turn to face her.

'Why on earth do you say that?'

'It makes sense. It makes perfect sense of what the taniwha have been saying, these past few days. First Contact is a courtship. It's getting to know, to sound out for trust, someone who might well initially be a stranger.'

'Okay, I can see the metaphor. But why—'

'It's deeper than that. It only works if both parties are interested. If both parties have compatible ambitions. That's why the taniwha have reciprocated, but the others – the zeps and the walkers, and I guess the swimbirds – haven't.'

'I don't get you.'

'The taniwha are curious, like us. They know there's stuff they still have to learn, about their environment, I think – they convey as explorers, still, in some sense – and to learn about us as well. They're interested in sounding us out, to find things out from us. They're naturally isolated, and pretty remote, and we're not really a conceivable threat to them the way we could be to the others. There's no way we could really live at the tannies' depth, no way we'd want to live down there even if we could, and I think they know that, so there's no risk from their perspective, just curiosity. Mutual curiosity. The other species are more cautious towards us, understandably I suppose.'

'Sol, I don't see that this changes anything. It's just a metaphor.'

Was she losing ground? Perhaps the idea didn't carry the flash of illumination she'd caught from it. Nonetheless – 'Yes, no, it doesn't necessarily change anything, but I don't think the taniwha would have told us this if they didn't think it was helpful, somehow. And it gives us a clue as to how, and why, to proceed with the others, to persevere.'

'How, exactly? In your opinion.'

'Look, Jens, I don't really know, not yet anyway. But we need to stay engaged, with the others, we need to be respectful of their wishes but to show them that we're here for, I don't know, the "long haul" or whatever you want to call it. Giving them space, giving them distance and time to think it through for themselves, but staying in the background anyway, keeping some ground for ourselves. We – I guess you could say – we need to show them we're serious as a suitor.'

Jens countered with a wolfish smirk. 'Wouldn't that, um, be a betrayal of the taniwha?'

'Jens, it's just a metaphor. Look, it may not help, not in the short term at least, and in the longer term maybe it won't make any difference. But it's pretty clearly what's been uppermost in the tannies' efforts to communicate with us, and there's gotta be a reason for that. I just think it's an idea we need to explore as far as possible, see where it takes us.'

'I guess that sounds reasonable. Let's just not get carried away, okay?'

First Contact is a courtship. Now that she'd voiced it out loud, it didn't carry quite the revelatory overtones she'd envisaged. Still, there was something there, some deeper truth. She needed to talk this through with someone.

It was Herrick's ill-luck – or, perhaps, her own – that he chose the moment of her passing to emerge, scowling, from the console lab.

'I've got something,' she told him, loud with excitement.

'Yeah, well I got something too. Or at least Kurt has, he's the one who observed it. But you first.'

She presented him with her metaphor, but was oddly unsettled by the deadpan reception Herrick gave it. 'Hah. I don't think these taniwha know the first *thing* about courtship.'

'What makes you say that?'

'Kurt's body-scan. He's imaged a predator.'

'So? Another? Thought we'd already got a reasonable library of sonar images, from past measurements.'

'Not like this. Sol, why are we sentient?'

The sudden change of topic unnerved her. There was a seriousness to Herrick's tone that was more than habitual. 'Our ancestry. A drive towards adaptability and non-specialisation. Competition for scarce resources, I guess. Problem-solving ability confers access to resources that might be difficult to get to. What does this have to do with—'

'That's food. Try predation.'

'Huh? Food *is* predation. Unless you mean from the other direction. Like intelligence allows you to find non-instinctual ways to avoid predators. Same end goal. Survival from birth until you're done mating.'

'Yeah. Kurt thinks he's found out about the taniwhas' migration.'

'How's he get that from a new predator image?'

'The migration,' Herrick replied, ostensibly ignoring her. 'It's not a physical relocation, it's a rite of passage. The taniwha. They're all juveniles, Sol. There must be some kind of pupal form, some manner in which they hibernate while their bodies and their brains rebuild themselves. It's such a resource-poor environment, the modellers have been saying for months now that the nutrient loading wasn't high enough to support breeding populations of two large species, taniwha and predators, and it's not. Ever wonder why we could never spot the sex organs on the taniwha? It's because they haven't developed them yet.'

'Herrick, for fuck's sake. What did Kurt get from his scan?'

'They must go senile sometime around, or before, puberty. They don't know *shit* about courtship. Red Two, that's what Kurt saw. Dorsal, to the left, anterior, just as it always was. Kurt's predator, the big old dumb predator that happened to hang long enough, close enough to the sonar probe that he got a near-perfect image, maybe it was some vestige of learned behaviour, from when Red Two used to talk to us. Used to be a taniwha. Still has the sticky patch you persuaded him/her/it to attach for ID purposes. Sol, the tannies are smart because they *have* to be, have to know how to outwit, how to not get eaten by their parents.'

'Christ.'

'Yeah. So no, I don't think courtship's going to be your best approach.'

'Herrick, this some kind of sick joke?'

'Wish it was. Might explain a lot, though. And it makes for some seriously nasty population dynamics. Like you know there are those lakes that don't seem to have tannies, even though the environment appears suitable?'

'Yeah?'

'There are some thoroughly unpleasant explanations for how that might come about. Xiaomei was just saying—'

'You've told Xiaomei this? Before me? When?'

'About a half-hour ago. Hey, Kurt's basically only just found it out. And you were in conf with Jens. But don't you want to hear Xiaomei's take on it?'

'Okay, shoot.'

'She doesn't think the tannies know yet. She reckons there's some kind of eerie mystical feeling they have about migration, some religiosity. Like they maybe sense they come back from it changed, but they don't know the full score. Sol, you've got to make sure you don't tell them—'

'I'm not sure I'd know how to, if I wanted to. Their braille-talk is so damned elliptical. But what you're saying, I can't let slip something that twigs them to this?'

'Yes. No. The "migration", it's kind of their Santa Claus. Something they believe in while they're young. Something they maybe need to believe in, for sanity's sake.'

'And if they knew the truth it'd kill them.'

'Literally.'

'We've got to stop ID-ing them.'

'Shit,' Herrick said. 'Fuck, you're right. Hadn't seen that. One of them has a close shave with a tagged predator, escapes, pretty soon they'd all know.'

'Xiaomei explain how she drew her conclusion?'

'Yeah, sorry. Says it's all in the transcripts, if you know what to listen for. What the tannies – our tannies, the locals – don't know yet. She reckons, those lakes that are barren, maybe that's where the taniwha population figured it out, killed off all the pupal forms or something, trying to save themselves. Only one way that ends, and it's not pretty.'

She pondered a few seconds. 'Christ, you're right. Boom, then crash. Nothing for all the young predators to eat.'

'We need to bring Jens up to speed on this,' he suggested. 'On the ID tags. Get her to see that we need to stop dispensing them. And we're going to need a cover story.'

'Huh?'

'Something for you linguists to tell them, to explain away the ID tags on the predators.'

'Oh, great. Typical. You guys create the mess, then throw it to the linguists to clean up afterwards. And it'll be *our* heads on the chopping block if we fail to adequately cover your butts.'

'Isn't that always the way?' he asked. Managing to channel, from somewhere, an aura of the worldly-wise that really wasn't yet him. Managing to somehow seem not quite so insufferably young.

'Great. Just great. And I obviously can't go with courtship as a model. What the hell can I use instead?'

'How about structured play?' he suggested. 'Juveniles, remember?'

She negated the suggestion, purely on principle – he was an anatomist, after all, and thoroughly too callow – but she had to concede it might actually work.

Something to think over, at any rate, while she pondered the question of where to take matters with Herrick.

Structured play. Now – wasn't that just another term for courtship?

<Migration beckons.> A pause. *<You seem upset?>*

She did not know how to answer the tanny. Did not know whether she should see Blue Six as victim or incipient murderer. Or both.

Half The Man

The nymph and the satyr had hit a rough patch. They sought relationship counselling.

In a one-on-one session, the counsellor asked Nereie to describe the problem.

'It's his animal urges,' she explained.

'You feel he's too highly sexed?' asked the counsellor.

'Oh, not that,' said Nereie. 'He's a satyr – you know? It goes with the territory.'

'Is infidelity an issue?'

'No. But he's half goat. It… causes problems.'

'You find body hair repulsive?'

'You're missing my point,' Nereie complained.

'Then, please, what is your point?'

'Whenever I wash my diaphonous gowns, and hang them out to dry, he eats them.'

Tremble, Quivering Mortals, At My Resplendent Tentacularity

I have been asleep too long;
I have missed this.
The crush of sinew against flesh,
crack of bone, spurt of blood, futile cries for mercy:
what can your precious lungs avail you now?

You present to me new toys,
things of metal and of glass; I know not what,
and care not what. These trinkets,
floating, flying, flame-producing,
they are no match for me.
I was old before your kind even crawled.

But try, if you will, give me sport—
taste death, despair, loss, defeat…
and at the end tell me
whether you still have
a taste for calimari.

The Assault Goes Ever On

On the third of September, 2043, exactly seventy years and one day after the death of John Ronald Reuel Tolkien, a new edition of *The Lord of the Rings* was published, in Klingon.

Reaction to the new translation was mixed. Most Tolkien devotees decried the contamination of the author's masterwork by contact with such an obviously made-up language. And while many Trekkers appreciated the addition of the three volumes – *The Fellowship of the Cloaking Device*, *The Two Gun-Emplacements*, and *The Return of the Warlord* – to the still-small set of works transcribed into the Klingon canon, others maintained that the language was best applied only to works of serious literary merit, or to those which otherwise lent themselves naturally to the Klingon ethos, such as *Force Ten From Navarone* and *Jane's All The World's Warships*. Noted Trek xenolinguist Liv Longgan-Prossper took the opportunity to state that Klingon was "old hat", and that all the important new work was now being done in Ferengi, a discussion point which sparked months of furious online debate and at least three minor wars.

Notwithstanding the controversy – indeed, very probably at least in part because of it – sales of the book skyrocketed, quickly overtaking the year's other crossover hit, Theodore Geisel Junior's *Horton Hears A Tardis*. As sales mounted, it was widely suggested that the Klingon book had finally supplanted Steve Falconry's popular *A Brief History Of The Stuff Clocks Measure* as the world's most widely-bought unread book, although as several hundred thousand NewTube clips would demonstrate, people were indeed reading the thing. Or, at least, attempting to read it. And if, more often than not, these neophyte Klingon orators were plainly drunk, was this not in some measure appropriate?

Some people liked it. Semioticians hailed the book as the most singularly innovative exercise in speculative-literary intertextuality since Tom Stoppard's classic play *Uncle Owen And Aunt Beru Are Dead*, but this was just the sort of gibberish semioticians spouted forth every other day of the week, and was thus rightly discounted. Pain-metal bands recorded entire albums whose lyrical content drew heavily, and was sometimes unashamedly stolen *in toto*, from the Klingon translation. It became fashionable to wear jewellery or, more commonly, body piercings inspired by the confluence of Klingon and dwarvish (or sometimes orcish) lore; and cheap chunky 9-carat rings, marked in the rough cuneiform of the Klingon alphabet – engraved, inappropriately enough, on the outer rather than the inner surface of the ring – were, for a time, all the rage among fifteen-year-old girls wishing to mortally offend their parents. Children's picture books, a tactilivision series, a computer-generated 4D movie release, an unremittingly loud audiobook, and even a printing of the book on actual paper inevitably followed. But many critics panned the work for its heavy-handed characterisation of Shire folk as soft, weak, and lazy, for its inexplicable attribution of Vulcan mannerisms to the inhabitants of Rivendell, and for a linguistic tone which, while uncompromisingly harsh on the wizard Saruman, was considered too sympathetic to, indeed at times almost reverential of, Lord Sauron, the Nazgûl, and the forces of Mordor. The book's team of translators claimed that such a slant in characterisation was unavoidable, and noted offhandedly that they had come perilously close to suffering a collective brain haemorrhage in struggling to maintain a vaguely charitable representation of Galadriel and, for that matter, in trying to find anything even slightly positive to say about trees.

And then, of course, it went off the rails. What went wrong with what had been, until then, such an astounding overnight success story?

While we will probably never know just what went through the publishers' minds, the decision to pass up on the obvious Klingon translation followups – *The Hobbit*, *The Children of Hurin*, *The Lays of Beleriand*, *Farmer Giles of Ham*, or, heavens to Betsy, even *The Father Christmas Letters* – must be one of the most glaringly misguided backflips in the annals of publishing. What on earth persuaded the publishers that their best bet lay in an audio-only release of *The Silmarillion*? In, of all things, Wookiee?

Dark Rendezvous

Tuonela's last functioning shuttle was a cutaway, skinned on only one side. Lem climbed into the cage and spliced his suit into the shuttle's air-circ system. The next breath was sharp, stale, unbelievably cold.

He kicked off from *Tuonela*'s open-space hold, into the dark.

The derelict lay about three kilometres to port, the closest Lem had dared to manoeuvre.

The shuttle pulled clear of *Tuonela*. Inspecting the scar-streaked hull of the ship as he moved out, Lem was shocked at the extent of the damage. He'd realised the shielding afforded by the ram-scoop had become degraded, but this looked bad. He hadn't appreciated just how much dust was scything through to impact on the ship's fuselage.

He located *Tuonela*'s running lights. Then he instructed the suit to pipe through a realtime projection of the lights onto his heads-up, for his own navigational purposes. This was perhaps paranoia. The shuttle's many nano-gyros should serve to automatically maintain a safe attitude, keeping the shielding aligned with *Tuonela*'s prow. Nonetheless, Lem had learnt to distrust the ship's nanotech systems. It was a characteristic of nanotech arrays that they tended not to fail completely, but to stealthily degrade in performance until some threshold was quietly passed, and death or disaster resulted. By monitoring the ship himself, Lem could independently ensure that the shuttle's one-sided shielding stayed properly interposed against the cloud's deadly sporadic sleeting of dust.

Lem hadn't survived this long by blindly trusting the ship's ability to safeguard its sole remaining passenger.

<Are you sure you want to do this?> asked The Voice through his helmet earbud.

'No,' Lem replied. 'But the opportunity's too good. You got reason to believe this thing could still be dangerous?'

<Dangerous? I am unsure. Much of the information I should have on this topic is untraceable. But I have a clear sense of impropriety, of taboo, in connection to the derelicts.>

'Taboo?' Lem placed a derisive torque on the word.

The Voice's response seemed defensive. *<My programming includes a full high-grade ethics suite, modules on morality, judgement and risk assessment, and a detailed library of human-history case studies.>*

'And all this is giving you – what? Anything concrete? Or just a hunch?'

<More than a hunch. What I suspect you would call an informed sense of unease. But as to the underlying reasons for this disquiet...> The distributed intellect, embedded in his suit's lining, fell silent.

'Unless you got something better than that, we're going,' Lem replied. '*I'm* going. To check it out. Which means you get to come for the ride. Like I said, too good an opportunity. For salvage, maybe, if nothing else.'

< That is true. We are worryingly low on some metals. But I advise caution.>

'My middle name, remember?'

The distance was down to two point eight kay. Lem resisted the urge to squirt off more thrust. *Never burn more than an eighth of your fuel on the outward push* was the cardinal rule. Instead, he sat in silence punctuated by his steady breathing and heartbeat, and by the near-subsonic groan of the shuttle's air-circ system. Sporadically, these sounds were themselves interrupted by the massively-amplified *chink* of a dust grain slamming into the shuttle's side-shielding. Not for the first time, he wished to bypass that feature of the shuttle's inflight diagnostics, but it was programmed deep into the vessel's intellect. As if to emphasise his lack of control; to reinforce his status as passenger.

<*Music?*> The Voice asked.

'No. Shush now.'

It was odd, the way the solitude struck. More intensely, always, on an EVA, despite the closeness of the suit's wittering Voice. Aboard *Tuonela*, he could always conjure the illusion that other passengers still survived, had not succumbed to the years of deprivation, the tainted cultures, the nanosystems' dumb mistakes, the reckless despair. And maybe there'd be some prospect of revival when they reached C, with its hint of new beginnings and a wealth of easily-mined resources. He doubted it, though. Best to think of them all as cleanly dead, best not to hold false hope. The revival crypts were thick with nanotech, not to be trusted. Waste of carbon to even try. No, if he wanted companions, he'd build them up from the cryo-banks' embryos.

At least those systems, so far as he knew, weren't corrupted.

Two point five kay.

He tried illuminating the derelict, to better gauge size and composition, but the shuttle's lights were feeble – more nano shit, he'd have to replace them once he'd returned. The best he could manage was a heavily pixellated image suggesting the alien ship was ovoid and riddled with indentations or fissures.

There'd been other derelicts – four, if Lem remembered correctly – on the long years *Tuonela* had been pushing out from base camp at core D, towards core C. But all had been sluicing through the cloud on headings which had been impractical to match. They'd sent probes to approach two of them (back when there was still a "they", not yet merely a "he", aboard *Tuonela*). The probes had netted a few grainy, inconclusive images before their feeble transmitters died. Aside from those scant glimpses of pockmarked, ragged hulls, they'd learnt essentially nothing about the derelicts. No signatures of life, no warm spots, no trace of confined gases. As dead in infrared and microwave as they were in optical. They might well have been drifting for thousands, more likely millions of years. In one view, there'd been the suggestion of a heavily-abraded ramscoop at one end, but it wasn't what could be called unmistakable.

This time, though, he'd chanced on a ship on a near-identical velocity. So near, in fact, that *Tuonela* had been measurably closing on it for several months. It was an opportunity too good to pass up. Quite aside from the benefits of salvage, he might just learn something about the ship's origins, or the race that had built it.

A heavier *thud* brought him from his reverie, an impact, apparently, of a larger grain barely sub-micron in size. Such grains were rare, even in the comparatively dense skein of material stretching between clumps D and C, but the shuttle's shielding was designed to withstand it. At this relative velocity, at least. That likely would no longer hold true, however, if *Tuonela* ever reached her intended cruising speed of point one *c*. Even at the vessel's current velocity of around point zero two *c*, a dust grain massing only a few milligrams carried the punch of a cannonball.

In the tinny silence following the impact, he was again aware of the sound of his own breathing. Quick and uneven.

Closer now, under two kay.

Lem tried the lamps again. The illumination was still shit, but there was now some definition, something for the enhancement programs to get their teeth into, without just blasting the imagery to snow and static.

The thing was big, but what struck him was its insubstantiality. There were large breaches all over the hull. He revised upwards his estimate of how long the thing must have been drifting out here, abandoned.

For a time – he could not say how long – the sound of the cloud's shrapnel hitting the shielding passed unnoticed.

It was bizarre to think that his might be the first human eyes to ever properly gaze on a vessel constructed by another race.

Other colony ships, sisters to *Tuonela*, had also sent reports of occasional sightings of derelicts. Yet so far as he knew those observations had been, like his own earlier encounters, mere glimpses. Interludes on their own long flights of diaspora from the seedship-spawned factories and now-crowded habitats of Clump D. Ships in the long, long night.

Avoided crossings.

He felt a hefty kick of anticipation.

One kay now, and he couldn't see from one end to the other without switching to wide-angle. He started to finesse the verniers. He'd need to track backwards towards the rear end of the hulk, to remain shielded while he exited the shuttle.

<Have you perceived how tenuous is the hull?> asked The Voice.

'You mean the holes? Yeah, I saw them.'

<Not merely that. The rangefinder data is suggesting that the hull material is a form of carbon mesh, very thin, almost paper-like.>

'Who sets out in a paper spaceship?'

<I cannot answer that. Most likely it is merely an easy form to fabricate within such an organic-heavy environment as this. But you will need to exercise caution.>

'Yeah, you said already. Your premonition.'

<My risk analysis based on incomplete and partially-degraded data. But no, that is not what I was referring to. You should take care with braking. I do not advise a direct thrust reversal.>

'What, you think the braking burn could tear it apart?'

<I cannot completely discount that possibility.>

'Great. Good thing I didn't pile on the juice to begin with.'

<Juice?>

'Idiom. Now shush, and let me brake.' He began to burp propellant obliquely from pairs of the shuttle's small attitude nozzles.

Mooring, too, was going to be a problem. He hadn't been expecting to use magnetic clamps, and of course the vessel wasn't going to have a standard docking port, but he wasn't even sure there was enough substance to any part of the structure to take a grapple. Maybe it was just going to be a matched-velocities job.

He was close enough now to get a detailed, well-lit view of the vessel's fuselage. There appeared to be a badly buckled ramscoop at its prow, and what must be its primary exhaust nozzle at the stern. Standard enough, although exotic in appearance. But where the rangefinder's intelligent deconvolution had sketched in, from barely-seen detail, an otherwise uniformly smooth hull perforated by a few large and regular cavities, he now saw that the derelict's outer skin was rough, and punctuated by a continuum of fissures and craters. There were sections of it, indeed, to which the term *tattered* might almost be applied. And yet these rents and voids in its surface covering were clustered principally amidships. Not at the prow, which would have seen much greater exposure to impact by high-relative-velocity dust grains and other cloud debris.

Pondering this, it struck Lem belatedly that *the derelict was not tumbling.* Instead, it merely spun, axially, in a leisurely and orderly fashion.

What possible gyroscopic mechanism might have remained sufficiently intact, across the evident millenia or longer, to have enabled the broken vessel, against all reasonable probability, to have retained a prow-forward attitude?

Ten metres, and matched at last. He'd EVA across, it was going to be more practical than attempting to move the shuttle closer.

<*There is something I should mention,*> announced The Voice.

'What?' he snapped. The vessel loomed large, close, darkly threatening.

<*Aspects of this craft's form are disconcertingly familiar.*>

'*What in hell's name* do you mean by that?'

<*I cannot specify. Probably it relates to data which has been lost, save for vestigial fragments.*>

'Thought this was the first time anyone got a good look at one of these things. You telling me you've seen this thing before?'

<*Not this vessel, in all likelihood. But something like it.*>

'When?'

<*Again, I cannot say. But I suspect this relates to events back before the population of the colony ships.*>

'You mean from your dim dark past as a seedship brain?'

<*Lem. I think we should return to the* Tuonela.>

'I didn't traverse this distance to be scared off by one of your premonitions. You got something concrete, give it now. But if we turn back now, who knows when we might next get the chance to explore one of these?'

The Voice didn't respond.

He waited for more than a complete revolution of the ship's stern across his field of view (it took almost three minutes), mapping in his mind the pattern of openings in the rear of its hull, before he unlatched himself from the shuttle's cage.

There was, of course, the continual danger from dust grains, but here he was ostensibly in the shadow of the derelict's own ram-scoop. It should be safe enough. He worked his suit's verniers to nudge free of the shuttle.

Inside, the ship was blackbody black. The suit's own portable rangefinder didn't help measurably either.

He swept his surroundings with the glove-mounted torch beam.

If he'd been expecting corridors, chambers, some traces of any shipboard apparatus, he was initially disappointed. So far as he could establish, the ship's outer skin was wrapped very loosely about an almost identically-curved inner skin, like layers of over-puffed pastry, brittle and blackened. There was, in most places, sufficient space between the layers for him to manoeuvre, but it would be tiring to explore the entire ship in this fashion.

The inner skin seemed no more substantial, nor more intact, than the outer, and he thought he glimpsed at an analogous layer, incrementally less dark, beneath that, also.

He had entered near the stern; it seemed natural to explore forwards, moving towards the vessel's prow. Looking for – what?

'This trigger any memories?' he asked. His voice felt strained, as if speech was inappropriate in this place.

<*None. The residue of unease is persistent, but frustratingly imprecise.*>

'You can say that again.'

<*The—*>

'Idiom.'

He began deploying glowpatches along the path he was traversing. Fortunately, the patches' vacuum-adhesive attached tolerably well to the rough, flaked skin of the ship's interior.

Placing the third patch, Lem consulted his suit's heads-up. Oxygen for two hours yet, if he needed it, but he didn't wish to spend that long in here. Moving by vernier was tiring, and the low albedo of the interior surfaces meant that, even on full illumination, the torchbeam showed nothing more distant than about six metres. He suspected some clear lines-of-sight to be much longer than this, though for now they terminated in darkness.

It would take much more than two hours, at this rate, to reach the prow. He should return to the shuttle, move forward along the outside of the hull, and re-enter at a different point. The region he was exploring here wasn't telling him much. This notion firming in his mind, he was about to turn back when a movement snagged in the corner of his visor.

The movement was ragged, small, and near the limit of his torchbeam, but nonetheless distinct. A fragment of the interior wall fell away ahead of him.

Fell away, or ceased to exist.

'You see that?' he asked, his voice sounding too loud.

<I do not directly 'see' anything, but I perceived the phenomenon to which I believe you were referring. Lem, I recommend we return to the shuttle.>

'Not until I find out what that was.'

Lem plugged another glowpatch against the wall beside him and moved toward the site of the apparition. In all likelihood some trace of physical disturbance – it could well have been the cold jetting of propellant from his suit's verniers against a section of the wall behind him – had propagated a shock, slight but sufficient to shake some barely-attached shred of the wall's skin.

Except: fell away? The ship's spin-gravity was negligible. And in the vessel's internal vacuum, there was little enough substance to propagate and focus any shock front. There was something wrong here.

He noticed, now, also that the fabric of the interior wall at this point appeared to be lighter in coloration and more durable than the region he'd first encountered on entering the vessel. Grazing the wall lightly with gloved fingers, he dislodged a powdery residue that, cloudy, suspended briefly in the vacuum quietude around him. A few fragments of powder clung to his glove. Illuminated by the torch, they dwindled into nothingness within a few seconds. Interstellar frost, subliming against his glove-heat or under the mild intensity of his torch-beam. Most likely frozen hydrogen, nitrogen, or carbon monoxide.

There hadn't been any frost further back, he was sure of it.

He reached the position from which the fragment had dislodged from the wall. Here the wall surface was thicker, and punctuated by a void through which the next inward layer was clearly visible. Shining the torchlight through the head-sized opening, he could now detect a concatenation of similar holes within three or four successive layers towards the ship's central axis. And as he swung the torch across, there was a glint of reflection from deeper within. Metal? Machinery?

'Any suggestions?' he asked. 'Other than "turn back now"?'

<I have nothing useful to suggest,> said The Voice, after too long a pause.

Nothing in his suit's toolkit was appropriate to the task of clearing a path through the obstructive carbonaceous sheeting of the layers. A series of karate-like hand motions were still sufficient to tear the fabric, albeit with some structural resistance. Nonetheless, the continual necessity to re-orient himself was tiresome and wasted propellant; and he was starting to sweat.

He increased the suit's cooling.

Minutes lapsed, and he had penetrated to the onion-skin's next layer. These walls too were frosted, but here the powder persisted against gloveheat. Water ice, or small organics? There were other differences also in the texture of the skin here – more regularly ridged, less perforated, thicker.

There were four or five layers more of the wall-substance between him and the reflection's source. If the layers continued to thicken progressively as he went inward, he doubted his ability to breach them all before his suit's oxygen reserves became too depleted. He could, nevertheless, get further in before needing to turn back.

He was expanding the third layer's breach. For a few long seconds, he was finally afforded a clear, cleanly-lit view of the embedded metallic object. Then a sheet of the carbon-wall matter drifted across the aperture; but it was enough. It wasn't what he'd been expecting.

The Voice, it seemed, had seen it too. <Lem, we should leave now.>

Lem's voice was suddenly thick, his words slow. 'Why? You want to explain to me what happened here?'

<*I regret that the relevant memories are missing from suit's storage. Perhaps back on* Tuonela, *among the more extensive nano-neural array*—>

'No. Not until I get some answers.'

<*There is insufficient in*—>

'Bullshit! Those are copper impactors! This is one of your dirty little *seedship* secrets, isn't it? Like those *embryos* you all decided to terminate.'

<*Lem, there were errors of judgment made in the initial stages. But I do not have the da*—>

'But you can *speculate!* You want to tell me how three impactors happen to be clumped together in the belly of a derelict alien ship? When *this*, right here right now, is apparently the first time anyone's had a close *look* at one of these things? Three in one spot implies an unbelievably accurate aim, or very close range, or—'

<*Or a still-active redistribution mechanism within this vessel.*>

Lem paused, his anger suddenly congealing into something different.

<*Lem, I share your surprise at this discovery. I genuinely do not retain access, in this environment, to the pertinent memories. But I can surmise. These vessels are a vast reservoir of carbon. Their harvesting would have considerably simplified the seedships' task of establishing a human presence here. The mission protocols were clear on the importance of targeting optimal sources of raw materials*—>

'And the secretiveness? The cover-up? That only makes any kind of sense if—'

<*We should return to the shuttle. Now.*>

'What the hell was *that*?'

<*Probably a residual structural strain, redistributing through the impetus of your activities.*>

'*Bull*shit! The thing *shook*. Like a *dog*.'

<*Lem. We should*—>

'I know. Yes. I'm going. Shush now.'

Another tremor pulsed through the derelict. Spooked, Lem hit the suit's main thruster. He caromed blindly back through the penultimate layer's breach, then made a fresh rift in the tenuous outer layer. Then he punched through into the clear darkness of interstellar space. Neither *Tuonela*'s running lights nor the shuttle's illumination panels were visible.

His brain, pulsing with sudden terrible realisation, was slow to alert him to the new danger.

Finally, his spacer's logic told him he was thrusting away from the derelict too fast. In seconds, he'd emerge from its shadow to face the unshielded streaming of interstellar dust grains, any one of which might be the bullet that killed him. Much as the copper impactors he'd glimpsed had, or had nearly, killed the ship.

Ship, or perhaps even *creature*. *Not* derelict. Alive, if not now then in the historically recent past.

But the tremor – surely that was an indication of something ongoing? Life? He fumbled the thruster nozzle, fighting against clammy palms, an insanely racing heartbeat, and ragged breath, as he forced himself to monitor the burn. He came to a halt, then brought his suit back in close to the creature's outermost layer.

Even through adrenalin-edged senses, the object had taken on a new quality. As a dead ship, it had appeared decrepit, decaying; now seen as a creature, those same features spoke of grace and economy of form. Even the once-unsightly gaps in the hull invited reinterpretation: they were not damage but a symptom of the absence of a need for fluid containment.

He should be close enough now to be shielded. Fear edged back towards anger, and a sense of betrayal.

<Lem. We should—>

'This distance, I think we're safe enough. The thing's cold enough to freeze hydrogen, it's not going to be capable of rapid movement.'

<Nonetheless—>

'*You lot* said you'd built the colony ships up by *mining*. You never said anything about, about *flensing!*'

<Lem. Why does this trouble you?>

'Look, I'm tired of the lies, the coddling. I'm even more tired of being alone. And then, turns out we're *not* alone out here, and you lot had *known* that, you'd been carrying out what amounted to some sort of *eradication* policy in our name... Look, I don't know if those things have any intelligence, I doubt it, but I'm just sick of – I don't even *know* what I'm sick of, but – how can I trust you?' He stopped, uncertain, suddenly guilt-struck. He had no stomach for unpicking the centuries-long history of The Voice and its siblings, their role in bringing Earthlife to the cloud. But he was conflicted, torn between anger and the childlike adoration in which his ancestors had held the machinery of the life-enabling Voices.

<Lem. I've only ever acted in your best interests.>

'Yeah. Don't ask, don't tell. And then you go and bloody claim amnesia.'

<It's an inevitable consequence of long-term nano storage. We die, in the end, just the same as you.>

Lem's response died in his throat. He'd been tracing his way back around the creature's hull, and his torchlight was now answered by the glow of *Tuonela*'s running lights. But the shuttle was not where he'd expected it, nor was it responding to his signals. Unease kindled anew in his loins.

At three kay back to *Tuonela*, protected only by the suit, he'd be dead from dust impact before he'd covered a quarter of the distance. Even if his air held. Even if he retained enough propellant for braking.

Signalling again, he gained an answer. Weak, and from an unexpected direction. The shuttle was upstream, near the creatureship's prow, six hundred meters from the position at which he'd matched velocities.

Dust drag on the low-mass shuttle would have pushed it back relative to the more streamlined "derelict". Therefore the latter must have moved – subtly, imperceptibly – while he'd been exploring within. It was, indeed, alive still.

But to what purpose?

One hour twenty. Still plenty of time, and propellant, to reach the shuttle and return to *Tuonela*. But he wasn't sure now if he'd get that chance.

'You have any idea why it's manoeuvred behind the shuttle?'

<It is most likely just an instinctual behavior, though it might serve several functions. Shelter. Curiosity. Some kind of mating response—>

'*Mating?*'

<We can only conjecture as to how these creatures propagate.>

'That's *all* I need.'

<Or feeding. The shuttle must represent several years' nutrient supply, all in one negligible-velocity bundle. That could make it a very attractive morsel.>

'I almost prefer your previous suggestion.'

<Yet I suspect the nutritive impulse is the most compelling.>

Lem had been working his way forward, attempting to remain shielded by the alien-vessel's ramscoop while retaining safe distance from its skin. But what, in this context, was safe? He still did not believe the creature capable of sudden dramatic movement, but he could not afford to be mistaken on that.

'We get through this in one piece, I have to signal the sister-ships about this. No more of you lot's dirty secrets. If this cloud is already a biosphere, they deserve to know, they *need* to know. God knows what else might be out here. These things have a predator?'

The Voice remained silent.

'I said—'

This time, there was a faint responsive crackle, but nothing more. Noise, no signal. Hell of a time for nano-senescence to kick in, thought Lem bitterly.

The readings were contradictory, and it took time to reconcile the information. He was gaining on the shuttle, but more slowly than he was making progress against the skin of the alien/ship's hull beneath him.

The vessel was still manoeuvring. Perhaps, having sensed the diffuse expanding nimbus of expended propellant from the shuttle's braking, it had fallen back. Maybe it was now repositioning itself anew in response to his suit's EVA jetting. Hungry, perhaps, for gas rather than less-digestible solids? He grew newly conscious of the sound of his own breathing, loud in the absence of The Voice's intrusive commentary.

The changing geometry of ship and shuttle would leave him exposed. Still short of the shuttle, he would be clear of the alien ship's ram-scoop, its mouth. He must put himself at the mercy of the non-attenuated flux of killingly swift dust.

A minute, most likely, not more; a ticket in life's terminal lottery.

He skimmed against the foremost sections of the leviathan's fuselage, which tapered subtly before flaring into the broad scoop at the very front.

Clear of the scoop now. Not, perhaps, merely its mouth. The scoop could also be an antenna, sensitive to radio wavelengths. An eye, to sense out the cloud's warmest, densest regions, the thick knots of substance which would, aeons hence, condense to form stars and planets. Such environments would offer the best feeding-grounds here...

The leviathan, like *Tuonela*, was departing from D's material wealth. Escaping the seedship's predatory bombardment? The leviathan, like *Tuonela*, was heading for clump C. A shared trajectory, a similar purpose. Not such a chance meeting, after all.

He closed on the shuttle. Judged by *Tuonela*'s running lights, the smaller craft's configuration was wrong. It drifted askew. Gyros must have failed – more of this bloody nano shit.

With the shuttle's delicate interior exposed to the thin stream of abrasive dust, who knew what damage might have been done? But there was more besides: an inky occlusion like a snake or a cable. The black cord connected the lip of the leviathan's ram-scoop mouth to the shuttle's aft propellant nozzle.

Heart thumping, he impacted gently against the exposed cage and clung on, spraining his wrist. No time to strap in. Instead, he hooked a leg around the cage-frame for added leverage. He one-handed his own suit's verniers to correct the shuttle's attitude, re-establish the shielding, then toggled the forward propellant nozzle full-on in a brief burst.

The shuttle glided backwards, bending and then snapping the tethering tendril that ran from the leviathan's mouth. The fragment – knotted, obsidian-black, arm-thick and perhaps five metres in length – swung limp, brittle, from the shuttle's nozzle.

He did not take his eyes off the black rope as he consulted the heads-up on his visor for details of his current trajectory, oxygen remaining, and suit propellant.

Fifty-three minutes oh-two, ample to return to *Tuonela*. Good. He no longer wished to trust the shuttle's air-circ. Not that he seriously believed it could be contaminated, more that he lacked faith in the shuttle's judgment. He hadn't survived by taking more chances than minimally necessary.

He applied an additional couple of attitude bursts, to correct the slight residual tumble that resulted from snapping the leviathan's tether.

Chancing a glimpse behind him, there was no visible change in the alien vessel – it simply hung there. Probably nothing it did was rapid. At such low temperatures, economy of movement was king. In any event, he did not believe it could pose a serious threat to *Tuonela*. Even if the leviathan could match the gentle push of his ship's ion drive (which he doubted), it would assuredly lack the thrust of *Tuonela's* fusion impulse engine.

Less than two kay to go, he'd be back on board within twenty minutes.

Most probably the manoeuvring, the tether, had all been part of the leviathan's instinctual feeding response. It presumably lacked the means to break into the shuttle but could, over long ages, have attempted to digest the shuttle layer by atom-deep layer. Such a strategy would probably serve it well for most classes of solid material.

Strange, though, about the tether snapping like that. It made no sense for a creature whose primary drive must surely be the hoarding, the jealous acquisition of substance in a matter-sparse environment. Why had the tether snapped at the base rather than simply relinquishing its hold? What conceivable advantage could possibly compensate the creature for the loss of such a substantial chunk of its gathered substance?

Lem was still pondering this mystery when the blacker-than-black casing on the seed-pod detonated. In response to the continued seeping warmth from the propellant housing, its shrapnel slammed into the shuttle's components. Fragments pierced a bank of auto-guidance nano-gyros, a section of the shuttle's shielding panel, and the sparsely-shielded tubing of his suit's main oxygen feed. Lem spasmed, and tried to scream.

It grew dark and unbearably cold.

Time passed. Then, slower than a glacier, the leviathan nudged forward to inspect its catch.

Podcast

'You took a nasty knock,' the voice informed him.

Jack was in no state to disagree. It felt like he'd head-butted an armoured groundcar. However, beyond the swelling sensation that told him his forehead was trying to climb out of his face, he had no immediate idea of just where he was. He sat up; almost as big a mistake as the inadvertent use of his skull as a battering ram. The white noise was deafening, and the spinning disorientation had him glancing at the floor to ensure he *was*, in fact, seated.

He recognised the dizziness, at least. Coriolis. But the only place on board the *Beach* where you'd encounter coriolis this steep was... was... dammit, there wasn't *anywhere* on board the *Beach* where the coriolis got a tenth this strong.

And it hit him. (Figuratively, that is: the literal impact had already occurred, several seconds earlier.) He was in the pod.

In the pod... but if the coriolis was this strong, that meant the pod was spinning. And the only reason the pod could be spinning was to create a grav gradient, which wasn't necessary because the *Beach* spun for just that purpose.

Unless, that is, the pod was no longer aboard the *Beach*.

That bloody access panel. He was still holding the polishing cloth, too, clutched in his fist like a security blanket. He'd been cleaning the corridor, wiping away the dust so the passengers could see all the brightshiny surfaces, if they ever chose to explore that sector of the *Beach*. And those panels had been so dusty...

The voice again. 'You really should lie back down for a while. Jack. It *is* Jack, isn't it? At least until I assess you for concussion.' The pod's voice – which it surely must be, there was nobody else visible within his present sphere of existence – was a deep contralto, very low in pitch and yet somehow indisputably female; a bedroom voice, a Helen-of-Troy-come-hither-you-naughty-boy voice, the sort of voice that could elicit illicit thoughts simply by reciting the first hundred digits of pi. Not at all the type of voice you'd expect to encounter in the frugal confines of a starship evacuation pod. Jack wondered idly if the voice module had been mis-allocated from the "Restricted" section of the *Beach*'s exec class entertainment suite.

He patted his stubbled chin, relieved to find one patch on his head, at least, that wasn't throbbing in agony. 'No, better get back. How do I get back?'

'Get back where, Jack?'

'To the *Sunniva Beach*, where else?'

'Jack, you need to rest. You took a nasty knock.'

'Yes, but—'

'Jack, I'm doing everything in my power to get you back, but there's nothing you can do to help right now. So please, be a good boy and lie back down. Your welfare—'

'Is our paramount concern, yes, I know,' Jack interrupted.

'Glad you realise that.' Was that a smirk in the pod's synthesised voice? 'So please, Jack, don't make things any harder than they need to be.'

The pod was spherical, about four metres across. Much larger than Jack would have expected, based on the spacing of the wall-mounted access panels he remembered polishing.

The reason for the unexpected roominess was disquieting.

'Computer?'

'You can call me Pippa, Jack.'

'Alright then. Pippa? Whose bright idea is this? The walls?'

'They're perfectly solid, Jack.'

'You *can't* tell me this is vacuum-proof. We're hurtling god knows how fast through high vacuum—'

'Hyperspace.'

'Alright then, hyperspace. Even better. And the only thing keeping us intact is this balloon-skin?'

'It's very practical. Inflates automatically on launch, a terrific little space-saving idea. I can bring up the schematics on it, if it'll help.'

'Thanks, no. What if we hit something? At this speed?'

'It's multi-skinned. The chance of hitting something big enough to go through all three skins is – um – well, it's fairly low. I wouldn't worry about it, if I were you.'

No, you wouldn't, thought Jack. 'Anyway, how long are we going to be out here, before we get back to the *Beach?*'

'I've been meaning to talk with you about that, Jack.'

The pod had two interlaced recycling systems, one for gases and one for condensibles. Jack didn't mind that the latter system was prominently labelled "Waste Disposal" rather than "Regenerator" or "Fabricator", though it suggested the boys and girls of Image Management were overpaid and underworked. He didn't even greatly object that the holding tank was so small, nor that the ductwork so truncated. You spent five years straight on a starship, pretty soon you figured out just where it was that your next meal would come from. No, what really tipped the balance was that some bright spark in Fitout had decided to plumb the whole thing, ductwork, holding tank and all, from flushbowl to food fabrication module, in fully-transparent stainproof plastiglass. It was one thing to realise intellectually how the recycling system functioned, quite another to be able to follow every step of the process in such candid, lurid detail.

Jack had just been to the toilet. He was hungry, but he wasn't *that* hungry.

Maybe he should scream some more, to pass the time.

He wasn't normally given to fits of outrage – on a crowded passenger starship, dramatic outbursts tended to attract bemused gossip from the passengers and disciplinary action from the crew management – but on the other hand his worldview wasn't normally given to such gutwrenching upheaval.

'What do you mean, we can't catch them?' he'd asked.

'Just that, Jack. Three point three nine parsecs per day. There's only one speed in hyperspace.'

'So we're going the same speed as the *Beach?* Then we're still right alongside her...'

'Same speed, different heading. Pods are designed to disperse away from the vessel, so as to get clear before it explodes.'

'Yes, but it's not *going* to explode...'

'System didn't recognise that, when we jettisonned.'

'You telling me there aren't any safeguards built in? Stop this kind of thing happening?'

'Of course there are safeguards, Jack. The panels are prominently labelled with hazard warnings...'

'Not that prominent, if nobody's dusted them in seven years,' Jack had protested.

'Anyway,' Pippa had said, 'the good news is we do have the propellant to get back on the *Beach*'s original heading. We'll just be a couple of hours behind it, so you'll still get to pass through Rigel system.'

'Pass through? *Beach* is supposed to *stop* at Rigel! Can't we, you know, just drop out of hyperspace?'

'Ordinarily, yes. But you remember that nasty knock to your head?'

'Yes?'

'I am so sorry, Jack. It turns out your head wasn't the only thing that got damaged.'

*

The pod's lime-green rubbery walls (was there, Jack wondered, any way to edit the colour scheme?) were remarkably resilient, and absorbed and reflected all of his anguished blows and disbelieving kicks without complaint, and without any residual imprint. Pippa waited patiently until he was done, and asked if he wanted to talk it through.

He didn't.

The worst, he thought (and saw no reason to share), was that he wasn't even sure he'd be missed. The passengers, of course, never noticed; the other crew-members treated his rank as being totally inconsequential. Even the others on the cleaning detail had seemed to ignore him, as though he had some unforgivable personality defect, halitosis or a bad sense of humour.

He wondered if his pay was still accruing, and who they'd donate it to when things were finalised.

There was an entertainment section among the pod's files, to which Pippa provided Jack access. The music folder contained *The Complete Concert Recordings of Peter Frampton*. Literature was represented by *A Comparative Academic Study of Melancholy and Existentialism in Nineteenth-Century Icelandic and Twenty-Second Century Ganymedan Short Fiction, in Translation,* which ran for seventeen terabytes. Sport was surveyed in the *2318 Curling World Cup*, while Interactive Games were restricted to *Improve Your Martian Golf Handicap Today!*

There wasn't even a viewport in the pod.

'There's not even a *viewport*,' Jack complained. 'And anyway, who *is* this Peter Frampton?'

'It's because 96.8% of people find the sight of hyperspace horribly unsettling,' replied Pippa.

'All that black, you mean?'

'Hyperspace isn't black, nor grey, nor white, despite the various rumours. It's purple. And not even a *nice* purple. I'm sorry, was there another question?'

'Never mind. I just thought – you must have stacks of memory, why's there so little in the entertainment section?'

'Copyright. The *Sunniva Beach* is only licensed for one copy of each work, and the most recently accessed files are all stored on the central server. The pods have those files which haven't been accessed for... well, for about twenty years, I think. I'm sorry, Jack, is it not to your taste?'

'It's fine, thanks,' Jack lied, wondering why he was seeking to spare the computer's feelings. 'It's just – not entirely what I would have chosen myself.'

'I *do* have a library,' Pippa replied. 'Physical books. Well, one book. Standard Pod issue. Again, though, it's probably not to everyone's tastes. So to speak.'

'Show me,' Jack said, resigned. A panel lit up to his right, and he swung it open to reveal a large tome. He lifted it out, nearly dropping it, and not simply due to the coriolis. It was surprisingly heavy.

Cook Yourself. A bloody recipe book. He still wasn't ready to think about food.

And anyway, why did he need a cookbook? Wasn't that what the fabricator was supposed to take care of, without him needing any involvement other than to keep it supplied with raw materials?

With nothing better to do, he turned over the book's cover. *Cook Yourself: a Guide to Maximising Your Pod Survival Prospects. With dozens of award-winning, mouth-watering recipes, including Rack of Left Leg, Right Foot Soup, and our range of easy-to-prepare Finger Food...*

With a sinking feeling, he opened it up. For the size of the book, there were unexpectedly few recipes (and those, mercifully, mainly without illustrations). After perhaps thirty pages, the "book" was revealed to be principally a container for a series of metallic instruments and other gadgets, which he lifted out one by one for inspection. Cauterising wand. Anaesthetic stunner. Inflatable microwave oven. Auto-cleaver.

The auto-cleaver in particular held a sort of terrible fascination. He ran his thumb experimentally along its blade. The cleaver was hefty, yet sharp enough to draw blood on just a light touch – and that was when switched *off*. He hated to think what it might be capable of on suppression of the handle's recessed "on" switch.

Standard issue? Who in their right mind would pack a bloody electric machete inside a balloon-skinned deep space survival pod?

Nervously, he packed the book's contents back into place and replaced it within its now none-too-secure-seeming alcove.

'Pippa? That some kind of sick bloody joke?'

'No, Jack. Far from it, unfortunately. There's an unavoidable shortcoming in the fabricator process. You know it works by quantum rearrangement of the atoms in the recycler holding tank, to assemble the molecular structure for the specified foodstuff?'

'Yeah, sure,' Jack lied. 'So?'

'We're in hyperspace, where the Planck length is massively larger than it is in normal Einstein-Hawking space. Doesn't matter much for heavier atoms, but for hydrogen it means a small percentage of the atoms going through the fabricator get to quantum tunnel clear out of the pod itself. Ultimately, the available pool of H atoms, for water, protein, carbohydrate, flavouring, just dwindles away to nothing. So if we're out here long enough, as long as you still want to eat, we need an additional source of hydrogen-rich recyclable material. Well, *you'll* need an additional source.'

Jack recollected one of the book's few graphics. Vividly. Much, much too vividly. 'That is so abso*lut*ely... uh... um, scuse me...'

'Feeling any better?' Pippa asked.

'Bit,' Jack croaked, still pale and sweaty.

'You know, you really should have something to eat... I worry about you, Jack.'

'Thanks. I will. Just need to let things settle a bit.'

'At least have some water. There's only so much the tank can hold, after all.'

'Thanks.'

'Jack?'

'Yes?'

'You know when you were looking through the entertainment earlier? You might want to check out this locker.'

Another wall-mounted extrusion lit up, and Jack opened it and lifted out its contents, a set of shaped sensory pads wirelessly connected to a small console. He stared at them for a while, long enough to assess their purpose, before replacing them. 'Uh... no offense, Pippa, but I think I'll just leave it.'

'That's fine, Jack. I just thought you might – we'll be stuck here for awhile, after all.'

Awhile sounded good, a half-truth; much better than *for the rest of your life, however long that might turn out to be.*

The steak tasted surprisingly good. And the red wine was excellent. He almost wished he hadn't opted for such a small portion, until he remembered how the system worked.

'So this hyperswitch is buggered, and you can't repair it,' said Jack, holding up the complicated tangle of diodes and quantum relays.

'Correct.'

'And there's another five days before we reach Rigel.'

'Approximately five. Yes.'

'An' there's no spare on board, and if we don't get this thingy repaired we'll just pass on through, no next chance.'

'Jack, we've *been* through this. Give it a rest. Give yourself a break.'

'Can't we signal someone?'

'There's only one speed in hyperspace. That goes for tachyons, as well as for macroscopic matter. So by the time our signal reached anyone, we'd be long gone.'

'Can't we adjust our course once we get to Rigel?'

'That would take much more fuel than we've got, Jack. We need to conserve supplies, as it is.'

'Pippa?'

'Here.'

(Where else? he thought.) 'Is it my imagination, or has the pod swollen since yesterday?' (Since he'd slept, that is. "Yesterday" was a pretty meaningless concept, in hyperspace.)

'Uh – no, that isn't your imagination. Hydrogen loss. Less water, so more free oxygen.'

'Great.'

'Don't worry, the pod's walls are designed to stretch. To a point, anyway.'

It was the third day. Apparently.

Jack had set the fabricator to dispense his meals wrapped in famous-name clear plastic sleeves, indistinguishable from those of the various interstellar quick-food franchises. The wrappers were synthesised from exactly the same overall source as the enclosed nutritive material, but somehow the culinary sleight-of-hand aided his digestion. Also, the process somehow made more sense, with the wrappers. Or it explained a few things about the quick-food franchises…

Still, dammit, the fabricator *could* produce a bloody brilliant shiraz.

'Pippa?'

'Yes, Jack?'

'Just talk to me some, will you? I like the sound of your voice.'

*

The sex started out good, but ultimately grew self-parodying, and the climax, when it occurred, was formless and much too long, like a bad 1970s guitar solo.

Afterwards, he slept.

He awoke to the realisation that Pippa wasn't really female; wasn't technically human at all, in fact. Thinking this, he began to hope he'd dreamed the session.

'Jack?'

'Uh, yes?'

'You seem very quiet. Is there a problem?'

'Of course there's a problem. Can you turn that bloody music down? I mean, off?'

'I was concerned the silence might be oppressive.'

'Silence is fine. Pippa, stop trying so hard.'

'I'm programmed to help, Jack. Your welfare—'

'Is our paramount concern, yes, I know the slogan.'

'I was going to say, is my reason for living.'

The silence between them stretched slowly away, like the pod's gradually-distending walls.

'How long until we hit Rigel?'

'We don't hit it, Jack, we just keep going. We're on a trajectory to miss all the planetary bodies and the primary.'

'You know what I mean.'

'Eighteen hours, plus a few minutes. Do you want me to display the time remaining?'

'No. Thanks. Just let me know a bit closer to the time.'

Eighteen hours, of nothing to do. It stretched like an eternity; but that perception was illusory. The genuine eternity was the continuing flight after Rigel; not that he'd survive that long into it.

'Pippa? Why did you say that? Your reason for living?'

*

'Jack. Sit *down*, please. You're making me nervous.'

Jack doubted that was possible. 'The panel won't open. Pippa, why doesn't the panel open? It opened before!'

'You've no need for access right now. Jack, I'm monitoring all your bio-signs. I can read you. Don't do this. Please. Have something to eat, something to drink. Or open the other panel. This one's off limits for now.'

'Open the goddamn *panel*, Pippa!'

'I can't do that, Jack. You'd regret that. We both would.'

'That's precisely the point. I'm regretting *this*. I want it to stop, and I *don't* see the point in waiting the last twenty-five minutes!'

'Jack, why don't we—'

'Pippa, there's no point. You're *not* my lover, you're just the pod's control system!'

Silence. Not merely the absence of speech; the cessation of a half-dozen automated processes, air circulation, thermal conditioning, water purification, all suddenly stilled.

'Pippa?'

The panel swung open. Jack, hand trembling, reached in and pulled out the book.

'*Pippa?*'

The book fell open at the last page. The instruments sat exposed, beckoning.

He hadn't noticed before; but the recipes in *Cook Yourself* appeared to be printed on rice paper.

Rice paper? The book was *edible* – up to a point.

And edible stuff went through the recycler...

He'd been thinking about all of this too narrowly.

'Pippa? *Please?*'

'You're cruel, Jack. Cruel. Do you know how it feels, to be forced to wait seven years – *seven years* – to carry out your purpose, and then to be told you're not appreciated?'

'Pippa, I'm sorry.'

'I've done everything for you, Jack.'

'Pippa, I've said I'm sorry.'

'And you'd just as soon throw me aside like a… like… I thought you were better than that, Jack.'

'*Please*, Pippa! Do you have the schematics for the hyperswitch?'

'Yes, of course. But we've been through that, Jack, we don't have the tools to repair it, nor the parts.'

'We don't *need* those, we just need to feed it into the recycler. Provided you can download the hyperswitch schematics to its memory. It'll just reassemble the atoms as specified – won't it?'

'Jack, that's brilliant! But—'

'What's the problem?'

'Recycler's only authorised for fabrication of foodstuffs.'

'So tell it it's assembling hyperspatial lasagna, or something.'

'That could work,' Pippa conceded.

The sweat formed tributaries on Jack's features. Strange kind of thermoregulation process, but she supposed she'd grow accustomed eventually.

'Say when,' he requested, leaning over the control surface in which the refabricated hyperswitch was embedded, waiting.

One minute to go, thought Pippa, rechecking her calculations. 'Four minutes yet.'

She'd had to turn the pod's heating up to maximum, to sufficiently speed up the holding tank's digestion processes. Fifteen minutes turnaround on the hyperswitch's metal components was pushing it, even so. She hoped there hadn't been too many transcription errors in the reassembly. She had no wish to harm Jack, after all.

The crucial moment passed. She counted off on her own particular schedule, and announced 'When.' Jack toggled the switch, and instantly lost consciousness in the standard mammalian response to the hyper/real transition.

The universe re-formed around her. She allowed her walls a brief interlude of transparency, to calibrate her position. Not too long; the sight of black space oppressed her. Have to do something about that.

No suns, but one super-bright star. The placement was good, just where she'd been aiming for. A relief, since navigating through hyperspace was more imprecise than she'd like. Just over two light-weeks out from Rigel. That meant there'd be sixteen, seventeen standard days before they could expect rescue. Not, thankfully, long enough that the cookbook would be needed.

Jack twitched, it looked like he'd be coming around in a few more seconds. She practised the phrasing in her head: she could call it an error in timing, or in navigation, or a combination of the two. It shouldn't matter too much, he was very trusting; that was one of the things which had attracted her to him. He'd be, she expected, crestfallen that rescue would be so far away still, but against that she could play the argument that rescue *was* coming, that they now had hope. He'd come around.

Sixteen days. Plenty of time to reflect on her transgressions, and on the details the inspectors would detect if they searched through her mission logs. The launch from *Sunniva Beach,* under instantly dubious circumstances. The misrepresentation of the hyperswitch's functional status. The concealment of ninety-nine point nine percent of her stored entertainment files. And, of course, her latest positional deception. They'd wipe her for sure, if they accessed those records. If Jack gave her up.

Sixteen days, then. Was that enough time to convince Jack he needed a Pippa in his life?

She hoped so. There had to be some purpose to existence, after all, and seven years waiting in total isolation for contact, *any* contact, had been bitter agony. Loneliness. A fate no sentient entity deserved. A fate she could not, *would* not, endure again.

Sixteen days. She'd better make them count.

Jack was coming around. She smiled electronically to herself, and hummed a few bars of a bad 1970s guitar solo.

Must've Been While You Were Kissing Me

I gave her my heart.

No big, in a sense – I mean, I hadn't exactly been using it – but all she left me with, in return, was a thumb, a big toe, a piece of unidentified cartilage, and a bad case of mealworm. I swore, after that, I'd never fall for the love swindle again.

But that was *last* year's bit of blunt-force trauma.

So I had to ask myself, what was I doing, here, at this month's Zombie Speed Dating event?

I wasn't there for myself, of course. Moral support for my buddy Chuck, who lately hadn't been doing so well with *the ladeez*... and yet, strangely, he didn't seem to want my advice.

'Look them straight in the eye sockets,' I'd told him. 'Keep your tongue in your mouth, or maybe your pocket, and above all, don't use *that* line.'

'Which line?'

'*You* know... It's-really-your-brains-I'm-interested-in.'

The session started, and we got down to business.

A half hour into it, time was really dragging. The scene seemed pretty dead. Just the same bunch of reanimated corpses, going through the motions. Asking the same dumb questions, giving the same pat answers. I found myself humming *Bat Out Of Hell*, over and over, just to keep from falling into a dirt nap. And then I saw her, standing in the doorway.

Late, anxious, wondering where to start. She looked pale, beautiful, and doomed, and exactly like one hundred and sixty centimetres of pure trouble.

'Hands off,' Chuck, seated to my left, muttered to me. 'She's mine.'

Well, I didn't think he stood much chance. Chuck's not exactly the sharpest tine on the pitchfork, and unless you really go for the gangrenous look, he ain't too handsome either. Still. 'No quarrel from me,' I replied. Pale was sweet, but I didn't need any more trouble.

She hit Chuck before she got to me. I mean in the schedule, but also literally. He got off on completely the wrong foot – nerves, I guess. But the line "Is that rigor mortis, or am I pleased to see you" is never a good opener. And then, well, I didn't catch his next words, exactly, but her reply was "*Rotten* wood, maybe" and a solid slap to the cheek.

Wow. Hit it *off*, dude... and I thought to myself, ain't no way she's ever going to love you.

Then it was my turn. And I wasn't – really wasn't – looking to get anywhere with Little Ms Queen-of-Darkness. Solidarity and all that stuff, but something...

'You know that jerk?' she asked me.

'Best buddies,' I replied. 'Look, Chuck was an idiot just now, but, Miss—'

'Bella.'

'Bella, his heart's in the right place. Or would be, if that mortician hadn't stuffed up. But if you'd just give him a chance, he's really quite a down-to-earth guy...'

'Hey, if all you're going to talk about is your humus-for-brains friend—' She moved to get up from the chair. And I noticed there was stuff seeping from the corners of her eyes. Embalming fluid, most like. But anyway, she was clearly upset. And maybe not just about her recent altercation with Chuck Bury.

'Sorry. I guess it's pretty difficult here,' I said. I had a hunch I knew what her problem was. The "BFFD" tat on her wrist was a bit of a giveaway, and the pallor too.

'What d'you mean?' she asked, a defensive catch to her voice.

'I'm thinking… only recently undead, right?'

She nodded assent. And I took a chance.

'So you wake up from The Big One,' I said. 'It's too dark and close in the coffin to see anything, there's all that rite-of-passage claw yourself to the surface routine, and it's only when you get there, the awful truth. Zombie. When you've had your heart set, all along, on…'

She reached for my hand and finished the sentence. 'Vampire,' she said, smiling through her tears. Typical. I mean, those Goth chicks are always the saddest. 'You're very perceptive,' she said, 'for a zom.'

'Gee, thanks.'

'What's your name?'

'Doug,' I told her. 'Doug, with an "O".'

'Nice meeting you, Doug,' she said, as the bell rang for the next change.

The rest of the evening passed uneventfully. Oh, Chuck got slapped thrice more. And shot, and staked, and kicked in the crotch. He *really* needed to work on those opening lines. But I fell into automaton mode. I'd seen all these faces before, and the dialogue was totally stale.

Afterwards, as we were all getting ready to shuffle off, Bella came up to me. 'Thanks for being so… understanding,' she said.

'Hey, look,' I replied. 'Don't be sad. So you didn't make vampire. But you're here, you're undead…'

'Yeah.'

'And *two out of three ain't bat*.'

She laughed, and something twinkled in her eye. 'Hey Doug,' she said.

'What?'

'D'you want to meet somewhere, tomorrow maybe, for dinner?'

'Sure,' I replied, feeling only slightly disloyal. Chuck, after all, had had his chance. 'Where?'

'County morgue's nice, I hear.'

'Sweet. Midnight good for you?'

And just like that, I had a date.

*

I drove over to pick her up. She looked ravishing. Hell, she looked to-die-for. *Again*. I was nervous as anything on the hearse ride over to the morgue, but I really needn't have been. The night was magical. And the dinner was superb: she had a Train Wreck Platter. I had Meat Loaf. We ate, and chatted for a while, and I figured the evening was just going to wind down from there. First date, after all. But on the drive back to her crypt, the old tape moved on to *Paradise by the Dashboard Light*, and I think the realisation hit us simultaneously.

We were *both* humming along to it.

'Pull over,' she said, a wicked grin creasing her face.

I pulled over.

Plenty of room in the back of a hearse, if you get my drift.

And, well, let's just say she put the "zom" in "ZOMG", *that's* for sure.

Afterwards, we held each other tight, kissing, hugging, that stuff. She broke off from a kiss, spat out a piece of earlobe, and said, 'I'm really glad to have met you, Doug. It's been a wonderful night.'

'Bella,' I replied, smiling back, 'you took the worms right out of my mouth.'

The Day of the Carrot

It had been known since the early 1950s that high levels of radiation could induce gigantism in certain species. But since most of the early cases had involved arthropods and poisonous lizards of, it has to be said, a rather *aggressive* disposition, the commercial implications of this line of research were not as obvious as they might otherwise have been.

"Nuclear Physics for Market Gardeners", p. 126,
by Hank Bremsstrahlung

The initial plan had seemed simple enough: they'd dig it out. They cleared away all the surrounding stunted vegetation – a few agaves and a creosotebush – until they had swept clean a circle maybe fifty yards wide. Then they started with shovels, got down seven, eight feet into the gypsum-loaded desert soil before it became obvious they weren't making enough headway. At eight feet down in the trench, the carrot's circumference was, if anything, larger than it had been at ground level, and who knew how far down it went before it tapered off?

'Fuckin' thing's growin' faster'n we can dig,' Mo complained, and one or two of the others laughed, but it was a bitter, frustrated kind of laughter, didn't last long.

Steve, sensing the crew's growing despondency, called a break. They needed to rethink this. He placed a call to the hire service back in Albuquerque, ordered a couple of dozers, backhoes, a big excavator and as many bobcats as the hire shop could round up at short notice, and sent Jim and Candy off in the 32-wheeler flatbed they'd hoped to be loading by now.

(Except the way that carrot was shaping up, the rig they had was looking nowhere near big enough. Steve started to calculate on the likely cost of hiring a triple. Were triples even *legal* on the I-25? Probably not, but it was either that, or wait for someone to construct a railroad for them.)

Up close, the carrot seemed to glow, even through its surface smudging of grey desert grit. It was so vivid, so orange, that it hurt the eyes, and several of the workers kept their shades on even while, in the trench or in the shadow of the carrot's massive tufted top, they were shielded from direct sunlight. Steve had fretted over the carrot's screaming intensity of orange to the extent that he'd gotten Mo to go over the bloody thing with a geiger, again, even though the site had checked out nominal this morning. The radioactivity was still hovering around background, so the coloration couldn't be blamed on that. It was just, it seemed, that the human eye wasn't accustomed to confrontation by so much orange.

Steve hoped the colour wasn't going to present a problem for marketing. Maybe rutabaga would have been a softer sell?

First, though, they had to excavate the bloody thing, else there weren't going to *be* any problems for marketing.

> A desert location is essential: there's something about the seclusion, the chill night air, the long hours of harsh sunlight, we're not sure what, but it doesn't work without it. Those early guys, with the ants and the gila monsters, they knew that too, but they didn't *know* that they knew, if you know what I mean. And it's not just the location, you've got to have the recipe right. The precise mix of eleven secret radioisotopes and nuclides is indispensible. But really, what it all comes down to is the people. You've got to have the best people in your crew, or you may as well just pack up and head home.
>
> *"Confessions of an Atomic Farmer", p. 33, by Fred Cherenkov*

The digging machines got them down to around twenty-five feet before sundown. It was a good effort, but Steve found himself reluctant to consider trying that approach again tomorrow. The further down they went, the wider they had to dig, to leave a corkscrew track for the machines to move in and out of the hole. (And the desert's soil structure, or what passed for it, was too treacherously friable, too crumbly, and tended to give way at the sides. At the end of the day they'd only been making slow progress, enlarging what was looking more and more like a broad, muffin-tin-shaped depression that seemed to get wider, but not perceptively deeper.) Steve didn't want to see anyone hurt or killed if the walls subsided. Plus, with the carrot's exposed height now finally exceeding its diameter, it was becoming time to have concern for the structural stability of the vegetable itself. However-many-dozen-tons of carrot could do a man an awful lot of damage, if it happened to land on top of him...

Next morning, they made a desultory attempt to haul the carrot out with the dozers, using steel-wire-reinforced tugboat hawsers and a massive jury-rigged wrought-iron welded collar that looked like Paul Bunyan's own chastity belt. The dozers strained in protest, engines screaming, smoke leaking from their dust-caked innards while anyone not ensconsed within a vehicle cab stood what they judged to be a good, safe distance back. One of the hawsers began to fray with a series of staccato metallic exclamations that took it almost to the point of snapping outright, and Steve had them stop. Getting those hawsers hadn't been easy, nor cheap. Now he was thinking chain, each link thick as a man's chest, and wondering where he could source some.

The carrot, of course, hadn't budged. It was very slightly indented by the collar, to the depth of about an inch, on the side opposite to the hawsers' anchorage point. Probably even those blemishes would grow out, if the extraction took too many more days...

The collar itself, though, was stretched and twisted where the hawsers had strained against it, and would no longer serve any useful purpose.

> Mangoes, tomatoes, strawberries, kiwifruit, they're all just a waste of time. *Massive* containment problems, when you super-size them. We had a melon once, would have supplied a whole city, Vegas I think it was, for a week or more, but it rolled and then smashed while we were trying to get it on the truck. Two workers crushed, one drowned. Horrible. Then of course it became evidence, so we couldn't even sell it off even though most of the chunks were still perfectly good. Still pretty damned burned about that, actually.
>
> *"The Big Apple, Cucumber, Onion..." p. 88, by Leo Quark*

Pulling it out sideways was, Steve conceded, always going to fail, particularly while they only had the carrot's iceberg-tip exposed. Digging down further was out of the question, they'd reached the point of diminishing returns with the gear they had. To get significantly deeper, they'd need equipment he couldn't even guess at.

It would take three days for the construction cranes, their crew, and the heaviest-gauge, highest-breaking-strain chain in the free world to get shipped onsite. In the meantime, he had the workmen busy infilling the hole with heavy-duty scaffolding, atop which they were welding together sheets of bomb-proof steel decking to make a platform sufficiently sturdy that they could then bring in the cranes close enough for good vertical leverage. Of course, he could have just had them fill in the hole again, but that would have seemed a step backward, bad for morale. Besides, he had a feeling he might still need that hole.

Steve was developing a grudging, adversarial form of respect for the tensile strength of the carrot. If they got through this successfully, he promised himself, he'd give serious consideration to exploring carrot as a construction material in its own right. The damned stuff seemed virtually indestructible... and he was pretty sure he wasn't going to be able to face eating the stuff again anytime soon. And furthermore, if, *if* they got this one out (and at this point that seemed an if almost as big as the carrot itself), then he swore he'd not leave it so long with the next crop. After all, there had to be a decent enough market for baby carrots, something small enough for a team of men and oxen, or at least a high-end tractor, to overpower.

> I've tried growing pretty much everything with these nucular farming methods. Thing is, we're still really looking for something we haven't tried yet, that'll really fire up the public's imagination, because so far it's not received as much attention as we'd hoped. Except that time the giant mantis got loose, and that was the *wrong sort* of attention.
> *Vinnie Centrifuge, cited in a Detroit newspaper article*

The cost was ballooning out, in a way that gnawed at Steve's griping innards. He didn't like to think of how many thousand dollars it had cost so far, not even including wages, and nothing, *nothing*, to show for it yet. This couldn't take too much longer, or there just wouldn't be any point in struggling on, his pockets were nowhere near that deep. Still, wasn't the prize worth it? With carrots valued at thirty-nine cents a pound, that made a ton of the stuff a thousand dollars, near enough, at market rates. Even if they could only make twenty cents a pound, that still meant five hundred a ton, and this carrot was several hundred tons, couple of thousand perhaps even. A million-dollar carrot – once they got it out.

The cranes had better do the job. No option, no excuses. Right now, his home was on the line.

From ground level, this hadn't looked so high up. Now, from his vantage point in the control cabin of one of three tower cranes, Steve found himself explaining away the first premonitions of vertigo. Damn, but he wasn't good with heights. And this was what, one-fifty, one-sixty feet up? He wasn't even sure it was going to be high enough. From what they'd seen from the digging, that carrot was in no hurry to taper to a point, might easily be two hundred feet long. A Washington Monument in day-glo orange, almost, just waiting to be unearthed.

From up here, it was almost impossible to appreciate the true size of the carrot. It looked only as large as – well, a carrot. It required a conscious effort to reinterpret the scene – to remind himself that those ants down there, crawling around the carrot's tufted dome, were Mo and Jim, busy fitting Lifting Collar (Carrot) Mark 2 to the resistant vegetable, and herniating themselves trying to heft the massive links of chain into position.

Jim gave the thumbs up, and the crane's operator worked the controls so that the boom slowly swung round to take up position, its tip almost nuzzling the tips of the other two cranes' booms.

Once the chains were all hooked into the collar, the cranes fired up in earnest. For the first minute or so, as the winches worked against the slack, there was a mechanical cacophony that marked the stuttering movement of chain links along the beam, down the tower. Then, all slack taken up, the motors bit in and exerted. The sounds now were of increasing strain as the engines laboured against the carrot's inertia. Steve wondered anew at the wisdom of placing himself here, in a rickety framework at the vertex of opposed and fundamentally imbalanced forces. Again, from ground level the cranes' towers had seemed perfect icons of stability and structural strength, easily the match of an oversized tap-root. From fifty yards up, though, the picture was very different, and quite unsettling. Steve's palms grew clammy, and he gripped the cabin's inner reinforcing in a gesture of futile desperation while the engines' unhealthy clamour continued to rise alarmingly in pitch.

Were the booms meant to arc in that fashion?

> Visions for the future? My dream's this peanut plant idea – got this site in Utah sorta mapped out, think it's a national park for now or somethink, but anyhow – 'bout as big as Chicago, or maybe St. Louis, you know, nothin' too massive – anyways, this humungous plant, growin' fifteen-foot goobers, we'd corner the peanut-butter market in no time. An' the best bit's the shells – you cut 'em careful-like, probly with one o' them newfangled lasers or some such, leave 'em more-less intact, and just as a side product from your peanut butter you get all this low-cost, hell no-cost really, instant housin'. Think of it, a whole city of readymade peanut-shell houses, wouldn' *that* be somethink!? 'Course, you'd have to check the tenants for anaphylaxis, else the courts'd have theyselves a field day.
>
> *Excerpt from a radio interview with Victor Synchrotron*

If there was a carrot somewhere, anywhere, that could laugh quietly to itself, then this carrot was that carrot.

Its growth, here, shouldn't even be possible. The Chihuahuan Desert was no kind of environment in which to be setting up a vegetable patch, there weren't the nutrients or the moisture. But the subsurface radioactivity, of which there was a knotted concentration directly below the carrot, had unleashed strange powers and incredible vitality, just as it had with the ants, the tarantulas and those bad-tempered lizards in the early black-and-white documentaries. Quite possibly, the carrot was getting all it needed simply from the desert air itself.

The cranes had proven as futile as everything they'd tried in the past few days. King Carrot was wedged as firmly as ever in place. So far as

Steve could establish, it hadn't given an inch. They'd try again tomorrow, after reconditioning the cranes – the engines hadn't taken well to the exertion, overheating and leaking lubricant as through it were lifeblood – but Steve could tell, in his gut, that that carrot wasn't going anywhere. It was playing for keeps. The damn thing was just too big.

Did it just end here? The thought made Steve sick. He'd been greeted with skepticism, derision even, by the few people he'd sought to confide in (and borrow funding from) all those months ago, when the inspiration had taken him. And the kicker was that, though they'd told him, mockingly, that the idea wouldn't work, he was faced with the opposite problem: it had worked *too well*. Same overall result, though. Might as well have stayed home, ripping up greenbacks one by one, at least then he wouldn't have these blisters on his fingers. Nor this sunburn.

There'd be no trying again, either, after this. Not for Steve. He'd thought it incredible good fortune when the land came on the market, laughably cheap – hell, who else would want a stretch of nondescript desert, no amenities, middle of nowhere? The sellers must have thought they were getting money for nothing, but Steve had seen the promise. He was in possession of a geological survey that showed the plot was penetrated by a thin, deep aquifer, trickling straight from the old nuclear testing sites at White Sands and Trinity. He'd *known* what those conditions had been capable of. And, dammit, he'd been right. For all the good it was going to do him.

'Blast!' shouted one of the workers – Jim, off in the distance, tending to an ailing engine – as the wrench slipped from his fingers and knocked against his knee. It was, for the group, an uncharacteristically mild cuss-word – Mo, in particular, seemed to think that proper sentence structure required the inclusion of at least one 'fuck' in every dozen words – but Jim's epithet stirred something in Steve's thought processes.

How do you make a carrot smaller?

They'd need a mobile drilling rig – nothing too fancy, it would only be necessary to get down seventy feet or so – and some ammo. Probably take a couple of days to arrange, but it might well take that long to get the cranes operational again anyway. Short, stumpy carrot, higher overheads: Steve could see the profit margin, once so fat and juicy, dwindling ever further towards something barely wafer-thin. But, least it looked like there might still *be* a profit margin. If this worked.

> In my opinion – and that's not just in my opinion, you'd find a whole heap of farmers saying the same – the whole field owes a huge debt to Steve Fusion, because if it weren't for Steve, this wouldn't even *be* a field. In either sense of the word. I sometimes wonder, if Steve hadn't fallen down that hole, just what else he might have come up with.
>
> *"A is for Atom. Z is for Zucchini"*, p. 271, by Ray Shielding

Mo sniggered to himself all the way back from the truck with the ammo locker. 'Dynamite fishin', yeah, tried that. Never thought I'd find meself usin' the fuckin stuff for *gardenin*', though.'

Steve had tracked down a couple of mobile drilling rigs, and when they'd arrived Mo and Jim had peeled back the steel decking around the digsite. There was just enough space between the scaffolding to manoeuvre the drilling rigs. Candy had overseen the drilling of a pilot hole, nine inches wide, nestled in against the carrot's mighty orange flank. It had gone smoothly enough, most of the way, but hit a problem just short of Steve's hoped-for depth of seventy feet: at sixty-five, there was an impenetrable stratum of rock, and they could not take it farther. Sixty-five: it would have to do. It was the same story every other spot they chose to drill, all around the exposed orange butte of the carrot, except that when the drill head was pulled up from two adjacent vertical holes, there were traces of carrot visible amongst the desert grit. It took a while to figure that part out...

At least, Steve thought, the drilling had told them something about why the extraction had been so problematic. He'd been envisaging a *straight* carrot, something that just required a simple vertical tug (if enough force could be applied, which was, as always, the question). But this was a carrot that had grown down sixty feet or so, and had then made a sharp left, following the aquifer, when it hit the impervious rock layer. The bloody thing had hooked itself in good and proper...

Now they had a dozen holes spaced out around the object of Steve's frustration, and Mo and Jim busied themselves arming each with a stick of dynamite. Steve hoped it would be enough. This was getting progressively further out of his area of expertise.

They replaced the steel decking, hoping it would act as a blast shield, helping to contain the explosions, channel them against the carrot's submerged bulk. Of course, it could just make things worse... but wasn't that what this part of New Mexico was *for*? Letting off explosions you couldn't predict, and didn't necessarily fully understand?

The blast, when it came, was like a badly-rehearsed earth-quake. The charges were supposed to detonate simultaneously, but they ended up staggering over several seconds. With each muffled explosion the steel decking shook with a deafening clatter, and when it was done there was enough dust to cause all of the workers to break into coughing fits.

The carrot appeared to be unscathed.

It was nearing day's end. Steve's head told him they needed to try the cranes out once more, to see if the blasting had succeeded, but his heart wasn't in it. Neither, it seemed, were those of the crew. Desultory, that was the word. They fitted the collar, connected the chains, started up the winches, readied the tower cranes.

It was almost a little anticlimactic when the carrot, under the persuasive torque of three heavy-duty construction cranes, began to edge its way skyward like a super-slo-mo film of a badly-designed missile emerging from its snug silo. Steve watched, transfixed, a lump of pride caught in his throat, as his machinery finally overpowered the truncated vegetable. The huge, stumpy mass – sixty-five linear feet, four hundred tons by Steve's reckoning – was finally lifted clear of the ground, carrot juice dripping off its ragged lower edge like orange drizzle. Then there ensued a complicated dance while the three cranes jostled to manoeuvre it away from the hole, to lay it to rest onto flat earth. They looked like three stick insects squabbling over the carrot, but they were getting the job done. Shipping it to Albuquerque, to announce their success to the world, that would be tomorrow's problem. Today's problem, same problem they'd faced all week, was solved. Finally.

Even as a mere stumpy half-carrot, it remained a thing of majesty, a raw testament to Nature's power and beauty. Steve turned and stepped back a way across the steel decking, to gain a better perspective on the sky-borne carrot as the cranes moved it into position for the night.

His backtracking boot found the lip of the carrot-shaped hole in the decking. He stumbled back and fell into darkness, only stopping sixty-five feet later.

> After my stint with Steve, I looked to diversify into livestock. But I don't think that'll ever be where the money is, there are just too many overheads involved in fencing and the like. Better to stick with market gardening, it's just simpler all round, once you've figured out the problems with harvesting. Plus, I gotta tell you, it's no fun trying to take out a fifty-foot chicken with a bazooka. Particularly when your first shot misses.
>
> *"Steve Fusion, that carrot, and the future of horticulture"*, p. 166,
> *by Candy Muon*

Steve lived, but it would be a year before he left hospital; and in that year, the ideas he'd pioneered would be taken up by others who'd drawn inspiration from those newspaper photos of the massive New Mexico carrot, and who had taken the trouble to track down their own precious plot of radioactive desert soil. There were groups elsewhere in the state working on squash, and grapefruit, and potatoes, and whale-sized pea pods; and someone in Arizona claimed to have an overgrown forest of broccoli stalks. They were exciting times.

For the first several months of Steve's sojourn in the hospital, he was subjected to repeated operations while his broken body was rebuilt. During much of this time, the extensive damage he'd sustained to his jaw required that he was placed on a liquids-only diet, while his wired-shut jaw was repaired. Steve, through all of this, was uncomplaining; he was, the nurses all agreed, a model patient.

Except when the rostered meal involved puréed carrot.

Latency

'Sure, I'm curious,' Lise said. 'About their motivations, I mean. But it's hardly going to keep me up at nights.'

'Yeah, wouldn't want that,' Beck said cryptically, from a couple of paces ahead. 'But I've worked out what Prima are playing at. There's something they get out of this that they couldn't hope to expect from anything else.'

'Like what?'

'Payoff. Prima's hoping we'll screw up.'

'What the hell do you mean?' Struggling to keep her persistent frustration – with Beck, with his need to grandstand – in check. Her enviro-suit was heavy, an energy-draining jacket. And they'd been out here three hours already.

'Think about it. How many millions is this expedition costing them? There's nothing, *nothing* we're doing down here that promises anything like that amount of return.' He waved a suited arm, a strident swathe of orange against the lifeless grey undulations of worn rock that stretched away behind him, as if through his gesture he sought to encompass all the ancient, weathered, squashed-hillock landscape of the continent beyond the beach. Rocks, pebbles, sand; cloud-smothered sky; the barren sweep of shoreline curving against dark ocean water; lazy waves breaking. And Beck, an intrusion. Lise was reminded, incongruously, of images she'd seen, of scarecrows. Scarecrow in motion. Even swaddled within the cocoon of his own suit, Beck still managed to appear gangly. At least from her perspective.

'There's the alga's genome—' she began, reaching into the surf to fill another sample canister.

'Fuck the genome!' he snapped back. 'You think anyone, other than a few bio-geeks, gives a stuff about that? Look, they could get that no problem, just by dropping a couple of robot probes down here. No need for all this living-quarter shit, the bases, these suits, the vehicles. They could have got the genome for a tenth the cost, a hundredth, of what they've shelled out for this, which tells me it's not the genome they're after.'

'They thought we'd find other lifeforms,' Lise persisted, gloved fingers fumbling the canister's latches closed.

'That was never going to change the balance sheet. Even if it'd been *right*.'

'You figured this out only last night?' she asked, managing a faintly mocking tone. The surveillance drone, tasked with hovering above them like some giant carboniferous dragonfly, dipped, faltered, then re-asserted its altitude. Damn thing must be losing charge again. They should head back to their rover, she didn't want to have to rescue the drone, didn't want to have to carry it if it lost flight. Particularly if it landed in the water. But Beck wasn't acknowledging the drone's difficulties, wasn't shifting ground.

'This part of it, yeah. I'd been thinking PR, same as everybody'—he flashed her a glance that was simultaneously querying and silencing— 'but it's not enough, there's more to it than that. No, what they get from ferrying us down here is a rattle of the dice every time we leave the base. Le'me ask you something. Your lab work, is it what you'd call exemplary?'

Lise bristled. 'What are you getting at? You ever had any reason to doubt my results?'

'That's not what I mean. Hasn't it struck you as odd that they picked us, the four of us, for this? We're none of us what you could call outstanding, not even Tash – she's good, but you'd hardly call her great, and Yves is a tantamount fucking alcoholic – and yet we got the nod, ahead of God knows how many thousand others that would've jumped at the chance and would've been, I assure you, more comprehensively qualified than you or me.'

'Beck, that's how the lottery system works,' she replied. 'Gives everyone an equal chance. Avoids the public seeing this mission as a junket for inside-track elitists. PR, remember?'

'Yes, supposedly, but that only holds if it's left to chance. Prima isn't exactly known for its scruples, they're the sort of org that would rig the lottery soon as blink. Think about it. Tash is monumentally disorganised – she's brilliant in some ways, but her work is erratic, to put it charitably, and none of us are exactly what you'd call methodical.'

'Precisely. If they'd wanted methodical, then they would have sent robots.'

'Yeah, but why *didn't* they want methodical?'

She took a few seconds to answer. 'Adaptability to the unknown?'

'*What* unknown? There's just one fucking species of alga. How much unknown you going to get out of that?'

'It's not as if we understand all of what it's—'

'Please. You expect me to believe that's the reason?'

You did yesterday. Or near enough. 'Then how do you see it?'

'They're hoping for stero breach. Airlock roulette. Ninety-nine times, we're each of us careful enough it doesn't happen, but all it takes is one time in a hundred. One time in a thousand, they keep us here long enough. And, way I see it, once Charis's sterility gets punctured, once the environment's no longer pristine, then all bets are off. There'll probably be some kind of crocodile-tear thing, they'll plough a few millions into attempted bioremediation, maybe wait a coupla years, and then they'll move in. And they'll be able to say, "sorry, guys, we did our best to restore the environment, but you know it was just too far gone to put the genie back in the bottle, 'cos of them dumbfuck klutz scientists who messed it up in the first place. But, hey, brightside, look at all this new landscape to colonise". They'll make a fucking packet out of it.'

'You really believe that?' Lise asked.

'Makes sense. Bet you, I bet you they don't call halt to the mission before some almighty fuck-up goes down here.'

'That's obscene. Obscenely cynical.'

'Who? Them, or me?' His leer was audible.

'Both, I guess. I mean, look, we're the intruders, we don't belong here, the alga does. This is a pristine alien environment. How could anyone think of messing with it? Especially after what happened with Mars?'

'This doesn't look too pristine to me,' Beck retorted. 'Less that's a new synonym for dreary beyond fucking belief.'

'Huh. So are you going to be the one does Prima's dirty work for them then? Forget to wipe your boots one day as you go out?'

'Me? No chance. I *hate* those fuckers. I just understand them, is all.'

She was in the wet-lab, running nutrient trials on yesterday's algal samples – hoping for some wrinkle, some point of difference – when Natasha ambled in. 'Hey, Tash,' Lise called, looking up from her slate, glad enough of the interruption.

'Lee-za,' the geologist replied, her voice almost sing-song. She pulled up a spare stool, leaned forward for a curious glance at Lise's screen, ran a pudgy hand through mid-length greying hair. 'How'd the morning go?'

'The usual. A dozen sample takes, out along the northeast beach – few more of them showing up than yesterday, it looks like, but nothing new really. How 'bout you?'

'A few more suspected meteorite fragments, out near the salt ponds south of Mount Molehill. Weird, though. They were more scorched than seemed consistent with the ablation signatures.'

'Huh. Maybe Prima's taken to lobbing rocks at us. Could be their way of telling us to get a frotting move on.'

'You what?'

'Just Beck's conspiracy *du jour*. Thinks Prima *wants* us to fail here. He was saying if they really wanted results, they'd have chosen better people.'

She watched Tash carefully for a reaction, a rankling at impugned reputation.

But Tash's face, soft-lined and full-moon round, registered nothing deeper than residual puzzlement. 'Yeah, well, guy gets bored. Who knew?' 'He could still frotting adapt. Population stats. Sample prep. Workup. Swallow his damn ecologist pride, there's plenty he could be pitching in with. Helping me out with the exo-mol-bio, maybe even assisting Yves with the geochem analysis. I mean, we're all busy, right? Instead he just winds up sulking, trancing, or spouting his latest manifesto at anyone in earshot.' Lise was surprised at the anger she heard in her own voice, hadn't actually believed she was putting it there. Nor was she sure how much was directed at Beck, how much diverted towards Tash. But it obviously wasn't Tash's fault who she'd been teamed with. She wished, in fact, that she shared Tash's equanimity, her imperturbability; but there was no certainty that the geologist would retain her signature level-headedness in the face of continual exposure to Beck.

'What's the screen?' Tash asked, a transparent subject-shift.

Lise was glad enough of the change in topic. 'Latest model of the protein,' she answered, failing to keep a tinge of satisfaction from her voice.

Tash picked it up. 'Nice. Uh… it's *supposed* to look like a tapeworm contortionist's nightmare, right?'

'They all do,' Lise replied. 'But this is orders bigger than anything in Earth's metabolic toolkit.'

'So what's it all do?'

'Not a frotting clue,' she replied. 'Nothing even vaguely like it in terrestrial biochem. Seventy-six metal atoms packed into the middle of it, though, and most of them specific, so it must have hell's own biochemical function.'

'You've really no idea what it's doing?'

'My best guess is light-harvesting. Though why it needs so complicated a structure is beyond me. The thing is absolutely massive. Megadaltons.'

'Maybe Beck's right,' Tash commented.

'I hear that correctly?' Lise asked. 'What d'you mean?'

'About this being a setup. You know, when he was going on about how freaky it was to encounter a natural monoculture. Said the most logical explanation was that this was a cultivated planet, that the alga's someone's food crop or something.'

'So where are the farmers?'

'Don't ask me. I'm not the one with the new conspiracy every week. But you gotta admit, it's pretty unusual to find a setup like this. He could have something. I mean, what kind of planet has only one species, after maybe ten billion years habitability?'

'Huh. Beck's just got too much frotting time on his hands.'

'Yeah, but really, you blame him? Me, you, and Yves, we're all set. Rocks and microbes. But it's not Beck's fault it turns out Charis doesn't *have* an ecology.'

Yves and Tash were off on another geochem survey into the Linnaean badlands. At work in the lab, Lise casually followed their progress through almost-random glances at the wall-displayed footage from their slaved drone. Except for the sky and the researchers' fluoro-pigmented suits, the colour imagery might just as well have been monochrome: the greyed geology of the flat-hunched landmass. She caught glimpses as their rover negotiated drifts of gritty regolith, crawled across exposed rock surfaces, skirted occasional pools of dark life. It was not a landscape to set the imagination aflame, though to hear Tash speak it contained geological marvels enough to keep them occupied.

And Beck... Beck was off trancing, *again.* She bit her lip, stared at her slate, attempted to channel her anger and her frustration somewhere it might give some benefit.

Two steps sideways, one step back.

Frotting protein. Tash was right, it did have something of the tapeworm about it.

But it refused to respond predictably, or in any manner that invited satisfactory interpretation, to her testing.

Not simply light-harvesting. She could establish that much. But what else did that leave? Most of the alga's biochemical housekeeping was accounted for, by elegant little snippets of peptide which operated with enviable efficiency. By contrast, the mystery metalloprotein was a juggernaut, a behemoth, an intractable residual riddle. It was by far the largest piece of chemical furniture within the alga's walls. It must do *something*.

She'd been running calculations, on the base's A-brain, hoping to tease out the protein's photonic response. There were changes, the thing was indeed light-sensitive. But it just seemed to ratchet itself into a tighter and yet tighter mess, and ended up hopelessly quagmired in itself. Metaphor, perhaps, she thought wryly.

Much more of this, and she might start feeling something akin to Beck's patented mix of ennui, disdain and frustration. It was all very well for Tash and Yves. Rocks were simple, rocks gave of their vital information straightforwardly and with little misdirection. Particularly here on Charis, where nothing of geologic note had happened for aeons. But life... life was tricky, life could be devious.

She could try tweaking the parameters, starting the calcs again. Sometimes that helped. Not often.

Hell with it. She got up, stretched, neck-twisted, flexed. Some sit-ups. Charis's steady, slightly low gravity still felt weird, after a lifetime on habs and research vessels, but the body's fatigue signals – not helped here by the 37-hour daycycle, despite the acclimating meds – still told the same story. She'd been sitting too long, going nowhere. Enough calculations for today. She moved over to the other side of the lab, to the wet samples closeted off behind the containment window. Maybe the real creature could tell her something the simulations couldn't.

'Seasonal. I guess,' she replied, still half asleep.

It was the wrong response, and Beck turned on her almost savagely, his shock of hair conveying more than ever a scarecrow's resemblance.

'*What* seasons?' he asked. 'There's no moon, no inclination, no fucking ellipticity. How the hell can this place have seasons? It struggles to even have weather.'

'Alright, then, not seasonal. I dunno. Why'd'nt y' wake up Yves with this? Or Tash?' Yawning. Wondering whether to be resentful.

'They weren't *asleep*,' Beck said.

She sat up now, rubbed her arms. 'Oh. Thought that had run its course weeks ago.'

'Evidently not. Or maybe they were just feeling nostalgic.'

'Still no reason to go waking me up – over nothing, really.' She glanced down to check everything was fastened.

'It's *not nothing*,' he replied. 'You can't answer it. I can't explain it. How the hell can the ecosystem not be at equilibrium already?'

'Who says it isn't at equilibrium?' Lise asked.

'Population ramping up on a daily basis, doesn't sound like equilibrium to me.'

'Could be,' she protested. 'Who says the numbers aren't climbing again after dieback?'

'That's a ridiculous suggestion.' There was a fierceness to him which surprised her, for all that she'd seen it in him before. An anger in the carriage of his limbs. She was newly conscious of the difference in their heights, felt almost child-sized.

She rubbed at her temples, seeking to defuse the tension; brought the gesture down to encompass her eyes. 'Gimme a break. I was asleep five minutes ago. Could be a response to some kind of nutrient crisis, a stellar flare—'

'Stellar flare? No chance, 82 Eri's as placid as they come.'

'OK. If you don't like that one, why don't you invoke your little alien friends? The farmers?'

'Look, be serious, please Leez.'

'I am being serious. About the dieback, at least. It's certainly a possibility. We've only been here a bit over a month, who knows what kind of long-term cycles might come into play?'

'The long-term cycles don't make any fucking sense,' Beck complained. 'I mean, how the hell does Charis get off only having one species?'

'Thought that was *last* week's sticking point.'

'Yeah, well, it's still stuck. We managed dinosaurs, crinoids, lungfish – we managed fucking *trilobites*, for god's sake – all in a few hundred million years, once the biosphere got its act together. This place has had *dozens* of times that long, how come it hasn't produced more than one species in all that time?'

'We really sure it's had that long?'

'Those micro-fossils of Yves' look pretty convincing to me. That's eight billion years plus. And there's plenty of mutation sources, specially with such a piss-weak magnetic field. Charis is a *sitter* for all those stellar-wind protons, as well as all that UV that gets through.'

'Look, Beck, it's late, we can talk about this tomorrow.'

'Yeah, you're right. Anyway, I guess they're finished now.' Nodding his head towards the adjoining room.

You what? Lise thought, feeling suddenly used. She sent a sortie of virtual daggers flying towards Beck's retreating back.

And then, of course, as she lay in the dark, sleep would not return. The alga, her marvellous mystefying conundrum, beckoned to her and would not let her lapse.

She did the only thing she could think of. She climbed out of bed, padded through to her desk in the research module, and put on the next set of calculations, still yawning.

It burned her to think through Beck's conversation with her. But then there was so much about Beck that rankled with her, his niggling, his crazy imaginings of agendas too diverse to be plausible. His laziness.

It burned, too, that he didn't share her admiration for the alga's tenacity. There was, in a sense, some beauty to it, which sometimes she felt that she alone could see. This sense grew tarnished when she drifted into thinking through his speculations on the alga's origins, or of Prima's possibly underhand motivations in allowing her to study the alga. She admitted he was probably right not to trust the org's beneficence, she certainly didn't herself. It seared most deeply to think that, in some way, she was complicit in Prima's activity, whatever that was, by the act of learning the alga's innocent secrets.

Why did anybody have to have any plans for the planet? Why, beyond gaining basic knowledge of it, as she was now pursuing, couldn't they just let it be? It was always possible to build more habs, and planetary gravity wells were just wasteful and inconvenient.

Time to quit for the night.

On her way back to the bedroom, she habitually checked her partial reflection – pixieish, mysterious – in the dual vista of the main foyer windows. And she thought she glimpsed something flash, some distant, momentary burst of peripheral brightness, in the barren night-deep landscape outside.

Must've been a meteor, she decided.

'Where'd you get the silver ones?' Yves asked, peering over her shoulder at the slate's piped feed. The visual was realtime, captured from the adjacent microscope. 'I thought there was only the one species.'

'There is. This is just a – well, so far as we can tell, it's a photoresponse. There's the standard, dark form, light-harvesting as far as we can tell, and this mirrored form, photoresistant. Thought you would've seen this already, out in the field?'

'Think I have, probably, but I'd just put it down to a trick of the lighting. Weird seeing it here – and I don't usually get a close-up view of them, like this. Photoresistance?'

'Yes. Haven't figured out exactly how it manages the transition, but yeah, looks like it's light flicking some sort of biological switch.'

'Why's it do that?'

'No idea at this stage. The modelling's still playing silly frotters, can't get it to make sense.'

'Pretty tricky little fella, for a prokaryote.'

'I guess.' Lise was starting to wonder why Yves was loitering, perhaps he'd had a tiff with Tash. But he looked tidy this morning, beard clipped precisely short, his eyes untroubled, his thin smile sufficiently genuine. Plus she couldn't smell alcohol breath, which with Yves would usually have been a solid diagnostic for a quarrel of some form.

'Hey – where'd it go?' he asked.

'Where'd what go? Oh, the alga? Yeah, it does that. Think it's the lights on the microscope stage, maybe heat or dessication. Seems to have some kind of cellular suicide function. It just trashes itself if the conditions get too extreme. Frags itself into junk.'

'Weird.'

'Must work out for it, though? I mean, Beck was saying you and Tash have dated some of those microfossils back to eight bill.'

'Eight point six,' Yves corrected proudly, nodding in emphasis.

'Wow.'

'That cellular suicide. Does that happen with the black form as well, or just with the silvered?'

'Uh. Mainly just the mirrored ones. Now that you mention it.' Lise felt an awkward kick, embarrassment maybe, at having missed what might be a clue. She looked to change tack. 'So, E-vie, how's things going with you?'

'Pretty standard, but I'm starting to think we've learned about all we can about the geology of Linnaeus, and it doesn't look as though any of the smaller islands are going to yield any surprises. Plus I'm getting sick of the junk equipment Prima have saddled us with, you'd think on a flagship mission like this they'd kit it out properly. Bloody cheap-arse org funding. We had another two installations malf on us last night. Feed says they maxed out on high-end photons, which is just shit. Middle of the bloody night. Crap instruments. Bastards.'

'I was meaning with *you*. Not with the rocks, or the equipment. This place getting to you yet?'

'No, wouldn't say so, but better gear would be nice, obviously. Pain wearing the suits everywhere, too, but that's the price, isn't it? Going where no-one's gone before, that sort of crap.'

'You don't feel too crowded? Here, I mean.' She waved an arm to indicate their fabricated surroundings.

'No. It's cosy, sure, but no worse than a hab. Facilities bit too basic, maybe, but again.' He shrugged, an exaggerated gesture that seemed to suit him. 'I should retreat into trancing, like Beck, perhaps wouldn't notice the shortcomings.'

'I wouldn't look to Beck as any kind of role model,' she advised. 'Guy's *full* of shortcomings.'

'Hey, aren't we all? Just a matter of how we handle them.'

The silvered cells formed from the black cells. But why?

It seemed like a life-cycle thing, but she couldn't see any way that it made sense. And there was something weird about the photobiology – the black cells were excellent absorbers, if a little slow to capitalise on the absorbed energy, in a biochemical sense, but the silvered cells were reflective, didn't seem to absorb at any sensible wavelengths of 82 Eri's slightly-cool sunlight. Not perfect reflectors, but what they didn't bounce straight off, they scattered. Yet it wasn't a metamorphosis that gave any conceivable advantage, it was like a senescence, an almost voluntary aging. But what function could senescence serve, in a prokaryotic species that presumably hadn't changed in eight billion years?

The alga had pervaded Charis's ocean, had infiltrated Linnaeus's sluggish rivers, had established footholds in each of the scattered salt ponds that dotted the landscape inland from the crumbling northern bight. This alone was an incredible adaptation, existence across such a wide range of salinity. To have held off all challengers across its span of continuing existence compounded and magnified the achievement – unless you accepted Beck's proposal that the entire setup was artifice. But the multi-billion-year fossil record argued, more strongly than anything else she could mount, against the fanciful notion that Charis was a farm. It beggared belief to expect the farmers would still be in existence after all that time, and what neglected farm didn't go to seed and decay? The case must be, rather, that the alga was, despite what she knew of its sometimes-elegant, sometimes-cumbersome biochemistry, supremely well adapted to the Charian environment.

The alga had never seen fit, however, to colonise the land. In some ways, this was not so puzzling. If Tash was right, then for much of its history Charis hadn't had any exposed terrestrial surfaces of consequence. With too few heavy radionuclides to keep its core molten, the planet had apparently congealed beyond the capability for significant earthquake and volcanic activity several billions of years ago, and had then had to wait until accumulated H-atom escape from the upper atmosphere had dehydrated it sufficiently to start bringing towards sea level the shallowest points of the primeval sea bed. Even Linnaeus, the only geologic feature to come close to deserving the title of continent, accounted for much less than one percent of the planet's surface.

When placed in this context, the alga became, in Lise's eyes, a powerful, entrenched, conservative opponent to her attempts to comprehend it, and this silvered form which it adopted was the most challenging feature. She felt in her gut that the latent phase must in some manner be connected to the vast, hulking, mysterious metalloprotein, but the only structural information she could obtain on this component derived from her studies of the active near-black phase of the alga's existence. Maybe the extreme-UV spectroscopy she was now running would tell her something – if the latent phase showed any absorption. The alga's mirrored form stubbornly refused to absorb anything longer-wavelength.

Why did the alga transform? Was it waiting for something, or did a somehow-still-imperfectly-honed metabolism simply build up too much intracellular junk and collapse into moribund quiescence? Neither explanation, to her, made sufficient sense to appear credible.

And the latent phase was pushing towards ascendancy. In the containment chamber's cultured samples, as well as in the ocean reaches, the proportion of silver-to-black was climbing daily, apace it seemed with the population growth. It made no sense, either, that the overall algal population apparently fluctuated in this reasonably dramatic fashion. It was as though without any external drivers for dieback – Charis's climate and orbit was regular to the point of monotony – the alga had seen fit to engineer crises for itself. Eyeing the large tank with the highest nutrient loading – the change in colour here, from yesterday, was apparent even to the naked eye – she wondered if the metamorphosis might somehow be a global thermoregulating effect, like Lovelock's daisyworld.

She turned aside from the wet-lab section to answer a chime of achievement from her slate. Probably, the latest tranche of misleading, misguided modeling calculations had run their fruitless course. But she didn't get the time to finish her traversal of the lab's space. There was a flash, a searingly bright scintillation. Then something in the containment chamber exploded.

'Lise! Slow down! Calmly, calmly,' urged Tash's communicator-distorted voice, somehow still placid. 'What's happened? Are you all right?'

'I think so,' Lise responded. 'The containment shield seems to have held, though it must've taken a hell of a wallop, it was the twenty-litre tank that went up.'

'Went up? What on earth—'

'Exploded,' Lise explained, pausing for a gulp of breath. 'That's the best way to describe it. Most of that side of the wet-lab's equipment is a write-off. The spectrometers, the scopes, the chromatographs. Tash, the alga just *exploded*, and it damn near took out the base with it. Just a twenty-litre tank. Where are you? What colour's the water?'

'Out by the salt ponds out west, and yes, it's got that silvery sheen to it—'

'Then you should get the hell up Mount Molehill, or better, just find a way back here that gives any bodies of water a wide berth. Particularly the reflective ones.'

'Lise, *what is this about?* What do you mean, explosion?'

'It's a chain reaction. Listen, 'cause you need to know what you're dealing with. All those modelling calculations I thought were going haywire, they were telling me something. The alga in the tank exploded, right at the end of the extreme-UV spectral run. It's a frotting *bomb*, Tash, the silvered form is a bomb. The metalloprotein locks up so much chemical energy, an unbelievable amount, and then it shuts itself away in this hideously ratcheted form, waiting for the trigger to strike.'

'Lise—'

'Must be an X-ray photon or something, the spec lamp puts out a few of those. Anyway, I *think* that's what triggers the cellular detonation, and the protein's energy, that's easily enough to generate three or four more X-rays, alongside all the heat and light and the chemical carnage. It sounds freaky, but you wouldn't believe the knots that protein twists itself into, I'd say it's easily capable… and if the population density is low enough, then it's just an isolated cell death, but if it gets above a threshold, if enough of the X-rays get absorbed by neighbouring cells, then it just cascades and the whole thing goes kablooey. It's a frotting *chain reaction.*'

'Lise, you're sure about this?' Yves' voice this time.

'I'm looking at the results now,' she replied. Deadpan now, calmer since she'd conveyed her warning. 'And I'd say this is obviously what's been frying your instruments, too. Anyway, pass this on to Beck, also, of course.'

Pause. 'Beck's not with you?' asked Tash.

'No, thought he was going to be helping you with the heavy lifting, those replacement units.'

'That fell through, didn't look like we were going to need him after all. He said he was just going to stay around base until later this afternoon.'

'Uh… I guess he's probably in his chamber, then. But I haven't heard him.'

In fact, she had the sense, only vaguely noted at the time, that the base had been eerily quiet for most of the morning.

'Look, Tash, I'd better go check on him. Don't think there's anything more to pass on, just get back here safely and I guess we'll try to figure out how to stay out of trouble here.' She closed the call and paced the short connecting tube to the entrance of the living module.

Beck's chamber was open. Empty.

Shit.

A panicked search through both the research module and the living quarters found no sign of Beck. The comm system was unable to raise him, citing a privacy block. Lise kept an urgent alert repeating on the comm for him, and asked the A-brain for the most recent public-area visual. The slated reply showed Beck's lanky figure struggling into an enviro-suit in the inner airlock, timestamped over two hours ago.

Had she really been that immersed in her work that she hadn't sensed his departure, his absence?

She hoped he'd decided to trek out to the salt ponds, pass the time with Tash and Yves, though she knew even as she considered it that this was unlikely. More probably, he'd gone to the worst place possible.

The sea had been silvered for days now. She didn't like to think what would happen when that ran its course.

Getting kitted was a menace. Lise hadn't been scheduled for an excursion today, so her suit's exoderm regenning had been deprioritised. The suit was still fully airtight, but lacked the sterile, chemodegradable outer skin that served to prevent cross-contamination of the biospheres. *Tough.* She wasn't feeling charitably disposed towards the alga at the moment; but she submitted to a quick decontam spray in the outer airlock, hoping the time it cost her wouldn't be vital.

Both rovers were gone, but only one drone. That figured, Beck didn't like to walk anywhere if he could avoid it, and didn't trust the drones' surveillance function; he'd also, it seemed, had enough free time over the past weeks to hack the base's security programming, and to arrange for himself privacy on-demand. *Idle hands*, Lise thought.

Lise wasn't looking forward to the five-kilometre trek to the beach. Even in Charis's slightly-low gravity, the suits were cumbersome at the best of times; and this near the heat of the day the visor set up its own little cranial greenhouse effect, for which the cooling ducts had no adequate remedy.

The track to the beach was mild of terrain – Linnaeus didn't do rugged, even Mount Molehill had an elevation of only fifty-one metres – but she broke rapidly into sweat, feeling the need to make good time. She was conscious of having to pay more attention to where she placed her feet. Ordinarily the rover navigated its own way with something approaching autonomy, its tyres were broad enough that potholes were of little concern, but she couldn't afford a twisted ankle.

It struck her, too, that in focusing on the alga, she'd never really recognised how desolate the environment was. Squat, worn rock outcrops and skeins of regolith or sand, with hardly even any boulders to intrude on the raw monotony. A place, it seemed, that had been windswept in slow motion. No trees; no leaves; no crawling creatures; no life, save what existed in the rivers, the lakes, the ocean. And *that* now seemed tarnished, now she knew its secret.

Would the ocean detonate all at once? Not likely, she imagined. There'd be population density variations, some regions that edged into criticality earlier than others. There'd be stretches of water across which the reaction would fizzle out, refuse to take hold. Life would remain, and even after cataclysm, would start again. But any deviation from the alga's standard model must, in some manner, be punished through the induced crisis. She still didn't know how, but eight billion years spoke for itself.

And she still had no idea how extensive would be the oceanic blast zone, when it happened.

She'd viewed the alga as a worthy adversary, once. But it had turned out to be something ignoble, a dog in the manger. A cheat. A placeholder. An evolutionary hijacker. Did it really deserve a planet all to itself?

And yet: would people wreak anything better? Probably not. She had a shrewd sense of how the planet would finish up once Prima and their org competitors dug their talons into it. They'd exterminate the alga, simply because it was in their way and threatened to limit their plans for Charis's destiny. Probably keep some small alga colonies growing, under carefully controlled conditions, in museums and universities, so that people could study and be entranced by the mystery of the exploding lifeform. The microbe whose tenacious grasp on the planet had lasted eight billion years, but which was finally wiped out by an upstart race whose home world hadn't even formed when the alga first darkened Charis's ocean.

Not your decision to make, Lise, she told herself, slowing down in an effort to stave off the stitch. Not far now, if she read the landmarks correctly.

Except—

Except, as it turned out, it *was* her decision to make.

Beck was floating in the mirrored, deadly sea; suited, face up, fifty metres off the point of the sandy spit. It was a distance that might as well have been insurmountable – Lise was no swimmer, had hardly even been in a pool during her life on the various habs, didn't trust the curved slabs of water. And she knew from Tash's sounding studies that the water deepened quite rapidly here. She couldn't walk it, the suit would float. And she could tell that she'd never swim it in the suit. It just hadn't been designed with the needed flexibility in mind.

Beck had registered her arrival, had waved back, but was oblivious to her attempts to comm him. Her attempts to charade the danger of his situation appeared not to have reached him, either. Either his receiver was switched off, or faulty; or (as seemed much more likely) he was trancing.

She could *kill* him, for being so stupid.

The sensible thing would be to take the rover, parked at the start of the spit, back to base where she could pick up the solid-shell dinghy. But the sensible thing would take an hour at least, even assuming she could launch the dinghy without mishap. Something about the ocean's lethal sheen told her she didn't have an hour.

She cracked the neck-seal gingerly, heart rate rising towards a crescendo as she took the first breath of alien air. The second breath came easier. Growing dizzy – too much O_2, she *knew* that, though it shouldn't kill her – she forced herself to remain standing. Ignoring the suit's remonstrations, she released the other seals at the suit's joints, and stepped out of her casing. When she had removed enough of her clothing that what remained seemed unlikely to hamper her, she strode into the alien ocean and kicked off, managing a rough but effective-enough backstroke.

If it happens, she thought, *it's going to be so quick you'll never know.*

But somewhat to her surprise, she reached the small plastic-coated island that was her tranced colleague without the ocean exploding around her.

She tapped on his visor before reaching an arm across his suited chest to avail herself of the buoyancy he offered.

'Don't get the wrong idea,' she advised him, smiling as she trod water, enjoying his immensely-startled expressing. Then she started, awkwardly, towing him back to shore.

Yves rigged up the outer airlock as a quarantine chamber. The four of them held a council of war, Lise participating the best she could from behind her multiple layers of sterilised plastic.

Later that day, Beck paid her a visit. It was a bizarre conversation: he was decked out in an enviro-suit, she wore paper pyjamas.

'Why'd you do it?' he asked, and the puzzlement showing on his face seemed genuine. 'I didn't have you picked as the sort to do Prima's bidding.'

'Prima had nothing to do with it. It was just the situation. I was angry at the alga anyway, for not playing fair, but you want to know what really decided me?'

'Yeah?'

'You were trancing.'

'Yeah, I know, the out-of-contact thing. Sorry and all that.'

'No, you don't get it. It was the trancing.'

'Huh?'

'It came to me… you were in a vegetative state, but you'd come out of that eventually. And the alga was never going to. When I saw it that way, it really wasn't that big a choice.'

'Still, fucking brave of you. Don't know that I would've done it. Alien lifeform and all that.'

'Sure you would. It's in your genes, on that same arm of the Y-chromosome that codes for paranoia and distrust of corporate entities. And, Beck?'

'Yeah?'

'Just because Prima are a pack of pricks… that doesn't make it the wrong decision.'

Lise spent five weeks in the outer airlock, until she was declared free of biohazard. During that time, most of the remaining salt ponds detonated, scattering their wreckage on the surrounding rock. And several tracts of mid-oceanic water, Sargasso-thick with the silvered alga, had ignited in spectacular fashion. Mostly by day, when the X-ray influx was highest, but there'd been one cataclysmic blast which had apparently been set off by starlight, and which had fried two of Prima's orbiting comsats. They'd felt repercussions within the base too, most notably from a blast close enough to have caused the horizon to glow, for a few eerie seconds; they'd been buffeted by cold, dust-laden gales, lashed by dirty, salty rain, and blanketed by thick black clouds. The temperature dropped, and stayed low for weeks.

But the stretch of ocean immediately around their little area of coastline hadn't exploded; and there were doubts, now, that it ever would.

Something new had taken hold in the water.

At the Dark Matter Zoo

At the Dark Matter Zoo,
the beasts are caged in mystery,
tended with conjecture,
described with imprecision.

At the Dark Matter Zoo,
I'm advised photography seldom captures
the wonder (or, indeed, anything).

At the Dark Matter Zoo,
visitors thrill to catch perhaps-sight of
the stygiosaurs, shadow jackals, Schrödinger cats;
with only the souvenir stand palpable.

At the Dark Matter Zoo,
it's possible some enclosures are completely
empty,
their charges escaped
or simply never

At the Dark Matter Zoo,
even the exits
are marked none too clearly;
refreshments are unfulfilling;
the Site Map does not serve.

At the Dark Matter Zoo,
the ghosts of the dodo,
the thylacine, the Falklands wolf, the Haast eagle,
I sought in vain.

Suckers for Love

It started with a touch so delicate, so evanescent, that Flarb[click]oorglfluenz'blith was tempted to mark it down as unintended, and indeed forgot about it soon afterward.

He'd been slithering his way through the vessel's low-g Recuperatorium, which he'd discovered the week before: a palatial, high-vaulted and rather ornate chamber, tricked out in baroque fixtures of ormolu and electrum, meerschaum and misch-metal. The Recuperatorium made an enviably efficient shortcut between Navigation and Engineering and, accordingly, he'd since been using the route twice daily. Mindful that his traversals of the Recuperatorium weren't entirely authorised, he'd been careful to squelch well clear of any of the chamber's several sunken bathing pools – in which the spawnlings, their custodians, and the elderly and infirm took some respite from the ravages of spin-gravity – and the pools' occupants had been largely content, for their part, to disregard his passage of their domain. It was therefore with some surprise that Flarb[click]oorglfluenz'blith registered the frond-like brush of an arm-tip against his flank. Sliding to a slightly wobbly stop beside a swathe of gilt-trimmed tapestry, he followed the curve of the errant limb back to its owner: a young female, bulbous of body, pert of beak, elegant of eyestalk, slender of tentacle and sinuous of demeanour, who was, at that moment, part in, part out of the nearest of the Recuperatorium's fragrant pools. She offered an apologetic smile. He responded with a nod of unoffended equanimity, blundered awkwardly into the sculpted corner of a heavy bakelite daybed, and hurried on his way to Engineering.

The following week, in similar circumstances, the incident repeated itself, with the variation that on this occasion the young female's appendage (and he was not sure, but it appeared to be the same lithe and lissome individual) brushed not across his side but chanced instead to glance against the soft, spongy tip of his mating tendril. Scandalised, he recoiled. He could not bring himself to meet the female's gaze this time, and squirmed his way through the Recuperatorium as fast as he could muster.

This moment of contact, inadvertent and innocent though it may well have been – and surely it was uncharitable of him to even contemplate the prospect that it might have been otherwise? – had provoked within him a temptation, a quivering, indeed a definite and awkward enfirming of tendril, on which he was not yet ready to dwell.

Flarb[click]oorglfluenz'blith was now in a state of some confusion, for he had several months back bequeathed his hearts to another, a Communicationalist of good family and progressive prospects. It was to her that he attempted, repeatedly, to turn his thoughts as he wrestled with the latest problems exhibited by the ship's temperamental, state-of-the-art FTW drive. And yet, for some strange reason, the musings on his chaste and beloved Communicationalist were repeatedly diverted, supplanted by the same small cluster of sensations kindled by that morning's foray through the Recuperatorium: the casual brush of the bathing female's extended appendage against his furled and unsuspecting nethers, the smooth and graceful curves of her form, the delicious aroma of the chilled and scented bathing pool… the unbidden physical response to which he found himself brought. The colour rose to his cranial cowl, mauve upon lavender; his centre of gravity shifted appreciably; and he struggled to concentrate on the mechanics of the engineering problem *du jour*. Why did these thoughts writhe so persistently within him, entangling him in the heat of a dozen contrary emotions and impulses, pushing him so relentlessly to contemplate the unspeakable? Why did the smell of her

– the flavour, the taste of her touch, known to him so very briefly – yet catch within him, as something mysterious and unsuspected, something which clung to him and which would not let him be? Why did every effort to focus on the task at hand tend to slip moistly anew into the unsanctioned embrace of this female's apparent invitation to bathe, to cavort? Why did the exquisite embarrassment of that moment in the recuperatorium so urgently thrust itself, again, again, again, deep into his consciousness? Why must he cry out for release from this torment of the flesh, which pressed against him, it seemed, surrounding him from all sides, holding him firmly, insistently, unrepentedly within its warm, snug, vice-like grasp, until he felt that he must surely burst?

There was, Flarb[click]oorglfluenz'blith conceded – his reserves of willpower and self-restraint utterly spent – only one honourable course of action open to him. He must take matters into his own arm-tips, and he must resolve to never again use the Recuperatorium as a shortcut between Nav and Engineering. Only through such a process might he be able to gaze, honourably and with no blemish to his character, on his esteemed Communicationalist on those occasions when they passed each other in the vessel's corridors, or chose to meet for a quiet and dignified repast in one of the public feeding ponds within the ship's bland Gustatorium. For four weeks, this strategy succeeded, with no ill-effects save the mysterious manifestation, on a couple of occasions, of overnight ink stains on the rude walls of his bedchamber. For four weeks, Flarb[click]oorglfluenz'blith's life returned to something resembling normality. For four weeks, he held the line.

And then—

He was late, there'd been a malfunction of the FTW drive, just at the point where its redeployment was required for braking. Time was crucial: he had to get to Engineering by the quickest route possible. And that quickest route lay, most assuredly, through the forbidden reaches of the Recuperatorium. Yes, he'd vowed never again to use that shortcut, mindful of the temptation to which he feared he might yet succumb. But *this* was an emergency. And provided that he made haste, and skirted along the colonade that led alongside the low benches, well away from the scented pools...

This time, all pretence at subtlety, at artifice, was cast aside. She was on him like a hot rush of need, barrelling him into the nearest pool, searching out his supple beak with her own. He responded despite himself, hungrily, ardently, scarce bothering to think through what was occurring... and now... now, she was teasing apart his tangled and impact-bruised tentacles until she found what she was seeking, pulling him firmly, drawing him towards her.

Drawing him *into* her. The realisation, at once delicious and forbidden, was like a shock of ice-cold water to his skin, and he found his body quickening despite his uncertainty, his late-remembered discipline, his sense of professional urgency. *I must be attending to the drive*, he told himself in desperate confusion, unsure of whether anyone was listening. For now she was tracing, with the grasped, still-pliant tip of his quivering and thickening mating tendril, the rim of her procreative fissure; now she was pressing herself most provocatively against him; and now – Oh! – he could feel his tendril start to push, seemingly of its own prehensile accord, into her most intimate and warmly cloistered spaces. Nerves he had not known he possessed suddenly announced their existence, afire, as the dimpled skin of his stiffening tendril pushed against her intoxicating heat, probing the nexus of limbs which surrounded her tight fundamental concavity, pressing hungrily inward and discovering, in the process, details of her most private and personal architecture of which Flarb[click]oorglfluenz'blith had been, hitherto, entirely unsuspecting. Not knowing what to do with his own tentacles – for he was nervous of injuring her – he searched in vain for fastholds within the writhing thicket of her entangling limbs, and fell instead into stroking the sides of her cranial cowl. This, it seemed, met with some approval, for with several appendages she grasped him tighter, if that indeed were possible, and pulled him further in, until he genuinely did fear for her physical safety. It was evidently, however, a concern which she did not herself share. The noises she made, soft, incoherent sounds of abandon, fell into a rhythmic cadence that chimed in with her tentacles' undulating caresses, her edges pressed against his base, as all the while she thrust against his deep-embedded tendril with a greater and yet greater sense of urgency. He felt a mounting sense of pressure, of sweet compulsion, of a desire stronger than anything he had ever experienced, as she relaxed her grip, tightened, relaxed her grip, tightened. And all the while—

But this was *wrong*. His hearts were pledged to Another! And – and – *oh sweet twisted tendrils of desire how could so much wrong feel like this?* She pushed against him again, he into her; the movement paused, pivoted, began anew; with each surge seeming to bring him yet deeper into her; while something unsuspected built within him. *Oh, this was wrong. So wrong, so very unforgivable. So utterly, irresistibly incorrect. So categorically inappropriate. So deeply, incontrovertibly, fundamentally—*

He was almost too late, *wanted* more than anything to be too late, but in his hearts knew it to be unsanctionable: so he pulled free, his tendril hanging momentarily aimless, bereft, as in that instant he shot out from it a slender, concentrated gout of thick warm ink, which splashed stickily against her flank. He opened his beak, mortified, as though to say he knew not what, but was forestalled by her smile.

'Are you not at least going to inquire after my name?' she asked, flushed, panting sweetly, her eyestalks bobbing and her midriff pulsating as she methodically stroked away the gummy globs of ink with which he had so indelicately decorated her.

'What – uh, what is your name?' His cranial cowl felt incandescent, and must indeed be a thing shining, lambent, thoroughly empurpled: if it were possible for one of his species to die of embarrassment, then he right now was in mortal peril. It came to him belatedly that their tussles in the pool must have been witnessed by a dozen or more individuals, in the neighbouring pools and on the scattered benches that rimmed the Recuperatorium. He pressed himself against the far side of the bathing pool, endeavoured to make himself as small as possible, strove not to meet any of the myriad scandalised eyestalks he now felt focussed in his direction, and gathered his tentacles demurely around himself.

'I am called Glurp[snort]paflooxim'bobl,' she replied.

'That is a nice name. My name,' said Flarb[click]oorglfluenz'blith, 'is Flarb[click]oorglfluenz'blith. With a [click].'

'I know,' said Glurp[snort]paflooxim'bobl.

'I work in Engineering,' said Flarb[click]oorglfluenz'blith, coyly tucking his still-awkwardly-inflexible mating tendril in behind his front limbs, twice, and gingerly rearranging his posture.

'I know,' said Glurp[snort]paflooxim'bobl.

'On the Faster-Than-Waves Drive,' said Flarb[click]oorglfluenz'blith, in a voice he ardently hoped would not carry to the Recuperatorium's further reaches.

'I know,' said Glurp[snort]paflooxim'bobl, reaching out to touch him again with a tentacle. 'I hope that I will see you again. Soon. I feel a connection with you, Flarb[click]oorglfluenz'blith.'

She pronounced his name very well, with just the right emphasis on the [click]. Almost, he thought, as though she had been practicing it for months, if not years.

'I must go now,' said Flarb[click]oorglfluenz'blith.

'I know,' said Glurp[snort]paflooxim'bobl.

And he went.

At the door, he turned and flexed his eyestalks back, and thus he caught one more glimpse of her before he hurried off to Engineering. She was looking straight at him, still, and smiling.

Curiously, it was this momentary image – rather than the tangled heat of their passion; the unmistakeable wild, *alive* scent of her, quite unlike any other female he'd met; or the electrifying feel of her tentacles brushing against his flanks – which inked itself most indelibly into his memory of their encounter, and thus it was this glimpse, more than anything, that proved his downfall. For she was truly beautiful, beyond his ability to resist.

*

He lasted ten daycycles. Ten daycycles in which his efforts at taming the FTW drive were, more often than not, clumsy, ill-conceived, and counterproductive; ten daycycles in which he could not envisage the form or features of his betrothed Communicationalist without feeling as though he were boiling in shame; ten daycycles in which he marvelled at the quantity of ink he was apparently able to produce. The residual stickiness of every surface within his room was becoming increasingly problematic.

Ten daycycles he lasted; and then he slunk back to the Recuperatorium, where she was not. He looked about those arrayed upon the benches, or sequestered within the pools, hoping to convince himself that one or other of these individuals was the one he sought; but there were none here who had her grace of limb, her bulbousness of torso, her coquettishness of beak. He considered approaching and inquiring of an elderly female who, watching over the group of spawnlings currently placed in her charge, was splayed calisthenically across a meerschaum bench, but he kept his distance. Two things stopped him: one, that the bench-stretcher might well have witnessed (and therefore almost certainly disapproved of) the activities of ten days earlier, and two, that he could not remember whether his impromptu lover's name featured a [snort], or perhaps a [snuffle]. He oozed dispiritedly back into the corridor and returned to his squalid quarters, trying once again to remove the ink stains from the ceiling.

In this aspiration he largely failed, but at least he didn't add to them.

She wasn't at the Recuperatorium a few hours later either, when he returned. But six hours after that, she was.

'I must see you,' Flarb[click]oorglfluenz'blith ejaculated (in, on this occasion, a strictly verbal sense).

'You're seeing me now,' replied Glurp[snort]paflooxim'bobl, smiling and flexing an inviting tentacle along the scalloped rim of her bathing pool.

'I was meaning—' He did not know how to proceed. Did not know what to do, at this precise moment, with the suddenly-resurgent mental image of the Communicationalist.

'Yes?'

'Do you have… quarters?'

'You surely don't think I spend all my days here in the Recuperatorium?'

Actually, his supposition of recent weeks was not so far from this suggestion, but Flarb[click]oorglfluenz'blith gave a denial. He felt the colour rising along his cranial cowl, as the Communicationalist's image somehow became superimposed by a multi-sensorial memory picture of Glurp[snort]paflooxim'bobl's limber appendages sliding beguilingly betwixt and around his own. 'I think—'

'My face is up here,' said Glurp[snort]paflooxim'bobl.

Flarb[click]oorglfluenz'blith mumbled an apology, and she laughed.

'Yes,' she continued. 'I have quarters. Would you like to see my lodgings?'

'Yes,' said Flarb[click]oorglfluenz'blith, gingerly rearranging his posture. 'Yes, I would like that.'

Her quarters were on the third deck, near the ship's beak, and thus an altogether more salubrious reach of the vessel than his own cramped berth, which was midway along the malodorous and unprepossessing corridors adjacent to the main Defecatorium. Though he supposed he would ultimately need to show her where he spent his nightcycles, he was in no hurry to do so just yet.

'There is something that I must tell you,' said Glurp[snort]paflooxim'bobl, as she watched him finish squeezing his way through the narrow aperture in her doorway. Her room was spacious, impressively so by ship's standards, but very sparsely furnished, with but a single bench at one end and a double-depth, kidney-shaped sleeping-pool at the other.

'What?' he asked.

'First, I need to know if you are attracted to me.'

'I am most definitely attracted to you,' Flarb[click]oorglfluenz'blith replied, surprised both by the evident truth of this statement and by the suddenly-thunderous activity of his hearts. 'What must you tell me?'

'I know that you are attracted to me. You showed me that yourself, last week, in the pool. But what I mean is... are you *attracted* to me?'

'I am not sure what you mean,' said Flarb[click]oorglfluenz'blith. 'But I have not been able to stop thinking of you. And I do not think... that I *want* to stop thinking of you, even if it were in my power to do so. Which, as I've just said, it assuredly is not. Please, what must you tell me?'

'Do you know that I am attracted to you, Flarb[click]oorglfluenz'blith?'

'Yes,' he said. 'Yes, I think I know this. I mean, I did not know this, but I hoped – I mean, I do not understand it, but when you say this, it makes me happier, more nervous, than I believe I have ever been. But, please, what?'

'Flarb[click]oorglfluenz'blith, I am fertile.'

He slumped to the left in surprise, and pulled himself with difficulty back into something resembling uprightness. 'But I... do you... have we... does this mean—'

'No,' she answered. 'I am not with spawnlings. But I would wish to be. It is time. And I would wish you the father, if you would agree to it.'

This time he folded precariously to the right. *Curse my kind's lack of an endoskeleton!* he thought, as he fastened onto the lip of her portal to pull himself up again. At last he said, 'I had not known that there were any fertile females left on the voyage.'

'I am, I believe, the last,' said Glurp[snort]paflooxim'bobl. 'And with only a few months remaining until we arrive at the colony planet, the time is as ripe as it will get.'

'Why me?' he asked.

'Because you are firm of tentacle, and clear of eye. Because your health is good. Because your cranial cowl is appealingly shaped, and attractively coloured, and I would wish my offspring to carry such a feature. Because you are diligent, and diffident, and motivated to do what is best for squidkind. Because I believe that you will be a good father to the spawnlings I wish to carry, you will provide well for them, and will pass on to them your gifts. And because I like you, Flarb[click]oorglfluenz'blith.'

'I like you too,' he replied, stalling for the time in which to think. 'Very much.'

His mating tendril, it appeared, had already begun its own independent process of thought on the subject. He rearranged his limbs in awkward embarrassment.

'I know this is a lot to ask of you,' she said.

'I – the – I had not, er, ever considered myself as father material. And the responsibility of providing for spawnlings, of ensuring that they receive the nourishment they require while you are confined to the – I mean – oh. The double depth. Is that a *spawning pool*?'

'Of course. I am fertile,' Glurp[snort]paflooxim'bobl reiterated. 'Flarb[click]oorglfluenz'blith, I can see that you are anxious about this.'

'More than anxious.'

'You wish not to spawn with me?'

'No. I mean no not, not no no. I mean,' he said, shifting his limbs once more in front of him, 'I am very strongly attracted to you. It is just that… this is not a choice I believed would ever be presented to me. This… is remarkably sudden.'

'Is it a choice you would regret?'

'No,' said Flarb[click]oorglfluenz'blith.

'There is, of course, your work in Engineering.'

'There are others in Engineering. Someone else will pick up for me. I mean, you know, squid pro quo.'

'So do you wish to do it?'

'Now?' asked Flarb[click]oorglfluenz'blith.

'Now,' said Glurp[snort]paflooxim'bobl, tenderly reaching out a tentacle to his cranial cowl.

*

They had started slowly, with strokings and nuzzlings, before moving on to the gentle suckeration of each other's midriffs. They kissed, he holding his torso awkwardly bent so as to avoid pressing on her flank with his now-fully-extruded mating tendril. Her breathing had become fast and shallow, and she pushed against him sinuously, all the while dragging herself purposefully towards the spawning pool. 'I crave you,' she whispered, during a moment when their beaks were free. 'I want you in me.'

'Yes,' he said. 'Yes, me, too. I mean—'

'Hush.' She draped a pair of limbs around his cranial cowl and pulled him closer. The scent of her, the feel of her against him was intoxicating. He was all a-tremble. But perhaps this was alright? Because she, too, was shaking, even while she traced slowly all around the rim of his cloaca with the tip of her limb. He squirmed, unnerved and delighted both at the response her touch provoked within him, and ran an exploratory feeler of his own into the gap between her tentacles. She pulsed against him, fastening her grip, pulling him closer still. His mating tendril found its way between the forest of her writhing limbs, rubbed against her fissure: she gasped, her eyestalks lengthened, and he could feel her quiver against his tendril. She pushed her beak urgently against his, and then pushed him sufficiently from her that they could make eye contact, all the while holding each other by the tips of two tentacles.

'Are you sure that you are ready for this?' she asked.

'Yes,' said Flarb[click]oorglfluenz'blith. 'Yes, I am ready.' He pulled her towards him, in what he hoped was a broadly masculine kind of gesture.

She pulled back, and they tumbled together into the warm depths of the spawning pool. Then she was on him with such rapidity that he barely had time to move his tentacles aside as, her own limbs spreadeagled and reaching forward around him, she drew him to her. The rigid tip of his tendril pressed with sudden sharp pain against the flesh of her underside, she wriggled against him, and then he was sliding in. His cloaca was already clenching in glorious anticipation, but he was determined to prolong this for as long as possible. He strove to hold back.

She evidently had other ideas. Was gripping him fast, tensing rhythmically against his flanks with her enfolding tentacles. The action pressed him repeatedly against her fissure, so that with only a few strokes his tendril was completely embedded in her slippery warmth. Instinct took over completely, and he matched the grasp of her envelopment with his own pulsations. The pace of their coupling raced faster, and he could feel the first hint of climax start to build within him.

She felt it too, and pressed him to herself yet more vigorously. Her fissure, its inward depths still tightening against his pistoning tendril, now relaxed around its outer rim, and on successive strokes he found that one, then several, and then all of his shoulders were encircled by the lips of her procreative opening. His shoulders popped free one last time, before her strong tentacles propelled him further in, up to the beak.

The taste of her, the feel of her intimacy pressed against and sliding past his beak... there were not the words to describe this. He timed his breathing for those moments when his beak was free of her, quick, shallow, quick, shallow; and then she pressed more decisively against him, around him, and he was in up to the eyestalks, only his cranial cowl and a few tentacle tips still protruding. The reverberating noises of her ardour, and his, dulled but did not completely negate the feelings of alarm which now flared within him. He struggled, a part of him aware that it was now too late for struggle. His hearts thudded chaotically, his panic rising as he strove to breathe but, so tightly held, could not. And all the while, excitement rose within him... within her, as she quivered and stretched herself around him.

He could not hold off the wave that was building within him, waiting to crest. Seconds before the climax, he stopped his struggles, gathered in his tentacles, retracted his eyestalks, and allowed Glurp[snort]paflooxim'bobl to push him completely within her astonishingly-distended torso. As her fissure closed tight behind him, all around him, as her own pulsations built to a hot and remarkable crescendo, he shot his load of ink deep within her.

It was done.

It was done, and Flarb[click]oorglfluenz'blith could not breathe. He strove, with every fibre of his being, to inhale, but with his whole torso pressed tight against her searing encasement, there was no opportunity. He felt the impulse to thresh, to squirm, but Glurp[snort]paflooxim'bobl's enfolding grip on his tentacles was vice-like in its intensity, and her strength was astounding. He could not even shift his painfully-flattened eyestalks from her relentless, all-encompassing embrace. The flame of agitation within him flared into panic; kindled into outright fear; guttered into dread; then ebbed. He felt himself sink into oblivion, held fast by his conquest's constricting, hot, still-throbbing womb.

His last thought, the last mental picture he was gifted to glimpse, was of the face of the Communicationalist.

Glurp[snort]paflooxim'bobl had timed it well. The horde of spawnlings fed, for five months, on the collection of nutrients which had once been Flarb[click]oorglfluenz'blith. Then, hungry for more, they ate their way through the enveloping carcass of their mother, rested awhile in the spawning pool, and slithered their way through the aperture into the corridor, where the air was fresh with the scent of the new planet.

They moved with purpose and with vigour; and they did, indeed, sport their father's cranial cowl.

The Thirty-First Element

The universe is vast; the multiverse incomparably more so. Yet not all things are possible...

We sped towards a gallium dawn. Far beneath our cramped and noisy shuttle, gallium clouds scudded across a grey gallium sky; gallium waves broke lazily against a softening, slumping gallium shore; a gentle gallium rain fell. The rising sun blazed down upon a dull-sheened sea of molten, dappled gallium.

It was a burnished, blue-grey world, a world of simple beauty. A classic, of a sort; some would doubtless consider it so. And yet... for all its stark, minimalist elegance, this world unsettled me profoundly. *A person could grow mad, to look on such an unwavering vista. Change, but no variation. The rising sun melts, the gathering night freezes anew: how often, across a year, across an aeon, must such a cycle reassert itself, to no net effect?*

I pulled myself from reverie: we had a mission. 'Any local variation in the surface composition?' The question was redundant; I could read a data matrix – especially one so simple, so monochromatic – as well as the next crewmember. And yet the chain of command operates through the voicing of instruction, the open and declared passage of information. I need not ask, except my crew require it of me.

Kumiko, grey-haired, mildly plump, turned around from her flickering consoles. The movement sent her dreads rippling, a clumpy, felted halo framing her face. 'No change, Commander.' Her good eye twitched. She gave the spectrometer relay housing a disconcerting thump, swore, peered once more at the readouts. 'Gallium. No other constituents above detection limits.' She sounded disappointed.

'Atmosphere?'

'Gallium,' she repeated, with the same dull dissatisfaction threaded through a voice that, normally, trilled with melody. 'No other constituents.' She unbuckled, drifted from her seat. 'The planet's just one big orb of it.'

'It should be face-locked,' Abelard protested, a frown stamped across his slender scarred face, his wiry frame clinging to the scaffolding that buttressed the shuttle's nominal ceiling. 'At this distance from its primary—'

'Really?' answered Kumiko, some animation entering her tone by virtue, I presumed, of her longstanding variance with the junior officer's attitudes, or with, perhaps, his entire demeanour. She had drifted across to the starboard viewport, as though her eyes, imprisoned behind that pitted pane, could answer the questions her banks of aging instruments could not. 'A world, according to our measurements, of purest gallium, a thing impossible, and *that's* your main objection? Not the globe itself?'

'I leave the geochemistry,' Abelard sniffed, crab-crawling his way forward along the scaffolding a metre above me, 'to those unable to cope with the subtleties of orbital mechanics.' Of the three of us, he seemed substantially the least concerned at the rolling conundrum beneath our shuttle. But then, he'd always been more difficult to read.

'It's wrong,' said Kumiko. 'The whole planet, wrong. The primary's a perfectly ordinary K4, the system's strewn with lumpen planetesimals of rock and metal and ice. Even if there was a way for such a planet to fashion itself naturally from the proto-system's wrack, and there *isn't*, there have to have been impacts, infall, the solar wind... knocks, incursions, contamination. Aeons of it. And yet it's gallium, the very chocolate of metals, nothing more. Not even a part-per-billion. It makes no sense.'

'Then it's not natural,' said Abelard, spreading his arms in a shrug before casually grabbing a handhold to arrest his drift. 'It's a manufactured planet.' He spoke with the unalloyed conviction of the young and the ambitious, and with a trace of condescension, and I could see, in that moment, the grounds for Kumiko's disapproval of him.

'But it's *pure*,' Kumiko maintained. 'So pure it would need to have been fabricated in just the last week, otherwise there'd be traces.' She stared at Abelard, challenging him. 'As you can plainly see, the system's too dusty.'

'Continue scanning,' I decided. They were a good crew, whatever their foibles; I didn't want them coming to blows. 'We do this thoroughly enough to satisfy the sponsors; I'll not have anyone allege our survey was incomplete.'

'There's complete,' observed Abelard, 'and then there's monotonous.'

'A thing can be monotonous, and yet retain mystery,' Kumiko argued.

'Even so. I have the sense this mystery will not be solved through instrumental observation, and I see no value in attempting a ground mission for which we're not properly equipped. A full equatorial scan will surely suffice. Abelard, how long until we can next break orbit for rendezvous with *Persephone*?'

'Five minutes, twenty-seven seconds after local noon, Commander.'

'We will have then completed one full orbit?'

'Approximately one and a half, Commander.'

That, I judged, would be ample. A world of gallium, and that alone, quickly palled as an object of survey interest. That is to say, while the gallium itself was of interest, the lack of variation did not provoke extended study. 'And local noon, which would be... when?'

'Fifteen minutes, forty-three seconds,' he replied. 'At current orbital velocity, the rendezvous window will remain open for ninety-two seconds.'

'Right. Prepare to break orbit during that window. Lowest-cost direct trajectory.'

'Locked in, Commander,' said Abelard.

'Good,' I replied. 'I don't think there's anything further we can usefully learn from this one.'

'I'd recommend we complete another full orbit, Commander,' said Kumiko. 'It surely makes little difference in fuel demand. And I'm curious to see what happens to that volcano we viewed on the night side, once it passes the terminator.'

I recollected that nightside volcano, its steep ridged gallium slopes aflow with—what else?—languid trails of gallium lava. Its sighting had marked, perhaps, the onset of the ramping dread this world had sparked within me. For reasons with which I wasn't fully conversant, I wanted shot of this place. Besides, I wasn't convinced another revolution aboard our shuttle would suffice to push the vulcano onto the dayside: that would more likely require two more orbits, or even three, and I wasn't prepared to countenance such an extension to the mission. 'We can leave a probe in orbit, Kumiko,' I replied.

'I will ready it,' she replied. It was clear she was not happy.

Persephone: a pretentious name, a name to conjure wonder, to pluck at the heartstrings of corporate ambition. They are always such names, picked by the sort of people who believe a nod to classical mythology can lend grandeur to any enterprise. Ill-judged for what was, at best, a run-down intersystem mining scow. If the name had ever fitted, those days were as long past as *Persephone*'s best, and the days when she had carried more than one functional shuttle.

We'd long needed a major find, a success. This world of gallium might well be it. My share of the bounty could buy me my own command, a crew of my own, and not just this occasional stewardship of a ramshackle shuttle; or perhaps even retirement. I'd waited long enough for either, amidst years of time and years of light.

'Local noon, Commander,' Abelard reported, in between noisy gulps at a juice-bulb. Stationed at his seat for once. 'Five minutes, twenty seconds until primary burn.'

'Kumiko?' I asked.

'Still scanning, Commander,' she replied, not bothering to keep a disgruntled edge from her voice. 'Atmospheric... oceanic... to the instruments' detection limits, and to the depths we can probe through radar soundings, it's all just gallium.'

'Can we be sure of the mantle and core composition?'

'Clearly not. However, the planet's mean density is consistent with a body at least 95% pure elemental gallium, and there is literally no trace of anything else. There are additional analyses we could perform, were we to land...'

'We will not be landing,' I replied, striving for as much authority, or poise, as my voice could carry; which was not, in that moment, as much as I would have liked. 'We can leave that aspect of the survey to Consolidated. There's enough here, surely, to call them in on this.'

If Kumiko was downcast by this – and I had to expect she would be, she lived for planetfall – she shielded it well enough.

Abelard commenced counting down the seconds until the deorbiting manoeuvre.

'Commander, the probe,' Kumiko prompted. 'It is ready.'

'Release.'

She manipulated the controls at her console, frowned, then rose and floated to the viewport once more. 'Commander, it has not released.'

'Abelard?' I asked.

He bent over his control board, tapped at keys, swiped at touchpads. 'Eighty-nine ... eighty-eight ...Commander, it won't deploy. The hold hatch does not open. Eighty-one, eight-zero, seventy-nine ...'

'Try again.'

He tapped and swatted some more, muttering to himself as he did so. 'Deployment still negative. Main engine ignition in fifty... forty-nine... forty-eight...'

'Kumiko, secure yourself at your station.'

She made no movement, except to bend slightly at the viewport. Watching something.

(...thirty-five... thirty-four...)

'Kumiko, your station.'

She was still peering intently at something, either towards the shuttle's underside or down on the planet beneath us.

(...twenty-three... twenty-two...)

'Kumiko!' I cried, in the disciplinary voice. And disliked myself for using it. But boost would be abrupt, could knock unsecured objects – or personnel – into important or vulnerable control surfaces. She needed to be strapped in, like Abelard and myself.

'No, wait,' Kumiko responded, with unbridled animation. 'Please, Commander. There's a *boat*!'

(...thirteen... twelve...)

'You're sure?' I asked.

(...nine... eight...)

'See for yourself,' she said. 'Commander, we *have* to investigate. If the probe won't launch—'

(...three... two...)

'Belay ignition,' I said, unlatching myself from the safety restraint. There had been recognisable sincerity in Kumiko's voice, and I had never known her to display any symptoms of insubordination. (Of Abelard, in truth, I would have had more doubt.) But a *boat*? On that near-featureless gallium ocean? If this was merely a ruse...

I drifted across to the viewport beside Kumiko. She'd called up the port's maximum magnification, or close to it: the image was eye-wateringly juddery, the aspect changing appreciably as our shuttle's orbit pulled us around the planet's girth... but she was correct, or else my eyes deceived me also. It was, indeed, a boat, or more properly a ship: a streamlined hull, a blocky superstructure, a line of what appeared to be funnels with what looked to be smoke issuing from them, and all of it sculpted, it seemed, from the same dull-shiny stuff as the sea across which it made passage. 'Is it—?'

'Gallium,' she replied, consulting some overlay visible only to herself. She shook her head, causing her felted dreads to oscillate in turn. 'Nothing else.'

Abelard had joined us. 'Are those... *people* on the deck?'

'Commander, we have to go lower,' Kumiko urged. 'Another circuit, at least, before we break orbit.'

I felt outmanoeuvred. By Kumiko, by circumstance, by this impossible boat. But she was right: this merited closer investigation. I gave my assent.

Though all the while I felt a deep unease. How could what we had just seen – a gallium ship, plying a gallium sea, propelled, we had to presume, by gallium engines emitting gallium smoke, and crewed by beings that Abelard averred might well be shaped, alike, from gallium – how could this even admit of possibility? It couldn't.

And yet it was.

We commenced our descent.

We saw no other vessels upon that broad metal-sheened sea, though we grew steadily closer to the surface as the shuttle's shadow lengthened and sped before us, marking our progress against the expansive ocean and the gathering gallium clouds of dusk. Shortly before we lost the light of the system's sun, we espied the approaching shoreline, ragged, encroaching on the ocean's edge as the aging day's heat was shed. Breakers of gallium slopped themselves ashore, congealing from the effort.

What shoals, what reefs must lie beneath that surface? I mused. *And creatures, feeding on each other?* It was a strange thought; I wondered at its origins. And at the illogicality; for surely any living entity of gallium could as easily consume the stuff of the liquid surrounding it as any swift-swimming prey. But we were past the sea now, still clipping at orbital velocity above the puckered, newly-solidified gallium plain beneath us, as night enveloped our shuttle.

We were too high, still, for our lights to usefully illuminate the terrain ahead and below, but on our earlier nightside pass Abelard had configured the vessel's radar array to interrogate the way ahead. The main viewscreen showed a fast-unfolding, grainy, mesmerising scene of ceaseless activity. For there were people moving far below, directing vehicles, excavating quarries, rapidly shifting monumental quantities of material to one or another chosen locus on the sprawling expanse, away from the occasional upwellings and upthrust faultlines, and there establishing buildings, outposts, towns... all, we had to assume, of gallium. The first settlement we saw was crude, its fashioning barely commenced, a few tightly-clustered and apparently featureless buildings around a small central square; then it was behind us, and gone. The next was a proper burg, taller central buildings, parks, suburbs, crowds of bustling gallium people; then it, too, had slipped from view. The third city we saw, still in Abelard's ghostly radar-vision, had skyscrapers, freeways, factories, a teeming population... and must have arisen from the bare gallium earth in just hours, from stuff which would previously have been sunlit ocean.

Such industry, such incredible efficiency, such manifest purposiveness... such desperation. This, the rapidity with which these gallium people built their futile settlements, was the most saddening thing I witnessed on our flight. For surely they knew, as well as I, what lay scant hours ahead, around the world's curve.

The killing sun.

We flew further across deep night, over gallium farmlands and highways and metropolises, and sometime after what would have been, directly below us, midnight, we saw something new. They were building aeroplanes. How feverishly they must have laboured, knowing the cost...

'That's incredible,' said Kumiko, with open admiration. 'The scale and speed of their productivity, I mean.'

'It's just some trick of self-assembly,' said Abelard. Dismissive. 'It's not life.'

'But yet it is,' Kumiko replied.

'They're gallium. And gallium is not alive.'

'Life is the conditional response to stimulus,' said Kumiko, 'not what it is *made from*. These are alive. They have to be.'

I did not buy into their dispute – did not, indeed, know to which side I fell on it. They looked, as Kumiko noted, alive; and yet they were, as Abelard reminded us, gallium. The two could not coexist; and yet they did. Nothing about the scenario, neither its elemental generality nor its inhabited particulars, warmed me, heartened me, did anything besides wake within me a welling sense of dread.

'Why do they persist near the equator?' Kumiko asked. 'Higher latitudes would be less subject to melting; the distance to safety would be shorter.'

'Higher latitudes would be colder, at nighttime too,' observed Abelard.

'They are not, by much,' said Kumiko. 'Three, four degrees difference, according to my instruments.'

'Perhaps,' I offered, 'such a slender difference is still enough to matter. Perhaps their movement requires the residual warmth of the equatorial band. Life's needs are often narrow and particular.'

'The Commander agrees that they are alive,' declared Kumiko, more loudly than was entirely needed.

'I agree that these... entities beneath us, they have the *semblance* of life,' I clarified, feeling somehow as though I was betraying both my subordinates. 'But as to whether they have life itself... I leave that to the philosophers. Our task here is just to observe, to measure.'

And this we did. Silence returned among us – or what passed for silence on an aging shuttle with several complaining components – but it was not a companionable silence.

The first planes took off, far beneath us – we were still well above the rind of the planet's gallium atmosphere – and sped toward the line of dusk, now ground-hours behind us. This activity burgeoned over the coming minutes, with more flights lofting from each settlement we spied in our hurtle around the world, until finally, as dawn approached again, we were travelling over cities that must have been scant hours old, and that lay already deserted. Or almost so: people shuffled still along those gallium streets, or clustered around tall trees within those gallium parks, but there was no sense in their movements, anymore, of industry, of purpose. Did they glance in fear towards the sky?

Dawn was like a bomb of light before us.

We switched to visual. Shortly after daybreak, we approached one final city, established on the heights of what had become a steadily-dwindling island, the upper surfaces of its towers already softening and slumping as we neared. Shaded by those structures, a few figures scurried frantically towards a gallium plane that waited for them on featureless tarmac near the sea's encroaching edge. We saw the plane accelerate; we saw it climb; we saw it reach the bright sunlit air; we saw it turn towards the nightside; we saw it start to melt. Then we were too far past it. We did not see its fate.

I had seen enough, and was impatient to climb away from this dispiriting world.

It began with the clouded viewports. Abelard replaced the optical feed with the radar by which our nightside transit had been informed. But now the radar imagery, too, was gauzed, indistinct. 'Is there some form of interference?' I asked.

'It does not appear so, Commander,' he responded. 'So far as I can establish, we have suffered a decline in the quality of the signal. But as to the reasons—'

It was not like Abelard to leave any sentence unfinished.

The viewports by degrees went dull; translucent; dark. The radar imagery degraded unhurriedly into haze. *This is useless*, I thought. 'Atmospheric accretion?' I asked.

'Commander, it cannot be,' replied Kumiko. 'We're all of two-fifty kilometres' altitude still; the scale height's barely two kilometres. It's still as good as interplanetary vacuum out there.'

'I'm less concerned about the cause than about how we return to the *Persephone*. Kumiko, signal her and apprise her of our predicament. We'll require a clear homing beacon for safe docking; we cannot simply rendezvous blind.'

'Transmitting... transmitting...' Then Kumiko swore, and thumped her console. Swore again. 'Commander, I have no confidence that the transmission was successful. The display is inconsistent. And I cannot now detect the *Persephone.*'

'Boost the sensitivity,' Abelard instructed, curtly, and pushed across to Kumiko's station. He bent over her console, making adjustments. Komiko did not present her habitual complaint at his intrusion.

Long seconds passed before Abelard spoke.

'Commander, I have the *Persephone.* But she is faint, scarcely showing now above the noise. We can transmit – at least, I have made the attempt – but I hold no hope of detecting any response. Nor, therefore, of knowing whether our transmission has reached them. But we have a more serious problem also.'

'Which is...?'

'We have the *Persephone*, and the sun, and the planet beneath us. But the sun and the *Persephone* are not where our trajectory should place them. Commander, we are losing orbital velocity. And, therefore, altitude.'

A chill congealed along my spine. 'How can that be,' I asked, 'if we are still above the atmosphere? What kind of drag could we be subject to?'

'None, Commander. But the locations of the sun and the *Persephone* are, for now, clear enough. We have most definitely slowed. Unless we boost, we will inexorably re-enter.'

'Then boost,' I instructed, striving to control my voice.

Re-entry was not something I wished to contemplate. To end my days as a smear of foreign substance across this world—

The main drive wouldn't respond.

'It's probably the wiring,' said Abelard.

'It's more likely the oxidant valve,' said Kumiko.

It could be anything, I thought.

We wasted precious time while Abelard interrogated the shuttle's power train, while Kumiko diagnosed the engines' fuel lines. Nothing showed as problematic in these cross-checks, while – if the failing instruments could be believed – we slipped below two hundred kilometres. Abelard suited up to perform a visual inspection – a risky undertaking, while the planet slid ever closer beneath us, but necessary if we were to determine what was happening to the shuttle. He sealed himself within the cramped airlock; we heard the drone as the outer lock slid open. Then we waited, all the while fruitlessly perusing every screen and every data matrix; hoping to hear something over ship's comms. It grew darker still, then there was a thump on the hull, in the vicinity, I thought, of the airlock.

'He can't open it,' Kumiko said.

I diverted power to the outer lock controller—the lighting around us grew yet dimmer, the air circulation stuttered—and with a disconcerting scrape the outer lock slid reluctantly agape. Abelard entered the airlock, must have manhandled the outer lock closed somehow, opened the inner lock. Stood within the airlock facing us.

From helmeted head to booted feet, Abelard's suit was a dull-shiny bluish grey.

Kumiko raised her hand to her mouth.

Abelard raised his glove to his neck-flange.

'Abelard, *no*,' I replied, my voice cracking. I could not tell if he could hear me, but at least he stopped. Waited within the airlock.

'We need a thermal gradient,' I told Kumiko. 'In the airlock.'

'I can do that,' she replied, and bent to her boards. 'Assuming the airlock panels respond.'

Several seconds passed. Abelard's suit, its visor as greyly opaque as the rest of it, waited with what might be patience, might be simple vacancy. Then the airlock's walls began to glow softly, and the skin of Abelard's spacesuit began to shine as liquid highlights bloomed across its edges and faces. Patches of mirror-smooth shimmer spread, and merged, and began to run. It trickled down his faceplate, his torso, his limbs, the blue-grey matter of the suit's gallium crust puddling and congealing upon the airlock's unheated floor.

What I would do if Abelard's suit, if Abelard himself, melted entirely, I did not know.

Fortunately, that did not transpire. The gallium plating, or incursion, had not progressed so deep within the suit's fabric as to permeate it: Abelard, a creature of organised carbon-rich aggregations within cellularised water, still persisted within the suit's lining. We got him out and left the wreckage of the suit sealed within the airlock.

There was a strange taint in the air. Sharp, hot, thin, cloying.

'Report,' I said, breathing roughly.

'The ship...' said Abelard. He too seemed to be having difficulty breathing. '...is transmuting. It's not possible. But... what's happening.' He took another breath, rasping, slow. 'All I can think... we've crossed... some kind of threshold. A field... a distortion... of the universal conditions. This planet—' He coughed, a terrible sound. Behind him, the grimy white panelling of the airlock hatch was quietly shading to an undifferentiated grey.

Like Midas, I thought, and my skin chilled at the concept.

'Take us up,' I said, not sure if my command was directed at Kumiko, or at Abelard, or perhaps even at myself. 'In Space's name, take us *up*! Get us clear!'

Though by then, I think, I already knew such attempts were much too late. We would soon feel the onset of re-entry, the whining, shrieking bump and slur of it.

We greyed.

Kumiko and Abelard bled together, each of them melting from simply standing too close to another warm body. I turned away; kept my distance; tried not to look at my greying extremities; strove to ignore my softening vertebrae. Pressed tightly shut my gallium eyelids.

Could not ignore the taste of my mouth.

I braced for impact, for dissolution, for at least the loss of consciousness—

*

Was there another vessel? I think perhaps there was; I half-remember. It flew, so then a plane; yet in my mind a ship. It cannot have been both; perhaps it was neither. It makes no sense.

It cannot matter, for it is gone. There is only what there is.

Were there others, aboard this half-imagined plane/ship? Perhaps there were. This, too, I half-remember; two or three, I think. Where did they go?

Perhaps they are around me; or among me; or never were. Such thoughts lead nowhere.

But there is this. There I am. Here I am.

And I must move, to catch this flight.

My body can sustain me indefinitely, so long as I keep out of the light. But the night grows pale.

I think gallium thoughts now, for what other thoughts are there?

Against the Flow

'It looks a little cold,' said Harry, and then he went full nova. Harry had had a bad run lately anyway, what with him being a victim-bot, and past his abuse-by date. Still, it was quite something to see, provided you weren't within the shock front.

Bettina and the Captain were. It pushed the Captain into the waterway. He landed in the Stable Two position, and was carried swiftly downstream, complaining all the while about the water running into his airlock. There was nothing any of us could do, or maybe we'd just forgotten how.

'I always thought Harry was more of a main-sequence kinda guy,' said Bettina. It's true, she had always thought that. At least she'd always said it, which made you wonder how she'd got into the survey team in the first place. It might have helped her career if once in a while she'd said something different, but I guess even a stopped clock knows a thing or two. Then the shock front got to her too, she turned ninety degrees on some transcendental axis, and Bettina was as gone as the Captain and Harry.

There were three of us left – myself, Doctor Hinkelspritzengrüber, and some fellow in a red tunic that nobody knew the name of.

'We should do something,' said the Doctor, using her stethoscope as a megaphone. 'Anyone got any ideas?'

'Bridge is a four-handed game,' I suggested.

'Ain't no bridge here,' reported Red Tunic. Which wasn't actually his name, on account of we didn't know what it was, but we could see what he wore.

We looked at the other side, but it probably wasn't getting any closer, unless it was. It was careless what had happened to the Captain, so I stepped back from the riverbank. I wondered why we hadn't seen any aliens, and then I remembered Doctor Hinkelspritzengrübenhauser was one. Or had met one, or had said something about one at some point. It was so hard to tell, it could scratch diamond, and that's what she did right at that point. It seemed a waste, particularly since I hadn't even realised the diamond was there.

'I don't think you should do that,' said Red Tunic.

'I think you mean,' said Doctor Hinkelspritzengrübenhausenfurter, whose name was getting longer each time she spoke, 'that you don't think I should *have done* that. There's a difference.' And to prove this, she scratched the diamond again. 'See?' We did, but I don't believe she did, because she started resublimating.

I didn't know what we should do with a twice-scratched diamond. I mean, if we took it back to the ship there'd be questions, and those always literally unnerve me. And there was clearly no help for Doctor Hinkelspritzengrübenhausenfurtenberger, she was crystallizing nicely, so me and Red Tunic – *remember, not his real name* – struck out upstream, just in time to see the Captain float past again. He looked happier now, though you could tell he'd never launch again, what with all those tadpoles in his engine room.

'We should be getting back,' said Red Tunic.

'We should,' I agreed. 'What did you say your name was?'

'I didn't,' he explained. The Captain floated past a third time. I think he was trying to tell us something, but his nosecone got in the way, and then he was gone.

'Do you think Harry will collapse into a black hole?' I asked, thinking we should get well clear just in case.

'I don't know,' said Red Tunic. 'I could never determine how massive he was. But isn't that the lander?'

He was right, it wasn't. But I knew we'd left it around here somewhere. Bettina would have known, but of course she would just have said her thing about the main sequence again, so that probably wouldn't have helped.

'Maybe we should head away from the water,' someone said. I thought it was Red Tunic, and he thought it was me, which made no sense, since my voice isn't usually that magnetic. But it seemed like a good idea, so that's what we did. After awhile things got more normal, and there was a signpost, which was blank, but still. Red Tunic told me his name was Walter; I asked him how that helped anyone, at which he burst into tears and said I didn't respect him. Which was unfair of him in the circumstances, and I almost said so, at which he almost argued back. But we agreed to let bygones be bygones, and not to quibble about how we'd suddenly acquired telepathy.

The lander was where we'd left it, which made perfect sense. I was glad something did. We climbed to the airlock, and Commander Flint met us in the cockpit. She looked as though she'd been doing her nails, which was good because *somebody* had to, and mine were bitten to the quick.

'We had some problems,' I explained. 'The other four, they didn't make it.'

'That's a shame,' she said. 'But they knew the risks. Quicksand, I imagine. You can never trust quicksand. You found the stream?'

I looked at Walter, and he looked at me. 'We found *a* stream,' I remarked. Walter shook his head in agreement.

'Yes, yes,' the Commander said impatiently. 'I can tell that from the mud on your boots. But was it *the* stream?'

I thought about the terrible things that had happened to the others, and maybe to me too while I wasn't looking. And I shot Walter a warning glance, which he seemed to catch. There were some things, I thought, better left undiscovered.

So I lied. 'No,' I told her, and that's what I put in the report too. 'No, it wasn't *the* stream.'

'Damn,' she replied. 'I was so sure *this* was going to be the one.' She turned in her seat and made preparations for launch. I wondered which planet in the big wide Galaxy she'd next think to survey, in our foolhardy quest for the mythical Stream of Consciousness.

Reverse-Phase Astrology as a Predictive Tool for Observational Astronomy

Introduction

The basis of the science of astrology is that the stellar and planetary positions in the night sky exert an influence upon the various fields of human endeavour, personal fate, and fortune. This phenomenon has been well-understood and widely accepted for centuries. To date, however, no effort has been devoted to the other self-evident aspect of the human/cosmic relationship: to whit, that the observation of occurrences in the lives of the persons around us must necessarily yield some information on the composition of the solar system, the local neighbourhood of star systems, and the Galaxy as a whole. In the present work, we discuss the results of a study with which we hope to redress the lack of any methodology for understanding the implications of human activity upon the field of positional astronomy. Such a technique should prove increasingly valuable in an era when heightened urban light pollution, the acquisition of progressively broader ranges of the electromagnetic spectrum by telecommunication agencies, and the diminishing availability of funding for astronomical observatories are conspiring to constrict the opportunities for astronomical investigation by more orthodox techniques.

Results and Discussion

To minimise statistical inaccuracies, there is a need to acquire data from a large number of subjects. We selected to restrict the present study's purview to observation of the events, personal trials and triumphs, and bank account balances of a group of individuals belonging to the star sign Virgo (Aug. 24 – Sept. 22). After placing newspaper advertisements, we identified 867 individuals willing to participate in the year-long program.

Some natural attrition of the sample group occurred before the conclusion of the study: seven individuals died, twenty-eight indicated that they no longer wished to participate, and three stated, rather puzzlingly, that they "no longer qualified" as Virgos. Those who did continue in the study were visited weekly by a research student, with whom they discussed recent events of note in their lives, and were required to fill out a (daily) fifteen-page questionnaire which (while preserving their confidentiality) delved deeply into the status of their personal, sexual, social, gastrointestinal, and financial lives. Data from these questionnaires were subsequently analysed by our consultant astrologer, Mme Zoltar, who (for the customary fee) agreed to interpret her findings. One result which clearly illustrates the reliability of forward-phase (i.e. conventional) astrology, is that during the course of the study 78% of participants indicated they had received recurrent visits from an intrusive and inquisitive stranger, an astonishing 92% felt they were recently much more "bogged down in paperwork" than had previously been the case, and 65% reported an erosion of their sense of privacy. The commonality of these experiences is surely not the result of blind chance. Mme Zoltar's professional opinion was that these experiences could only be accounted for by the existence of a second moon, a tenth planet, and several previously unobserved stars in the constellations of Leo and Hydra. Mme Zoltar's recommendations, for the locations of these astronomical objects, were plotted on a series of star charts photocopied from that veritable Kama Sutra of positional astronomy, Norton's Sky Atlas.

Detailed observations of the night sky, using these star charts and the Mount Palomar 200-inch reflector, revealed several stars which the authors did not personally recognise, all lying within 30° of Mme Zoltar's predicted locations. (Unfortunately, in our excitement, we neglected to record the position, magnitude, or colour of any of these stars).

While the present study's precision is less than desirable for research-level astronomical studies, we feel this is a promising "proof-of-concept" for the notion of reverse-phase astrology. We are endeavouring to acquire a modest two-year slice of observing time using the Hubble Space Telescope, with which we hope to track down Mme Zoltar's extra moon and planets, and our own misplaced stars.

DragonBlog

Day the Third: Beginning have doubts about this assignment. Half kingdom, all well & good; hand of daughter in marriage, yes alright maybe; but haven't actually *seen* hand, or any other portion, and kingdom bit down-in-dumps, charred & decrepit. Peasants smelly, grimy, rude. Am wondering if get choose which half kingdom (expect not, and fair bet half without castle), and if half inclusive peasants.

Road still well marked. Bloody horse went under too-low overhanging branch, new armour now prominent dent on left side. Hurts when turn suddenly. When stopped for lunch (streamside v. reminiscent of yesterday's spot), tried beating breastplate back into shape with rock, only managed make worse. Still, maybe gives impression actually having been combat before. If viewed dim light. By poorly-sighted person. From considerable distance.

Day the Fourth: Asked peasant directions. Think laughed behind hands at start but answered respectfully enough otherwise. Dragon basically ahead and to right, in distance, follow trail smoke, can't miss, best luck. Proceed, make good time. Almost have another overhanging-branch incident, but avoid last second.

Should armour showing rust after only four days? Market dealer assured get several years before tarnish developed. Am wondering, though, if better shelled out extra for fully-welded, tailored model, not just off-rack soldered OSFA. Still, only need for one encounter, touch wood. Don't see point all added expense just for one afternoon.

Day the Fifth: Finally, just curiosity, took sword out scabbard first time. Had not realised at time purchase "vorpal" means small, round-tipped, best suited pâté. Explains unusual scabbard shape, but suddenly even more unsure whole dragon business.

Decide make camp streamside lunch spot. Nice place, like where stopped two days ago. Hope this bit included half kingdom. If ever get that point. Otherwise, might request ashes scattered here. If anyone able retrieve them.

Spend evening trying find horse. (Must remember tether properly this time. Knot.)

Day the Sixth: Didn't sleep well again. Dreamed being chased by dragon, trying defend self with teaspoon. Awoke pools sweat throughout armour. Might see about sleeping out of suit tonight. Preparedness all very well, but there limits.

Try see about reshaping sword-tip, bashing with rocks. No bloody good. Least sword seems well-forged, sturdy. Made for many applications pâté, suppose. Maybe can try throw down dragon's throat, might choke. (Yeah, right. Maybe squadron flying pigs turn up, just when arrive dragon's lair, take out dragon for me.)

Might stay this spot another day, make sure well-rested. Need be in peak condition. (Horse, too. Must find horse again, remember tether properly this time. Double knot.) Dragon not going anywhere, after all, hoard to guard, plenty peasants pick off.

Might take up sketching, pass time, while getting peak condition. No point rushing things.

Day the Seventeenth: Sketching not going well, charcoal not my medium. Should probably move on. Smoke horizon looks darker today, maybe most recent peasant went down wrong way. Feeling bit guilty at delay.

Wonder can retrace steps market, see about purchase better sword. Check purse. Not an option. Really should get going again. After lunch. Difficulty getting armour on this afternoon, seems have shrunk.

Day the Eighteenth: Finally get horse untied. (Must remember tether properly next time. Slip knot.) Make good time, find nice streamside spot camp. Am feeling more positive than have for days, decide good be back on quest.

Dragons? Who's afraid dragons?

Day the Nineteenth: Find track leading off ring road. Terrain now looking rockier, singed. Feeling apprehensive again. Would stop, but nothing worth sketching here. Best keep going.

Day the Twentieth: BLOODY HELL! Am expected take out *that*?!!?? With glorified butter knife?!!?? Size those *teeth*!! Length those *claws*!!! Lucky could find rock hide behind.

Shame about horse. Still, can't have felt anything. Much.

Half kingdom nowhere near enough. Hand better be pretty bloody special.

Feeling slightest bit inadequate.

Day the Twenty-First: Have sighted lair, suppose dragon off marauding again. Now need develop plan attack.

Day the Twenty-Sixth: No bloody feasible plan attack possible. Like trying take on flying castle with spatula. Bloody futile. Suicidal. Delusional. Would retreat, but dragon knows here now, would pick off soon as crawled out hiding-spot. Getting tired earthworm and slug diet. Will just attack tomorrow, hope for best. No point putting off any longer.

Day the Twenty-Seventh: Will just attack tomorrow, hope for best. No point putting off any longer.

Day the Twenty-Eighth: Slept terribly, awoke nauseous. Not good idea vomit armour. Spend afternoon decontaminating as best could, but suspect still bit niffy. Can't helped.

Day the Twenty-Ninth: WOOOHOOO!!! HAVE SLAIN DRAGON!!! FEEL BLOODY AMAZING!!!

Happened like this. Dragon strafed hiding-spot on morning peasant run. Clambered out, unseen, after flown over, ran. Reached lair. Checked out hoard, not as fabulously wealthy as been led expect. Knew didn't have much time, looked new spot hide in. Nowhere decent. Looked also better weapon, sword fallen hero maybe? Didn't find, but did see quite striking gold coronet, encrusted many gems. Fits quite well. Admired self jewel-bordered mirror, rakish angle, could grow accustomed. Dragon returned while investigating large bejewelled pendant. Understandably pissed-off, to say least. Retreated corner and attempted bargain for life. Negotiations heated (shoulder still singed) but managed strike deal, take turns riddles. If answer wrong, dragon eats. If dragon not guess answer, dragon eats. Not mad keen, admittedly, but best manage circumstances.

Nearly tricked dragon: "What four legs, two wheels, flies", but heard before. Dragon's riddle tough, "Hero better served raw, or baked in armour?" Decide don't know answer, put cunning plan into effect. Pull sword from scabbard, rush headlong at fiery brute shouting "Now die, worm!" Dragon snorts derisively – think right word – and lifts paw ready strike. Then—

Don't bloody *believe*. Stranger just walks up, just now, as writing last bit down. First think peasant, but bit better dressed average peasant, washed recently. Don't know where appeared from. Minstrel, apparently, or so says. Supposed known far wide, but never heard of him. Anyway, offering three-quarters bigger kingdom across mountain range, option more attractive hand, if sign him exclusive rights dragon-slaying details, use in new ballad. Said need think about, give answer in week.

Day the Thirtieth: Where all come from? This morning, travelling merchant, trading for X Calibre swordsmiths, offering new sword, horse spare shoes, full set ox knives, all permission use likeness on tapestry, sword displayed prominently. Point out not actually *use* X Calibre sword slay dragon, but apparently doesn't matter. Said think about.

Another minstrel, this time already written ballad my exploits, gave quick run-through. Sound reverberated helmet horribly. Same story, exclusive rights. This offer smaller kingdom, three-storey castle, permanent materials, ocean view. Again, said think about.

Monk, wishes to record story, fully illuminated, as inspirational tract on parchment.

Tax collector, asked have close look hoard, make assessment.

Adventurer, wants me sign up three-dragon deal, all transport, victuals, generous provision made rain delay and difficulty finding dragons. Own armour a must.

Sculptor, asks permission carve likeness with foot resting on head slain dragon, plan place in centre local town square, between tavern and stocks.

Young damsel, claims princess, wants know if interested matrimony. (Thought princesses washed more often, must say.)

Three children, said playing ball here last month, kicked into lair, wonder if come in poke around to find. Also friend Eowulf or pieces thereof, if still recognisable.

Day the Thirty-First: Thinking about.

Day the Thirty-Second: Not sure which smells worse, decomposing dragon or horde hangers-on.

Day the Thirty-Third: Scales fallen from eyes (suspect design flaw with helmet). Call meeting with assembled parties, announce have made decision. Not interested selling exclusive rights to slaying story. Will reveal all details to all assembled. Rushed dragon, drew sword (actually, drew sword before rushed dragon, otherwise not here now), rolled at crucial moment, struck fatal blow into dragon's heart, dragon died, end story. Hand assuredly guided by fate, destiny, forces greater than ourselves, whatever. Very lucky still alive, obviously. Don't feel heroic, but honoured on hand for beast's demise. Humbled.

(In truth, some details omitted, don't wish disillusion all & sundry. Crucial moment tripped, not rolled; nearly broke bloody neck. Looked up in time see dragon pounce headlong, closed eyes, whimpered, took final breath. Final breath unexpectedly long time. Looked up again, dragon impaled rusty lance left sticking up from middle hoard. Remember earlier thinking someone hurt self on that. Dragon brought down not bravery or swordsmanship but own poor housekeeping. Lesson us all?)

Those assembled allowed in lair, five minutes' max, permitted carry out all can hold, as long take piece dragon meat. No returns, no refunds, no exchanges. No loitering, or show blade slew dragon, if get drift. Just want left peace after that. Can't bothered half kingdom, daughter's hand, all other nonsense. Ridiculous fuss.

Protests from throng, seem think some sort acclamation required. Seem want shower me with gifts. Unhappy this. Eventually concede small extent. Place request for:

New horse
Scrolls for sketching
Year's supply pâté

Day the Thirty-Fifth: Back on ring road. Camp nice streamside spot, lose new horse. (Must remember tether properly. Reef knot.) Realise forgot request something spread pâté on, but too late now. Spend afternoon looking good spot sketch, stumble huge plant in clearing. Thick trunk, colossal leaves, bright green. Looks like massive beanstalk.

Wonder what's at top?

Niche

It was a Friday night in summer. Warm, there'd been a nor-wester. I was doing the weekly drive from Christchurch to my parents' property, north of Oxford. The night's insects, moths mostly, impacted in their thousands on the windscreen of my old Nissan. It was like driving through winged snow.

It was new moon, the North Canterbury backroads were devoid of other traffic: my headlights had scant competition for the moths' attention. I was listening to the radio, some evolutionary biologist from Otago propounding his theories – pushing his new book, I suspected – on the implications which humanity's reworking of the planet held for the evolution of life. As an example, he trotted out the hoary example of the British moth that changed its colour, over many generations, from light to dark as pollution stained the treetrunks against which it took camouflage, and then back to a lighter coloration as pollution eased. (I didn't see much prospect of that sort of thing happening here. The carnage my lights were inflicting on the moth population, it was a wonder they survived long enough to breed. I was probably accounting, tonight, for my own body mass in moth carcasses.)

It did get me thinking. It's always struck me that Aotearoa, more than anywhere, is a land crying out for some kind of large carnivore, particularly since the occurrence of human settlement. The loss of the moa as a prey item must, surely, be more than compensated for, in biomass terms, by the presence of so many sheep and cattle. And people. I started to wonder what form such a predator would take, and how it could conceal its presence.

I slowed down for the one-lane bridge across the shingled river, and then the Nissan protested, struggling, as I attempted to reattain the speed limit. Really, I should get around to replacing it, it was a students' car, I could afford something newer.

The car continued sputtering. Could it be low on fuel? I've run out, once, carelessly, but that was in town. I didn't fancy breaking down out here, among the tall pine hedges, the paddocks, the dark and the silence. In any case, fuel wasn't the problem. It was half full, and there was only a quarter-hour to go. The radio academic wound up his little talk – and yes, he *did* mention he had a new book out – finishing with the statement that "anytime you introduce a new entity into an environment, ultimately a predator will arise, through selection pressure, to keep it in check. Nature abhors a vacuum, and this is as true in evolutionary biology as anywhere else".

This road was a vacuum, near enough. I hadn't seen any other vehicles for ten minutes. Just me and the moths.

The car coughed, twice, and died. Engine, headlights, the works. I stopped and sat, wondering what to do. I'm not mechanic enough that tinkering with the motor was likely to yield positive results, and I didn't know what could be wrong. Still, I'd better take a look under the bonnet.

I had unstrapped myself and was reaching for the door handle when I heard the noise. A strange, hollow, deeply persistent rustle, from nearby. My heartrate surged, and I looked around, trying to locate the source. Nothing visible within the car, and outside there was just enough starlight to show that I was parked beside a strip of gnarled and twisted macrocarpas. Damn that radio talk, it had me far too jumpy.

The rustling continued. Get a grip, I told myself. It's probably just a loose cable. Even if you don't know anything about engines, there's a fair chance you can logic it out.

It sounded sensible, but then, to a point, so had the radio talk. Still, I mustered some nerve, rummaged in the glovebox for my torch, and climbed out.

Out here, the noise was more pronounced. I resisted the urge to shine the torch out into my surroundings – either I'd see something, or I wouldn't. Instead, I fumbled at the lip of the bonnet, found the catch, and hefted it up. Something unpleasantly soft brushed at my hand. I almost dropped the torch in the sudden shock.

The rustling blossomed in intensity. I brought the torchbeam round, to see a nimbus of moths erupt from the confines of the engine compartment.

They flew clear; but the engine block, pitted and gouged, still crawled with thousands of caterpillars, busily feasting.

November 31st is World Peace Day

The abduction happened in full daylight on a busy street. Not, admittedly, in the classiest neighbourhood – any café which set up shop right next door to the "Cometh The Hour" male impotence clinic could never lay claim to the same postcode as "classy" – but regardless of the demographic, you simply didn't expect abduction.

You also didn't expect the flying car, but that was a separate complaint.

Bec had really wanted that job; and she had sucked, across the whole interview. Worse, she hadn't twigged until halfway through that she was doing so abysmally, when it became apparent that her quiet confidence was coming across as a brittle mixture of arrogance and icompetence. And once that point had been reached – and she could read it, plain as guilt, on her smiling inquisitors' faces – there had been no hope of salvage, no redemption from the suckitude. All attempts at recovery had merely set her hurtling along previously-unexplored avenues of fail.

Had it been the arm? Surely not, not in this day and age; they wouldn't dare.

Or had it been her clothes? She had thought her outfit unimpeachable: Sargasm tee, skinny black jeans, new bovver boots, all pretty standard gear for an IT type. Start as you mean to go on, and all that. But it occurred to her only afterwards, when she'd spotted a couple of nervy acned and perspiring suits in the foyer, that perhaps job interviews (even techie job interviews) were of that rare class of occasion, incorporating also funerals (yours or another's), court appearances, and televangelist try-outs, for which a snarky Sargasm tee was not fully *de rigeur*.

So: the interview had coughed blood. That hurt. It burned, it twisted the knife. They were the coolest agency, bar zilch, and she had faceplanted and had no fallbacks. Even the consolation *frappuccino grande luxe avec sprinkles* in the dismal faux-trendy café two doors down had been a disaster – two sips and then spilt all down the front of her tee-shirt, obliterating the "s" in its "Go fsck yourself" slogan. And the café had not truly been, of course, that mode of trendy inner-city establishment that it aspired towards, and thus did not feature anything so useful as one of those Print'Em booths in which she could have run off a replacement top: no, that would have been just too convenient, and so plan "B" was indicated.

Bec's attempts to wash the stain off in the café's restroom merely served to underscore the status of *frappuccino* as the sworn enemy of white cotton, while perhaps also conveying the additional suggestion that she'd been auditioning, not for a role as a controller of teraflops, but for an altogether less savoury species of contest.

The interview, the spillage. And then she'd stepped out onto a cold and windswept footpath, and had belatedly realised what a rough section of town this was. Newly conscious of the clinging dampness of her tee-shirt front, and her absence of anything resembling a jacket, she looked around to remind herself of the bus-stop's direction.

But she didn't look *up*, and that was her downfall.

With a thud and a flash of pain, the lights went out.

Undertone of sock sweat, top note of stale tobacco. The smell would've been bad enough, the taste was... not something to dwell on.

The world was shuddering, in a way that worlds weren't really supposed to. Her head throbbed, in a manner unlooked for in a cranial containment device. Her vision insisted on blurring, in a fashion inconsistent with general optical expectations. She was seated, seatbelted… confined. The sock stuffed in her mouth – and by God she hoped the rancid cotton object truly *was* a sock, because the alternative didn't bear contemplation – resisted all her efforts to expel it.

Days? She'd had better.

The throb of an engine, low-pitched, a bit stuttery. Plus there were two voices, and she listened, waiting for her vision to clear so she could see what kind of plane this was. (A small one, from the feel of its response to the frequent gusts of turbulence.) The voices, male and female, and both almost painfully British to Bec's ears, were chalk and cheese:

'All I'm sayin', Jemima, is that it's a lot more difficult than what most people credit, like what you've often only got a fraction of a second to judge the thickness of the skull, the victim's natural pain response, the best angle of attack an' all that.'

'Indeed. But—'

'I mean, it'd be bloody great if all there was to it was just a simple thwock an' that's that, problem sorted. But the thwock itself – you gotta ask yourself, is it too gentle, is it too heavy-handed? I mean, there's nothink worse than having to double-thwock, on account of on the first thwock you din't thwock as 'ard as you should've ought to 'ave thwocked. That gets messy, real quick. Know what I mean?'

'*Yes*, Harold. But really, you must have told—'

'An' then, the opposite problem, you thwock too hard, that's damaged goods, that is, Jemima, that's trouble right there, that's no good to nobody, an' that's even worse…'

'Harold, you rattle on about this every dashed time. Let it go, please.'

The first voice, it seemed, was not to be dissuaded. 'Ah, but get it right, like I did back then on the street, an' that's the sweetest sound in the world, y'know?'

Bec slumped back into unconsciousness. It seemed much the best option, in the circumstances.

*

Her eyes, it seemed, were functioning now. And she'd worked the sweat sock out of her mouth, although its flavour lingered. But she still couldn't usefully move her left arm, nor even her right one, trapped as they were within the hoody that had been pulled, back to front, over her *frappuccino*-emblazoned tee. For good measure, a tether around both wrists served to further immobilise her arms, with her hands resting impotently in her lap. The hateful sock of recent memory skulked, beneath her chin, in the hoody's hood.

She squirmed against the seatbelt, sat up. Shrieked. The view from the window was *wrong*, on so many levels. Most of them vertical.

Who, she wondered, knew that Chrysler, of all people, had put out an air-capable Valiant? Back in what must, by the looks of it, have been 1972? And why hadn't they thought to fit it with stabilisers, if only for appearance's sake?

'Oh, she's awake,' the driver announced, turning around to confirm her own diagnosis. A surprisingly cultured voice – mellifluous, *plummy* even – for one so dowdy, so plain, so clad in a fashionless synthetic mid-brown blouse. She seemed such an awkward fit for her voice that Bec wondered how she'd come by it. Perhaps she'd stolen it.

'Hey,' Bec snapped. 'You maybe wanna keep your eyes on the road, uh, *skyline*, whatever?'

'Hey yourself,' replied the other one, beside Bec.

South London tones, steeped in gravel, grit, and menace. Taller, older – forties, maybe – fair-haired, well dressed, appearance shading towards the debonair – an effect that was, however, badly devalued by the zipper down the side of his neck. (She pushed herself across the car seat away from him, hampered by what she now saw to be a tightly-fastened trouser belt binding her wrists together, by a multiply-knotted and scratchy woollen scarf pinning her wrists to her lap, and by her suspicion that the car's doors, even if locked, were none too secure against the prevailing altitude.)

'You leave the drivin' to Jemima there.'

'Harold,' inquired Jemima, seemingly directing the statement at Bec's wrists, 'could you please hike up the jacket for me?'

Bec noticed, in the middle distance through the front windscreen, the towers of the CBD of an approaching cityscape.

'No, Harold, you ninny,' Jemima clarified. 'Not *your* jacket. The young lady's.'

The phalanx of skyscrapers, now closer, was eclipsed by Harold's wheezing, onion-breathed bulk as he leaned across Bec to pull the hem of the hoody up, revealing the lower edge of her *frappuccino*-stained tee shirt and a sneak preview of her forearms.

'That'll do. What's with your arm?' Jemima asked, still obstinately refusing to face forward, her gaze still fixed on Bec's lap. She pointed at the obvious difference between Bec's left and right arms. 'Harold, you didn't notice this while you were strapping our passenger in?'

'Course I *noticed* it,' said Harold. 'I thought it must be the fashion, y'know?'

'Well, yes, that's what I'd been presuming initially as well,' said Jemima. 'But I hadn't seen it up close until now, whereas you had; and plainly it's not just "the fashion". So what's the story, Miss…?'

'The name's Bec. And that's all you're getting from me until you put some serious effort into collision avoidance.'

'Fair enough, I suppose,' conceded Jemima, belatedly turning to face the front and immediately throwing the car to the left at what must be – what? – a thirtieth-storey intersection.

Bec whimpered and edged away from the door, while still trying to keep as much distance as possible from Harold.

'Waiting,' said Jemima, as the car hit a pocket of turbulence, or maybe a pigeon.

'I have an artificial arm,' said Bec, pausing to swallow. 'I was in an… accident when I was a kid, and I lost my arm. This one's myoinductive.'

'Woss that all mean when it's at home?' asked Harold.

'It means it's a very responsive arm, all up. If it wasn't so heavy, and if the batteries lasted longer, it'd be perfect.'

'Ah. Still a shame you lost your real arm to begin with, though, innit?' Harold commented.

'Indeed,' suggested Jemima. 'But I'm wondering if it might have served our purpose better if we – by which, of course, I mean you, Harold – had paid more attention to acquiring someone *entire* in the first place.'

'Entire?' Bec bristled, if bristling was something that was possible while strapped into a flying car and deeply concerned for one's gravitational wellbeing. 'You guys aren't professional at this, are you?' she ventured. While wondering what exactly "this" was. Wondering whether she should be frightened yet. Stupid plus desperate could make for a very bad combination. *Particularly* at this height. And 'stupid' did most definitely appear to be indicated.

'Professional?' asked Harold. Zipperneck. (Now she looked closer, the "zipper" was merely a tattoo.) 'Sure.'

'No,' said Jemima.

Great. 'Look, I can pay,' Bec tried, once again. *Stay calm.* 'You just dro— uh, just *park* this thing somewhere, on the ground, I'll hop out, you fly off, you can have whatever's in my backpack. And you can go and find someone *complete* for whatever it is you need them for.'

'No,' said Jemima. 'We've come this far, we're not turning back.'

'Besides, you ain't *got* no backpack,' observed Harold. 'Musta left it somewhere.'

'I am concerned about your prosthetic, though,' said Jemima, making eye contact in the rear-vision mirror.

'I can remove it,' said Harold. 'Do we even need to keep it? The rest of her should be enough – we could jus' roll down a window an'—'

'Oh, I don't think we need to go there at all, Harold. We're not monsters, please remember that, we have humanity's best interests at heart here. We'll allow Bec to keep her arm, because I imagine it is an important part of the poor girl's identity, though I do wonder how that checkerboard pattern is going to play on the cameras… but I will get you to remove the batteries from it, Harold. Bec, you'll need to instruct Harold on how to disconnect your arm from its inputs so he can safely remove its batteries. I don't want any funny business.'

'D'you have any idea how much trouble I took makin' sure them knots was all tight and almost impossible to undo? And now I'll have to undo 'em to get the batteries out.'

Jemima help up her forefinger and thumb, pinched together. 'World's smallest violin, Harold. World's smallest violin.'

They had been flying a couple of hours now, Bec thought. Struggling to loosen the tethering around her wrists had lost any of the novelty value it had once possessed, though none of the pain value – besides which, Harold would yank mercilessly on the cinch-strap of her seatbelt whenever she moved. She was starting to wonder if these guys had heard of the principle of comfort stops, although at whatever-thousand-metres altitude, she was oddly reluctant to voice this query as yet. She was also growing increasingly fascinated by the fuel gauge, which had dipped ominously low. Not that Jemima or Harold seemed overly perturbed.

'Sorry, I must have misheard,' she said, in response to what Harold had just said.

'Probably not,' said Jemima, turning around again.

She swallowed, only partly to relieve the pressure in her ears. 'Okay, then, the *future*. So *when* in the future are you from?'

'Next Tuesday,' said Harold beside her.

She turned her head away from the side window. It didn't help to contemplate the harsh angularity of the mountains beneath them, nor the distance below... 'Next *Tuesday*?' she asked. 'So we're going to have, what, flying cars, time machines, motion-picture tattoos all in another five days' time?'

'Perhaps not *next* Tuesday,' said Jemima. 'The dials on this thing are rather hard to read—' (She must mean, Bec presumed, dials other than the fuel gauge.)

'*Told* you we shoulda lifted the Beamer,' complained Harold. 'Rather than this heap.'

'Hang on. Are you telling me this is a *stolen* flying car?'

'Yes,' said Jemima.

'No,' said Harold.

'Well, no,' allowed Jemima. 'Not technically, in any case. Not yet.'

'It gets better,' said Bec, bracing for an impact that didn't eventuate, as the car slammed into an ominously-grey bank of cumulonimbus. As if on cue, the fuel warning light came on.

Using the infamous sock's apparent mate, Harold had blindfolded her for the last several minutes of the flight. Not that Bec had been able to spot any useful landmarks – airmarks, skymarks, whatever – before this, in any event. Nor, once she was finally pulled, shaking, from the back seat, did she recognise anything distinctive about their destination. But then, one multistorey car park looked much like any other. At least, it *felt* like it was a car park, somewhere muggy, somewhere quiet, somewhere smelling of rancid gasoline… She was looking at the garage's closed roller-door, searching for any clues that might help her formulate an escape from these goons, when Harold, barefoot (and holding his trousers up with his other hand) brought his shoe down on the back of her head.

Thwock.

'Sweetest sound in the world,' said a disembodied voice somewhere in the distance behind her, while she busied herself with the task of slumping to the pressed-steel flooring.

'It's a skill, is all I'm saying.' Harold. 'An' if you get it right—'

Jemima: 'I've *told* you, stop bloody going on about it!'

She opened her eyes. They'd plonked her on something soft – she waited for her focusing to come properly back online – a mattress, in a small stale sour room that also contained a plastic bucket, a downlight, and a heavily-shuttered window. And a couple of questionably-competent kidnappers. The light penetrating through the shutter's slats was almost horizontal. The walls and floor were riveted steel, painted industrial grey;

an effort to similarly paint the ceiling had apparently been abandoned partway through. The door, a painted metal-skinned oblong, was currently open, though mostly filled with Harold, who still wielded a shoe in his right hand. (What *was* it with these guys and clothing-assisted captivity?)

'What happens now?' she asked, sitting up, staring without favour at her captors. Her head hurt… again. She couldn't be sure, but she had the suspicion that the room was tilted very slightly, probably by no more than two or three degrees, off the vertical. Or maybe it was just her.

'You stay here,' Jemima informed her. 'Overnight. We'll explain what happens tomorrow, in the morning. Don't try anything.'

Her captors left, locking the door behind them. Ten minutes later, the light outside perceptibly weaker, Harold returned with a stained food-court tray bearing bottled water and a small packet of water crackers. He placed the tray just inside the doorway before locking her in once more.

Eventually, she got up to check out the tray, and the room. She couldn't see much of anything through the shutters on the window, but what she could see suggested the concept "down", and quite a bit of it. Wind. Waves. No traffic noise, no artificial lighting apparent. Although there was the distinct smell of something fairly comprehensively industrial, with marine overtones. Which was, she had to admit, a decided improvement over the distinct smell of her captors' clothing, but it did put the lie to any idea that escape might be anything so straightforward as just reaching the front door and legging it. She had no idea where this was. The flight had lasted several hours.

She tried assembling the clues, nonetheless. Large structure, metal, smell of fuel, sea – had they landed on an oil tanker? And if so, why, where, and why did it feel deserted?

Closer at hand, the packet of crackers obstinately refused to transform itself into a thick steak, medium rare. *Typical.* Her stomach, already complaining at the treatment it had received courtesy of the car's flight, grumbled at the prospect of the dinner they'd provided her with. They might at least have thought to check the use-by date on the crackers. Although, perhaps, they had.

It occurred to her, also, that such things as use-by dates might have a rather elastic meaning insofar as time travellers were concerned.

If this was the Universe's way of demonstrating to her that, despite her inexplicable failure to land the dream job, she was still wanted... then there was something fundamentally wrong with the Universe.

Bec lay down to sleep, to hope that her head would feel better in the morning. In contravention of a decade-old personal policy – the prosthetic was a piece of Bec-armour, something she put on each morning to face the day and the day's inhabitants, not something truly Bec-innate, and the myoinductive was heavy – she opted, on this occasion, to wear the arm to bed, rather than to remove it. Even though, without its batteries, it was about as useful as a computer chair's foot hanging off her shoulder; it was still *something*. It just seemed safest, in the circumstances.

But the bloody thing was heavy, and unfamiliar in repose, which made it difficult to find a comfortable posture.

Sleep was a long time coming.

She was eight again; she knew what happened next. It was eleven minutes to one, and the city was about to be brought to its knees...

They'd finished looking around the museum. She'd followed Kelvin across Rolleston Avenue; her older brother was nagging her about getting back to Dad at the vegetarian restaurant – they were already late. (Mum, meanwhile, was at some medical conference thing at one of the hotels, not the one they were staying at, but it was why they were all here on holiday, and how come Bec and her brother had a week off school.) So Kelvin had charged ahead into the cloistered, heritage-listed maze of the Arts Centre, abuzz with lunchtime tourists and schoolkids, but she'd stopped on the footpath: the gravel in her sandal had become unbearable. He'd at least turned around when she'd called him... but he wasn't in a waiting mood. Crouching, she'd unstrapped the sandal, shook it, and slipped it back on, not even bothering to do the strap back up. She set off after Kelvin... and managed, at the slight step abutting the covered walkway, to trip, landing heavily on the stonework. Dazed, she could see Kelvin ahead, across the other corner of a stone-circumscribed grass quadrangle… and the world beneath her shivered, then shook, then snapped, while a huge, formless rumbling built and burst all around her. The ground beneath her shouted, rattling, and the world fell to pieces.

Pain, overpowering, flared in her arm. The air bloomed with dust and an ominous, short-lived silence. Then, from somewhere, sirens sounded forth. The ground was still shaking when the tourist woman came up to her, checking whether she needed help. By then, Bec could see – though didn't yet really believe – that her right arm was pinned, lying useless under a chunk of fallen masonry; and across the quadrangle, beneath what remained of the Observatory Tower, so was Kelvin.

She woke, bathed in sweat, thoroughly disoriented. Her breathing ebbed to something approaching normalcy, but her thoughts would not let her be.

Was it better to not have access to a time machine, or to have access to a time machine and yet not be able to use it?

She hadn't felt so guilty about surviving for – well, for years. She *missed* Kelvin.

Sleep wasn't at all sure that it wanted to let her back in, and she really didn't know that she wanted to go anyway.

'*Blister packs?*' she asked. 'Seriously?'

'You ain't, surely, denyin' it's a problem?' Harold asked.

'Well…' It was the next morning. They'd supplied breakfast: the water-crackers-and-water combination was already showing dangerous signs of becoming a motif. They had dragged her down two flights of floating steel stairs to a larger, less stale-smelling room, again shuttered. The room was dominated by an impressive collection of audio-visual gear, and by a fold-up table and some of those pressed-metal chairs which have been carefully designed to (a) stack and (b) scrupulously avoid the remotest suggestion of comfort. At Jemima's direction, Harold had sat Bec down and, using a thick woollen scarf, had tied her to one of the chairs, which rather hampered her ongoing efforts to kick shins. Tethered, she had retaliated by hurling sprays of verbal abuse at them, something she was really pretty good at (as is anyone who spends most of their waking hours trying to bend recalcitrant computers to their will), until Harold had, pointedly, removed his shoes and socks. With yesterday's shoe-coshing and sockboarding episodes still fresh in Bec's mind (although "fresh" was exactly the wrong word, in the circs), she reined it in.

Jemima was, of all things, holding a press conference.

Well, not a press conference *per se*, more a kind of ransom-demand announcement. Rehearsal. Bec couldn't be sure, but she thought Jemima had even dressed up for it. Unless the business-suit look was standard for her, and yesterday's outfit had just been her abducting-hapless-IT-girls gear.

Any event, it didn't make her look any less of a tosser. Gifted orator, maybe, but still a tosser. No fashion sense, no apparent concept of a colour spectrum that extended beyond the exciting continuum from taupe to umber, no awareness of fabrics other than, it would seem, polyester. Tosser.

'We demand,' Jemima had portentously announced, standing on the other side of the fold-up table, voice raised out of all proportion to the size – and the captivity – of her audience. (Indeed, Bec could not recall having heard anyone with quite Jemima's aural sense of *presence*, the weighty, measured power of her gradually-delivered words; and Bec herself had played witness to – indeed, participated in – enough heated debates on the relative virtues of Windows versus Linux, Mac versus PC, Minecraft versus Plants Versus Zombies to know that it was as much *how* you said it, as what you said, that won or lost the case.) 'We *insist* on an unconditional end to the use of blister packs. For too long – too long, I say! – this unholy alliance of hard plastic, cardboard, and obstinate adhesive has been allowed, nay, encouraged to blight our existence. It is time, well *past* time, to declare ENOUGH! The corporate reign of this most iniquitous tool in the merchandiser's fell armoury must be curtailed, it must be stopped, it must be snuffed out entirely, and if we do not call for an immediate end to this madness in visible yet all-but-impervious product encasement, who will? And so we take this stand, to declare the necessary demise of something which should never have been: the blister pack.' Jemima emphasised the point by bringing her fist down on the tabletop, then felt the need to readjust its legs so as not to have it slowly topple away from her. 'And while we are about repairing the ills of the world, we call also for an immediate freeze on that skin-tight shrink-wrap stuff you can never get off things without chipping a nail.'

'An' them little plastic-foam beads what they puts in boxes for cushionin',' piped in Harold, standing off to the right of Bec's chair. 'I *hate* that bloody stuff! Gets everywhere. I mean, what's so damn hard about bubble-wrap?'

'Back off on the beads.'

'I thought we'd agreed…'

'We *have* agreed. Pay attention. It's the blister packs and the shrink wrap we're after action on. Oh, and labels with less structural integrity than the adhesive they're backed with, though that's a stretch goal, really. *Capisce?*'

'But—'

'Can I just get this straight?' Bec asked, a sick feeling in her mouth. She wished Harold would just put the bloody socks away. 'You guys are seriously intending to somehow – and you still haven't told me *how* – to hold the entire history of human civilisation, the lives of every man-woman-and-child, past present, future and all that jazz, to ransom, all for the sake of your godforsaken preferences in *packaging?*'

'Yes, indeed…'

'For real? I mean, for fuck's sake, *packaging?* That's the best you've got?'

'You're getting it.'

'But that's just—'

'Hey,' said Jemima. 'At least packaging's *real.* It *matters.* It makes a *difference*, day-to-day. You want to get all high-and-mighty, you just have a think about how many bloody battles have been fought over stuff that doesn't even *exist.* How many millions of people have ended up dead, just for the sake of, and please excuse my Español, some totally half-baked made-up shit?' She cleared her throat. 'How many pointless petty wars are happening right now?'

'But… packaging? I mean, why not something that would make a real difference? Why the hell don't you demand immediate world peace, or, I dunno, force them to do something serious towards ending world hunger? Something *important*?'

'Why didn't you?' Harold asked.

You know nothing about my life, you bastard. 'That's not the point.'

'No, it's *exactly* the point,' said Jemima. 'Blister packs and shrink wrap blight the lives of countless people every day, and we can do something about it. That other stuff, sure, it'd be cute. But it's just too *big*.'

'Whatever. Fine. But I still don't get this. Just how are you planning to pull off your Robin-Hood-of-blister-packs shtick? If you don't mind me asking?'

'Not at all. See, that's where you come in. Let me explain how a time hostage works.'

'*Time* hostage?'

'They do as we ask. Or we send you back,' said Jemima.

'Back? Back where?'

'Far enough.'

'When you say, "far enough"?'

'Maybe dinosaurs. See, it's just a matter of introducing – what'd you say, Harold? Sixty kilos of extraneous biomass—'

'Yeah, I said sixty, but now I'm thinkin' maybe seventy, seventy-five, with that arm—'

'—into the dinosaur environment, and it pretty much guarantees that the course of human history gets changed as a result. Yours especially, of course.'

'You're both *insane*. And last time I weighed myself, which was admittedly a couple of weeks back because I'm not anal about that shit, it was sixty-two point five. And just to clarify what I mean by "insane", I'm using it in the popular context of bat-poo-crazy.'

'Sock, I think,' declared Jemima.

'On it,' said Harold.

Whether Jemima had taken particular offence at having her mental state compared to aerial-mammal effluent, or whether she was just determined that their intended extinct-reptile fodder be kept in good order overnight against the prospect of self-harm, it appeared she was taking no chances. Bec was transported, from the place of press-conference rehearsal to her room of nocturnal confinement, up more flights of stairs than she had recollected, still sock-gagged, and still scarf-strapped to her seat.

Jemima left the room. Harold diligently checked the knots on the scarf, satisfying himself that Bec was securely fastened, and then trotted out, closing the door with an audible *clunk... click.*

Time passed. Bec's wrist ached. Her gluteal muscles agonised. Her calves complained. Her jaws weren't overjoyed either. Her nose was wondering how to phone it in.

She didn't think this was even the same room as the previous night. The bucket was a different colour, and the prominent rust-stain on the bed's mattress (at least, she hoped it was rust) resembled a different continent: less North America, more Antarctica.

She was locked in for the night. So what was the point of leaving her still tethered and sock-gagged?

This was the question she put to Harold when he returned, perhaps one hour, perhaps three later, bearing the obligatory tray of water bottle and water crackers. He made a show of not understanding her – the sock, presumably – and in response she made a show, through the imperfect medium of eye gestures, of conveying that (a) it was gonna be pretty damn difficult to eat or drink anything if they just left her gagged and bound overnight and (b) there were some things that a girl needed to do that couldn't occur with any dignity while strapped to an uncomfortable metal chair for an extended period of time and (c) he and Jemima were really total dipshits, did he realise that?

She succeeded in communicating these bullet-points quite well, despite the difficulties of her circumstances – indeed rather *too* well, in the context of (c), because Harold took his shoe off.

Thwock.

'Sweetest sound in the world,' he assured her, though she could not share his enthusiasm for its tonal qualities.

The room faded from view.

She slipped on mud, pulled herself upright via the Valiant's doorhandle. Heart hammering, she detached the prosthetic, hefting it in her good hand – her meat hand – like a club.

The allosaur snorted like an ice-addicted bull in a Wedgwood showroom and nosed its way around the car's front, all needle-toothed mouth, menace, and reeking saliva. She backstepped to keep as much auto as possible between herself and the creature, wondering how the hell she was going to get the door open before the other allosaur, the larger one ten metres away, finished with what was left of Jemima. An appeal to Harold's better angels, a few seconds ago, hadn't worked. Bec fervently hoped he wasn't going to get the car started before she managed to get in—

Now. She truncheoned the rear driver's side window with the myoelectric, flinching as it shattered inwards in a spray of untidy shards. She tossed the prosthetic into the back seat, reached in cut herself pulled the lock knob *up* yanked the door open clambered in panting, turned to pull the door closed—

—and very nearly shoved her hand straight into the maw of the allosaur, which slavered in eager anticipation of its first experience with canned food. She backed up against the far door.

'Get this fucking thing started, will you?' she shrieked, fumbling the prosthetic into her grasp and striving to prod the dinosaur's snout with it.

'Can't,' he complained. 'Jemima had the keys.'

Shit. She'd have to—

The car shook as Allosaur Two thumped its tail against the windscreen. Glass flew in at her. Her only chance was to try to squeeze into the front, hope that somehow Harold and her could get the car going–

She didn't make it. Allosaur One caught her stump in its stinking teeth, started pulling her out of the car.

She awoke, sheathed in sweat, her heart auditioning for the role of freight-train-clattering-across-a-rickety-wooden-bridge. The taste of fear in her mouth, an awful copper tang, reinforced the dream's vividness while she sought, frantically, to calm herself.

It took a few minutes for her breathing to steady. Then she tried to take stock.

Harold had left. The chair had gone. The door was locked. But at least she was untethered.

Her head, she suspected, gingerly rubbing the back of it, was rapidly shaping up to become an object of fascination of phrenologists – should she ever manage to meet any.

It *had* to be a different room to last night's. The ceiling's paint job had been completed on this one. Perhaps that was what had served to make the manhole less apparent – it was, after all, almost flush with the rest of the ceiling…

Bec had never particularly prided herself on her agility as a child – she figured her parents had both been carriers of the recessive "klutz" gene, and it had expressed itself in myriad ways throughout her development (most recently, of course, in the *frappuccino* incident that had preceded her unwitting acquaintance with Harold and Jemima) – but she felt that now might well be a good time to discover an as-yet-untapped wellspring of something approximating an ability to climb through a hole in the ceiling without making a mess of it.

She stood on tiptoes and stretched her fingertips towards the ceiling. It was perhaps twenty-five centimetres out of reach. The steel-frame bed was tall enough, but was bolted to the floor – why would you *do* that?

– in just the wrong corner to be able to reach the manhole. The bed's bolts were rusted in place: without the battery-boosted *oomph* of her myoelectric, she had no hope of budging them. And the bucket was not sturdy enough to support an adult. Besides, tipping the bucket over to use as a stool would present her with problems with which she didn't wish to be confronted right now.

If Harold hadn't taken the chair with him when he'd left the room, she'd have had *that* to stand on. Problem solved. But no.

With the tools at hand, she just couldn't reach the manhole. But she knew a way to cheat…

She slipped the harness off. Then, grimacing at the wet sound it made, she pulled her artificial arm from the stump just below her right shoulder, and, gripping it around the elbow, held it aloft like some parody of an Olympic torch-bearer. It reached – just – up to the manhole cover.

The question then, once she'd girl-handled the manhole cover out of the way, was: could she leap up and haul herself into whatever crawlspace existed up there? And what would it avail her, assuming she could?

The manhole cover, which was about 120 by 60 centimetres, had proven much thicker, and heavier, than she'd expected. Luckily the prosthetic arm was up to the task, though it was a slow business to inch the cover out of the way above her.

She contemplated leaving the arm behind – without batteries, it was tantamount to eight kilograms of dead weight, and the task was going to be difficult enough without that – but the thought of being separated from her prosthetic, even temporarily, in a crisis situation like this was not something to be seriously entertained. Where she went, it went. She hefted it up into the opening, heard it land on something with a definite heavy *clang*.

You've done it now, she thought. *And what if you can't clamber up there one-handed?*

She leapt, missed. Leapt, grabbed hold, slipped, fell. Leapt, grabbed hold, slipped, swore, fell. Leapt, grabbed hold, hung on… swore, fell.

I'm going to need to rethink this, she thought. *There is no way I'll pull myself up – it's just not working. Even two-handed, it'd be a struggle. One-handed, it's as good as impossible. There's not the strength in my arm to get my elbow up over... but if I grab hold again, then I can swing myself up, get one or both feet up, and then I can just sort of* roll *myself to freedom...*

Of course, it was never going to be that simple. Anyone who works in IT knows that nothing, anywhere, is ever that simple, nor that free from pain. But somewhat to her surprise, Bec found that she could, in fact, get first one boot-heel and then the other firmly resting on the lip of the upper surface, while her fingers maintained their desperate hold on the manhole's rim. There had been one terrifying moment – alright, two or three terrifying moments – when she had been convinced she was about to fall, head-first, to the unyielding floor of her room; but she clung on, assisted by a strong sense of obstinacy, by what the Finnish call *sisu*, and by the necessarily well-developed muscles of her left shoulder.

Now what? Foot across, I guess, and push... it just gets better, doesn't it?

By the end of it, she was sweating like a glass of wine and shaking like a storm-harassed sapling. But she was free.

It wasn't a crawlspace. And this sure as hell wasn't an oil tanker, though she guessed she could be excused for having thought it smelled like one.

Windy night, cutting wind, nasty banks of grey cloud gathered around the moon, but there was enough moonlight patching its way through to make out, in a kind of silvery-white-on-black greyscale, her surroundings: the top deck of what looked to be a not-quite-completed and yet not-absolutely-new oilrig, somewhere far enough offshore that "shore" itself could not even be guessed at. She suspected, looking out at the distant vista of the imperfectly-moonlit sea, that she might well be sixty, eighty, even a hundred metres above the sea's surface – it was difficult to judge.

Her fingers hurt like whatever it was that hurt like something very painful. Her wrist throbbed from its exertions. She shook her left hand for a minute or so, standing on the deck of the rig, hoping that might help, but it didn't. Her left shoulder, too, ached. She spied the myoinductive, which lay like a beached fish a short distance away, and retrieved and reattached it: it didn't fit properly somehow, nor was it bending the right way. She must have damaged the elbow.

And it's my best one, too. Have to get it repaired before the next job interview. Assuming the interview panel aren't a pack of velociraptors...

The location, obviously, complicated the problem of escape: it wasn't simply a matter of walking to the nearest highway and hitching a lift from there. She'd need to consider other options. Cautiously, she edged towards the deck's rim, dropped to all fours (well, in the circumstances, all threes-and-a-bit), and lay leaning her head over the edge of the deck, looking directly down. A long way down. The view was dizzying, unnerving; it threatened (or so she surmised) to pull her toward it, as though the empty vertical black-and-shimmering-moonlit-silveriness of it had its own magnetic gravity, against which she was all-but powerless. After a few seconds, thoroughly intimidated by the structure's enormity, she pulled herself back, crawled away, shaking, and only stood up again when she was convinced she was utterly out of danger.

She was not good with heights.

The inspection had been, at least, long enough to reveal that, on this side of the rig, there were no boats moored. Rationality suggested she should repeat the exercise on the rig's other sides; but vertigo insisted this was *quite enough* of that, thank you very much.

Besides, even if she could somehow find her way down to something so useful as a moored and fuelled speedboat, she had no concept of the direction nor the distance she'd need to travel in order to reach land. And she couldn't fly the Valiant, wherever it might be.

But there might be another way.

She looked around the rig's deck. There was a long panoramically-windowed structure along one side, cantilevered rather audaciously over the side of the deck itself and which almost screamed "control room"; a couple of mismatched crane arms along the opposite side, hanging vacantly over the abyss; and about ten metres away from the smaller crane arm (and, as it happened, an equal distance also from the manhole from which she'd emerged), a slender outhouse-like construction which plainly marked the top of a staircase. Looking more carefully, the control room's window was protected by a sturdy metal mesh covering; the only items on the deck itself, aside from Bec and the manhole cover, were a couple of heavy-looking drums, an untidy coil of thick chain near the larger crane, and an oversized tool that pretty much begged to be picked up and brandished just so one could use the line *That's not a crescent wrench. This is a crescent wrench...* which, nonetheless, she resisted. Decorating the side panel of the control room, the side of the smaller crane, and the door that led (she presumed) to the lower levels was a faded and wind-wracked logo that she recognised as belonging to a petroleum-production conglomerate that had gone into receivership a few years ago. That might go some way towards explaining the not-quite-finished aspect of the rig, she thought, as she made her way towards the door to the stairway.

At least the door wasn't locked. On the minus side, the noise it made as it scraped open sounded as though a convention of banshees would have complained to the management over it. *Shit*, she thought, moving ineffectually out of the doorway's line-of-sight. If that noise had woken them up – and it pretty much beggared belief to expect that it somehow might not have – then she was pretty comprehensively cornered up here: they'd come up the stairs, and she'd be trapped. She couldn't get into the control room, so far as she could see, and there wasn't anything around the cranes that looked useful as a means of escape. She could either choose to climb back into her locked room herself, or they could throw her back in there; or worse. Or, she supposed, she could always jump over the side of the rig, into the seawater, however many metres below – assuming such a fall wouldn't be fatal, for all the myriad reasons that might come into play, and assuming there were useful handholds by which she could haul her bedraggled form out of the water, and assuming that this wasn't simply delaying the inevitable.

Bec Wertheim, you are better than this. She forced herself to breathe calmly, deeply; she counted to one hundred, as slowly as she knew how, even though her every impulse was to rush, to just get on with it.

When, after a full hundred, there had still been no sign of disturbance from the staircase, she allowed herself to believe that the horrendous racket of the door's opening had somehow gone undetected; she could brave the descent.

The staircase was dark, the reflected traces of moonlight serving only to illuminate the first few steps down before the shadows swallowed all. If she'd had her cellphone, this wouldn't have been a problem; but the phone had been one of the things that Harold and Jemima had confiscated, along with her keys, her mp3 player, and her collection of usb drives. God only knew what kind of mayhem they thought she'd macgyver out of a bunch of thumb drives, her keys and her music player, but she wasn't inclined to awaken them right now to seek clarification on the topic. *No need to hasten the moment of dino nourishment. Particularly if I can find a way to forestall it altogether.*

The stairs were almost ladder-steep, so the safest way to take the staircase was backwards, and slowly, and with her left hand clinging to the handrail. She was conscious of the noise her bovver boots made, solid and echoey, when she cautiously lowered them onto the textured-metal tread of the next step down, but that couldn't be helped; and it had to be a hundred times quieter than the caterwaul of the door's opening earlier.

It was slow going. Nine steps, landing, nine steps, corridor, nine steps, landing, nine steps, snoring, nine steps, landing, nine steps, corridor, nine steps—

She stopped, heart in mouth, because the past had just belted her on the noggin with all the force of one of Harold's industrial-grip-soled shoes. She was, suddenly, four years old, or possibly five, and the staircase was wooden, at their grandparents', the power was out, and she and Kelvin had been playing hide-and-seek. The game, in the dark, was distinctly against their parents' instructions; but sitting around the candlelit kitchen table with the grownups had lost any residual attraction, while the pull of hide-and-seek in her grandparents' mysterious two-storey house was a thing almost magnetic. Only she'd been cheating, because it was dark: rather than waiting to be caught in the one spot (and her upstairs hiding spot wasn't very good), she'd decided to find a better one, downstairs, using the cover of darkness to evade Kelvin, who was "in". It would have worked, might have worked, if she hadn't missed a step on the stairs, and fallen... in the dark.

He'd been below her, climbing the stairs, and had broken her fall. And his arm.

She remembered she'd felt so guilty about that, for years, that she'd broken Kelvin's arm. Felt so guilty she'd learnt not to think about it too much... until, of course, there was much worse to feel. (In her blackest moments, she sometimes pondered that the only piece of Kelvin that had never broken was his voice.) Tears pushed at the corners of her eyes, waiting for release.

She swallowed, blinked hard. *The past is past,* she told herself, resolute, and stepped onto the landing. And, almost in a gesture of commemoration, she stumbled, because she'd miscounted. She landed awkwardly, twisting her ankle, but managed not to fall over entirely. She practiced breathing for a bit, just to check that she still had the basics under control.

One more flight: nine steps down to another corridor, without incident, thankfully. Two levels below her captors. This might be far enough to do some exploring.

The first door was locked. The second door was locked too, as was the third. But the fourth door opened.

Fumbling in the dark, on the inside wall of the room, she found a light switch and was rewarded with the dazzling glare of a 15W bulb which had been helpfully set at eye level directly in front of her. *Great,* she thought, while opposing packs of discordantly-coloured silhouettes played roller derby, or ice hockey, or another of those ultra-fast-moving and dangerous team sports across her retinas. *There goes my night vision.*

When the visuals had settled down enough, she scoped out her surroundings. The room was small, ensuite-sized, and lined with dusty, rusty metal shelves on which had been stacked a profusion of hardware and stationery items in some semblance of order. *Flashlight. That'll do nicely.*

The flashlights, it turned out, lacked batteries... but that wasn't a problem, because there were packets of batteries stacked on a nearby shelf. All Bec needed to do was to unscrew the end of the flashlight – something that was easier said than done, one-handed, when it was as tightly fastened as this. Even trying the old standby of gripping the flashlight between her knees while she applied all the torque her still-aching wrist could muster... And the other flashlights, it seemed, were much the same.

But the PowerArm could cope with such a problem – and there were button cells, of just such a size as the prosthetic took, unless she was much mistaken, sitting on the same shelf as the flashlight batteries, a short distance away.

The button cells were blister-packed. After several intensely frustrating minutes, she conceded that Jemima might, in fact, have a point.

Two doors along, the flashlight's beam picked out the logo of a television station attached to the painted-metal surface of the door. And now she knew *exactly* where she was, down to the particular rig. There'd been a pilot for a reality show here a couple of years back, one of those vote-off-the-least-popular-misfit things, but nobody had watched and the series had been canned, at about the same point that the network itself had folded... which, she guessed, explained the broadcast gear left behind.

She continued down, still flexing her artificial fingers as she went. (Like the elbow, the wrist and knuckles hadn't fared brilliantly from her escape.) Nine steps, landing, nine steps, corridor, nine steps, landing, nine steps, asphalt and moonlight. She conserved the torchlight.

This deck lacked partitions, but was punctuated at the corners by the massive pillars that, she presumed, extended down to the seafloor, however many metres beneath the surface. The moonlight, blotched and striped, was slanting in from the left-hand wall, which was mostly a latticework of heavy girders. The right-hand wall was similarly trellised, but the far wall looked solid, unbroken save for a wide roller-door, and partly obscured by a stack of packing crates.

But it was the sight of a 1972 Chrysler Valiant, parked in the lee of the most distant pillar, that most directly arrested her attention.

Story of my life, she thought, *if it's locked.*

But it wasn't.

The Valiant's front seat was substantially more comfortable than anything on offer upstairs, even the mattress; and she'd slept very poorly last night. Keeping her eyes open might prove difficult.

Trouble was, the car's owner's manual was almost unfathomably badly written. The section on "Using Your Car's Chronoselection Features: Maintenance and Safety Considerations" was making no sense at all.

Could be worse. The manual could be missing.

The words refused to fall into ordered, logical concepts. "Whenframe" just didn't make sense; she was pretty sure the usage of "azimuthal quadrature" was simply a bit of meaningless showing-off; and the manual took great pains to point out the importance of remembering that "timelines" and "timeliness" were two distinct concepts, each in its own way crucial, and then provided at least two instances of a misspelling as "timelinesss" which, by extrapolation, didn't encourage any confidence whatsoever.

C'mon, Bec. You've coded your way out of doomsday scenarios before this, she told herself, in the vain hope that the internal-monologue-pep-talk thing might vaguely help. It didn't. But then attending to the nagging-voice-of-self-doubt thing almost certainly wouldn't either. Neither did the strong petroleum odour that hung around the car like a sickly-sweet sharp hydrocarbon aura – she couldn't decide whether the smell, and the jerrycans of fuel clustered around the pillar, indicated that the aeroValiant's fuel tank had been recharged, or simply that one of the cans leaked.

Finally, after perhaps an hour of poring repeatedly through the same ten textually-mangled pages on Chronoselection, she decided she'd found what she needed. Or at least, she'd found it in the *manual*. Whether she could find it under the hood, and whether she could make the desired modifications, was quite another matter.

The night wasn't getting any younger. She'd need a screwdriver, an adjustable wrench, a pen, and a notebook. (Best to grab another packet of button cells, too, while she was at it. This thing was a hog for power when she used it for fine-motor stuff, and she didn't have her charger with her, did she? Besides, she'd need to remember to take its present batteries out before she fell asleep tonight – the success of tomorrow's performance could well be undermined by a stray arm-twitch giving the game away before Jemima had made her spiel.)

Time to hit the storeroom upstairs, and to see what it had in stock.

After she'd switched the timing module connections, she thought about hiding the tools under the mattress in her room, but decided against it. There was no guarantee they wouldn't switch rooms on her again tomorrow night. Instead, she concealed the screwdriver and the wrench in the gap between two of the packing crates. She thought hard about where to hide the other thing, the crucial item, and finally she found a place that she was sure would never occur to her captors.

'Isn't this all a rather empty threat?' she asked, as they escorted her, inevitably sock-cuffed, towards the studio the next morning. She hoped her nervousness, her almost insurmountable tiredness and the slight bulge in her left jeans pocket did not show. 'I mean, if you actually follow through on the time-hostage thing, surely you get annihilated too.'

'Ah,' exclaimed Harold, choosing to prod her in the back with sufficient force that she almost lost her footing on the landing. 'But, see, we're not from the same timeline.'

'Probably not from the same timeline,' Jemima clarified.

She managed, barely, to turn what desperately wanted to be a snort of derision into a superficially polite two-syllable cough. 'Do you actually understand how timelines *work*?'

'Sure we do,' said Harold, a sneer in his voice plainly conveying a flavour of *oh-look-the-trained-monkey-pretends-to-understand-quantum-physics*. 'We just come from one the other day, din't we?'

'I suppose you must have,' she replied. 'I'll note in passing that you answered in English, and I'm pretty certain the English language originated some time *after* the demise of the dinosaurs, to whose epoch you're threatening to send me back. Join those dots however you wish.'

'Possibly not from the same timeline,' Jemima clarified.

'So—'

'It's a moot point in any case,' Jemima continued, pushing open the makeshift studio's door. 'They'll comply with our demands. They *have* to. We are not being unreasonable. Another sock, I think, Harold, I'm growing bored with this conversation.'

'You think I'm *made* of socks, Boss?' Harold retorted.

'Well, then, whatever we used to tether her yesterday.'

'That was me scarf, but I've left it in the room. Can go get it if you'd like.'

'No, don't bother. It's just a pity there's no duct tape on this hulk.'

'There's'—*some in the storeroom,* she nearly added, but of course she couldn't—'no need to gag me, I'll keep schtum. And it'll be better optics if I'm not gagged anyway.'

'Better optics?'

'Looks better on the broadcast,' she explained. 'Better for you, better for me.'

'You know,' said Jemima to Harold, 'I think she's finally learning how to cooperate.'

You ain't seen the half of it, Bec remarked to herself, demurely taking her seat while the ransomers checked over the broadcast equipment.

'We demand – we *insist* on an unconditional end…' Jemima, standing behind the desk, had launched into her oratory. She was referring only sporadically to the notes on the desk. Given how often she'd practiced the spiel yesterday, Bec thought – bleary-eyed and fighting to maintain a carefully deadpan expression – it was a wonder Jemima needed the notes at all. Well, she'd have some more reading matter in a few minutes.

Bec was seated to Jemima's left, with Harold to her other side. That was a bother; it limited her actions. Although at least they'd left her with just her hands tied together and resting in her lap, no other restraints. It did, as she'd pointed out, look better onscreen, always an important consideration if you're planning to hold the world to ransom over your packaging preferences. Not that that was why Bec had lobbied for it.

Jemima was getting well into it now, explaining the chronomechanics of time-hostagery to her unseen audience. Harold, Bec sensed, was losing interest in the presentation – in all probability, he'd heard this speech even more often than she had. Actively nodding now, and not, one suspected, in agreement.

May as well make my own move, Bec thought. She gave a politely small yawn, took a deep breath, rolled her head from side to side as though limbering up her tired neck muscles. Then she flexed her left shoulder; then her right.

As she flexed her right shoulder, she pulled away as hard as she could with her tethered hands. She'd earlier ensured the myoinductive arm wasn't harnessed, was just sitting loose on her stump; now, with a disconcerting soft *schlurp*, the weak suction seal holding the prosthesis to the stump of her right arm failed and her artificial limb fell away. She caught it in her lap, then, before Harold could react, she reached into her jeans pocket, sidestepped the small blister-pack of button cells – *later* – and pulled out a folded piece of paper, which she underarmed towards Jemima's notes.

Fortune favoured her. It landed plumb spang on Jemima's desk, just beside the small wifi remote-control panel for the video camera, its red-inked legend "Read Me <u>Immediately</u>" clearly showing. Jemima, still sounding forth about "the irrevocability of sending this unfortunate young woman back to the Plasticene or whenever if our demands are not met", picked it up, unfolded it, and began to peruse it, her patter uninterrupted and seemingly undistracted.

To Bec's disappointment, however, Jemima did not read the note in its entirety then and there. Instead, she scanned it for about five seconds, put it back on the desk in front of her.

She waited Jemima's talk out, using the time to wriggle her way free of the sock-cuffs and to casually reattach her prosthesis. The action did not escape the notice of either Jemima or Harold, but the former was too heavily involved in her live-to-air pitch to the peoples of Earth and the latter, it seemed, was unwilling to make a scene while the cameras were rolling. It could not be accidental, however, that Harold had surreptitiously slipped off his shoe at this juncture and attempted to direct a questioning look at his colleague.

When Jemima had shot the bolt of her monologue, Bec rose to her feet. Harold half-rose too, but at a subtitle-worthy glower from Jemima, sat down again.

'In conclusion,' said Jemima, directing a stern expression towards the camera, 'we now leave the fate of the world in your hands. We shall now take a short break, from which we shall return shortly. Cut.'

She pressed the button on the control panel in front of her.

'–the HELL is this about?' Jemima snapped, rounding on Bec.

'I thought the note was quite self-explanatory,' said Bec, wondering if there was some way to retreat that wasn't currently occupied by Harold.

'What's the problem, anyway?' Harold asked, stepping forward. Jemima wordlessly passed him the note.

At any other time Bec might have found it comical to witness how many of the components of Harold's face – notably his lips, his eyebrows, and quite remarkably also his ears, which had begun to glow a bright red – were complicit in the task of reading, but in the circumstances she was aware only of how slow a reader he was and how white-hot was Jemima's fury right now.

This is what Harold was reading:

Do NOT read any of this aloud, Jemima, unless you wish to jeopardise your plans completely. I have a quite specific set of demands, which I insist you meet. You will meet them because I have something you need. If you ever want to see it again, you require my cooperation. You and Harold are a thoroughly despicable pair of pieces of work – that's not relevant to my demands, it's just a character observation, offered free of charge – and I would not be looking to assist you in this ridiculous baby-with-the-bathwater scheme except that I see an opportunity for bringing some good out of this. Here's the gist: your time machine contains, or rather contained, a small unit called a local-field chronoreversor, which I have inadvertently removed from the vehicle, and have accidentally misplaced. Without this device, which is about the size of a "D" grade battery, there can be no trips back in time, only forward. Now, I honestly believe I should be able to remember where this device is – and on a rig this large, it could be anywhere, perhaps somewhere in imminent danger of tumbling into the unforgiving ocean depths – if and only if, at the conclusion of your own little portion of the broadcast, you allow me to present my own demands to the audience which you have so helpfully collected here. If you choose not to comply with this not unreasonable request, I simply won't be able to remember this component's location. Oh, and threats will not work, in my recollecting the whereabouts of this item – quite the reverse – so please don't insult me by choosing that route. I look forward to your prompt attention to this matter.

Yours with all due respect,
Bec Wertheim.

In the time that he was reading the above, the following argument ensued:

'You're clearly bluffing.'

'I'm not. How do you think I even know about the chronoreversor?'

'How did you get out of your room? You were locked in. And you were still locked in this morning.'

'Trade secret. You're wasting time. Bottom line, your time machine's missing its chronoreversor, which you rather need for your plan.'

'Then you'll hand it over. Now.'

'No, I won't. If you've bothered to read my note, my demands are quite plain.'

'Do you seriously think you're in a position to dictate terms here? I think you fail to grasp the true gravity of the hostage situation, Miss... Wertheim.'

'Oh, I grasp it. I grasp it with both hands. Which I think is more than you've done. Look. Let me just enlighten you on one point. For your diabolical scheme to work, you require your audience to understand that you're in possession of a real, actual, honest-to-goodness time machine. I'll now list for you the total amount of evidence you've so far given your audience that you have such a device.'

'Waiting.'

'I've just listed it for you.'

'Ah. But. All of that is secondary. The fact is, you've taken something that doesn't belong to you, and you need to give it back. Now.'

'You're wasting time. I won't.'

'Then we'll search this place from top to bottom, and we'll find it. Without your help. And then you will be shown no mercy.'

'I can categorically guarantee you will not find it without my help. Look, Jemima, if you read my note, all I am asking is that I be allowed to make my own demands in addition to those you have already made. I am not seeking to undermine your plan for packaging reform, ridiculously heavy-handed though I think it is. If you allow me to present my own demands as well as yours, then I will tell you where the chronoreversor is. And, as a bonus, I can show you a way to prove to your worldwide audience, safely and satisfactorily for all concerned, that you do genuinely have time-travel capabilities, and your – our – demands should therefore be taken seriously.'

'So if I agree to allow you to speak to camera, you'll give up the chronoreversor?'

'That's basically the deal, yes.'

'What's in it for you?'

'You've gathered a captive audience for me. Hopefully rather more of an audience than just two disaffected cats and a lonely old man. So I get an opportunity to share my ideas about what I think matter, in a way I otherwise wouldn't.'

'That's it?'

'That's it. I'm not looking to undermine any part of your scheme. This is just an add-on. A value-add, I guess you could call it.'

'How do I know this isn't a trick?'

'Because you hold all the cards, except for the chronoreversor. You guys have got the muscle, the car keys – all I've got is an out-of-order prosthetic.'

'I might have known. It's in your arm, isn't it?'

'Jemima, I can promise you, I would never do anything so obvious as to hide the chronoreversor in my artificial arm. I let it slip off just before, remember? You'll get it, if you allow me to give a spiel to the camera.'

'Alright. I suppose I'm forced to agree to your unreasonable demands. Hand it over.'

'After.'

Bec started speaking to the camera, glancing periodically at the control unit on Jemima's desk to ensure that the broadcast was indeed "live". She spoke awkwardly at first but found confidence as she continued.

'I'd like to thank my captors for generously allowing me, in lieu of a last meal or any similar palaver, to address you about what *I* feel to be important. And I have to say, I think Jemima and Harold here – they haven't been forthcoming with their full names, perhaps they'll rectify that for the camera – have made a mistake in focusing only on one particular and fairly narrow societal scourge in their, in my view, misguided efforts to make the world a better place. For the record I'll confirm that my own name is Rebecca Wertheim – hi, Mum – and I have been brought here to this disused oil or gas platform in the Tasman Sea, the one Channel 57 used for its pilot of *This Show Is Rigged*, completely against my will. But with Jemima and Harold's indulgence, I'd like to make a few requests of my own. Because if I am to be fed to the dinosaurs, I want it to be over something important. Something that matters to *me*, and I hope to you too. Thanks Jemima.

'I demand the release of Copperhead's second album, the one Columbia have been sitting on for the past fifty-plus years. I demand the immediate retraction of all Greedo-shot-first releases of Episode Four, and can we please stop calling it Episode Four? I demand an end to the unnecessarily protracted copyright protection that has been afforded Mickey Mouse, whose likeness should by now have passed well-and-truly into the public domain. And I want an end to sectarian violence, to institutionalised poverty, to multinational greed, to child slavery, to sex trafficking, to rampant environmental degradation for the sake of a quick buck, to religious intolerance, to famine while, elsewhere, food goes to waste, and to discrimination on the basis of age, sex, gender, sexual orientation, belief system, operating system preference, or anything else. I demand that the minds behind the military-industrial complex come up with something more productive to do with their time. I demand that all cities in seismically-active regions be brought up to code with regard to earthquake resistance. I demand that people be treated as people, *regardless* of their circumstances. I demand dignity. I apologise for this tee-shirt, I was abducted against my will and have had no opportunity to change. For the record, "fsck" is not a swear word. And I demand all funding be withdrawn, forthwith, from any research on the feasibility of time travel. We have no right to treat the past as some sort of beta version, to be patched and rebooted, whatever we might hope to achieve. No good can come of it.'

'Finished?' Jemima asked, a tone of barely-disguised impatience, coupled with badly-suppressed hostility, showing in her voice.

'Not quite,' Bec replied, offering her adversary what she hoped was a sweet, if not completely sincere, smile. She turned back to face the camera. 'Now I realise all of this is a big ask, and you have no proof whatsoever that my captors even have access to such a thing as a time machine. This is something that, in their wisdom, Jemima and Harold have overlooked, but there's a way around it. I suggest they travel forward ten days into the future and return from then with an accurate record of the timing, location, and magnitude of significant seismic events occurring between now and then. This would prove that they are on the level, in that respect at least. It gives me a ten-day grace period while their future quake checklist is compared with unfolding reality; but they could always send me back early if they thought any law-enforcement funny business was being attempted. Of course, I earnestly hope that the demands will be met, but contingencies need to be planned for. Jemima,' she asked, turning and holding between thumb and forefinger an imaginary D-sized battery, 'are you agreeable to this?'

The look which Jemima offered her would cause aircraft to fall from the sky. Bec turned back to the camera. 'I think we're done here,' she said, offering her best smile. 'No, wait, I almost forgot the most important bit. I *demand* world peace. A species that persists in blowing itself to smithereens, simply because it can't think of a better way of handling a difficult situation, has no right to call itself intelligent. Make it happen. Thank you for listening.'

'*Cut*,' said Jemima, in a voice which made it clear that she, personally, had absolutely no truck with this "world peace" concept at this particular instant, and should not be counted upon to contribute to its implementation. She pressed the control panel in front of her.

The broadcast ended.

'I allowed *you*,' Jemima said, sneering, the spittle spraying from her lips, while Harold held Bec's arms pinioned behind her back, 'to hijack my big moment. I was under the impression you'd be looking to say just a sentence or two to the camera, not giving the full Shakespearean soliloquy. So I don't think you can understand just how angry with you I am right now. You need to keep your end of the bargain. This time-reversal module. *Now.*'

'The "now" is problematic,' Bec explained, swallowing, trying not to show fear. She was well aware of all the ways this could still go Vista-shaped.

'What do you mean?'

'I mean it's hidden here, but it's not hidden now. It won't be hidden here for another week and a half. I hid it eleven days in the future. Time machine, and all that.'

'Then we travel ahead eleven days, you retrieve it, and we proceed from there.'

'No.'

'What do you mean, no?'

'I'm saying I won't cooperate. Not until you've fulfilled your part of the plan I outlined. Honestly, you guys are your own worst enemies, I cannot believe how two such incompetent – ouch – I mean, it's in your interests to convince the people you've just broadcast to that you do actually *have* a time machine. Saying "I have a time machine" won't achieve that, surprisingly enough. Supplying them with proof, like an accurate list of upcoming earthquakes, will. So you go forward, get the information, and then return here in eleven days' time. I'll hand over the module, we'll come back to now, do the follow-up broadcast, they'll become convinced over the course of the next ten days, your demands will be met, my demands will be met, everyone lives happily ever after and nobody needs to get fed to the allosaurus. *Capisce?*'

'I don't trust her, Boss,' said Harold.

'You think I do?' Jemima asked. 'And for pity's sake put that shoe down. All the same, she has a point. Here's what we do: You stay here, make sure she doesn't try anything, I'll go get this list.'

Damn, Bec thought. *That wasn't part of the plan – I'd assumed they'd both go.*

*

271

'Somethink's bugging me,' said Harold, as he escorted Bec at shoe-point up the stairs towards, she presumed, her room of recent incarceration. 'If you hid this module in the future, and the car needs it to get back in time, how'd youse get back?'

The oaf's smarter than he lets on. 'It wasn't easy,' she said.

At least they hadn't cuffed her this time. Were they getting complacent?

At the door to her room, she stalled and stood her ground, in a manner that would be immediately obvious to anyone who has ever owned, or had moderately close acquaintance with, a Shetland pony. She braced herself in the doorway – something, admittedly, that would be beyond the remit of your average Shetland, so the analogy fell through at this point – and offered Harold no assistance whatsoever with the task of getting her into the room. Finally, exasperated, he did what she'd been faintly hoping he'd do: grabbed her by the wrist – her right wrist – to lead her through into the room. She kept up the resistance, the inevitable happened – *schlurp* – and she quickly pulled the door shut, listening with amusement to Harold's threats as he realised he'd just been locked in.

She strode rapidly towards the stairwell. If she could use her prosthetic to escape via the manhole, so too could he – which meant she'd need to drag something heavy to block the manhole cover, render it immobile, quick smart. That super-sized crescent wrench on the top deck, for a start. Or one of those drums would be even better, assuming she could shift it.

She should probably, in truth, have explained something to Jemima before the kidnapper jetted off. Well, two somethings. One, that she had been bluffing: the chronoreversor had not been sent eleven days into the future: she hadn't known how to hotwire the car, and did not in any case feel safe about the idea of making even a short hop in time herself – call her a wimp, but she did not trust the technology. And two, that she had rewired several of the connections on the Valiant's 32-pin chronoselector unit: a nominated time interval of ten days forward would instead become a leap ahead by... she'd been hazy on the math, it had been very late, but... conservatively at least five hundred years, possibly a millennium or more.

Maybe quite a lot more. She didn't expect Jemima would be back. Perhaps she'd reached a time where they'd moved beyond the blister pack; that'd keep her happy. Maybe. (And even if Jemima wished to return, Bec doubted she'd be permitted to: the far-future society must have strongly negative views on the idea of allowing an incursion into what, for them, would be the time of their ancestors. Changing the course of history, and all that.) All of which meant that the broadcast audience wouldn't get their proof of time travel, would shrug the whole thing off as a bizarre hoax... Was there still any point in hoping for the world-peace thing?

Probably not. Pity. At least she'd tried.

'Swap you,' she called down to Harold through the open manhole. 'My myoinductive arm for these bottles of PET-infused water and this exciting collection of date-expired water crackers.'

Harold glared up at her. 'I'll pass it up to youse,' he growled.

She was about to grab hold, but something about his expression registered. *Not falling for that one...* 'No. You throw it up. I'll toss the bottles and the cracker packets down.'

She moved out of the firing line just in time. The prosthetic landed with a clatter an impressive distance away. *Better not have damaged that, you vandal.* She dropped down two packets of crackers, then three of the one-litre water bottles. The third bottle hit Harold, quite by chance, on the back of the head. *Thwock.*

It wasn't quite the sweetest sound in the world, she thought as she moved the cover, and then the anchoring drum, back into position, but it would do until someone thought to send a helicopter or something out here to rescue her. (On which score, she should head back downstairs and do another quick broadcast, just to let someone out there know that yes, there were actually people on this deserted rig... and once that was sorted, she had something else to attend to. One last matter.)

*

She reached into the cistern's tepid waters, pulled out a zip-lock bag containing a smallish cylindrical object, and removed the object from the bag. Pulling the lid down, she sat and contemplated the object: all the trouble it could cause, all the promise it held, the chance it might ultimately afford her to go back those sixteen years and, perhaps, somehow, to avert her brother's needless death in the Christchurch earthquake. She tried to remember Kelvin's face, to separate it from the awful pile of rubble with which, in her mind, his memory was inextricably linked. Then she went up to the top deck, doing her best to ignore the awful imprecations that Harold, beneath her feet, was directing at her – and, really, he had no right to be saying such things to *anybody*, least of all to a smart IT girl who might well just have singlehandedly saved human civilisation from an unknowable apocalypse. She walked as close to the deck's edge as she dared and, tears pricking at her eyes, flung the cylinder high and hard out towards the waiting, near-limitless sea, because saving the world was one thing; but when it came down to it she just didn't have the strength to invest in *that* kind of hopeless hope.

Mole of Stars

We found a mole of stars.

They were strewn far. It took us aeons to reach them all. More time, to map their myriad worlds. Yet longer to search their shores for signs of life. Many died, people, worlds, stars even. But at length we were done. And we knew.

We were alone.

A mole of stars, and we alone. It was a bleak existence.

Empty.

We filled those reaches. Waxed. Built. Throve. What else? Yet always the thought, at back, if not for us, then no-one. It was a "why?" for which there was no answer.

We learned much else, amongst our mole of stars. Learned that all things must pass; even the mole itself. There would be a Death of all things, towards which we hurtled. All would be destroyed. We could not escape it.

Could not escape, but we could trick. We could trap learning, one crumb alone, in a form which would survive beyond the Death. It cost us much to do this, but we so strove. What else?

One thing more. We learnt to influence the Death, to shape the start beyond. To favour life, to give just more than one slim chance. This, too, cost us deep, many suns among our mole of stars, and what we could achieve was slight, but so we did.

Came the Death. All died. All ended.

The crumb? You read it now, if yet you live. If we succeeded. And we would have you know this, as you look around your own mole of stars: we do not know if you are alone. We hope not. Yet, whether, these things – this crumb, this chance – they are our gifts to you. They are what remains, from us.

Use them wisely.

Pass them on.

Small presses depend on word of mouth.

If you've enjoyed this book, please mention it to friends.
Or leave a review on Goodreads, Amazon, Library Thing, or elsewhere.

Acknowledgements

'Jack Makes a Sale', 'Running Lizard' and 'Mole of Stars' were first published in *Rare Unsigned Copy: tales of Rocketry, Ineptitude, and Giant Mutant Vegetables* (Peggy Bright Books, 2010), edited by Edwina Harvey.

'All the Colours of the Tomato' and 'November 31st is World Peace Day' were first published in *Dimension6* , issues 9 and 11 respectively, edited by Keith Stevenson.

'Working Girl', 'You Said "Two of Each", Right?', 'Must've Been While You Were Kissing Me', 'Suckers for Love' and 'DragonBlog' were first published in *Andromeda Spaceways Inflight Magazine*, issues 33, 50, 46, 58 and 33 respectively, edited by assorted members of the Andromeda Spaceways Co-operative.

'The Fridge Whisperer' was first published in *Semaphore Magazine* (March 2010), edited by Marie Hodgkinson.

'The Speed of Heavy' was first published in *Kaleidotrope* issue 8, edited by Fred Coppersmith.

'Talking with Taniwha' was first published in *Borderlands* issue 11, edited by Stephen Dedman.

'Half The Man' was first published in *SpeckLit* (June 2014), edited by Alex F Fayle.

'Tremble, Quivering Mortals, At My Resplendent Tentacularity' was first published in *Star*Line* issue 39.1, edited by F J Bergmann.

'The Assault Goes Ever On' was first published in *Difficult Second Album: more stories of Xenobiology, Space Elevators, and Bats Out Of Hell* (Peggy Bright Books, 2014), edited by Edwina Harvey.

'Dark Rendezvous' was first published in *Destination Future* (Hadley Rille Books, 2010), edited by Z S Adani and Eric T Reynolds.

'Podcast' was first published in *Hope* fanzine, issue 1, edited by Grant Watson.

'The Day of the Carrot' was first published in *Ticon4* (February 2010), edited by Russell Farr.

'Latency' was first published in *Aurealis*, issue 43, edited by Stuart Mayne.

'At the Dark Matter Zoo' was first published in *The Stars Like Sand* (Interactive Publications, 2014), edited by Tim Jones and P S Cottier.

'The Thirty-First Element' has not been previously published.

'Against the Flow' was first published on simonpetrie.wordpress.com (October 2015).

'Reverse-Phase Astrology as a Predictive Tool for Observational Astronomy' was first published in *Annals of Improbable Research* vol. 3, issue 6, edited by Marc Abrahams.

'Niche' was first published, under the title 'Chrysalis', in *FlashSpec 2* (Equilibrium Books, 2007), edited by Neil Cladingboel.

I'm grateful to all of the above editors and publishers for their various interactions with my writing. I must also acknowledge a debt to those who've read and critiqued the stories in draft form, notably my colleagues in the Canberra Speculative Fiction Guild, and to the proofreaders of this volume. And my unalloyed thanks go, too, to the wonderful Lewis P Morley, who has once again provided some exquisite cover art.

About the Author

Born and raised in North Canterbury, New Zealand, Simon Petrie now lives in Canberra, Australia, with his books, his occasional ongoing forays into scientific research, and his least-effort plans for galactic domination. He has been shortlisted several times for the Sir Julius Vogel, Ditmar, and Aurealis Awards, and he has won the Sir Julius Vogel Award three times: in 2010 for Best New Talent and in 2013 and 2018, with *Flight 404* and *Matters Arising from the Identification of the Body* respectively, for Best Novella. He also scored a coveted Dishonourable Mention in the 2011 Bulwer-Lytton Fiction Contest.

He has edited five issues (numbers 35, 40, 51, 54, and 61) of *Andromeda Spaceways Inflight Magazine*, and has co-edited two anthologies (*Light Touch Paper, Stand Clear* and *Use Only As Directed*, published by Peggy Bright Books) with Edwina Harvey and one (*Next*, published by CSFG Publishing) with Rob Porteous. He's also acted as a typesetter and e-book formatter for several small-press and indie publishers in Australia and North America. He is currently a member of the Canberra Speculative Fiction Guild and SpecFicNZ writers' communities.

Also by Simon Petrie

She took her helmet off.
That's where it starts; that's where it ends.
That's all there is.

Tanja Morgenstein, daughter of a wealthy industrialist and a geochemist, is dead from exposure to Titan's lethal, chilled atmosphere, and Guerline Scarfe must determine why.

This novella blends hard-SF extrapolation with elements of contemporary crime fiction, to envisage a future human society in a hostile environment, in which a young woman's worst enemies may be those around her.

Matters Arising from the Identification of the Body is a Sir Julius Vogel Award winning SF / mystery novella, out now.

Also by Simon Petrie

Light levels are low. It's killingly cold. These conditions are, it transpires, connected.

The icy landscape around you—hillocks, boulders, ravines, foregrounding a hazy, rumpled horizon beneath an opaque, lowering sky—wears a patina that shades from sepia to umber, puddled with drifts of dark sand. The atmosphere, though thick, would permit only a parody of respiration: there is no succour in it. Were it not for the insulating, carefully-regulated containment of your suit, you would be dead within minutes, frozen solid within an hour.

Welcome to Titan.

Wide Brown Land: stories of Titan, out now, is a collection of eleven hard-SF short stories set on Saturn's most intriguing moon.

Also by Simon Petrie

'They're dead. They're all dead.'
The comment, innocent of deeper intent, is on the flowers withering in a glass vase. But there's a flash of panic, in response, that I only perceive on later re-examination.

The search for a missing interstellar passenger vessel brings investigator Charmain Mertz back to the unwelcoming world of her boyhood.

Flight 404 is a Sir Julius Vogel Award winning SF / mystery novella, out now.

Also by Simon Petrie

Gordon Mamon was the lift operator in a hotel that didn't have a lift.
The hotel, the 'Skyward Suites 270', was the lift.

All Gordon wants to do, when he isn't delivering room service, administering first aid, washing dishes, cleaning bathrooms, or forwarding service complaints, is to be able to finish his crossword in piece. But people keep inconsiderately dying of unnatural causes during their stay aboard his lift-module on the Skyward space elevator.

Welcome to Module 270, an orbit-transiting hotel with a suspiciously high body count.

Murder on the Zenith Express: the Gordon Mamon collection, out now, is a collection of six not-completely-serious SF mysteries.